D0231343

m. B
QK

Aberdeenshire Library and Information Service
www.aberdeenshire.gov.uk/libraries
Renewals Hotline 01224 661511

15 DEC 2018
16 FEB 2018

1 9 MAR 2008   08. JUL 08
2 2 MAR 2008   15. NOV 08.

1 4 APR 2008   1 0
1 2 MAY 2008   2 1 JUL 2008
- 9 JUN 2008   1 0 DEC 2008
2 6 MAY 2008   09. AUG 08   10. JAN 09
                20. AUG 08

                12 SEP 2008   06. FEB 09
1 0 JUN 2008

                               19. OCT 2016
                               2 4 APR 2017
                2 4 FEB 2017 JUN 2017

FAIRSTEIN, Linda A.

Killer heat   2 1 NOV 2017

                               1 7 APR 2018

ALIS

2607448

KILLER HEAT

ALSO BY LINDA FAIRSTEIN

The Alexandra Cooper Novels

FINAL JEOPARDY
LIKELY TO DIE
COLD HIT
THE DEADHOUSE
THE BONE VAULT
THE KILLS
ENTOMBED
DEATH DANCE
BAD BLOOD

Non-Fiction

SEXUAL VIOLENCE: OUR WAR AGAINST RAPE

KILLER HEAT

Linda Fairstein

Little, Brown

LITTLE, BROWN

First published in the United States by Doubleday,
an imprint of The Doubleday Broadway Publishing Group,
a division of Random House, Inc., New York.

First published in Great Britain in 2007 by Little, Brown

Copyright © Fairstein Enterprises, LLC 2008
The moral right of the author has been asserted.

*All characters and events in this publication, other than
those clearly in the public domain, are fictitious
and any resemblance to real persons,
living or dead, is purely coincidental*

No ced,
store any
pe be
oth or
cove and
conditi chaser.

ABERDEENSHIRE LIBRARY AND
INFORMATION SERVICES

2607448

HJ	624163
MYS	£12.99
AD	SOAF

A CIP catalogue record for this book
is available from the British Library.

Hardback ISBN 978-0-316-73171-3
C Format ISBN 978-0-316-73172-0

Typeset in Sabon by Palimpsest Book Production Limited,
Grangemouth, Stirlingshire
Printed and bound in Great Britain by
Clays Ltd, St Ives plc

Little, Brown
An imprint of
Little, Brown Book Group
100 Victoria Embankment
London EC4Y 0DY

An Hachette Livre UK Company

www.littlebrown.co.uk

FOR KATHLEEN HAM

Courage, a cold case – and, at last, a conviction

And I fear, I fear, my Master dear!
We shall have a deadly storm.
    — BALLAD OF SIR PATRICK SPENCE

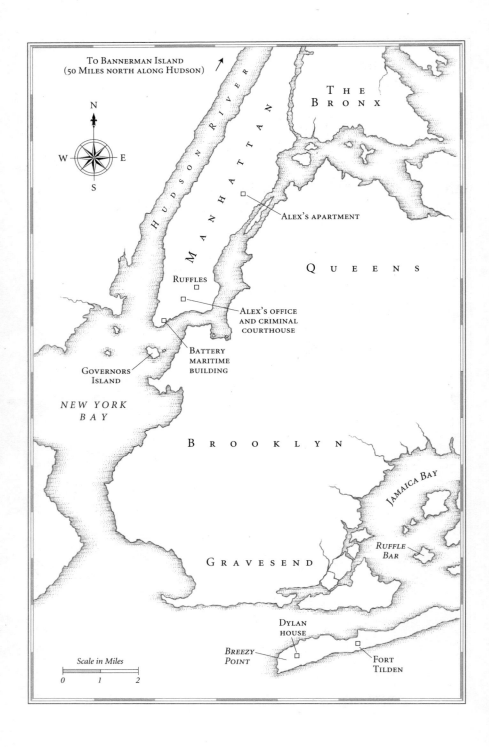

To Bannerman Island
(50 Miles north along Hudson)

N
W   E
S

HUDSON RIVER

MANHATTAN

THE
BRONX

□ Alex's apartment

QUEENS

Ruffles
□

□ ———— Alex's office
          and criminal
          courthouse

□

Governors
Island

Battery
maritime
building

NEW YORK
BAY

BROOKLYN

JAMAICA BAY

GRAVESEND

RUFFLE
BAR

DYLAN
HOUSE

BREEZY
POINT

□

□ FORT
   TILDEN

Scale in Miles

0   1   2

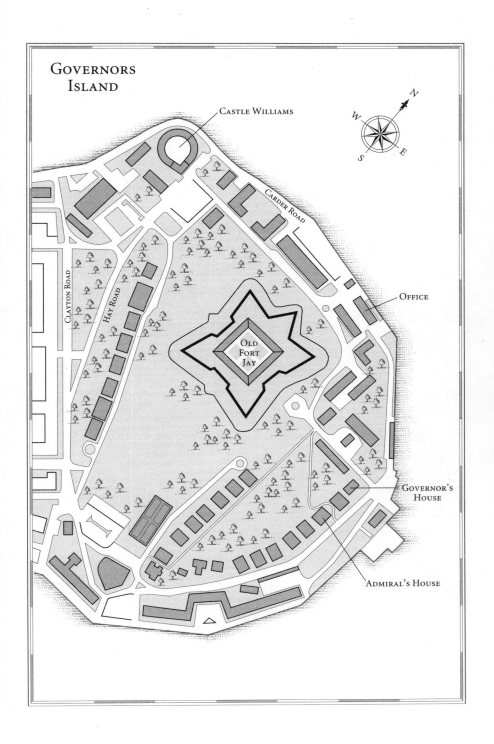

GOVERNORS
ISLAND

CASTLE WILLIAMS

CARDER ROAD

CLAYTON ROAD

HAY ROAD

OLD
FORT
JAY

OFFICE

GOVERNOR'S
HOUSE

ADMIRAL'S HOUSE

N
W   E
S

1

Mike Chapman bit into the tip of a Cohiba and held the match to the end of his thick cigar, drawing several deep breaths to make certain it was lighted.

'Take a few hits, Coop,' he said, passing it to me.

I shook my head.

'The stench from that corpse is going to stay in your brain for weeks unless you infuse it right away with something more powerful. Why do you think I've always got a couple of these in my pocket?'

I took the cigar from Mike and rolled it between my fingers.

'Don't look at the damn thing. Smoke it. That broad's been decomposing for days in an empty room during a summer heat wave. Wrap your lips around that sucker and inhale till the smoke comes through your nose and ears, and maybe even from between your toes.'

I put it to my lips, coughing as the harsh tobacco taste filled my mouth and lungs. There were no overhead lights above the concrete barriers we sat on at the intersection of South Street and Whitehall, which dead-ended at the East River, near the southernmost tip of Manhattan. 'There's no air out here. Not even a breeze off the water.'

'Almost midnight and it's still ninety-seven degrees. She's cooking in that room,' Mike said, tossing his head in the direction of the crime scene that he'd been working for the last three hours. His black hair glistened with sweat, and the perspiration on his shirt made the cotton cloth cling to his chest. 'Whatever body parts were left intact will be fried by the time they bag her.'

'Are you going with the guys to the morgue?' I asked.

'Might be the coolest place in town tonight. You into refrigerated boxes?'

'I'll pass. Are they almost done?'

'The ME was ready to call it quits when the maggot maven showed up.'

The putrefaction of the woman's body, which had been left to rot in the abandoned government offices over the old ferry slip, offered an irresistible opportunity to swarms of summer flies, which entered to lay their eggs and leave their offspring to nourish themselves on her flesh.

The blast of the horn from the Staten Island Ferry, its giant orange hull sliding out of the pier from the enormous modern terminal just twenty yards downriver, startled me. We were half a mile south of the bustling marketplace that had once been the South Street Seaport, flanking the glittering towers of Wall Street, outside what seemed like the only building in the downtown area that had been neglected alongside the water's flotsam and jetsam.

I stood up from the concrete barrier and looked over my shoulder at the entrance to the deserted slips – three vaulted openings that led to the water, supporting a raised porch and the offices in which the body had been found, centered between forty-foot-tall columns that faced Whitehall. Crumbling wooden pilings bordered the walkway behind me, while trash floated and bobbed among the large rocks in the water ten feet below.

'Jumpy already?' Mike smiled at me as he held the open collar of his shirt between his thumb and forefinger, waving it back and forth as though the cloth might actually dry out despite the oppressive humidity. 'You don't even know what happened to her yet.'

'Has he got any ideas about how long the woman's been dead?' The cigar smoke filtered up through my nostrils, overwhelming the pungent odor of death.

'Bug juice, Madam Prosecutor. The good Dr. Magorski likes to bring this whole thing down to when he figures the flies laid the maggots which finished feasting and then sat on the floorboards and pupated. He's picking up the pupal cases to take to his lab. It's a slow process,' Mike said, dismissing the expert with a flip of his hand.

The forensic entomologist had been called to the scene by the young medical examiner who first responded to the detectives' notification. I had watched Magorski work several other cases, clipping a pair of lenses that looked like tiny microscopes over his thick eyeglasses while he scoured the body and its surroundings for signs of insect life – with its predictable cycles that might help establish a time of death.

'I understand. But do you think he's useful?'

'I want you to keep puffing on that thing till you turn a pale shade of green.'

'I feel like I'm coming up on chartreuse,' I said, brushing wisps of damp hair off my forehead with the back of my hand.

'Personally, I think he's a waste of resources. Is she dead more than a week? Yeah. Less than two? My money's on that. The only reason everybody south of Forty-second Street didn't notice the odor is because this place is so isolated, except for the decaying fish remains and sewage right below where she was found.'

'That's still a pretty big window of opportunity.'

'Once we ID the broad, it won't take long for some joker to tell us the last time she showed up at work or a girlfriend to say what domestic tiff sped her out the door of her apartment. Stick with real detective work, kid. I never met a bug with a gold shield.'

I had seen more than my share of bodies as the prosecutor in charge of the Sex Crimes Prosecution Unit in the Manhattan District Attorney's Office for the last decade. The black humor of many cops and colleagues, an effort to defuse these ugly situations, did nothing to ease my revulsion.

'Hey, Chapman,' a rookie in uniform called out to Mike from the porch of the old ferry slip. 'They're bringing her out now. You and Ms. Cooper can come back up.'

On the roadway opposite the aging terminal, the Franklin Delano Roosevelt Drive sank below ground to loop under the Battery and reemerge as the West Side Highway. The far side of the tunnel entrance, dozens of glass and steel office towers – many of their windows still lit – formed the dense, narrow canyons of the city's financial district.

'Sorry to drag you down here. I really thought it might be your girl,' Mike said. He knew I had been assigned to an unsolved case involving a young woman who'd gone missing the week before.

We watched as the MEs van backed into the loading dock and the attendant opened the rear doors, ready to receive the body bag.

'Looked like a good possibility till the wig came off and we realized her hair wasn't red,' he went on.

Mike was a second-grade detective assigned to the Manhattan North Homicide Squad. His usual turf stretched from north of Fifty-ninth Street, uptown through the Harlems and the Heights to the narrow waterway that separated the island from the Bronx. But the end of summer, despite the spike in murders that usually accompanied a dramatic rise in the temperature, was also the time many cops took their vacation. The two squads, now short of manpower in late August, combined forces to respond to every murder in Manhattan.

We stopped talking when four men – one from the medical examiner's office and three uniformed officers from the First Precinct – emerged from the dark mouth of the building with their charge. There were no other spectators, no need for them to walk as though they were pallbearers, struggling to balance the coffin. The foursome loped along with the body, heaving it onto the stretcher inside the van, jerking it from side to side to position it before they strapped it into place for the ride up the drive to the morgue.

'None of these "ologists" can help with the more important questions,' Mike said as the driver slammed the double doors. He wiped the sweat from his forehead with his handkerchief, then passed it to me. 'Who the hell is she? What brought her to this godforsaken place? Why hasn't anybody noticed she was out of commission before tonight? What kind of monster am I looking for? I can't even think straight it's so hot.'

'No other missing-person reports?' I pressed the damp cloth to the back of my neck.

'Nothing that fits. Two African-American women – one from the Bronx and the other a chronic runaway from Queens – an Asian tourist, an old lady with dementia who hasn't come home in a week, but definitely a blue-rinse dye job. Your case is the only one that seemed a possible match.'

As the assistant district attorney who supervised sex crimes, I had partnered with Mike for more than a decade. I was at my desk in the criminal courthouse when he called me several hours earlier, asking for more details about the physical description of the twenty-two-year-old woman – Elise Huff – who had gone missing more than a week earlier. The investigation had been handed to me two days after her disappearance by my boss, Paul Battaglia, now in his fifth term as Manhattan's district attorney.

'Elise is a redhead. Natural.'

She had disappeared after a night of barhopping with a girl-friend, who split from her at 3:00 a.m. when she had been unable to convince Elise to go home. Elise's parents had pressed their congressman, in Tennessee, to lean on Battaglia to ramp up the search for their daughter, assuming that she might have been the target of a sexual predator.

'That's why I called you out. This one,' Mike said, pointing at the taillights of the van that carried the woman away, 'was a redhead when I showed up, till the medical examiner rolled her face to the side and the damn wig fell off.'

The synthetic auburn mane had been straight, lustrous, and obviously expensive when I looked at it earlier with the aid of Mike's flashlight. It had covered a shock of short curly hair – dark brown – the only distinguishable feature still visible on the head and body.

Mike took the cigar from me as we walked under the archway and back into the terminal, toward the staircase. His cheeks hollowed as he sucked in several deep breaths before handing it back. 'Inhale once more, Coop.'

Climbing the steps behind Mike, I smiled at his constant attempts to protect me from the more horrific parts of our job. Hal Sherman was setting up the battery-run lighting system that would allow him to take dozens more photographs of the grim room from which the body had been removed. Within the confines of this space – no more than thirty feet long and twenty wide – the Crime Scene Unit investigators would look for any speck of evidence that might lead to an identification of the victim, her killer, and whatever connection linked them to each other.

'So what's the weapon?' Mike asked.

'Maybe the butt of a gun caused the fracture. Maybe a hammer. The autopsy'll tell you more than I can.' Hal put a ruler on the floor, next to what looked like a bloodstain, before he leaned over to snap his picture.

The young ME was certain that the woman had died from a blunt force injury, an impact that had depressed a portion of her skull on the left temple and caused the fatal damage to her brain.

'You make anything of the marks on her face?'

'Yeah. Scope the personals for a guy who likes to dance. Too bad there wasn't much skin left. The bastard must have stomped on her face after he whacked her. I don't know if there's enough of a pattern to get a shoe print, but I shot it from every angle.'

I stood still while Mike geared up again – rubber gloves and booties – to go back over every crevice of the dusty room.

'And when uniform arrived?'

'Obliterated everything on the stairs,' Hal said, sweeping his arm around the room, then wiping his moustache with his sleeve, 'and all over the place.'

The glass in each of the five windows that faced the river was shattered, much like the bones of the dead woman's face.

'You guys find anything?' Mike asked the two cops who had been assisting Hal.

'Double-checking. Nothing so far except this – I don't know – looks like a knotted strip of leather. Like the end of a key chain or something.' One of them held up a two-inch piece of rawhide.

'This guy was good,' the other said. 'Must have had lots of time. Maybe even got away clean.'

Each man had examined half of the room, and now they switched positions to go over the other's territory. Mike stepped around Hal and stood behind an old wooden desk. He opened the four drawers, flashing his light into them and slamming them shut.

'Government offices. Seems like whoever winds up designing stuff for the city has to take a course in how to make it look dismal.'

'What agency was this?' I asked.

'Ports and Terminals.'

Three chairs with broken backs lined the far wall. Mike lifted each one and replaced it. He moved toward several crates piled in a corner.

'Don't bother, Chapman. They're as empty as your pockets.'

'What did you think about those lines on her wrists?' Mike was crouched on the floor now, measuring the coating of dust with a gloved finger.

'Some kind of ligature. Maybe even cuffs. Hey, Alexandra, you want to wave that cigar around. Where did you get such a good one, Mike?' Hal asked, sniffing the air.

'Coop's boss. All his friends stockpile him with the best Cubans. Only the feds prosecute for trading with the enemy. Not Battaglia. He just lets the evidence go up in smoke.'

'You think she was killed here?' I asked.

'Nah. She's a dump job.'

'No signs of any struggle, but then that's pretty tough to do when you're bound,' Mike said, agreeing with Hal. 'Maybe still alive when he brought her up and left her to die. That's why there's blood.'

I looked through what was left of the window. The river was dark, a slight chop from the current kicking up an occasional whitecap. A few small boats criss-crossed the harbor, illuminating narrow lines over the water with their headlights.

'Not a trace of her clothing anywhere?' I asked.

'Zip. Looks like we're dealing with a pro, Coop. Felony frequent flier miles. C'mon, I'll put you in a cab. You've got court in the morning.'

I said good night to Hal and his crew and went downstairs, careful to avoid the powder on the banister where crime scene cops had dusted for prints.

As we emerged from the mouth of the archway, under the faded print of the sign that said BATTERY MARITIME BUILDING, one of the crime scene cops was waiting for Mike.

'There's something snagged in one of the long wooden splinters of the pilings, Detective. Take a look. I've photographed it there, so let me know if you want me to fish it out.'

I followed Mike to the north side of the old structure. He

leaned over the wire fencing and his hair gleamed as the officer held a flashlight above his head. I could see an object floating on the surface of the water, its many thick strands splayed like the tentacles of a sea creature.

'Bring it up, Jenks. You got something to hook it with?'

The eager kid ran to the department station wagon and brought out a long metal pole. He disappeared inside the bay of the old terminal and reappeared on the far side of the fence. He walked along the edge of the building, carefully stepping down and out onto the planks between the tall pilings.

After several attempts to snag the mysterious object, Willy Jenks triumphantly lifted it out of the river, swung the pole over the fence, and dumped it at Mike's feet.

I kneeled beside him and tried to figure out what I was staring at. Mike removed another rubber glove from his pants pocket and slipped it on before he began to separate the tangled strands.

With his index finger, Mike found what looked like a handle, pulling on it to stretch it out toward my foot. Then he started to count the strips as he spread them apart on the ground. 'One, two, three . . .'

I could see that they, too, were made of leather, knotted like the piece the cops had found upstairs. 'What do you—?'

Mike held his finger to his lips to quiet me as he continued to count. 'Six, seven, eight.'

The ninth length of rope was missing its knot.

'What is it?'

'Guess you never saw a cat-o'-nine-tails before.'

Mike picked up the whip by its handle, shook off the water, then raised his arm and cracked it against the asphalt walk. The sharp sound split the still night air like a gunshot.

'Bound. Tortured. Killed. It's not a pretty way to die.'

2

'Ms. Cooper, are you withdrawing your offer?'

Alton Lamont had taken the bench minutes earlier, just after court officers had uncuffed the prisoner and seated him next to his lawyer.

Although the odors of the waterfront and the grisly scene of the previous evening lingered in my mind's eye and brain, I tried to concentrate on the pretrial proceedings under way in Lamont's courtroom.

'That's not a real plea bargain she suggested, Your Honor,' Gene Grassley said, pointing his stubby forefinger in my direction. 'It's Ms. Cooper's version of a death sentence.'

'Mr. Grassley knows we're going forward.' We had spent most of the day selecting a jury and were finishing up the afternoon with some last-minute housekeeping before setting a timetable for opening statements. 'My victim boarded her flight in Seattle at dawn – the offer's off the table.'

Floyd Warren was studying his copy of the indictment as his lawyer talked about him. 'My client turned sixty-one last week. He can't serve out thirty years in state prison.'

'He's looking at fifty if this jury convicts him,' Lamont said, smiling at Grassley. 'I expect he'll try to do the best he can.'

Warren looked up at Lamont, scowled, and licked his front teeth.

'I don't mean any disrespect by this. I know you've been a judge longer than I've been practicing law.' Grassley had started his career with the Legal Aid Society a few years before I became an assistant district attorney. 'But sixty-one-year-old men simply do not, can not – well, they're not your typical rapists.'

'May I be heard, Your Honor?'

'Let me finish, Alex.' Grassley was a head shorter than I. He liked to keep me in my seat once jurors were in the courtroom, as though he feared they would be swayed by my arguments because of my greater height. 'I know what she's going to say, Judge. There's no such thing as a typical rapist. I've heard her spiel before.'

'May I—?'

'Okay, so older guys are still capable of molesting children or beating their wives,' Grassley said, as though those were insignificant criminal acts. 'I'm not saying such things are impossible. But Mr. Warren is charged with climbing up three stories on a fire escape, squeezing through a small window, struggling with a healthy young woman to rape and sodomize her. Suppose for a minute he even did those things – when was this? Thirty-five years ago. *Thirty-five years ago*. He's not capable of doing them now. He's not possibly a danger to anyone. There's a legal doctrine Alexandra Cooper has no respect for. You need to help her with it.'

'And what is that, Mr. Grassley?' Judge Lamont took off his glasses and rubbed the bridge of his nose.

'*Rachmones*, Judge.'

'Rock what?'

Alton Lamont was an African-American, a former defense attorney who had been elected to the Supreme Court – New York State's highest trial court – more than twenty years earlier. He cupped one hand to his ear and shook his head.

'Compassion. It's the Yiddish word for compassion.'

The heavy door creaked behind me and I turned to look over my shoulder. A young man dressed in a T-shirt and jeans walked down the short aisle of the small courtroom and sat in one of the empty rows of benches.

'A few months back, Mr. Grassley, when you were here with Ms. Cooper on another matter, you were complaining she was *too* soft, a bleeding heart, if I'm not mistaken.'

'Yeah, you're right. But she only bleeds for her victims. Try to talk logic to her about an alleged offender and you can't even get ice water from the tap. She's got blinders on.'

I was saving my arguments for the serious legal issues ahead. Judge Lamont could handle this.

'And what's your logic this time? Seems to me Mr. Warren could have had this all behind him if he'd stayed in town after the first trial.' Lamont was studying the court file. 'Looks like the jury almost let him walk.'

Floyd Warren put his elbows on the table and rested his forehead in his hands.

Grassley passed behind me and leaned against the rail of the jury box. 'They were hung nine to three for an acquittal.'

'Doesn't make sense that your man skipped,' Lamont said. 'The prosecution case never gets better the second time around.'

'There was another rape charge filed before a date for the retrial was set, Judge. Kings County,' I said from my seat. The defendant had been identified by a woman in Brooklyn who saw his photograph in the newspaper.

'And even then my client was still free on bail. Couldn't have been such a big deal.'

Lamont rested his head against the back of his tall leather chair. 'Those were different times, Mr. Grassley. 1973, I'd venture to say there weren't a dozen rape prosecutions successfully brought in this entire city that year. Archaic laws, no Special Victims Units, and DNA hadn't been heard of yet. There wasn't a lawyer on either side who could have dreamed that science would give new life to these old cases.'

'Alex and I were still in diapers, Judge. Ancient history.'

Warren glanced at me and sneered again.

'What are you looking for here, Mr. Grassley?'

'Give him a couple years, maybe three, and membership in AARP,' Grassley said, laughing nervously. 'He'll go back to his wife and his little suburban house outside Birmingham. Whatever you think he may have done, Judge, he's retired now. Out of the business. For the last ten years he's lived quietly, supported himself as a landscape gardener. Where's your *rachmones*?'

Lamont looked over my head as the door opened again. Another young man walked in, dressed like the first, and took a seat behind him. I assumed there were cases on the calendar late in the day that the judge would hear after he finished our arguments.

'You're putting on a good show for your client, Gene,' the judge said, waving at the court reporter to tell her that he was going off the record, 'but your bullshit – sorry I don't have a legal term for it, it's just plain bullshit. And it's so far over the line that it's insulting to me and to the – how many victims, Alex?'

'Forty-two and counting.'

'Alleged victims,' interjected Grassley. 'My client hasn't been charged in any of those cases yet.'

'In 1974, Mr. Warren jumped bail before his retrial here – almost certain to be acquitted – and began a rampage more devastating than the worst hurricane on record. He left New York and – Alex, refresh my recollection, will you?'

'He moved south and became the Philadelphia "Strip Mall" rapist – about a dozen cases reported there over the next eighteen months. Then he continued on to the DC area, where DNA has recently confirmed that he was the Chevy Chase "Carjack" rapist – head count still growing from police there and up the road in Silver Spring – before going on to terrorize the academic community in North Carolina as the "Chapel Hill Campus" rapist. Patterns all along the East Coast throughout the next twenty years.'

'And if you and your cops are so damn smart, how come nobody identified him in all that time?'

I was standing now, and my slim five feet ten inches of indignation towered over Grassley's short, pudgy frame. In the seventies and eighties, Floyd Warren had moved around the Southeast like a chameleon, changing his name in every location. When SVU detective Mercer Wallace backtracked to collect the evidence from three decades of closed cases, he found local records that matched a transient calling himself Warren Floyd, who later became Floyd X and a variety of aliases before settling in Alabama and adopting the name of the late judge before whom his case had been tried – Howard Rovers.

'Surely you haven't forgotten, Mr. Grassley, that the defendant attacked all of these women before 1989, which was the first time DNA was accepted as a valid scientific technique in any courtroom in America. And that it was another decade before databanks were established in many of the states in which he was most successful. God knows what we'll find when Alabama links up to CODIS.'

The Combined DNA Index System was making it easier for communities all over the country to identify offenders from evidence submitted to a centralized FBI computer program.

Floyd Warren licked his front teeth again, staring at me as I spoke, and then tapped on the table to get Grassley's attention. He wrote something on a piece of paper and slid it across to his lawyer.

Gene Grassley looked at the note and shook his head.

Floyd Warren started to get to his feet and the two court officers standing behind him stepped forward to hold him in place. 'Judge Lamont. Yo, Judge.'

Lamont banged his gavel. 'Stay seated, Mr. Warren. Tell Mr. Grassley what you want to say. It's really not appropriate, nor is it smart, for you to speak directly to me.'

Grassley slipped into his seat and tried to calm his client.

Floyd Warren wasn't interested. 'Judge, what about my statues?'

'I'm warning you, Mr. Warren. Speak through your lawyer.'

'Don't you have no damn statues in this state?' He held up the piece of paper he'd just written on. 'Statues of limitation?'

'Statues? You mean statutes?'

'Yeah, that's what I'm saying. Statues.'

The court officers were trying to keep Warren in place by holding on to his broad, powerful shoulders. They were waiting for a signal from the judge to use more force.

'Hasn't Mr. Grassley explained this to you?'

'He hasn't 'splained nothing to me. I got rights, don't I?'

'Of course I've told him,' Grassley said, as the court officers shoved him aside so they could keep their hands on the defendant.

Lamont banged his gavel again. 'Shut up, Mr. Warren. This isn't going to be a free-for-all in front of the jury. Not in my courtroom, I can promise you that. Handcuffs and leg irons come next.'

There was a momentary silence and the officers let Floyd Warren settle back in his chair. His face was rounder now than in the mug shot taken at the time of his arrest so many years ago, and his dark skin wrinkled. He seemed to like being the center of attention.

Just as quiet resumed, the doors opened again and a third young man stepped inside, scoped the situation, and joined the others in the rows behind my seat. All three were wearing bright yellow T-shirts.

'Perhaps, Judge, you can repeat for Mr. Warren what I've already brought to his attention several times.'

'I'd be happy to, Mr. Grassley.' Lamont checked with the reporter to make sure this would all be part of the official record. 'In New York State, until quite recently, there was a statute of limitations on rape cases, just as there are for all other violent felonies, with the exception of murder.'

'I didn't kill nobody,' Warren said, in a stage whisper meant for all of us to hear. He picked his teeth with the tip of his lead pencil.

'Because of the advances in DNA technology – the certainty of that science – many state legislatures have eliminated those five-year statutes. The district attorney is now able to bring charges on sexual assaults that occurred yesterday, even if they aren't solved for another fifty years.

'But that's a new law, Mr. Warren. That wouldn't apply to your old case. The sole reason Ms. Cooper is able to go forward now is because of your own actions. You kept this case alive all by yourself, all this time, by jumping bail and fleeing the jurisdiction.'

Even if a second jury had convicted Floyd Warren three decades earlier, the sentences imposed on rapists were so light then that most were released to parole within five to ten years. The recidivism rate – the rate at which they repeated their offenses, often using exactly the same modus operandi – was staggering.

Lamont stopped speaking as the doors opened and swung shut again. I turned my head and saw two more young men, both yellow-shirted, walk in and take seats with the others. The judge removed his glasses and looked at me quizzically. I realized these kids must not have been there to see him, and I shrugged my shoulders.

I looked back once more. There was something written on the

front of the T-shirts, but the five solemn onlookers were sitting with arms crossed over their chests and I couldn't make out the words.

Lamont went on. 'The statute was tolled by your very—'

'Told what?' Warren mumbled. 'Nobody told me nothing.'

Lamont pretended he hadn't heard the belligerent prisoner. He wagged a finger in Warren's direction. 'The effect of the statute was suspended by your flight. That's what has kept the case alive.'

It had been dead in the water for thirty-five years, until the day a few months earlier when Floyd Warren, aka Howard Rovers, stopped at a dealer's outside of town to buy a shotgun. Confident that he had eluded law enforcement for over three decades, he submitted his fingerprints for the application. When he returned to make the purchase, the local police were waiting. The New York warrant for bail jump had appeared as a match in the automated fingerprint system when Warren's background check was run. After the NYPD's Special Victims Unit was notified, Mercer Wallace asked me to dig through the archives to find the old trial folder, in hopes that some evidence still existed to send to the lab for DNA analysis. A crumpled pair of cotton underpants gave us our break.

'Ms. Cooper, Mr. Grassley – are you clear with the rest of my rulings?'

'Yes, Your Honor,' I answered aloud, and Gene Grassley nodded.

'And I want the record to reflect,' Lamont said, standing so that he could gesture with both arms, expressing the enormity of his outrage, 'that I consider it shameful, a morally offensive blot on the legal history of this state that I am obliged by the Constitution to take this woman's testimony according to the laws of 1973.'

'Objection, Your Honor,' Grassley said. 'Most respectfully, I don't think—'

'Save that nonsense for the jury. I'll say what I damn well

please when they're not here. I was practicing law back then, Gene. You understand that when a stranger climbed through the window of your home and held a knife or a gun against the body of – of your mother or your sister or your wife, that woman, no matter how saintly she might have been, couldn't go to court unless she could prove she had struggled against her attacker, even when he threatened to shoot or to stab her? There had to be *independent* proof of who this animal was? That the testimony of *every* raped woman was deemed incompetent as a matter of law?'

'Judge, my client—'

'All that changed, as you both know, in the mid-1970s, before either one of you came to the bar. Yet I'm bound by those rules today. How foolish is that?' Lamont asked, tapping his gavel lightly against the copy of the penal law on his desk. 'More than thirty years have gone by, the legislature finally caught up with reality, but I'm forced to make my rulings based on what the laws were when this attack took place. And I must say that is really a disgrace.'

I couldn't tell whether Alton Lamont was truly outraged or not, as he placed his right hand over his heart and patted his chest several times. But I knew this statement would read well on his campaign materials when he stood for reelection in another year.

'Ms. Cooper, does your witness realize that I have no choice but to follow the old law?' He looked at the name in the indictment. 'Miss Hastings, is she set to go?'

'Yes, she is, Judge. She understands.' I didn't need to add that she was terrified at the thought of being in a courtroom with her rapist again. I didn't need to allow Floyd Warren to gloat with pleasure at the prospect of subjecting this woman to the same humiliating ordeal she had undergone a lifetime ago.

'Then we're good for tomorrow morning at eleven? That gives you time to settle in with Ms. Hastings first thing.'

The judge knew that Kerry Hastings had flown in twice from

her home on the West Coast to meet with Mercer Wallace and me. The first time, after so many years of silence had led her to assume the case would never be solved, was to give her own saliva for the DNA analysis of her clothing and bed linens. The second was for our initial preparation for trial.

'That leaves just the rape shield issue, Judge,' I said.

Lamont cupped his hand to his ear again. 'Didn't catch that, Alex.'

As soon as I spoke, the five men in T-shirts had started to cough. Fake, exaggerated coughs that were loud and disruptive. I tried to ignore them.

'I said we need to address the question of the rape shield law, Judge.'

The hacking noise made it impossible for Lamont to hear me. He wiggled his finger at the captain – Louie Larsen – who was standing near the last row of benches. Larsen began ambling to the well of the courtroom.

I looked to see whether Floyd Warren was communicating with the quintet of young men, but he never turned his head.

'Gene, Alex. Come up here to the bench.'

I walked forward while the two officers behind the defendant closed in around Warren, anticipating that he might have had a way to orchestrate the small commotion.

'You know these guys?' Lamont asked me.

'No, sir.'

'Grassley, they have anything to do with your client?'

'Don't look at me, Judge. They're sitting behind Alex. Thought she imported some cheerleaders to buck her up.'

Louie Larsen took his place between Grassley and me. 'Pablo Posano.'

'What?' My head snapped around and I studied the faces of the five young men. None of them looked familiar.

'You've gone white, Alex,' Judge Lamont said. 'Who's Pablo Posano? Is he here?'

'He was the leader of the Latin Princes until we put him away this spring. He's in Attica, Judge. Posano's got to do all his time in maximum security. He raped a twelve-year-old girl as part of an initiation rite. I tried the case, Your Honor. Posano hates my guts.'

The Princes were among the most dangerous drug gangs in the city. For every member jailed or killed on the street, ten more seemed to sign up the next day. Posano's posse had threatened the trial judge and intimidated several of the witnesses, who thereafter refused to testify in my case. I was as chilled as though someone had held an icicle to my spine.

'How do you know they have anything to do with Posano?' I asked Larsen.

I swiveled to take another look at the unwelcome spectators. I had given Floyd Warren too much by reacting to the punks. He was staring me down.

The kid in the second row stood up, the others behind him rising as if on cue.

'It's on the back of their shirts.'

'What is?'

'Pablo Posano. That's what's printed there.'

'Stop!' Alton Lamont said, banging his gavel on his desktop.

The five gang members paid no attention.

Now I could see that the black letters on the front of each yellow shirt spelled a single word: FREE. As they turned their backs to Lamont to follow their leader out of the courtroom, the judge got the message as clearly as I did. FREE PABLO POSANO.

Floyd Warren licked his front teeth and laughed. He could see the fear in my eyes.

3

'They didn't threaten me. They're way too smart for that.' I dropped the case folder on top of my desk.

'Why can't Lamont just boot their asses out?' Mercer Wallace asked.

'They didn't *do* anything. Nothing except sound effects that won't show on the record. By the time we figured it out they were gone.'

'And tomorrow?' Mercer was a first-grade detective assigned to the NYPD's elite Special Victims Unit. He had painstakingly reconstructed the case against Floyd Warren and wanted it to proceed without complications.

'Lamont says he'll deal with it if they come back. It's a public courtroom. He can tighten the security but you know he'll never seal it.'

'More than that, I know you can't play with the Latin Princes, Alex. To Posano, you're the face of evil. You're the one who put him in jail, when he figured he had everyone else scared away. You stood in front of him day after day, building your case and arguing to the jury, dancing circles around his mouthpiece. It became way too personal with him.'

'He's got years to get over it.'

'His crew is too vicious. They may not realize you've got some tough innards beneath that pretty packaging. And some powerful reinforcements covering your tail.'

I didn't question Mercer's warning. In the last year alone, the Dominican gang leader had ordered the unsuccessful hit of a federal judge who had presided over a drug case that sent three of his lieutenants to jail and intimidated scores of witnesses from appearing in a handful of related grand jury investigations.

'If harassing me is what they wanted, consider it done.' I sat down in front of the air conditioner and lifted my hair to let the cool air blow on the back of my neck. 'What's the word on Kerry?'

'The flight is on the ground in Chicago. Severe thunderstorms. I don't think she'll land before ten tonight, but I'll pick her up and take her to the hotel.'

Kerry Hastings was a twenty-two-year-old graduate student when Floyd Warren broke into her Greenwich Village apartment and raped her. The 1973 trial had been another assault – on her truthfulness, on her integrity, on her spirit – and when the jury failed to agree on a verdict, she retreated from her once pleasant life even further. Mercer was one of the few people who had engendered her trust, from the time of his first phone call, astounding her with the news that she might achieve some measure of justice after all these years.

'I'd still like to have her here at seven thirty in the morning. I want to go over her testimony once more.'

'I have the feeling she'll be better rested than you.'

'I'm set. Who could imagine that this case would be easier for me to try now than it was for my predecessor thirty-five years ago? Easier for Kerry, too.'

'Chapman's here to suck a little more of that energy out of you.'

'Where?'

'Down the hall in the conference room. Got someone with him.'

I stood up, fanning myself with the manila folder that held Pablo Posano's posttrial motions and his inmate number at the maximum security prison where he was serving time. 'I'll check it out. You want to call Attica for me? See if we can get a list of Posano's visitors and his phone log?'

'Sure.' Mercer reached for the file as I walked out of the room.

The corridors emptied out earlier than usual during the hot summer days. There were fewer trials as lawyers, judges, and witnesses escaped the city on vacation. Government workers were allowed to leave their offices on afternoons when temperatures, threatening to overload the electrical power grids, climbed above ninety-five degrees. It was six fifteen and the executive wing of the trial division was quiet.

I pushed open the door and saw Mike sitting across the conference table from a young woman who was talking to him. A handful of snapshots were spread out in front of her, and Mike was studying two of them as she spoke.

'Here she is,' he said. 'Alexandra Cooper, I'd like you to meet Janet Bristol.'

The most obvious thing about her when she looked up was the redness and swelling around her eyes. I wasn't surprised. It was rare for me to meet someone for the first time, professionally, who had much to smile about.

'Janet showed up at the First this morning,' Mike said. 'She saw the squib in the *Post*. The one about the body.'

'I haven't had a chance to read the newspapers today.'

Mike handed me a story – three short paragraphs – buried deep in the back of the news section of the tabloid. 'MARITIME BATTERY . . . AND ASSAULT: TERMINAL. The naked remains of an unidentified woman were found yesterday evening in the abandoned offices above the aging ferry slip . . .'

'Janet's afraid the victim might be her sister. We may need you on this, Coop.'

'Thank you for coming in. I know how difficult it must be for you.'

'I doubt that you do.' Her comeback was fast and sharp.

'We're on our way to the medical examiner's office. Janet's going to try to make an ID.'

Standing in front of the morgue's viewing window was one of the most painful steps a family member was forced to endure in the course of an investigation. Nothing could prepare Janet for the condition of the face and body she was about to see.

'How can I help?'

Mike got up. 'Let's step out and I'll—'

'You can repeat what I said.' Janet Bristol reached into her pocket for a tissue and blew her nose. 'I know that's why we're here.'

'Can you tell me why you think this might be your sister?'

Janet blotted her eyes and looked down at the photographs, handing me one. 'That's Amber about a year ago.'

I studied the image. The resemblance to Janet was striking. Long, narrow faces, lightly freckled skin, and thin, tapered noses. Everything was consistent with the shape and size of the woman we had seen last night.

'We're not close, like I told Detective Chapman. But we had this deal that we always went out together on our birthdays,' she said. 'Her birthday was the Sunday before last. She just turned thirty-two.'

By this past Sunday, the woman decomposing behind the cast iron façade of the old building had already been dead for more than a week, if Mike and Dr. Magorski were right.

'When's the last time you spoke to Amber?'

Janet straightened up. 'Christmas. I think it was right after the holidays. I had gone home – to Idaho – to see the family. I called her when I got back.'

'And not once during the last eight months?'

'I told you, we're different. We don't really get along.'

'Can you tell us something about her?' I sat down next to Janet to look at the other photographs. I wanted to know what would lead this woman to the conclusion that her sister had been the victim of a murder, rather than that she simply chose to celebrate the event with someone else.

'Amber is – well, she's quirky, like I told the detective. She moved to New York about nine years ago, after college. Worked for a temp agency. Wound up doing word processing at a law firm. That's where she's been for the last five years. Masters and Martin.'

'One twenty Wall Street.' The offices of the small firm that specialized in patent law placed Amber a short walk from where the body was found. 'And how long has it been since she showed up there?'

Mike crossed his arms and sat on the windowsill. 'She was let go in July.'

'She quit,' Janet said defensively. 'That's what the receptionist told me.'

'Have you called her at home? Or gone to her apartment?'

'Her answering machine is full. It's not taking any more messages. And her cell phone is shut off.'

'Are there neighbors?'

'She didn't have any friends in the building, really. I called the super. He hasn't seen her since last week.'

'I've got the address, Coop. The East Nineties. You should know they wanted her out of there.'

'Behind on the rent?'

'Nope. People didn't like the company she kept. If Janet can

– well, if she's able to make an ID,' Mike said, 'we'll go straight there.'

'Did you have a plan to meet on Amber's birthday?'

Janet shook her head. 'I started calling on that Friday. Left a few messages then that she didn't return. We go to the same place every year. I just assumed she'd show up.'

'Where's that?'

'Dylan's Brazen Head. It's a pub on First Avenue, near her apartment.'

I glanced at a photo of the two sisters together, both smiling for the camera. Behind them was the mirrored wall of a bar, lined with bottles of booze. The Brazen Head had been in business for more than twenty years, a magnet for prep school kids from the Upper East Side because of the affable owner's willingness to turn a blind eye to underage drinkers. It was named for the oldest pub in Dublin, which dated back – according to legend – eight hundred years.

'Did you go?' I asked.

'Yes. I went early, at six, and waited there until ten o'clock.'

'Tell Ms. Cooper why Amber picked Dylan's.'

Janet looked at me sideways before she answered. 'Jim Dylan and Amber – well, she's been, I guess you'd say, dating him for three years.'

'What she means is that Jim Dylan has a wife and six kids, three of 'em still at home in the nest,' Mike said. 'So I wouldn't exactly call it "dating." '

'Did you ask Mr. Dylan about your sister?'

'He told me he hadn't seen her since May. Jim didn't want to talk about it there. One of his sons was tending bar.'

'Is there anything else about your sister that you think puts her in harm's way?'

'Like I told you,' Janet said again. 'Amber's quirky. I'm afraid this stuff might end up in the newspapers. I just want to protect her if I can.'

'What do you mean?'

'My sister supplemented her income with another job, Ms. Cooper,' Janet said, blowing her nose again. 'She tried to talk me into the same thing a couple of years ago, but I thought it was disgusting. It broke my heart to think of what she was doing.'

'What kind of job?'

'A dating service.'

I wanted to find a tasteful way to get Janet where she was going. 'An escort?'

Mike lifted his blazer from the back of the chair, slipped his finger under the collar, and draped it over his shoulder as he stepped behind me.

'I told her how dangerous her lifestyle was, and nothing I said could get her to stop.' Janet rested her head in her hands and started crying again. 'Doesn't matter what you called her, she laughed it off like it was a compliment. An escort, a prostitute, a whore, a hooker.'

Mike leaned over and whispered in my ear. 'I'm thinking she's a dead hooker now.'

4

I walked Janet Bristol to the rest room to wash her face, then returned to wait for her in my office.

'You've got to give me a hand tonight,' Mike said.

'What am I missing?' I looked from him to Mercer.

'We're going to get a hit at the morgue,' Mike said. 'I can taste it. I just look at that beauty mark on the side of this broad's neck and picture the one in the identical place on her sister. A patch of skin untouched by the bugs. We got hold of Amber's dentist an hour ago – she had sent Janet to him for an abscess last year. He's faxing over her records to Dr. Kestenbaum.'

'And if it's a match?'

'Janet tells me that if we're not the first ones to get hold of Amber's little black book, this case will rocket from oblivion to the headlines. Good morning, Idaho. This is your wake-up call.'

'Does she know her sister's clientele?' Mercer's six-foot-six frame towered over Mike, and his ebony face was sweating heavily.

'Not specific guys, but according to Amber's stories, they're what the newspapers refer to as boldface names. Lawyers, businessmen, politicians. I want you to come uptown with us, Alex, if Janet makes an ID,' Mike said. 'You're the one who's going to have to run interference with Battaglia if this investigation takes a detour.'

'Don't be luring Coop away from my case,' Mercer said.

'You told me this trial would be over in two days.'

'It should be,' I said. The courtroom circus created by Floyd Warren's defense attorney had prolonged the proceedings for two weeks back in the seventies. Now, the powerful addition of DNA to the prosecution case would change the focus – and pace – radically.

'So by this time Thursday evening, Ms. Cooper, Floyd Warren will be one more notch on your belt and you'll be looking for something to take your mind off the much more important fact that you've got no social life. I can fill all those empty hours for you, kid,' Mike added. 'Me and my rapidly growing summer-in-the-city body count.'

Mercer knew why Mike wanted my company. Mercer and I spent countless hours handholding survivors of violence who needed emotional support to get through the unfamiliar clinical steps that marked their introduction to the criminal justice system. It took as much time, sometimes more, than working the investigation.

Mike was impatient in that role. He was at his best when he set himself up against an unknown predator, teasing secrets from the dead to offer up cold, hard evidence that would lead him to the suspect.

'You want Alex to take charge of Janet Bristol tonight?' Mercer said. 'And if the little black book has some dynamite in it, you want her to sit right on top of that keg?'

'Or stick it in her pocket. Give me a curfew, man. I'll have her tucked in. She's so overwired for this trial, you can't be worried about it.'

'You want to go with them, Alex?' Mercer asked.

'Sure.'

'See you here at seven thirty. You get some sleep.'

I straightened up my desk and, when Janet Bristol returned, went with her and Mike to his car. The ride to the six-story blue brick building that housed the morgue took only fifteen minutes. The deputy medical examiner assigned to the case, Jeff Kestenbaum, met us at reception and took us into his office. A lanky man with the serious mien of a scholar, he was always gentle with family members, who usually came to his office for terrible news.

Kestenbaum explained to Janet how the viewing would occur. He tried to tell her, more graphically than Mike had done, how the skin and soft tissue of the woman he now believed to be Amber had been devoured by insects after her death. He confirmed that the dental records matched the work in those teeth that had not been kicked out of Amber's mouth by her killer.

'Do I – do I have to look?'

The office required that at least one person known to the deceased attempt a physical identification. Stories were legion about people with similar characteristics – build, coloring, crowned wisdom teeth or abdominal surgical scars – who were mistakenly identified because of confusion about these traits.

'Before we release the body to you, yes, you must.'

We took the short walk to the window that separated Janet from the corpse. It would be cleaner now, after the autopsy, with some of the facial wounds stitched together, than when Mike had called me in the night before.

The green curtain was drawn back and Janet reacted immediately.

'Oh, my God,' she said, pressing her face against the glass. 'Yes, it's my sister. Oh, my God, yes.'

Now the resemblance was even more obvious, with Janet's cheek in profile to us, matching the outline of the bone structure of Amber's face. Her knees buckled and Mike picked her up in his arms before she could hit the floor.

We followed Kestenbaum down the hall and Mike rested Janet on the sofa in the small lounge that was set aside for grieving families. She was alert almost at once, and the men left the room while I sat beside her, stroking her hand and trying to calm her for the tasks ahead.

'Is there someone you'd like to have here with you?'

'No. There's no one. It's my mother I've got to call.' She took a deep breath and leaned her head back against the arm of the sofa.

'Any friends who can keep you company?'

'I don't want anyone to know, don't you see?'

'To know that Amber's been killed?'

'That'll be news soon enough. I don't need them to find out how she lived.'

'Anything I can do to—?'

'Would you please step out for a few minutes? I'd like to be alone here for a while. To think about Amber, if you don't mind.'

I closed the door behind me and walked to Kestenbaum's office. The doctor was standing at his desk, organizing autopsy photographs – a male victim of a gunshot wound – probably for a court appearance. Mike had his feet up on the side of the desk, surfing channels on the small TV.

'Janet ready to go?' he asked.

'Wants a few minutes to collect herself.'

'I'm itching to get my hands on Amber's client files.'

'You'll have a laundry list of some of her johns, a married lover, the disgruntled landlord, an ex-employer, and maybe a random stranger who carries the tools of torture with him,' I said, counting on my fingers the directions Mike's investigation might now take. 'Where to begin?'

Mike raised the volume and Alex Trebek announced the Final Jeopardy category. ' "Famous Americans," folks. Let's see what you're willing to wager.'

'I'm in, Coop. Twenty bucks.'

Not a gruesome crime scene nor the solemnity of a morgue could keep Mike from watching the last minutes of *Jeopardy*. He had majored in history at Fordham and he loved to show off his extensive knowledge of a variety of trivia subjects.

'I know, you're about to tell me it's inappropriate,' he said. 'You're about to tell me even hookers got sisters with feelings. I'll have your money before Janet powders her nose.'

'Twenty for me.'

'Doc?'

'Got to concentrate, Mike. I'm working on an exit wound,' he said, making notes as he held one of the enlarged photos. ' "*Taceant colloquia. Effugiat risus.*" '

Mike's Latin was better than mine, from years of parochial school. He, too, recognized the translation of the words posted over the entrance to the medical examiner's office. 'Let conversation cease. Laughter, take flight. This place is where death delights to aid the living.'

'You're just taking a pass 'cause the question isn't some brainiac scientific thing, Doc. You blew us out of here with that one about injuries to the fifth metatarsal. A Monto fracture or whatever it was.'

Trebek was back on cue. 'He was only the sixth foreign-born individual to be declared an honorary citizen of the United States by the president, pursuant to an act of Congress.'

Two of the three studio guests eagerly scrawled questions on their screens. One cocked his head and stared blankly at the camera.

'I'm sorry, sir,' Trebek told the kayak instructor from Indianapolis. 'Winston Churchill was the first to receive the honor. In his lifetime, actually, in 1963. We're looking for the sixth person. No guesses?'

The bank teller from Long Island had also guessed incorrectly, and the beekeeper from Dallas didn't bother to take a stab at the answer. Neither did Kestenbaum or I.

'Who is the Marquis de Lafayette?' Mike said. 'Major General Marie Joseph de Lafayette, hero of the American Revolution. Valley Forge. The Yorktown campaign.'

Trebek nodded at the camera as the board behind him revealed the answer. 'Yes, indeed. George Washington's great friend, only the sixth foreigner so honored. Churchill, Mother Teresa, Raoul Wallenberg, William Penn – and his wife, Hannah – and then the young French nobleman who came to America's aid. Not chronological, obviously, folks.'

Mike shut off the television to continue our history lesson. 'Yeah, if Cornwallis hadn't surrendered at Yorktown—'

'Excuse me,' Janet Bristol said, pushing open the door to Kestenbaum's small office. 'Would you mind telling me exactly – well, exactly how my sister died?'

Mike took his feet down from the desk and held back a chair for Janet.

'Not at all,' Dr. Kestenbaum said, stacking the photos he'd been working on into a pile.

'Did you reach your parents?' I asked. She was pale white and still sniffling, and even more agitated than when I had left her minutes ago. Her cell phone was clasped tightly in her hand.

'Not yet. I'm not ready to do that,' she said, looking at her watch. 'I decided to wait another hour, till my father gets home from work. I want them to be together when they get the news.'

The cell phone in her hand rang. She flipped it open and looked at the incoming caller's number. 'It's Jim Dylan. I don't need to take it. He can just rot in hell,' Janet said, dropping the phone into her tote.

'Why do you think he's calling you now?' Mike asked.

'Oh – well, I just left him a message about Amber. About her murder.'

Mike grimaced and tried to hide his displeasure. 'From here on, Janet, I don't want you talking to him, or to any other people who might be witnesses, okay? I need to know exactly what you said to Dylan, and then I'll take it over now.'

She pointed at me. 'Ms. Cooper didn't tell me I couldn't speak to people about Amber.'

'I'm sorry. It didn't occur to me that you would try to reach anyone but your family.'

Janet's red-rimmed eyes were more focused now. 'That prick has some answering to do, Mr. Chapman. For more than a year he'd been promising Amber he was going to leave his wife. We talked about it – we *drank* to it – on her last birthday. On Sunday, Jim told me he didn't want me to mention her name, that she wasn't welcome in his bar anymore. Well, let him come down here and take a look at what he drove her to.'

I doubted it would be as simple as the formula to which Janet seemed to reduce Amber's fate.

'Does Dylan have a key to her place?' Mike asked.

'I don't know. I doubt she gave keys to a living soul. She didn't even give one to me,' Janet said. 'Not exactly the kind of habits you'd want someone to walk in on.'

Mike was eager to get to Amber's apartment before anyone else tried to enter. 'Why don't we start on up there.'

'I want to know how she died, Doctor.' Janet's hand trembled as she brushed a lock of hair out of her eyes and lowered her voice. 'Do you think she suffered much?'

There was no way to soften the blow. The best that forensics could do was to explain the manner of death, the mechanism that had cut short Amber's life. But the length of time Amber Bristol was in the company of her killer and what had happened to her while she was still conscious – the answers

Mike Chapman wanted – would undoubtedly prove even uglier.

'It's quite possible that she did suffer,' Kestenbaum said. 'Your sister was – badly bruised, Ms. Bristol. Most of the injuries occurred before she died.'

Janet winced and breathed in deeply.

'The newspapers – will there have to be stories about this? About Janet and her, uh, her lifestyle?'

'Hard to know,' Mike said, pacing behind Kestenbaum's back in the narrow room. 'Right now, there's no reason for any sensational press.'

'Is there DNA?'

'It's unlikely that anything Dr. Kestenbaum recovered will identify the killer.'

'Then at least she wasn't raped.'

A little bit of television forensics was a dangerous thing. Maggots had done their work well, moving into body openings and cavities, destroying what the killer might have left behind.

'Do you have more, well – something else to go on?'

'Look, Janet,' Mike said, leaning his strong forearms on the desk. He was impatient to get on his way, to get to work before the next shift brought him more cases. 'We don't know the first thing about Amber. Till you walked in the station house today, we didn't have a clue to connect her to a name. There wasn't a shred of identification, not a piece of clothing, not a blessed thing—'

'There was the whip, wasn't there?' Janet said.

Mike lifted his head to glare at me. I shook mine back at him.

'What whip?' There was no sure way to link it to Amber's death at this point, and it was the kind of detail that investigators would withhold from the public for as long as possible – something about which only the killer might know.

'The sergeant,' Janet said, 'the man at the desk in the station house. He told me the cops fished a whip out of the river. He was trying to calm me down, telling me he hoped it wasn't the killer's.'

Mike put his hand on the doorknob and held Janet's chair as she stood up.

'Be sure and look over Jimmy Dylan when you talk to him, Mr. Chapman. He's not what he appears to be – just a charming barkeep,' Janet said. 'He knew all about Amber, and he did nothing to stop it, nothing to help her. Jimmy knows that's what people paid Amber to do.'

'What do you mean?'

'My sister's a dominatrix, Detective. She liked to hurt people – took pleasure in it. I'll bet if that whip had anything to do with Amber's murder, it belonged to her and not the killer.'

5

Amber Bristol's studio apartment was on the third floor of a walk-up building on East Ninety-first Street, near the corner of Lexington. The superintendent, Vargas Candera, had admitted us with a spare key that he said she had given him, reluctantly, after a kitchen blaze in one of the other units had forced the fire department to break down a door. He waited for us in the hallway.

Janet sat downstairs in a patrol car with two officers while Mike and I put on plastic gloves for a first look around.

'I'd say Amber was either a meticulous housekeeper or somebody else made a clean sweep around here,' Mike said, adjusting the dimmer to its brightest position.

The kitchenette was to the left of the entrance door and the bathroom to its right. A curtain of black wooden beads separated the foyer from the king-size canopy bed just beyond. Mike held the swinging beads aside and I followed him in.

'Early American brothel. I guess you can take the girl out of Idaho, but you can't take the ho out of Ida.'

The trim on the bedstead was a simple calico pattern that matched the cushions on the two armchairs. A hooked rug in the same pastel shades covered most of the floor. The walls were decorated with paintings of horses and mountains in cheap wooden frames meant to look rustic and folksy.

'No sheets?' I asked.

The quilt – a modern reproduction of a classic wedding ring pattern – was folded neatly in the center of the bed, which had been stripped even of its mattress pad.

'Maybe she was abducted on her way to the Laundromat. That's a route you've probably never taken, Coop.'

'It's not only that it's been sanitized, Mike. This room is completely sterile. There's nothing personal on any surface.'

'Remember, it was Amber's office. I'd hardly expect her to have photos of Ma and Pa on display. No pictures from the prom, no old boyfriends.'

'I was counting on a computerized version of a little black book.'

'You're a little late.' Mike moved one of the bedside tables. The lamp and window air conditioner were plugged into a surge bar on the floor. So was a six-foot-long cable connector that fed the empty cradle of a PDA.

I looked around for a telephone and answering machine. There was a space on the small table, between the lamp and a decorative candle, and the line that fed the jack also snaked along the rug, attached to nothing.

'Somebody's taken stuff out of here. Anything that could connect Amber to her business,' Mike said.

He was opening drawers. First, next to the bed, where I could see that she kept her supply of condoms, and then her dresser.

Underwear, sweaters, and three drawers of negligees below that.

I pulled open the closet door. Slacks hung with skirts in a variety of lengths, everything black except for the blue jeans. Shoes were lined neatly on the floor – flats in front, backless pumps with high heels behind them, and six pairs of leather boots. There were a bunch of empty hangers and lots of large hooks affixed to the back of the door.

'Nothing unusual?' Mike asked. 'No sex toys? No other obvious equipment?'

'I'll confess ignorance. I wouldn't know what it's supposed to look like.'

'Right. And you're the expert.'

'Sex crimes, not games.'

'I love it when you play the dumb blond. Those are the rare times I feel most connected to you,' Mike said.

'There's plenty of room to hold stuff – big hooks and lots of wire hangers. But that would be just a guess 'cause there are normal things that would fit right in.'

Mike scratched his head. 'Maybe Janet's wrong. Or nuts.'

'Or Amber didn't work out of her home. Or she retired.'

The beads made a clicking noise as I brushed through the curtain to look in the refrigerator. Vargas Candera leaned against the doorjamb.

'No, *señora*,' he said laughing. 'She not retired. Amber, she's a very busy lady.'

Mike leaned his back against the wall and crossed his arms. 'Doing what?'

'*No se*. Plenty of men, they come and they go,' Vargas said, playing his fingers in the air like they were climbing up and down the stairs. 'I'm not supposed to know nothing, right? I jus' work here.'

'Must have been noisy,' Mike said.

The skim milk was ten days past its sale date and the butter gave off a sour smell.

'Ms. Amber, she paid me to extra-soundproof the apartment when she move in,' Vargas said, stroking his moustache. 'She tell me she likes to play her music loud. Paid me good to double Sheetrock. Put in 'coustic tile.'

'Was noise a problem in the building?'

Vargas rubbed his grease-stained thumb and forefinger together, suggesting that he had been well compensated for his ignorance. 'I never heard no music after that.'

'When's the last time you saw Amber?' Mike asked.

'Not for a week. Maybe more.'

Vargas started to walk into the foyer. 'Stay right there,' Mike said. 'Don't put your hands on anything. I need to get some guys here to dust for prints. When's the last time you were in this apartment?'

'Me? She don't ask me in much,' Vargas said, one side of his mouth pulling up in a smile. 'I can't afford it.'

'Enough to know if anything is missing? If it looks the way Ms. Bristol always kept it?'

'Not my job.' He held his hands up, palms outward, the strong, thick fingers in front of his face. 'I don't go in there since I fix her toilet last summer.'

'Do you know any of her friends? Any of the people who came to see her regularly?'

I thought of the doormen in my high-rent high-rise building, only twenty blocks away. The sharpest ones held dozens of secrets – infidelities and betrayals by neighbors – thirty floors' worth of them.

'I not a busybody, lady.'

'You live in the basement here?' Mike asked.

'*Si*. I got my television, my girlfriend, and my six-pack. I do my work and I keep to myself.'

'Anybody else have a key to her apartment?'

'How would I know? If a key work, nobody bother me.'

Mike's frustration was growing. 'Dylan. There's a bar around

the corner called Dylan's. You ever seen that guy visiting here –
the guy who owns the joint?'

'I got no idea who you mean. Dylan what?'

'Men pay you to forget they were here, Vargas? Is that how
it goes?'

'They don't have to do nothing, Detective. Ms. Amber takes
care of me very good not to hear nothing, not to see anybody,'
Vargas said, cracking the knuckles of his left hand in his powerful
right fist. 'That girl and trouble, they was always together.'

6

I sat on a bar stool at Primola, sipping my sparkling water like it was aged Scotch. Mike was next to me, stirring the ice cubes in the vodka with his finger. Every table in the chic East Side restaurant was full of people escaping the August heat with a good meal.

'Is the air-conditioning blowing on you, Alessandra?' Giuliano asked. 'I'll have a table for you in five minutes.'

'We're fine right here.'

The owner had been my friend for many years. He was used to seeing me with Mike or Mercer and kept us well fed through many long nights of highly charged casework.

'Fenton,' he said to the bartender. 'Give Signora Cooper a drink. On me.'

'She's like Ali before a big fight, Giuliano. Can't be flirting with a hangover when she faces the jury in the morning.'

'I'll take a raincheck,' I said, nibbling on a bread stick as thin as a straw.

Mike turned to me and rested his feet on the rungs of my stool. We made an odd couple, from backgrounds as different as anyone could imagine, but had forged a real intimacy over a decade of working on some of the grisliest cases the city had seen.

'Have some pasta, Coop. You need the carbs.'

'I just want a bowl of gazpacho. It's too hot for anything else.'

He turned back to Fenton. 'I'll start with linguine. White clam sauce. Then I'll have a veal chop, thick as they come.'

Murder never got in the way of Mike's appetite. His father, Brian, had been one of the most decorated cops in the NYPD's history, retiring after twenty-six years on the job. Mike had been weaned on investigative skills and instincts, but he was also the first in his family to attend college. When Brian died of a massive coronary less than forty-eight hours after turning in his gun and shield, his only son became even more determined to follow in his footsteps. Immediately on graduation from Fordham, where he had waited tables to supplement his student loans, he, too, joined the department.

'Have you ever been to Dylan's?' I asked.

There weren't many watering holes in Manhattan that Mike had missed, between his personal barhopping and the complex directions of many of his cases.

'Too preppy for a blue-collar guy like me.'

'How did an Irish pub get to be so preppy?'

'When I was in college, the place had more of a neighborhood feel.' He had turned thirty-seven the previous fall, six months before me. 'Jimmy Dylan was good to the cops. Happy to have guys from the precinct going off duty drop in when he was trying to get the drunks out at the end of a long night.'

I chewed another bread stick and leaned closer to Mike, trying to hear over the laughter of the patrons at the closest table. Mike's eyes were almost as dark as his hair, and I was pleased to see that they had regained some of the sparkle that had disappeared for the better part of a year after the accidental death of his fiancée, Valerie.

'Dylan started to make some money for himself, so he began to send his kids – the oldest three are sons – to private schools. Junior – that's what they call the eldest son – he must be almost thirty now. All his high school pals hung out at the joint, 'cause Jimmy served them liquor when they were too young to get it anywhere else. He didn't really give a damn what anybody thought. Once you had all that teenage testosterone mixed in with a little alcohol, Dylan's became a magnet for the prep school girls, too. Fancy broads like you, looking to get lucky.'

'I didn't—'

'Yeah, sorry. You were too busy memorizing Shakespeare sonnets and sublimating your sexual desires swimming laps to hang out at pubs,' Mike said, opening one of the linen napkins on the bar and spreading it across my knees as he saw our waiter, Adolfo, approaching with my chilled soup.

I had been raised in Harrison, an affluent suburb of New York City. My mother was a registered nurse who stopped working to raise her three children – my two older brothers and me. My father's medical career took a radical upturn when he and his partner designed and patented an innovative device that became a staple of cardiac surgery. The Cooper-Hoffman valve moved us to northern Westchester, where much of my adolescence was spent training for swim team competition, and paid for my superb education at Wellesley College and then the University of Virginia School of Law.

Mike tucked his napkin into his open shirt collar and started twirling his linguine-filled fork against a large spoon, even as steam still rose from the clam-covered pasta.

'You ever see the bodies on the guys who swim the thousand-meter crawl?' I asked, reaching out to pinch Mike's side. 'Totally buff. No NYPD doughnuts. No chips.'

'They're always soaking wet and they wear bathing caps. Nothing sexy about it. Soup cold enough for you?'

'Very refreshing. Does Jimmy Dylan know you?'

'Nope. He knew my pop,' Mike said. 'Brian worked on a case back when I was twelve or thirteen. Two kids who met at the Brazen Head, drinking at the bar. Girl wound up dead in Gracie Square Park, just south of where the mayor lives.'

'And what did Dylan have to do with it?'

'Nothing. And everything. The boy was nineteen years old, just off the boat from Ireland. Brought a mean cocaine habit with him. Both he and the girl were underage, but Jimmy's crew made them welcome at the bar. Three parts cocaine, two parts tequila shots, and one part homicidal rage when the girl tried to say 'no' transformed the perp into a cold-blooded killer – alcohol courtesy of Jimmy Dylan.'

'So you'd think the SLA would have shut the place down,' I said. The State Liquor Authority licensed every drinking establishment.

'All the publicity just gave Dylan's more cachet. Jimmy paid a big fine, I think, and by then kids from Connecticut and Jersey were queuing up around the block, fake IDs and all, just 'cause the place had its fifteen minutes of fame.'

'Are you going to try to find him tonight?' I asked, wiping some sauce off Mike's cheek with my napkin while he sliced into his chop.

'Yeah. Spoils it a bit, though, that Janet gave him a heads-up.'

'I guess I'll be paying you back on that one for a while.'

My cell phone vibrated on the smooth varnished surface of the bar. I picked it up and noted the district attorney's home number in the illuminated display before I answered.

'Good evening, Paul.' I plugged a finger in my left ear and walked out to the vestibule, through the crowd waiting for tables, so Battaglia wouldn't hear the background noise.

'How come you're not home yet? I tried you there first. Don't you have a big day tomorrow?'

'I'm on my way. Just having a bite to eat.'

'Don't let Chapman's appetite run up your bill. You'll go broke feeding him.'

Someday, if I lived long enough, I might get to tell Paul Battaglia something he didn't already know. The longtime prosecutor had developed an incredible array of sources in the unlikeliest of places, and he delighted in putting the information he gathered to good use – to solve crimes, respond to critics, engage reporters, or simply amuse himself.

'I'll cut him off at dessert.'

'Why didn't you come by to tell me about the case Mike brought you in on last night?'

'I didn't think it was going anywhere, Paul. I was in court all day on Floyd Warren. We never expected to get a name on the woman so fast.'

Now I was sweating again. There was no fan in the hallway and the hot air coming in from Second Avenue was stifling. So was the thought that I had done to Battaglia what he liked least – let him be the last to know.

'This Amber Bristol, how was she killed?

'Bludgeoned to death.'

'With what?'

'Don't know yet.' Never a good answer to give the district attorney.

'Figure it out, will you? The story's already out on the wire services,' Battaglia said, pausing between sentences. 'I'm going to tell you something that has to be held in strictest confidence.'

'Of course.' I walked to the sidewalk and seated myself at one of Giuliano's café tables. It was too oppressive for any customers to have eaten outside.

'Have you ever met Herb Ackerman?'

'No. I've seen him at a few of your press conferences.' Damn,

46

the last thing Mike needed was one of the city's best investigative reporters breathing down his neck so early in the process.

'He's going to be in your office first thing tomorrow morning. You need to talk to him.'

Battaglia knew all about the Floyd Warren trial. It was the most dramatic cold case we had solved, with national consequences, and he had used it as the best example of his leadership in the recently completed drive to eliminate the New York State statute of limitation for rape.

'It's the main testimony in my case in chief, Paul. I'm meeting with our victim at seven thirty.'

I was close enough to know that Ackerman had been one of Battaglia's earliest supporters on the editorial board of the *Tribune*, the most important local weekly news magazine. And I was keenly aware that their relationship had taken a bad turn two years ago, when the coverage of a vigilante subway shooter in Ackerman's influential column had resulted in a series of critical pieces about the DA's office Major Felony Project.

'I'll tell him to be there at eight. I'd like you to keep him waiting,' Battaglia said. 'Just give him fifteen minutes before you go up to court. And don't forget that he screwed me on the Metz case.'

The district attorney's memory was infallible. And payback was one of his strongest motivators.

'I've got nothing to tell him, Paul.' It was uncharacteristic of Battaglia to let his prosecutors meet with the media before a trial. He was the master of the well-timed leak, but I had no information to give away.

'He's not coming to get a story, Alex. We're in the driver's seat this time.'

'Why? What's he got?' I asked.

'What Herb Ackerman's got is a problem. He tells me he was a client of Amber Bristol's.'

7

Kerry Hastings's hands were trembling as she lifted the coffee mug to her mouth. It was eight-thirty on Wednesday morning, and we had spent the last hour in my office with Mercer Wallace, reviewing the questions I intended to ask her when I called her to the witness stand.

'It's going to be very different this time,' I said to her. 'I wouldn't urge you to go through with your testimony if I couldn't promise you that.'

Thirty-five years earlier, Hastings had told her story to a jury, answering questions about the crime that were virtually the same as those I had framed for her now. But her cross-examination had gone on for two days, and I expected that the tactics that had worked so well for Floyd Warren's defense at the first trial wouldn't fly today.

'I don't want to look at him again, Alex. I've spent all these years trying to erase the image of his face. You can't imagine how agonizing it is to be back in a room with that man.'

Kerry Hastings was one of the most intelligent witnesses I had ever worked with. She knew she would sit only a short distance from the man who had forever changed her life in the course of their forty-five-minute encounter. She had been told that she would be asked to point out her attacker, if she could – even though his DNA now resolved the issue of identification.

'I know that. I'll do everything in my power to make this easier for you.'

'Do I get to tell the jury how Floyd Warren has affected every single day of my life? That not once in the three decades since he awakened me and held a knife to my neck have I been able to sleep through the night?'

She didn't have to tell me that the crime itself and the shame that society imposed on rape victims of Kerry's generation had combined to prevent her from ever developing a successful intimate relationship in the intervening years.

Mercer was sitting behind her, off to the side. He leaned forward and rested his hand on her shoulder. 'Judge Lamont will hear all that, Kerry. Alex will get her conviction and you can say what you damn well please in your impact statement to Lamont.'

It wasn't often in a prosecutor's career that the outcome of a trial could be predicted. Juries were fiercely independent, as this victim had learned so harshly the first time out. But the science of DNA and the rapidly evolving technology of computer-generated matches made it ever more difficult for a defense attorney to suggest reasonable doubt when identification of the perp was the sole issue.

I handed Hastings the photograph that had been taken at Bellevue after the rape. She would have to authenticate it for me in court. The black-and-white shots of the slashes on her neck, made by the sharp blade of Warren's knife as she struggled to get away, would corroborate the deadly force he had used to subdue her.

'You think anyone will believe that this is the same woman?' She smiled as she showed the picture to Mercer.

Twenty-two-year-old Kerry Hastings was tall and slightly over-weight, her pretty round face accentuated by short curly hair held back on one side to allow the photographer to capture the wounds that circled her neck. The hospital gown hung loosely and topped her knees. Bruises were visible on the shins of both legs.

The fifty-seven-year-old who sat between us had lost all the baby fat in the intervening years. She had taken up running, training for marathons as a way of focusing her energy and chan-neling her anger into a more positive goal.

'You look just great,' Mercer said.

'Youth, middle age, and "you look just great," ' Kerry said, turning the photo facedown on the edge of my desk. 'Those must be the three stages of life, Mercer. There's only so much you can humor me.'

'There won't be any surprises in my direct examination.'

'And Mr. Grassley? Is he going to do what they did to me back then?'

'He's not required to tell me that in advance, Kerry. I'm hop-ing not.'

'You'll hear Alex shout "objection" any chance she can,' Mercer said. 'Don't you even think about answering if you see her on her feet.'

The three-volume transcript of the first trial was part of my case file. The cross-examination was one of the ugliest I'd ever read.

'Four men on that jury thought I was a prostitute,' Kerry said. 'Four others figured that I might have simply fabricated my story.'

'Rape shield laws have saved victims from that kind of horror,' I said. They had been enacted in every state in the country, but too late to help Kerry Hastings.

Floyd Warren's first counsel had claimed that his client was a pimp and that the seemingly demure young woman on the witness stand had actually worked for Warren. He had peppered Kerry with hours of questions about their supposed relationship, suggesting that she was racist as well and that the argument in her tenement apartment – the one that had caused a concerned neighbor to call 911 at 4:23 a.m. – was about money she had refused to turn over to Warren.

'Did you know there was only one other woman in the entire courtroom in 1973? Just one juror, a few years older than I.'

'The legal system wasn't very friendly to us back then. This office had a staff of two hundred lawyers, and only a handful were women. That district attorney didn't think lady lawyers should be exposed to the blood and guts elements of violent crimes or to any discussion of sexual predators. There were very few women on the bench or at the bar, and it was still a novelty for them to serve on juries. Not much different than in your field.'

Kerry Hastings had been in the first year of a master's program in neurobiology at NYU – a brilliant student who excelled in a specialty dominated by men – when the break-in and rape occurred. She was one of the first women in her field to get a doctorate, returning to school after a three-year hiatus when Warren's mistrial – and his subsequent flight – caused her to leave Manhattan for the West Coast, fearful that he would find her again.

I held up the clear plastic sleeve that contained the pale blue cotton underpants in which the evidence was found that linked Floyd Warren to scores of cold cases.

'I'll ask if you can identify these.'

Kerry bit her lip as she looked at the panties and nodded. She had worn them to the hospital after the attack, where they were taken from her. Her initials were written on the label in black marker, and a hole was cut in the crotch where the semen stain was found.

'I've tried so hard to forget all this, and now the memories come flooding back in,' she said, closing her eyes and taking several deep breaths. 'It's amazing that someone had the foresight to save my underwear all these years.'

'I wish we could tell you that's what happened,' Mercer said. 'The guy who used to have Alex's job? Just thank your lucky stars he was sloppy. When Warren jumped bail, the prosecutor dropped the trial folder in the back of his file cabinet. If he'd followed protocol and returned the evidence to the property clerk, it would have been thrown out years ago.'

The telephone rang and before I could reach for the receiver, I could see from the light on the console that Laura Wilkie had answered. Seconds later, she opened the door and greeted us. 'Mercer, it's for you.'

'Have any other women come forward, Alex? I mean, here in New York?'

'Let's talk about that after you're off the stand.'

There had been a perp walk when Floyd Warren arrived in New York in police custody from his home in Georgia. Mercer Wallace had escorted him from Central Booking to the street, where an eager group of paparazzi waited to take pictures to run alongside his original mug shot. Women who had never dared report the crimes decades ago called the Special Victims Unit to unburden themselves of the pain of their experience.

'The whole thing's so damn unfair,' Kerry said. 'His lawyer was free to make up the most outrageous lies about my life, yet I'm not allowed to mention that Warren raped God knows how many other women – stabbed two of them. They were allowed to think that he's the virgin and I'm the roundheel. Your legal system makes no sense.'

Battaglia had appointed me to head this specialized bureau after my rookie years in the criminal court. All the groundbreaking work on these issues had been done by prosecutors who preceded me – the tedious labor of changing laws and the harder task of educating the public about these highly charged crimes.

Mercer opened the door and signaled me to join him.

'I promise you, you'll know everything I do by the end of the day,' I said as I walked past her to leave the room.

'That's the warden at Attica, returning my call about Pablo Posano,' Mercer said. 'We've got to look somewhere else inside the Latin Princes for the problem. Looks like this monster has grown a new head.'

'Why?'

'The order to stalk you couldn't have come from Posano. He's been in solitary confinement since two weeks after he got there. Tried to jump a guard and they jammed him up. Twenty-three hours a day under bright lights – no reading material, no communication with the outside world. If he hated you before that, imagine how it's festered now.'

'So he didn't give the orders himself this time,' I said. I thought of the tall, solidly built Posano, with dark curly hair that had undoubtedly been shaved by the guards, and the intensity of his light eyes, which bored through me when he stared me down. 'One of his homies is looking to make points by getting back at me?'

'Bank on it, Alex,' Mercer said. 'You're the devil who put Pablo Posano in a black hole.'

8

'Alex, there's a gentleman waiting for you – he says he's been here for an hour, but he won't give me his name. I've got him in Maxine's office,' Laura said. 'He says you're expecting him. And he's terribly nervous.'

Max, my paralegal, was on vacation. Her quiet office around the corner was the ideal place to meet with Herb Ackerman.

'Mercer, why don't you explain to Kerry that there may be some ringers in the courtroom this morning and that it has nothing at all to do with her case?'

'Fine. And I'm calling Lamont's clerk. I want to make sure they'll have your back covered.' Because Mercer was a witness in this trial, he was not allowed to be in the courtroom while the other witnesses testified.

The corridor was busy with the nine o'clock arrival of lawyers and support staff, most with cardboard coffee cups and paper bags stuffed with bagels or doughnuts in hand. This floor of the huge criminal court building housed the executive wing, public relations, the trial division chiefs, and the bureau that handled appeals for the six hundred prosecutors who served at the pleasure of the district attorney.

I opened the door of Max's office. Herb Ackerman had helped himself to her telephone, standing behind her desk, talking to someone in his office about the fact that he'd be late.

'I'm sorry. Sorry. Ms. Cooper?' he said. 'I'm Herb Ackerman.'

'Good to meet you.'

He was a short man in his early sixties with a pasty complexion and a receding chin. His neck stretched up and out at me as he talked, like a turtle extending its head out of the shell. He had reddish brown hair that looked like it had been dyed with shoe polish and eyeglasses whose lenses hadn't been cleaned in months.

'Have a seat, please, and tell me why you're here.'

'Didn't Paul explain?' he asked, preferring to stand and pace.

'He told me that you wanted to see me. About Amber Bristol.'

'No, I didn't want to see *you*, frankly. I wanted to meet with him,' Ackerman said, jabbing his finger in the air.

The ratty tweed jacket he wore with a button-down shirt, too tight at the collar and frayed at the cuffs, seemed a poor choice for yet another hot, humid day.

'Well, then, perhaps I should just direct you to his office,' I said, rising from my chair.

'No, no. He told me you'd have to handle this. It's just, well, it's embarrassing to discuss these things with an attractive young lady.'

I'd made a career dealing with men who'd done embarrassing things. 'This is my job, Mr. Ackerman. For the moment, whatever it is you're going to talk about stays between us.'

His neck elongated itself as he peered around the dingy room, ringed with old green government-issue metal file cabinets, which held a history of the depravity of Manhattan's sex offenders since the unit was created. 'You're not taping me, are you?'

'No, sir. I'm not.'

'I suppose you know who I am?' His nose wrinkled and he pushed his glasses back in place.

'I do.'

'I've known your boss since he was a kid, Ms. Cooper. I've been very good to him over the years,' Ackerman said, hiking his pants up over his potbelly and tightening his belt. 'I hope that counts for something.'

'Mr. Battaglia told me that you knew Amber Bristol. Why don't we focus on that?'

He paced again, away from me, and lowered his head. 'I'm not a crime reporter, Ms. Cooper. I've written about significant cases when they've had an impact on social issues. My experience is more, shall we say, global than street-smart.'

'How did you meet Ms. Bristol?'

'At a cocktail reception. Yes, about a year ago. A cocktail party.'

'Where was the event, Mr. Ackerman?' There was no need to scare him off yet by taking notes. 'I need to know exactly how you became acquainted.'

'Um. Let me think. Must we be that specific?'

'We certainly must.'

'No, I guess it was online. I must have met her online. I'm mistaken about the party.'

It was going to be a contest with Herb Ackerman. He was going to test me to figure how much he could fudge without giving me the facts I needed.

'Do you remember the site?'

'Probably she just began a correspondence because she admired something I'd written. One of my columns,' he said. 'People write to me every day, Ms. Cooper. I couldn't possibly keep track.'

This interview was clearly not going to finish before I had to go to court with Kerry Hastings. I needed to take better control of the witness and let him know that the tabloids would like nothing more than to make this arrogant intellectual fodder for their gossip columns, if not their crime headlines.

'That's not a problem for us. Our forensic computer cops can retrieve documents – even things you've deleted – once we get hold of your hard drive.' I smiled at Ackerman as he squirmed and turned to face me. 'The technology is amazing. Your people probably do it at the magazine all the time, just to find drafts of old copy.'

'You'll – uh, you'll actually look for, um, proof of what I'm telling you?'

'So far, sir, you haven't told me anything. I just thought that if you were having difficulty remembering how you and Ms. Bristol got to know each other, we could try to support your memory with paperwork. From the little I know about her, I suspect she wasn't a regular correspondent with your editorial board. I just assumed you might have met in a chat room or something of that nature.'

He exhaled and his chin settled down into his collar while he thought about what he wanted to tell me.

'You could be right, Ms. Cooper. I spend such a lot of time on my computer. Perhaps I'm confusing her with someone else. Yes, yes – I might have come across her while I was surfing the Web.'

The Middle East peace process, car bombings in Iraq, UN peacekeeping in Africa, poverty in urban America – and an escort service in New York, with a possible emphasis on sadomasochism. A natural progression in an Ackerman online search.

'Here's what we'll do, Mr. Ackerman. I'll go up to court and try my case, because that's extremely important to me right now. I've got a woman who actually wants me to help her. You think about this again and when you're ready to have a candid conversation, just give me a call.'

'Please don't go,' he said, reaching his hand out to grab mine. 'Do you understand how difficult this is for me?'

'Amber Bristol is dead, Mr. Ackerman. How tough was that for her?'

'I called Paul Battaglia because somehow – somehow I became involved in a relationship with Amber,' he said.

I tried to look him in the eye as the words spilled out more quickly, but the thick line of his bifocals distorted my view.

'I was in my office last evening when the story about her murder came over the wire. I was mortified, naturally, and thought that if I reached out for the authorities instead of waiting for them to find a reference to me in her Palm Pilot, there might be a way for me to keep my name out of this.' He met my stare. 'Do you think there is?'

'I obviously don't know enough to give you an answer to that. I'll start with you now, but you'll have to talk with the homicide detective, too. He's got the lead on the case until we get to the arrest phase.'

'You're close to an arrest?' Ackerman was breathing deeply. 'What can you tell me about that?'

'You've got this backwards, sir. There's nothing I can tell you.'

'My name? Do the police have my name?'

'Assume that they do, Mr. Ackerman. When's the last time you saw Ms. Bristol?'

'It was a Friday night, the week before last. It was always a Friday. Her Palm Pilot has everything in it. It's where she kept all her information.'

Two nights before her birthday, before she was supposed to meet her sister, Janet, at the bar.

'Where was that, Mr. Ackerman?'

'In my office. We met in my office.'

I would need Battaglia to sign off on a forensic psychiatrist to work with me. I'd need to understand the risks Amber Bristol had been willing to take with her life. Now the case would be

58

confused with psychobabble about why one of the most distinguished journalists in the city would meet with a hooker at the *Tribune*'s power offices.

'Always at work?'

'Amber's been to my apartment from time to time,' he said. 'I'm a widower, Ms. Cooper. I invited her there occasionally, but then there are doormen to deal with in my co-op, you understand.'

'And her home?'

'Never. I don't even know where she lived.' He clasped his hands together and appeared to be confused by that question. 'Well, if she ever told me, I've forgotten. She had a boyfriend. Obviously, she didn't want our paths to cross. I thought maybe he lived there with her.'

'You know his name?'

He shook his head and his wrinkled neck jiggled. 'I never asked. I think he worked in a bar. At least that's what she said. It's a problem for me to separate the stories she told me – which ones were real and which were, well, fantasies.'

'It must have been even harder to get her past security at the *Tribune* than into a residential apartment building. Wouldn't she have to sign some kind of log?'

'Indeed, I'm sure there's a record of her visits,' he said. 'But believe me, if Herb Ackerman called down to say I was expecting a guest at nine or ten o'clock, and a well-dressed young woman showed up with a press pass, then—'

'A press pass? Did you help arrange that?'

He waved his hand across the desktop. 'Any kid can put his or her hand on one of those. Summer interns, students at local schools, freelance writers.'

'You got one for her?'

'Yes.'

'With a photo and the magazine logo and her name?'

'Yes. Well, that was part of the game we played.'

'Game?'

'She didn't use the name Bristol,' he said, with a chuckle that I could only hope was a nervous reaction. 'Amber Alert. That's what she called herself when she was with me.'

Perhaps this small-town girl with an unhealthy imagination liked the fact that her alias appeared on billboards all over America.

'Let me ask a few more questions, Mr. Ackerman. Then we'll make an appointment for a longer interview.'

'I'd like to get this done now.'

'The last night you were with Amber, did you and she engage in any sexual acts?'

'Sexual? Oh, Ms. Cooper, you're completely mistaken,' Ackerman said, his chin crawling back down onto his short neck. 'Our relationship wasn't about sex.'

I stood up to conclude the meeting. 'I was counting on your candor to help us, Mr. Ackerman. That's the only way we can be of any use to you.'

'But Amber and I never had sex,' he was almost whining as he looked at me.

'Then you tell me what your get-togethers were like.' I didn't want to give him any information about whips and handcuffs until he raised the subject himself.

Ackerman reached under his glasses with the thumb and forefinger of his left hand and massaged his closed eyelids.

'She diapered me, Ms. Cooper. That's what she did.'

'She *what*?'

The forensic psychiatrist I had in mind, an expert in psychosexual disorders, would probably double his rates when I gave him the case hypothetical.

'It's a – a problem I have.'

'A medical problem?'

'No. No. Nothing I need,' he said softly. 'I like to be diapered.'

'Amber Bristol diapered you? In your office at the *Tribune*?'

I had been taught in my early years never to appear to be judgmental, but sometimes it was harder to feign indifference than others.

'Yes.'

'And there was no other sexual contact of any kind?'

'None. None at all.'

'Did she bring anything else with her when she visited you?'

'What kind of things do you mean?'

'You mentioned the word "fantasy." Any objects that went along with what you two did. And how was she dressed, Mr. Ackerman? Did she carry a handbag? Did she bring any kind of tote with her?'

'Amber was dressed – we laughed about it, actually. She looked like something off a sailing ship, is what I told her. She had just bought herself a jacket – sort of white cotton, double-breasted affair. It had gold buttons and epaulets, with some gold braid on the shoulders. I made fun of it, I guess, but she thought it was quite the style.'

The short-waisted military-style jacket had been the rage in the spring, sold all over town by department stores and boutiques knocking off the high-end version.

'The last I saw of her is when she walked out of my office. I saluted her and told her she looked like a ship's captain.'

The description of the clothing might be useful if it turned out Amber Bristol had been killed that night.

'Did she carry a purse?'

'Yes,' he said, nodding at me. 'Always did. One of those great big things, with long straps on her shoulder. Did you find that? It's where she kept her Palm Pilot.'

'Suppose we found it, Mr. Ackerman. Why don't you tell me what else was in it?'

'Do you enjoy doing this, Ms. Cooper?' He sat up straight and thrust his head forward again. 'Humiliating me like this?'

'That's not my plan, sir. I'd prefer not to be asking these

questions.' They didn't seem a fraction as mortifying to me as the thought of seeing him undressed on a sofa in his office.

'Look, Mr. Ackerman. We know that Amber was also into sadomasochistic liaisons.'

He wagged a finger in my face. 'Not with me. I'm not involved in any business like that.'

'But she was,' I said. 'That's an indisputable fact. And we believe some of her own devices may have been used to kill her.'

'I never touched them. None of them.'

'None of what, Mr. Ackerman?'

'Handcuffs, then, okay? Is that what you want? Yes, she brought handcuffs with her sometimes. But I swear we never used them. She took them out of her bag occasionally to show them to me, but that wasn't my thing. God knows what else she carried around with her.'

He was distraught now, his head nestled back down onto his chest.

'Anything else?'

'No. Nothing at all.'

'Was there anything you would characterize as violent that occurred between you and Amber?'

'Absolutely not. I'm not like that, Ms. Cooper.'

I was trying to get a clue as to what Herb Ackerman really *was* like.

'You understand that we're going to have to get a sample of your saliva, for DNA,' I said, in case any other evidence developed. 'The detectives will do that later today.'

'I'm not a common criminal, young lady. I won't be treated like one.'

Many of my witnesses started with that attitude. The idea of Mike Chapman venturing into the *Tribune* building with a Q-tip to take a buccal swab from Ackerman made me think we'd find a more cooperative way to get it done.

'Did you speak with Amber again after she left your office?'

'You heard me, didn't you? I didn't hurt that young woman. I had nothing to do with her death. And no, I never heard from her again.'

'Did you try to reach her? Did you leave any messages for her?'

He tilted his head, ready to test me again. 'I don't remember.'

'I haven't listened to her answering machine or her cell yet,' I said, happy to be bluffing him. 'Perhaps I can refresh your recollection after I do.'

'Maybe so.'

'Other than your office and your home, did you ever go anywhere with Amber? Did you ever take her anywhere else, like out to dinner?'

Ackerman shook his head. 'She was a nice girl, Ms. Cooper. But our relationship only had one purpose.'

'How much did you pay Ms. Bristol?'

Another deep breath. 'Two hundred fifty dollars, in cash. That bought me an hour of her time. And I must tell you something else that you haven't asked.'

'Yes?'

'You'll see, if your detectives do their homework, that I wrote about that place where Amber's body was found in an article that was published this winter. In my column,' he said.

'Trib-ulations' was Ackerman's sounding board, a weekly opinion piece that let him take on issues of local or national importance.

'The Battery Maritime Building?'

'Precisely.'

'You've been to the terminal recently? I thought it's abandoned and—'

'Ferry service to Brooklyn stopped in 1938, as you probably know. But the army used the slip for years when they owned Governors Island. I've been writing, advocating about converting the empty space for other uses.'

Mike would be as interested in the military history of Amber's death chamber as in Ackerman's familiarity with it.

'Is that something you and she ever talked about?'

He puffed himself up now, unable to resist the opportunity to gloat. 'She made it a point to read everything I wrote. Quite a bright girl. I don't remember discussing that column in particular, but Amber would have been certain to see it.'

'You were smart to call the district attorney, Mr. Ackerman. This way, I can arrange for you to meet with Detective Chapman, and we won't have to come looking for you at an inconvenient time.'

'There'll be no calls to the office, then?' he asked as I stood up. 'No leaks to the media?'

'Mr. Battaglia controls that pretty well,' I said, knowing that my boss played the press like a Stradivarius.

'When Amber left you that evening, what time was it?'

'A little after midnight,' Ackerman said. 'She arrived at eleven o'clock, I'm quite certain of that.'

'There'll be a record of when she signed out.'

'Probably so.'

'And you, did you leave with her?'

'Oh, no. No, no, no. I see where you're going with that, Ms. Cooper. No, no. Even if I walked her out to get a cab, which I may have done. I sometimes did that, as a gentleman would. But I'm sure I went back to my office to lock up.'

'Did Amber tell you where she was going?' I asked, my hand on the doorknob as I tried to escort Herb Ackerman from the room.

'She was meeting someone for a drink. She was mad at her boyfriend, I know that. I think she was planning to meet someone at another bar. Maybe she was trying to make the man jealous. Amber knew just what buttons to push.'

9

'Today we're going to travel back in time,' I told the jurors. Sixteen people in the box, twelve regular jurors and four alternates. There were an even number of men and women, a racially diverse mix of New Yorkers, but only four of the group had been born at the time Kerry Hastings was raped.

There were few spectators in the room. The trial of an aspiring rap star who had shot up a Midtown nightclub when the manager tried to throw him out had drawn reporters to the courthouse across the street.

That was good news for Hastings, who had no interest in reliving her assault so publicly. But I couldn't ignore the presence of a young man who glared at me from the front-row bench. I recognized him from yesterday's pack of Latin Princes. He had passed through the hallway metal detector, which gave me some level of comfort, but I knew he wasn't there to root for my case.

'The events that the witnesses will describe to you took place in the early morning hours of July 10, 1973. You will meet Kerry Hastings,' I said, outlining some of her background in my opening statement for the people who would soon hear her story, 'who was twenty-two years old on the night that Floyd Warren changed the course of her young life.

'Let me give you some context of the times during which these crimes occurred. The president of the United States was Richard Nixon,' I began. I had tested the almanac listings of that year on my summer intern, a college student. She didn't seem to know who Spiro Agnew was, so I left out the fact of his resignation and the subsequent Saturday Night Massacre. The ceasefire ending the involvement of American ground troops in Vietnam didn't register very well either, in light of more recent military engagements.

'A first-class stamp cost eight cents, Elvis – Elvis Presley, not Costello – was a sellout nearby at the Nassau Coliseum, and *The Godfather* won the Oscar for the year's best movie,' I said, making eye contact with the several jurors who had listed film as among their favorite hobbies in the voir dire questions. And I nodded at number six, the bus driver who spent most of his afternoons at an Off-Track Betting parlor in his neighborhood, when I told them that Secretariat had captured the Triple Crown, the last time that feat had been accomplished in horse racing.

I told them what the prosecution case would prove, in colder, more clinical terms than the excruciating details they would hear from the mouth of Kerry Hastings. I read to them the charges – rape and sodomy, burglary and robbery – in the indictment returned by a grand jury, what used to be called a 'blue-ribbon panel' of carefully selected citizens during the thirty-year reign of District Attorney Frank Hogan.

'We will prove these charges by the testimony of witnesses who will tell you what they experienced through each of their five senses: what they saw, heard, felt, tasted, and smelled on that unbearable morning – and in the days and years that followed.

'You will hear from police officers, a doctor, and forensic biologists. You will see crime scene photographs and physical evidence that you can examine yourselves – things that will take you back to the tiny room in which these life-threatening acts occurred.'

I was standing in front of the jury box as I turned to the defendant and his counsel. I started to walk toward Gene Grassley, knowing that the sixteen triers of fact would follow my movement, would look at Floyd Warren when I pointed at him and accused him of the crimes.

'You will hear from police officers – now retired – who responded to the 911 call made by a neighbor when Kerry Hastings's muffled screams pierced the warm night air. They will both tell you how they chased this defendant from the front door of Ms. Hastings's building, as he crossed the street and vaulted a chain-link fence, trying to escape them but getting caught less than a city block away. He had six dollars in his pants pocket, and there was a serrated steak knife that he had discarded on the ground in the course of his flight.'

I watched as the jurors looked at Warren. He was dressed in a denim shirt, with an orange macramé kufi cap. He met their stares head-on, shaking his head from side to side. He no longer looked able to scale a seven-foot schoolyard fence.

'And while Kerry Hastings's case grew cold, while justice stalled, science kept moving forward with a revolutionary technology called DNA.'

I gave the jurors the bare bones of the people's case. I wanted to pique their interest, engage them on the victim's behalf, and impress upon them the facts we would present.

'And I will stand before you at the end of this case, when I have proven Floyd Warren's guilt beyond *any* doubt, and ask you to convict him of each of these crimes with which he is charged.'

As I took my place at counsel table, I noticed that two more of the Latin Princes had entered the room. There were no words emblazoned on their chests today, just the image of a dagger, half covered in blood, on the black background of the T-shirts. A court officer stood behind my chair, facing them. I tried to concentrate on Grassley's opening.

His remarks were short and he spoke in generalities, urging each of the jurors to keep an open mind. He knew that my evidence was overwhelming, and he was up against the dazzling science of genetic fingerprinting.

'You may call your first witness, Ms. Cooper.'

'The people call Kerry Hastings, Your Honor.'

One of the court officers went to the side door that led to the witness waiting room. When he came back in, every head but mine turned to Hastings, to inspect her, as she walked into the well of the courtroom, approached the stand, and was sworn in.

I rose to bring my notes to the lectern. I could see now that there were eight gang members in the room, along with a handful of my colleagues. It worried me that the group would try to stage any kind of outburst while Kerry Hastings was testifying.

For almost fifteen minutes, I took her through the basic information of her background – her education, her training, her impressive résumé of publications and academic awards. Her poise and dignity belied the anger that she had described to me, the anger she had carried internally for three decades. This jury was meeting a mature adult, robbed of a life she had planned for herself when her youthful dreams were shattered by Floyd Warren's brutality.

I had her describe how she went to sleep the night she was raped and what had awakened her.

'I heard a noise on the fire escape. My bed was right next to the window, and because it was such a warm night, I had left it open.'

As she answered my questions, the young man in the front row began to cough.

'What kind of noise was it?' I asked her.

'It sounded like something rattling against the metal grating. That's when I opened my eyes.'

'And what did you see?'

'I saw light – like flames – just outside my window. I sat up in bed because I was afraid that something was on fire.'

'What happened next?'

'There was a man sitting on the window sill. He already had one leg in my room. The flames came from a cigarette lighter that he was using to see his way in the dark.'

'What did—?'

'He dropped the lighter and grabbed my hair with his left hand. He pulled me toward him and held the point of a knife against my neck. "Don't scream," is what he said to me. "Don't make me use this."'

Kerry Hastings was almost mechanical in her recitation of the story. She was determined, this time, that she wouldn't give Floyd Warren the satisfaction of seeing her cry. I needed to slow her down and make her wait for me to finish my questions.

Several of the young gang members appeared to be having coughing fits.

'Were you able to see the face of the man who held the knife to your neck?'

The judge banged his gavel three times. Hastings jumped, surprised by the pounding noise directly behind her head.

'Let's have some order here.'

'I saw him for less than a minute. He put—'

'Hold on, Ms. Hastings, will you?' Judge Lamont said. 'I can't hear your answers.'

Floyd Warren was smirking, pleased to see that the witness was rattled by the disruptive spectators.

Louie Larsen approached the kid in the first row and exchanged whispered remarks. Then Larsen walked to the bench and said something to Lamont.

'Carry on, Ms. Cooper.'

'Had you ever seen the intruder, the man who came through your window, before?'

'No. I didn't know him.'

'Let's go back, Ms. Cooper. I didn't get what she said about seeing the man.'

Hastings turned toward the judge. 'I only saw him for a few seconds. He put a pillow over my face before he turned me on my stomach. He didn't want me to see him.'

'Wait for Ms. Cooper's questions, please.'

So much for my smooth direct. Kerry Hastings's calm was dissolving rapidly.

The lead Latin Prince had another coughing spell, doubling over and clapping his chest.

Alton Lamont stood up and pointed at the door with his gavel. 'Take it out of here, young man. Captain Larsen, let's clear the courtroom.'

One of the officers directed the jurors to rise and file through the door behind the witness stand. Several of them stooped to pick up bags and backpacks, fixated on the confrontation between the judge and the Latino loudmouth.

'It's a public trial, Your Honor. I know my rights.'

Another officer took his place beside Kerry Hastings, who looked shell-shocked by all the activity going on around her.

Larsen had the leader by the arm and was trying to drag him out of the room. Half the jury members were still watching, still listening, even as they were being herded along.

'Ms. Cooper's trying to railroad another brother, Judge. She's a liar! Liar!'

The other gang members were on their feet, pushing one another to get to the door ahead of Larsen and his charge.

'Arrest him, Captain. He's over the line. Arrest him.' Lamont banged his gavel again.

'Arrest my ass, Judge. She's a liar!'

One of the others slammed the door open and the rest followed into the hallway. The heavy wooden panels swung back and forth several times, echoing with the sound of the eight-foot-tall metal detector as it crashed to the floor, flipped over by the fleeing Latin Princes.

Kerry Hastings looked at me, blinking back tears. I had promised her the trial would be easy. I assured her nothing would traumatize her like the first time. Today I'd been wrong.

10

'No, Judge, I don't want to move for a mistrial. Let's just go forward,' I said.

It was an hour later. Lamont had granted a recess while we regrouped. The Latin Prince who'd been arrested, Ernesto Abreu, had been charged with harassment and taken away in handcuffs. The broken metal detector meant that any spectators would be patted down before entering the courtroom, and I knew that Louie Larsen would slow that process sufficiently so that we could carry on without incident or unwelcome visitors.

The jurors were given a curative instruction. They were told to ignore the outburst that had occurred and not to discuss it among themselves. Most of them were no longer smiling at me as they had during voir dire, some undoubtedly wondering whether what Abreu had shouted was true.

Kerry Hastings had been rattled by the interruption. Despite her resolve, she was more nervous now, and more emotional.

The jury was riveted by her testimony, moved by her valiant effort to get away from her assailant despite his repeated threats to kill her.

'I'm going to ask you to look around the courtroom today and tell us whether you see the man who attacked you in 1973.'

Hastings shifted her lean body and looked at Floyd Warren. 'I can't tell you that I do. I couldn't identify his face then, and I can't do it now.'

Several of the jurors looked at me to see if this was a setback for the prosecution. They didn't understand, yet, that DNA made this case stronger than an eyewitness identification.

Warren stared his victim down and shook his head from side to side.

I finished my direct with questions about the medical examination she underwent that night and the clothing her assailant had worn.

'That's his,' she said, when I handed her the long-sleeved yellow shirt with large white polka dots. 'I could see the pattern in the dark. I watched his hand, even when I was face down on the bed, because I kept trying to see what he was doing with the knife.'

'Did the defendant take anything from you?' I asked.

'Yes, Ms. Cooper. He stole six dollars – all single bills – that were in a handbag on the chair next to my door.' Kerry Hastings looked back at the jurors. 'And he stole my life.'

'I have no further questions, Your Honor.'

'Mr. Grassley, are you ready to proceed?'

'Yes, sir.'

Grassley had been watching the jury's reaction, trying to gauge whether the old-fashioned attack on this victim's character would work. He was clever enough to realize that it probably would not. Instead, he opted for the classic post–rape shield law defense – that Kerry Hastings had indeed been subjected to a devastating experience but that Floyd Warren had been railroaded by the prosecution – an argument made even easier by Ernesto Abreu's well-timed courtroom explosion.

The cross-examination of Kerry Hastings, the experience that had crippled her so completely at the first trial, lasted only twelve minutes this time. No one was more surprised than she when Judge Lamont told her she could step down from the stand.

The afternoon moved just as quickly. We were barely into the evidence before Rosemarie Quiggley, a forensic biologist from the medical examiner's office, testified about her analysis of the stain found on Hastings's underpants. Although she, too, had not even been born when the rape occurred, Quiggley described the robust nature of seminal fluid – its ability to be a viable test source after three decades in the back of a file cabinet – and the DNA profile it yielded.

'Did you also examine the swab taken from the mouth of Floyd Warren after his arrest by Detective Mercer Wallace?'

'Yes, I did.'

'And were you able to compare those two samples?'

'Yes. I compared the two DNA profiles and determined that they were a perfect match at fourteen of the loci studied.'

'Would you please tell the jury how many people in the world,' I said, 'exactly how many people on this planet, would have a profile identical to this one?'

'Ms. Cooper, if you looked at the DNA of a trillion – with a "t" – that is, *one trillion* people, you would never see another that matches Floyd Warren's genetic profile. You'd have to find 166 planets the size of Earth, with billions of people on each, before you'd encounter something like this.'

The day ended at five forty-five with Mercer's testimony about the arrest of the defendant.

When Mercer and I got back to my office, there was a note taped to my door from Laura Wilkie. She assured me that Kerry Hastings had been driven to her hotel by two detectives from the

District Attorney's Office Squad and that Mercer should call her there.

He picked up my phone to dial just as Mike Chapman entered the room.

'Heard you had a good day in court, if you don't count the shout-outs.' Mike was wearing a navy blue windbreaker, with the crisp white logo of the NYPD on his chest, and jeans with a freshly pressed crease down the front.

'Even better for Kerry. I think she's really relieved.'

'You got your summation ready for tomorrow?' He knew my habits. I'd been taught by the great litigators who broke me in to craft my closing arguments before the trial began. It always gave tighter structure to the presentation of the case.

'Would you like a sneak preview, Mr. Chapman? I could use some practice on a thoroughly skeptical citizen of the state.'

'No, thanks. Floyd Warren's dead meat, unless you blow it for us.'

'You taking Mercer for a drink? That's a very dressed-down look for you, Detective.'

'It's my body-in-a-swamp best, Coop.'

I lowered my summation folder and looked at Mike. 'What body? What do you mean swamp?'

'This time it's Elise Huff.'

Mercer hung up the receiver. 'Where?'

'An anonymous call came into 911 an hour ago. Some old guy found her body in a desolate corner of Brooklyn, off the Belt Parkway, wrapped in a blanket and dumped in a muddy stretch of reeds and weeds.'

I closed my eyes.

'It won't be yours, Coop. But if you want to see the scene so you can report back to Battaglia, you'd better come along with me now. The Brooklyn DA is holding a press conference at nine tonight. This one's on his turf.'

11

A phalanx of police cars was parked along a dead-end street not far from the Belt Parkway. Huge spotlights rigged atop Emergency Service vehicles brightened the area as the late-summer twilight descended on the city. Cordoned off beyond the last patrol cars were the vans of camera crews from local news channels.

I couldn't see the water of Jamaica Bay, but I could smell the salty sea that was only hundreds of feet away, where the marshy stretch of land bordered on an inlet.

Mike led Mercer and me onto the path that had been trampled in the tall grasses by the first-response teams that had recovered the body. Crime scene tape was wrapped around the lone telephone pole on the side of the road and draped loosely over the bushes. We followed its yellow plastic trail.

'What brings you to the sticks, Chapman?'

A pudgy red-faced man, not quite as tall as Mercer's six foot six, waddled toward us. It was hard to walk in the muck without lifting one's feet above it with each step, and his extra weight made his movements even harder.

'Somebody has to make sure you get it right this time. Dickie Draper, this is Alex Cooper. I think you know Mercer.'

'Pleased to meet you,' he said, removing a small aerosol can from his pants pocket and spritzing it around his head. 'You could survive a gunshot wound to the head out here and these frigging mosquitoes would still kill you with West Nile.'

'The Huff girl, that's how she died? A gunshot wound?'

'Nah. I'm just saying, you don't have this kind of real estate in Manhattan. You need safari gear to survive out here.'

Draper lifted his feet, one at a time, and made an about-face.

'Where's the girl?' Mike called after him.

'At the morgue,' he said with a wave of the hand. 'Had to get her out of here before the press ghouls overran us.'

Rising above the brown tips of the reeds, off in the distance, I could see rows of uniformed cops. There were dozens of them, walking in two lines perpendicular to each other, arm's length apart, flashlights in hand. They formed grids, combing the wild landscape for clues, in this unpopulated area east of the parkway and west of Kennedy Airport.

'You want to tell us about it?' Mike said.

Dickie Draper looked like he had twenty years of experience or more under his imitation alligator belt. 'You got a need to know, or you just slumming?'

'Paul Battaglia assigned the investigation to me when Elise went missing. I've interviewed some of her friends, which may be helpful to your guys. And I'd also like to be able to give my boss a report tonight. I know he's been talking to her father since she disappeared.'

Draper took another step away from us. 'CPL 20.40. We got a body, we got the case.'

'You're quoting the criminal procedure law to Coop?' Mike said. 'Maybe if the bar association has a prom this year, you two can take each other. Talk the law. Recite CPL passages.'

'I don't want your case, Detective,' I said. 'It's obvious, unless you've already got a suspect, that this one has to be worked from both ends. Elise was last seen by her friends in Manhattan, and no matter where she was actually murdered, I realize the fact that her body is here gives you jurisdiction.'

'Mr. Raynes will be by in an hour,' Draper said. 'He's made it clear he wants the ink on this one, okay?'

'Even if it means hauling himself off a bar stool to get it?' Mike said. 'I'm impressed.'

The rivalry between the district attorneys of New York and Kings County had been long-standing. Battaglia's prestige was unparalleled, both for the many violent crimes that he vigorously prosecuted and for the innovative methods he undertook to police the white-collar community. Jerry Raynes had been in office for almost as long but had never achieved the same prominence. Both men had six hundred lawyers to do the heavy lifting, but Raynes constantly struggled for press coverage to further his political ambitions.

'I didn't say he'd be sober, did I? I just said he'd be here,' Draper answered, looking up at a low-flying 747. 'And I don't think he's looking to share the stage with Battaglia.'

'How'd she die, Dickie?' Mike asked.

'Looks like a blow to the front of the head. Three or four of them, maybe. Blunt force trauma. Maybe bashed in with a rock or a brick.'

Mike and I exchanged glances.

'Badly decomposed?'

'Not so bad as you'd think,' Draper said, swatting the side of his neck. 'Especially with all these bloodsuckers around. She was

78

wrapped up in a blanket – olive green, old army style. It's back at the station house. Red hair all over it, clumps of it. All that red hair is how come we could ID her so fast.'

'Is there a label on the blanket? Something to trace?'

'Partial. There's some really faded writing. I got it in my notes.'

'Any sign of sexual assault?' Mercer asked.

'The kid was naked, there was duct tape covering her mouth, and there were marks on her breast – scratches or bites. We won't know about DNA till the ME does the internal exam.'

The last piece of the sun – a glowing red ball – was setting behind us. Like clockwork, jumbo jets passed overhead every few minutes on their way to the landing strips.

'Who found Elise?' I asked. 'Why would anyone be out here?'

'Raynes is gonna offer an award to the caller at the press conference tonight. Whoever was sniffing around this place didn't want to leave his name. Got in a car and drove to a diner more than a mile away, but directed us right to the spot.'

'What is this here?'

'No-man's-land, stuck between some low-end housing projects,' Draper said, gesturing off in the distance, 'and the bay. You know Arlington Cemetery?'

'Sure.'

'Well, this is where the Brooklyn mob likes to bury its dead. Hallowed ground to them. The Mafia has probably dumped more bodies here than we'll ever be able to find. It's the only marsh I can think of where you can go bird-watching and find big old Sicilian canaries wrapped in cement overcoats.'

'Your guys pick up anything yet?' Mike asked.

'Nope. Did I mention her hands and feet were tied?'

'Cuffed?'

'Not exactly. Plastic ties. That's the only thing we've got so far. Like one of them was caught up in the fabric of the blanket. There was some of her hair stuck to the tape, too.'

Bound. Undoubtedly tortured. Killed.

'How far back off the roadway was the body?' Mike asked.

'Thirty feet, at least. Somebody had the confidence to park at the side of the road and carry the girl all the way to this drop.'

'And you think she's been out here for a few days?'

'Hey, everybody has to be somewhere. She's certainly been dead for a while.'

'Have you had any other squeals like this?' Mike asked.

'Brooklyn SVU's lookin' for a phony livery cabdriver picking up teenage girls. Taping their mouths and binding their hands. Rapes them but lets them go alive.'

'Could be the others never struggled and this one did,' Mercer said. 'Huff was out bouncing with her friends. Where are your witnesses from in the livery case?'

'All started out in Queens, the opposite direction,' Draper said. 'Three of them.'

'No open homicides?'

'Nothing close.' Draper made a circle in the mud and started back toward his car. 'This stuff is for the young pups. I'm outta here.'

'We've got a dump job in the South,' Mike said.

'Any of this ring a bell?'

'Blunt force. Restraints. Not a fresh kill, either. Naked – and the guy cleaned up after himself pretty well.'

'DNA?'

'Nothing by the time the docs got to her.'

'A little early to be thinking serial,' Draper said.

The FBI tagged serial killers – a term coined in the 1970s – as those who had committed three murders over an extended period of time, with cooling-off periods in between, during which their other actions seemed to be normal.

'I guess that's how you do it in Brooklyn, Dickie. Just sit back and wait for a third body to show up. Beats working for a living. I'm not saying it's the same guy yet, but maybe you haven't seen the end of us.'

Dickie Draper was breathing heavily from the exertion of the short walk. He opened the door of his unmarked car and sat in the passenger seat. Rolling down the window, he passed a handful of Polaroid photos out to Mike and me.

The last friend to have seen Elise Huff alive had taken a snapshot with her cell phone just hours before they parted ways. I had downloaded the close-up, which showed Elise's laughing eyes and big smile, and tacked it to my bulletin board. I had studied the picture, and I knew her face.

There was no mistaking that the body was Elise, despite the grotesque injuries. Now both eyes were swollen and discolored, the nose appeared broken and twisted to one side, and blood was caked over the crown of her head, which seemed to have been splintered like a broken lightbulb.

Two overheads, a profile from each side, and long shots of the battered body lying against the drab green cloth that had covered her were Draper's unofficial record of the scene. Tomorrow, in the morgue, after she'd been cleaned up, she would be posed for 8 × 10 glossies in the room where her autopsy would be performed.

'The 911 call came in at 5:08 p.m.,' Dickie Draper said, flipping open his pad. He thumbed through several pages before handing out another Polaroid that was clipped to the paper. 'Here's your clue, Sherlock. Run with it.'

Half of a short white label was still affixed to a corner of the blanket with tight, tiny stitches. The other ragged edge looked like it had been torn off over time. The lettering had faded and I could barely make out a word.

'Give me your flashlight, Dickie,' Mike said.

He shined the beam at the photograph and I read aloud what was left of the maker's name. 'There are three letters, the end of a longer word, obviously,' I said. 'L, A, N – before the abbreviation "Bros."'

'Hey, Chapman, did I tell you about the sand?'

'What sand?'

'On the blanket. There was a lot of sand clumped on it. Maybe this scumbag was into picnics at the beach.'

I looked down at the muddy rims of our shoes, then up at the horizon.

'Not here, Ms. Cooper. But you oughta come back for a swim some afternoon. We got some nice beaches in Brooklyn,' Draper said. 'Now why don't you tell me what you know about this Huff girl?'

I started to fill in some information about her background and her disappearance.

He looked over my head at the flashing lights that signaled the arrival of a high-ranking official.

'That'll be the district attorney pulling in,' Draper said, reaching into his pocket for a glassine envelope as he picked up my hand. He shook some sand into my palm. 'See this? You've got nothing like it in Manhattan, young lady. You tell Mr. Battaglia to stick to the pavement. Mr. Raynes and me, we're on the job.'

12

'We know that DNA is good science,' I told the jurors the next morning. 'It works when it exonerates the innocent, and it works just as well when it points a finger directly and reliably to those who are guilty.

'You could fill the 56,546 seats at Yankee Stadium every day for the next fifty thousand years,' I said, speaking to the majority of jurors who had listed themselves as baseball fans, 'and the possibility simply doesn't exist that you will find another human being who could be linked to the seminal stain that Floyd Warren left behind the night he raped Kerry Hastings.'

Just in my time in the practice of law, science had changed the way sexual assaults were being tried. That was not true for the victims of acquaintance rape or domestic violence, who were still subjected to rigorous crosses about their relationships with the alleged abusers and the degree to which they had consented to some kind of sexual encounter. But in cases of stranger rape, victims had historically been vulnerable to defenses of mistaken identification. DNA took that issue completely out of the line of attack.

The crime that had condemned Kerry Hastings to self-doubt for thirty-five years had been retried in a day and a half.

I was grateful that none of the Latin Princes had appeared in the courtroom this morning. I was hoping that no juror had been affected by the chanting gang member who had screamed out that I was a liar.

Judge Lamont took the jury through the legal definitions of first-degree rape and sodomy. I could recite those lines as easily as a three-year-old could sing the alphabet.

'The penal law defines dangerous instrument as follows: any instrument – like a knife – under the circumstances in which it is to be used, attempts to be used or threatens to be used, is readily capable of causing death or other serious physical injury.'

I watched the jurors absorb the information. How had I missed the nut – a well-educated housewife and mother – who had hung one of my cases two years earlier because the victim had not been stabbed by the knife-wielding rapist? Using a knife, she had argued to her eleven frustrated colleagues, didn't mean just holding it against someone's neck. If the defendant had wanted to *use* it, he would have killed the woman against whose throat he had held the blade.

The charge went on for more than an hour. Often, at this point in the trial, I used my legal pad to make lists of the groceries I had run out of during prolonged litigation or the names of friends whose calls I'd neglected because of the intensity of the case.

Today, glancing up from time to time to try to read the expressions on the jurors' faces, I was charting the similarities – and the distinctions – in the circumstances of the deaths of Amber Bristol and Elise Huff.

'You have the obligation to deliberate, ladies and gentlemen, and to attempt to reach a verdict that will be fair, both to the people of this state and to the defendant, a verdict that will reflect the truth based on the evidence in this case that you believe and on the law as I charged it, whether you agree with that law or not.

'Now, Ms. Cooper and Mr. Grassley, will you approach the bench?'

Several jurors stared at Floyd Warren as he shifted his chair to face them. He tapped his pencil on the table and then again started picking at his front teeth with the lead point. If they were trying to discern what had driven this man, who had never opened his mouth to speak throughout the trial, to commit such a brutal crime, they would have to do a lot more than consider his now benign appearance.

'Any exceptions to the charge? Any requests?'

Each of us answered, 'No.'

'Then I'll send them inside to begin. Their sandwiches have already been delivered, so they'll start out with lunch,' Lamont said. 'This could be a quick one. You both in the building this afternoon?'

Gene Grassley and I nodded and stepped back to our places.

'That concludes all our business, ladies and gentlemen. You will now retire to begin your deliberations.'

We waited until the twelve jurors were excused and the judge asked the four alternates to wait in the witness room. 'I'll see you both later,' Lamont said as he dismissed us.

'Locking up?' I asked Louie Larsen.

'Yep. You can leave your files. Mercer's in the hallway to take you downstairs.'

'None of my amigos lurking today?'

'Three of them showed up in the middle of Gene's argument,'

Louie said, shrugging his shoulders. 'I didn't have the personnel to do any manual searches, and they're the jerks that broke the machine, so I told 'em they'd just have to wait. Guess that didn't suit them.'

'You get that group ID'd yesterday?'

'Only the ringleader, the kid we locked up. The others ran too fast. I gave Mercer the information about Ernesto Abreu.'

'Priors?' I said, opening the courtroom door.

'Drugs, drugs, and more drugs. Felony arrests all knocked down to misdemeanors.'

'How'd it go?' Mercer asked. 'You got a slam dunk this time?'

'Fingers crossed. Don't jinx me.'

'Kerry's in the conference room. She wanted to be here this afternoon, to wait out the verdict with us.'

'I like that. Have you spoken with Mike today?'

'Yeah. He's home, waiting on the results of the Huff autopsy.'

The phone was ringing as I stopped at Laura's desk for my messages. 'Hold on,' she said. 'Alex has just come in. Let me ask her.'

'Who's that?'

'It's Ed, the intake supervisor from the Witness Aid Unit,' she said to me, holding the receiver aside. 'A young woman tried to get in to see you this morning. Lobby security knew you were in trial and sent her around to them to see if they could offer her some counseling.'

'Why does she want me?'

Laura started to repeat the question but the person on the other end had obviously heard what I asked. 'Ed's telling me she wants to report a rape. That the advocate at St. Luke's told her to ask for you specifically, because she's ambivalent about going forward and they want you to encourage her. Doesn't want her parents to know, so you'll have to explain the realities of a prosecution.'

'Can it hold for another day?'

86

Ed was talking to Laura, who repeated to me what she learned. 'Yeah, that's fine. She's been examined and all. Wants answers about what's involved before she makes her decision about pressing charges.'

'You're the keeper of my book this week. What have I got?'

The only thing I knew for certain was that Friday evening – the next day – the new guy I had met a couple of months ago was coming to town and I was determined to make time for dinner with him.

Laura had my appointment book open in front of her. 'For tomorrow, there's still a big question mark next to Floyd Warren's name. I guess that's in case the jury's still out. Then you've got it highlighted from eight to four, if the trial's over. Says you're accompanying Mike to the range. Rodman's Neck.'

'I can put that off.' The notation referred to the NYPD's shooting range, where officers were required to go twice a year to qualify with their handguns.

'Not again,' Mercer said. 'You made a solemn promise, Alexandra. Joe Berk and his cronies almost put your lights out. Mike insisted he'd teach you how to use a gun at the end of that case and I do believe I heard you say "amen."'

'Just a minute,' Laura said to Ed, the social worker who was trying to book the date. 'We're just checking Alex's availability. Let's try for next week. Can it wait until Monday, at eleven? And why don't you tell me the young lady's name?'

'I hate guns,' I said to Mercer. 'You know that.'

Laura was penciling in the appointment. 'Clarita Munoz. That's confirmed. You'll send up the paperwork and her contact information, Ed? Thanks a lot.'

'You're around guns too much not to know what to do with one,' Mercer said as I opened the door and went to my desk.

The red light on my telephone hot line – the intercom that linked the district attorney directly to my desk – was flashing as I walked in the room.

'Paul?'

'What the hell went on between you and Herb Ackerman?'

'I had no time to tell you. You weren't in yet when I went up to court this morning.'

'Come on over right now,' Battaglia said. 'I need to know what he's got to be so sorry about.'

'What do you mean?'

'That's the note he left. "Sorry for everything." Herb Ackerman walked out your door, went up to his office at the *Trib*, and swallowed a bottle of pills. I didn't tell you to kill the man, Alex, did I?'

13

'Madam Forelady,' Judge Lamont asked at 5:22 p.m., after waiting for Gene Grassley and me to arrive back in the courtroom, 'has the jury agreed upon a verdict?'

'Yes, sir, we have.'

'Please rise, then, while my clerk records it.'

The jurors had filed in like a prosecution panel. None of them were smiling and none attempted any eye contact with the defendant. I stared straight ahead, my heart pounding as the first juror rose to deliver the news.

'How say you as to Floyd Warren, charged with robbery in the first degree?'

'Guilty.' Her voice was strong and clear. Off to my right, Warren moved his chair closer to Gene Grassley and mumbled something.

'How say you as to Floyd Warren, charged with rape in the first degree?'

'Guilty,' she said, even louder this time.

'Bullshit.' I could hear Warren clearly now, and so did the two court officers standing behind him. Each took a step closer in.

For Kerry Hastings, who had never expected to see it, there would be some belated satisfaction. Floyd Warren would spend the rest of his life in prison.

The word *guilty* was repeated again and again. Sodomy, robbery, possession of a dangerous instrument – they had convicted him of every count in the indictment.

'Ladies and gentlemen of the jury, hearken to your verdict as it stands recorded,' the clerk said, continuing the official business of the trial.

Lamont made short work of thanking the jurors and dismissing them. He wanted the defendant put back in the holding pen as quickly as possible. Tomorrow, they would all read newspaper stories reporting the conviction and the links to more than fifty other brutal crimes from this city south to his adopted home in Georgia.

'I'm going to suggest to you, Gene, that we put this matter on the calendar for Monday,' Lamont said. It was the practice to have three to four weeks between the verdict and the sentencing. 'I've got more than enough to work from, and I'm not going to ask Ms. Hastings to make another trip cross-country to present her impact statement. Ms. Cooper says her witness is willing to stay for the weekend and get this whole thing behind her. You going to fight me on this?'

'I hear you, Judge. That's fine.'

Floyd Warren pounded his fist on the table.

'I'll take your motions then. If there's nothing further,' Lamont said, 'we stand adjourned.'

I didn't break a smile until Mercer came into the courtroom and embraced me. 'This one must feel good,' he said.

'Especially sweet when you tally up the years and the number of victims. I want you to be the one to tell Kerry.'

He helped me pile my case folders and trial exhibits onto the shopping cart and wheeled it off to the elevators. 'We'll do it together.'

'Did you get an update from Mike on Herb Ackerman?'

'He'll live. They pumped his stomach at Roosevelt Hospital. His shrink told Mike it's the classic "cry for help." We should be able to see him in twenty-four hours. Don't let Battaglia's finger-pointing get to you. Take your victory lap tonight.'

Kerry Hastings was waiting for us at the elevator bank when the doors opened. She reached out to put her arms around Mercer's neck when he gave her a thumbs-up, crying as she buried her head against his chest.

'Let it out,' Mercer said. 'You've had all that emotion bottled up for way too long.'

'I may actually sleep through the night. You two have given me that privilege again.' Kerry Hastings was sniffling, still, but she was smiling through her tears. 'I know there used to be a tradition here, Alex. I never got a chance to participate in it the first time around.'

'What's that?'

'There was a little restaurant behind the courthouse. The cops said if we got a conviction, we'd all go there to celebrate. Does it still exist?'

'Forlini's. It was just a little hole in the wall back then,' I said. 'You bet it's still the best place in town to celebrate.'

Every DA in the office and every cop who'd ever testified at a trial had lifted glasses after victories, drowned their sorrows when bad guys beat the rap, and awaited verdicts late into the night at the restaurant that had been run by four generations of Forlinis since it was first established opposite the detention center known as the Tombs.

'Only if I can buy the drinks,' Hastings said.

'By the time we cross the street and walk in that bar,' Mercer said, 'the whole Sex Crimes Unit will be waiting for Alex. They'll be drinking to you whether we show up or not, Kerry. That's a tab you don't want.'

Laura had been fielding calls from my friends in the unit most of the day. Catherine Dashfer and Marisa Bourgis, Ryan Blackmer and Evan Krupin, Sarah Brenner and Nan Toth – one of the perks of Battaglia's office that outweighed the low salaries was the intensity of the camaraderie. These lawyers had seen me through the darkest hours of my career and were always available to cheer for one another when the guys in the white hats won a round.

It was almost six thirty by the time I closed up my office and took the short walk to Forlini's with Kerry, Mercer, and Laura.

We walked in the main door to the restaurant, but I could hear the crowd in the bar as soon as we entered. Mercer led Kerry past the jukebox and into the back room, jammed with regulars who stopped in most days for a cocktail on their way home, as well as with the people waiting for us.

When Ryan saw Mercer he started to cheer, and most people who recognized the popular detective joined in with applause. He got our drinks, rapped on the bar to quiet everyone, and held up his glass to clink against both of ours. 'To Kerry Hastings – for your courage. And your patience.'

She was overwhelmed by the reception, pleased to take her place on a stool and be congratulated by prosecutors and cops, most of whom were too young to fully comprehend the enormity of her triumph.

Mercer and I were making dinner plans with Hastings when the bartender handed me the portable phone.

'I tried your cell,' Mike said. 'You probably can't hear it over the noise of all those ice cubes knocking around in your glass. Nice job, Blondie.'

'This was a good win. You want to meet up with us?'

'I'm working. I just asked Dempsey to turn on the TV for you. You're in for twenty bucks.'

'Mike, forget it. We'll do it another time.' I looked up at the small screen mounted on the wall above the end of the bar. The Final Jeopardy answer was about to be posted.

'I gave you a pass last night. What's your bet?'

'Tonight,' Trebek said, 'the category is "Leading Ladies." "Leading Ladies."'

'Double or nothing,' Mike said. If he wasn't reading treatises on military history in his downtime, he was watching old movies.

'You're on.'

'Put your money on the bar where Mercer can see it.'

I took two twenties out of my pocket as I explained to Mercer what the call was about and pointed at the screen. Both he and Kerry laughed and put up forty dollars each.

Just as we saw the printed statement against the bright blue square of the game board, Trebek read it aloud. 'Hernando Cortés proclaimed that God and this woman were responsible for the Spanish conquest of Mexico.'

Mercer and I shook our heads, while the bartender interpreted the cash on the bar as a request for another round of drinks and served us a refill.

'How misleading is that?' Mike said. 'They're not talking about a film.'

'I thought you knew every bit of history from the conquistadores to the Alamo.'

Kerry Hastings offered a question, just as the three contestants were chided for their faulty guesses. 'Who is *La Malinche*?'

'What'd she say?' Mike asked.

'The correct question is, "Who is Doña Marina or, as the Aztecs called her, the traitorous *La Malinche*?" That's right, the young woman given to Cortés as a slave, who became his mistress and helped with his conquest of Mexico. She's very controversial, folks, but an important figure in history.'

Mercer handed Kerry Hastings the money. 'We'll get the rest of the pot from Mike.'

'I read all I could find about strong women who overcame adversities when I was trying to grope my way out of the dark,' she said. 'Cortés' mistress was one of them. She was called a harlot, too.'

'What do you say to dinner, Mike? I've got to get off the phone.'

'I hope you don't think the only reason I called is to keep you up to speed on your trivia. Dinner is you and me, kid. I'll buy whatever you want from the vending machines in the Twentieth Precinct. Looks like you messed up another interview.'

'Thanks for letting me have a couple of hours to relish my verdict. What now?'

'I'm trying to broker a peace. I've got Elise Huff's father here,' he said. 'And her best friend.'

'Barbara Gould? Mr. Huff's known her forever. She told me they're very close.'

'Maybe they were – until she lied to you last week, Coop. You'd better get up here right now and straighten this mess out.'

14

'Where's Barbara?'

'Cooling her heels in the squad room. Talk to Arthur Huff first. The girl can use the time to lose some attitude.'

I followed Mike up the staircase to the third floor of the old station house on West Eighty-second Street. Elise and Barbara had shared an apartment just blocks away, on Amsterdam Avenue. It was Barbara who had called the Huffs when Elise had not come home for two nights.

Arthur Huff was sitting in the captain's office sipping coffee from a mug when Mike opened the door for me.

I had been spared the heartbreaking assignment of telling him the circumstances of his child's death. Detective Draper and his team had delivered that news the night before, dashing the family's hopes – against most odds – that Elise would be found alive.

I introduced myself and offered words of consolation for his unimaginable loss. He had heard the same thing too many times today for it to have any meaning.

He had just come from his daughter's apartment, collecting a few of her personal effects that he wanted to keep with him.

'I forgot to ask about her little ring,' Huff said. 'Did they find anything on – on Elise?'

'No, sir. You can tell me about it if it's something you think she was wearing. Perhaps it will turn up in the investigation.'

'She never took it off, from the day her grandmother died four years ago. My father was a West Point man, Ms. Cooper. Graduated in 1943. The cadets all had rings back in those days. That's the USMA emblem.' Huff held out his hand to me to show me the writing on his father's ring, a thick gold setting with a yellow stone. 'Mine's a citrine, like hers, only larger. When the men became engaged, they had identical ones made for their fiancées – miniatures, of course. Elise wouldn't go anywhere without her ring.'

'I'll add that to the report. We'll certainly return it to you when we find it.' I wasn't hopeful that it would ever surface in the Brooklyn marshland.

He removed a pair of hoop earrings, a cameo pin, and a thin gold necklace from his pocket and cupped them in his hands. 'Not much to go back home with, is it? Her little sister's going to want these things. She worships Elise.'

'I'm sure she has good reason to do that.'

'I'd like to know why I can't talk to Barbara again,' Huff said, adopting a more businesslike tone. I guessed him to be in his early fifties – with red hair the color of his daughter's – although the fact that he hadn't slept in a week made him appear older.

'It's important that we get some information from her first,' Mike said.

'I think you've had your chance to do that, Detective.'

'She wasn't honest with you or your wife, either.'

I had met with Barbara Gould for an interview when Battaglia first assigned me the case. She repeated to me then that she had called the Huffs at the end of the preceding weekend. She told them, and then the police, that she and Elise had gone out drinking after work. But she lied about the time of night they parted company, where she last saw Elise, and how intoxicated both young women were.

'Barbara's like my own child,' Huff said, dismissing Mike completely. 'She'd never lie to us.'

'Well, we're going to try to find out why she did.'

'I spoke to the captain tonight, before he left,' Huff said, getting up from the desk and walking to look at the pegboard wall behind him, which was covered from floor to ceiling with artists' sketches and mug shots of wanted perps. 'He told me about another girl – another body found somewhere downtown this week.

'Tell me, Detective,' he said as he turned back to Mike. 'You don't think these two cases are connected, do you?'

Mike brushed back his hair with his hand. 'Too early to say. More likely just a coincidence that—'

'Good. Because I don't expect my baby had anything to do with a man who was killing whores. Do you understand that, Mr. Chapman? Elise is – Elise was a good girl, and I don't want the Huff name mixed up in that other woman's business.'

'We don't spend a whole lotta time blaming our victims, Mr. Huff,' Mike said. 'We just leave that to the newspapers. Are you comfortable here while Alex and I have another run at Barbara?'

He slumped back down into the chair. 'I want answers, Detective. I've got our congressman putting some heat on y'all. I expect results. I'm expecting you to solve this damn thing quickly. My wife and I would like some closure. And we'd like it soon.'

'Closure,' Mike said, shutting the door behind us. '*Closure* is the most bullshit word in the English language. I'll find this beast and you'll send him up the river for the rest of his life. The day of the verdict, Huff will have that short-lived rush of happiness that comes with a homicide conviction. Some news jock will stick a microphone in his face on the courthouse steps and ask how he feels about the conviction and he'll tell them it's great and now he's got closure. Next day he and the missus will wake up and realize their kid is still dead. There's no such thing as closure when you lose someone you love to a murderer.'

I knew that, too, and it was part of the reason it was so much more satisfying for me to work with survivors of sexual assault, who never forgot what happened to them but were most often able to move on with their lives.

'Heads, you can be the good cop,' Mike said.

'Not a contest. I want another shot at her.'

'Bad cop it is. This kid doesn't know yet what it's like to be in your crosshairs, Coop.'

Barbara Gould was in the small cubicle used by the Twentieth Precinct detective squad for interrogations. It held a table and four chairs, and the walls were completely bare. Her head was resting on her forearms until she picked it up when we entered the room.

'Hello, again,' I said.

'Hello. Look, Detective, if you give me back my cell, I've got to be going now. It's almost nine o'clock and I've got a lot of stuff to do.'

The twenty-year-old had practiced her pout well. The moment she recognized me, she put it on and began to pull and twist a strand of her long brown hair around her forefinger.

'Ms. Cooper needs to talk to you,' Mike said, leaning back against the door.

'We've had that conversation.'

'And now we're going to have it once more. Only this time you're going to tell me the truth.'

'I tried to tell Mr. Huff. So I was wrong the first time,' Barbara said, rolling her eyes toward the ceiling and clicking her tongue against the roof of her mouth. 'What happens if I leave? Can I just go now?'

'No, you can't leave.'

I had no authority to keep the petulant young woman in the station house, but she accepted my answer and didn't move from her seat.

I started, calmly, to go through the story she had told me originally. 'We're going to start over, Barbara, from the time you and Elise left your apartment.'

Two years younger than Elise, Barbara had come to New York first and was about to enter her junior year at Marymount College. Elise had finished college in Tennessee and landed a job working at La Guardia Airport as a counter agent for Jet Blue.

The first part of the story was consistent with what she had told me a week earlier. Elise had come home from work at seven, and after eating a light supper together they went out to meet friends. Barbara was dressed in leggings and a tube top, and Elise had kept on the navy blue pants and crisp white short-sleeved uniform shirt – complete with small gold wings on the collar – that she wore at work. She liked to do that, Barbara had said with a laugh when she first talked to me about Elise, because guys often took her for a flight attendant.

'What time did you leave your apartment?'

'I don't know. Around eleven, I guess. Between eleven and twelve.' What passed for closing time in many other parts of the country was the hour at which Manhattan's cosmopolitan young ladies set out to meet guys.

'Where did you go?'

Barbara looked over my head at Mike, still twisting her hair. 'I told you.'

'Tell me again.' I needed to know how much of the original story was true.

'Gleason's, over on Columbus. Just around the corner from our apartment.'

'What did you have to drink?'

'White wine.' She had surrendered her fake ID to me when I first met her. It was a forged driver's license, readily available almost everywhere in the Manhattan bar scene.

'The same for Elise?'

'Yeah.'

'How many glasses?'

'Two. We each bought a round, and then some guy was hitting on me. He bought us the third drink. But we hardly touched them.'

'I wish I could get a refund for every glass of wine a witness tells me she ordered but never touched,' Mike said. 'Eight bucks a pop, I could retire tomorrow.'

'Did you see anyone else you knew?'

Barbara thought for a few seconds. 'No.'

'How long did you stay there?'

She rolled her eyes again. 'I'm not sure. It's like more than a week already.'

'And your friend Elise is dead. Mike and I need a timeline for everything she did that night. I'm not asking you about ancient history, Barbara. Think hard.'

'An hour. Maybe a little longer. You're like really pushing me.'

'Then where did you go?'

'There's that little place I told you about, like halfway down the block from Gleason's, with an outdoor café. We went there, so we could sit outside. Columbus Café.'

'Did you order anything to eat? Or to drink?'

'Nothing to eat. Just another glass of wine. I only had like half of it.'

'And Elise?'

'Same thing. She didn't drink that much.'

'Did you know anyone there? Talk to anyone?'

A few seconds of hesitation, again. A few too many. 'No.'

'Barbara, who did you see?'

She lowered her eyes and changed hands, twirling the hair on the left side of her part. 'Oh, God, I don't want to bring anybody else into this.'

'That's not a choice you have, don't you understand?'

'It's not going to bring Elise back,' she said, as tears welled up in her eyes. 'Nothing's going to do that.'

'It's about the truth, dammit. Who are you trying to hide from us?'

'Nobody. Why can't we just leave my statement the way it was?'

'You didn't split from Elise at that café, did you? You didn't leave her there and walk home, like you told me last week.'

'What happens to me if I change my story?'

'If you do it now? Nothing. If you wait until you've testified falsely under oath, then we get to figure out if you've committed perjury.'

Barbara pulled the strand of hair across her lips and began to chew on it.

'You're doing a lousy job, Coop. You're gonna give bad cops a good name,' Mike said, stretching his arms out and cracking his knuckles. 'Isn't this when you tell her to get the friggin' hair out of her mouth and stop whining about herself?'

Barbara's face soured at the sharp sound of his words.

'It wasn't my idea. Elise was the one who wanted to go downtown. I told her it was stupid.'

'Every minute you waste, you make it harder for us to find her killer. We've had detectives in and out of Gleason's and that café every night since Elise went missing,' I said. No one recalled seeing anyone fitting her description in the early hours of the morning, either with friends or alone. 'I believed you, Barbara. I believed that's where you left her. Obviously it's not true. Now, when did you leave Columbus to go downtown?'

'I don't know.'

'There's a little operation called the Taxi and Limousine

Commission, Barbara. They've got the trip sheets of every yellow cab – where and when the driver made his pickup and where he dropped his passengers off. I'll have those records tomorrow.'

'Really?' She twisted her neck and screwed up her mouth.

'It's all in their computer by now. I just have to give them the address of the café and ask for the fares that got in after one a.m. The TLC will tell me how many riders, and where they went.'

'Okay, all right. There were three of us. Is that what you want to know? I hooked up with this guy I knew at the Columbus Café.'

'What's his name?' She was watching Mike as he took out a pad from his rear pants pocket and began to make notes.

'He doesn't want to get involved.'

'He's involved up to his eyeballs, simply because he was with you and Elise. Maybe he saw something or someone you didn't see.'

'He's going to hate me.'

'Did you hear what Mike said? This isn't about *you*.'

'Look, I told Mr. Huff tonight. I told him I forgot that we stopped at another place downtown. I just didn't remember at the time is all. It seemed so unimportant, and I was so upset.'

'Who's the guy?' I asked.

She picked up her sunglasses from the table and put them on. 'Cliff. His name is Clifford Trane, okay?'

'Take those off, Barbara.' I needed to see her eyes. I needed to gauge whether she was feeding me more nonsense.

'I don't have to take them off. I don't have to be here if I don't want.'

'Tell me about Cliff.'

She wiggled her head back and forth, as though deciding what to tell me.

Mike took three steps forward and pulled the sunglasses off Barbara's nose. She was beginning to cry.

'He plays basketball for St. John's. He'll be a senior this year.'

'Coach would flip out if his name was in the paper anywhere but the sports pages, I guess. Booze and clubbing don't fit with preseason training,' Mike said. He would have to fill me in later on the college basketball scene. 'Sometimes I think the media drives the criminal justice system, everybody worried about their fifteen minutes of fame instead of doing the right thing. That didn't hurt much, did it? Give Coop the rest.'

'Why did you leave the Columbus Café?'

'Because of Elise. She wanted to meet somebody downtown.'

'It's a big place, downtown. Where?'

'The Bowery. A bar called the Pioneer.' The strip of land that ran from Canal Street up to Cooper Square had been skid row for more than half a century. Gentrification and the spread of yuppie hangouts across SoHo had encroached on the once-dangerous avenue, replacing some of the flophouses and home-less shelters with pubs and clubs.

'Who was she going to meet?'

'Kevin. She said his name was Kevin. Or Kiernan. Maybe it was Kiernan. I don't know him, all right? I don't know anything else about him.'

'You, Cliff, and Elise – you all took a cab together?'

'Yes,' she said, whining more heavily now.

'What happened when you got to the Pioneer?'

'It's a bar, Ms. Cooper. Get it? We ordered drinks,' Barbara said. 'Cliff was doing tequila shots. I think I had wine. I don't know about Elise.'

'Why not?'

'She was upset, that's why. We stayed at the bar and she sat down at a table against the wall. She was talking on her cell.'

'To whom?'

'Kevin, I guess.'

'For how long?'

'Five minutes, maybe ten.'

'Then what happened.'

'Elise and I had an argument,' Barbara said, as tears streaked down her cheeks.

'About what?' I kept digging at her rather than letting her pause to collect herself. The floodgates had opened and she was telling us the real story for the first time.

'I was mad at her for dragging us all the way downtown, like practically half an hour in the cab. I was really pissed off.' She wiped her nose with the back of her hand.

'Why?

'Because I wanted to go home with Cliff, that's why. I think Elise was jealous of me,' she said, growing more sullen as she tried to justify her annoyance at her dear friend. 'I mean, I don't know if she made up this Kevin or Kiernan or whoever he is. We went out of our way to go with her to the Pioneer, and the damn guy never showed up. Was I supposed to wait all night?'

'Did she know you were mad?'

'Yeah. Like I said, we had an argument.'

'Inside the Pioneer, in front of other people?'

Barbara lowered her head. 'In the bathroom. I don't think anyone else would have heard us.'

'How did it start?'

'I told Elise that Cliff and I were leaving. It was after three o'clock. I was tired and starting to feel – you know, sleepy,' she said. 'I asked her what was up with this Kevin guy, and she like blew me off. Told me to go ahead without her. That'd she'd be fine getting home. I tried to get her to come with me, I really did.'

'How hard did you try?' Mike asked.

'I didn't like drag her by the arm and all, okay? Was I supposed to carry her out?'

'Did she know anyone at the Pioneer? The bartender?'

'We'd never been there before. Neither one of us. We only went 'cause this guy Kevin told her he'd meet her there.'

'How did she know him?'

'Some party the week before. She said a girl she knew from work introduced her.'

'Was she drunk when you left her?'

'Buzzed. I'd say Elise had a good buzz on.'

'Was she still drinking?'

'Cliff bought her a glass of wine. Left it on her table. I don't know what she did with it. He was only trying to be nice.'

'Where did you tell her you were going?' I asked.

She rolled her eyes once more. 'Cliff wanted to come to our place, okay? I told her we were going home. I didn't care whether she came with us or not.'

'How big is your apartment?'

Barbara blushed. 'It's a studio.'

It would be hard for two kids their age, one still in school, to afford more than that on Manhattan's Upper West Side. But the situation didn't offer much privacy when one of them hooked up with a guy.

'Maybe she felt like a third wheel,' Mike said.

'I can't help that. This isn't my fault. I didn't kill Elise and I don't know who did.'

'The last time you saw her, where was she and what was she doing?' I asked.

'She was at the same table against the wall. Sitting there by herself,' Barbara said, giving us an additional fact each time she opened her mouth. 'I even called her from the cab, just to see if that jerk ever showed up.'

'Did you talk?'

'Yeah. She told me she was going to take a walk, go to one of the other bars down there to find him.'

'Which one?'

'I don't know, really. I told her not to do that. I told her it wasn't safe to walk around alone down there at that hour,' Barbara said, rubbing her eyes. 'I told her that I'd stay over at Cliff's place instead. That she just ought to get in a cab and come home.'

The detectives would have to play catch-up. Nights wasted in the chic eateries on Columbus Avenue would now be spent in the uneven mix of spots – upscale and lowdown – that book-ended the Bowery. Bartenders, bouncers, patrons, and passersby would be canvassed anew. The photograph of the smiling girl in the white shirt, wings on the collar – and the description of her outfit, including the crested gold ring on her finger – would be posted in the Pioneer and in the other bars on the blocks around it. They'd have to find Kevin – or Kiernan – or whoever it was Elise expected to meet.

'Did you talk to Elise again? Did you try to call her after that?'

'No.'

'Weren't you worried when she didn't come home Saturday morning?' I asked.

'I had no idea she wasn't at our apartment,' Barbara said. 'I didn't get there myself until Sunday night.'

'You spent the weekend with Cliff Trane?'

She rested her elbows on the table and placed her forehead in her hands. 'Yeah.'

'I don't get it, Barbara. Who are you protecting in this?'

'Cliff's going to be so mad at me,' she said, sliding down in the chair and twirling her hair again. 'He was suspended from school sophomore year. Some girl claimed that she was date-raped by his roommate and that he was an accomplice.'

I didn't know where to take this next and looked over to Mike for help.

'The charges were dropped, Ms. Cooper,' Barbara said. 'But if he's connected to another scandal he'll be thrown out this time.'

'It'll be up to Dickie Draper, from the Brooklyn homicide squad, to figure out how connected your man is,' Mike said. 'In the meantime, you'll be working 24/7 to help the detectives find out who the guy is Elise was supposed to meet.'

'I don't want Mr. Huff to hear this,' Barbara said, lowering her voice. 'I don't know if Kevin or Kiernan even exists, Mr. Chapman. Like the way she told guys she was a flight attendant? Elise was making things up all the time.'

15

The hundreds of gunshots that erupted continuously in the still, muggy air of that August morning sounded more like a war zone than an old park grounds in the Bronx. I waited with Mike at the entrance to the pistol range at Rodman's Neck, the training base run by the NYPD Firearms and Tactics Section, just over the drawbridge that led to the little village of City Island.

Large signs that said RESTRICTED were posted along the roadway that separated this isolated area from Pelham Bay Park, of which it was once a part.

'There's a first time for everything, Coop,' Mike said, leading me up to a table in front of a low wooden building that looked like an old stable. We both put on padded ear protectors, although they did little to muffle the constant sound of gunfire. 'Settle down.'

He knew me as well as I knew myself. I didn't like it here. That was evident from the expression on my face and the stiffness of my body.

I was scoping the vast property as we walked through the stall to the place where we would stand for my first lesson firing guns, which I had promised Mike and Mercer I would take after a confrontation with an armed killer.

We were both in jeans and polo shirts already coated with a fine layer of dust from our walk from the parking lot to the area where dozens of cops were lined up side by side, shooting hundreds of rounds of real ammunition as cartridges discharged around us.

'I'd rather be talking to Herb Ackerman. Or checking out Bowery bars.'

'Later for that. You do well in school and I'll take you bar-hopping. Okay, we're starting with a revolver.'

One of the instructors came up behind me and Mike introduced us. He was dressed in the standard uniform of the firearms squad – all khaki, instead of the dark blue that street cops wore, with crossed pistol insignias on the collar. His name was Pete Acosta, and he had a revolver for each of us.

'But you don't even use one of these anymore.'

'I started with this because my old man swore by his. Once upon a time, everybody on the force used a .38. Cops love them 'cause they always fire,' Mike said. 'And for beginners like you, they're usually easier to handle. Now there's too much fancy hardware on the street and these just can't keep up.'

The day after rookie police officers were sworn in, there was a weapons selection event at the academy. It had become increasingly rare for young cops to choose to work with these guns, once thought to be more reliable, though much slower, than semi-automatics.

'Don't look so frightened,' Mike said, prodding me in the back. 'Step out there. No one's going to shoot you.'

He loaded his revolver with six rounds while Pete loaded mine.

To both sides of me, only eight feet apart, were officers firing their guns, maybe a dozen men and women in all. In front of each position was a target, set in the ground about thirty feet away.

The human form, a drawing of a life-sized figure in sharp black outline, was pointing his gun at us. Every cop was blasting away at his chest or head. Most of the rounds were smacking into their paper targets, killing the gun-wielding menace again and again. Some missed high or wide, and you could see the dust kick up on the dry mounds of dirt that formed a perimeter to the rear of the range.

'Go ahead, Alex,' Pete said, smiling at my hesitation. 'Eight million rounds are fired here every year and nobody's ever been hit.'

I looked from side to side at the men practicing around me and raised my arm, lining up the notch on the tip of the revolver through the sight.

'Get the thug,' Pete said.

'What?'

'We call him the thug.'

I pulled back on the trigger and the gun discharged.

'Sweet Jesus,' Mike said. 'Check with the Montauk police, Pete. Somebody might be sitting on his deck, gunshot wound in the middle of his forehead. She sailed that one right out of the ballpark. You check your vision lately, Coop?'

The sound of the constant gunfire unnerved me. I had never heard anything like it. I picked up the revolver and aimed again, or so I thought. The bullet lodged somewhere in the dirt beyond the thug's shoulder. He wouldn't even have needed to duck.

Mike stepped in closer behind me and put his arms over each of mine. 'You see that guy on the target? He's aiming to blow your brains out. Think of it that way.'

He was trying to keep my arms in place after I sighted the chest of the paper figure. 'Pull back.'

I fired once more, into the mound off in the distance, and now the cops on either side of me stopped to watch. Then I tried the last three rounds, but none of them came close.

'You do it.'

Mike stood beside me and pointed the revolver. He let off six rounds, before refilling the gun with a speed loader that Pete handed to him with another six. Every one of them made its mark somewhere on the threatening thug.

'Maybe you'll like the semiautomatic better,' Pete said. 'What do you use, Mike?'

'A Glock 19,' he said, unholstering his gun from his ankle.

Pete walked inside the stable with the revolvers and returned with a different gun for me. 'Try this. It's a Sig-Sauer. A nine millimeter semiautomatic.'

'Too many moving parts for her. This is a broad who can't operate a DVD player, Pete. She may never get it, but Mercer and I are determined to try.'

More men were turning to watch me now – mocking me – as Pete explained the differences between the guns.

'There's one bullet in the chamber,' Pete said, 'and fifteen in the magazine. It requires good isometric tension to use one of these, Alex. There's a lot of jump in the recoil.'

I could guess from firing the revolver what recoil was, but I didn't have a clue about isometric tension.

'Put your right index finger on the trigger,' Pete said.

Mike moved in again to position me. He had put his own gun back in his ankle holster. 'Stand with your legs apart, arms straight out.'

'Why don't you just let Pete do this with me, okay?'

'Put your right index finger on the trigger,' Mike said, ignoring me as he was not unused to doing. 'Both thumbs on the left side of the grip. No, no, no. You can't cross them like that.'

The guy to my right stepped back, with good reason. I pressed hard on the trigger, and when the gun discharged, my arms flew up with the kick and pulled to the side. It seemed like I had grazed the thug's kneecap, although I had been aiming for his chest.

'Look, I can't do this with everyone staring at me.'

'You? I'm thinking your dream gig is to try a four-perp murder case that's televised on Court TV. What's with the shy shooter thing? You giving up?'

'Not yet. Is there any other way to do this without an audience?' I asked Pete.

'FATS. That's an indoor facility. Let's go over there. It's the Firearms and Tactics Simulators,' he said, pointing to another area of the vast operation.

I returned the Sig and ear protectors and started to walk with Mike.

'You two head over,' Pete said, stepping into an office as we passed through the stable to the far side of C-range, the designated pistol target area at which we'd been firing. 'I'll put these away and be right there.'

'It's amazing no one's been killed here.'

'Shot, no. Killed, yes,' Mike said. 'Thirty years ago, one of my father's friends was blown up.'

'What do you mean?'

He walked backwards and squinted to look off to the south, beyond the pistol range. 'There's a huge crater they call the Pit. It's on the southernmost tip of the peninsula here, that juts into Eastchester Bay. The bomb squad detonates all the devices that are recovered in the city. They've done it since the days of the Weathermen. One of the earliest bombs they brought here detonated prematurely, and Brian's friend didn't make it away in time.'

'How horrible,' I said. 'Is that why the range is restricted? The bomb danger?'

'This whole enclave is the NYPD's practice territory for urban warfare,' Mike said, to the background noise of gunshots. 'You've got all the special weapons that the antiterrorist squads use – MP5 submachine guns and Colt rifles and Ithaca shotguns. There's a helipad for the department's choppers. You got Aviation and police boat docks, the Bomb Squad, Special Ops, Highway Patrol, all hidden in this out-of-the-way place that nobody seems to know about. It was even an emergency base after 9/11.'

The range was a beehive of police activity. We passed a mess hall and a gun shop and the entrance to an underground bunker that Mike said held at least one of every kind of firearm ever manufactured, including rare World War II weapons.

There was a series of prefab shacks lined up in a row, and the fourth one of those had the FATS logo hanging over its railing.

I scooped up a handful of empty cartridges from the ground as Pete jogged toward us. 'Don't get too attached to those,' he said. 'I've got my lead poisoning test next week.'

I opened my fingers and watched them drop.

'Takes a lot more than that. But we were losing police dogs at a terrifying rate. Turns out they were absorbing the lead through their paws.'

I winced as he opened the door to the small cabin. The overhead lights were on when we entered. Pete turned them off so that the three of us stood in complete darkness.

'Private enough for the princess?' Mike asked.

'It might not make any difference in my shooting skills that I can't see, but I think some light would be helpful.'

Pete stepped over to a computer monitor and played with the controls. The entire far wall became an enormous screen, and the first frame of a movie was frozen against it.

'Move over behind here, Alex.' He guided me to a large, empty oil barrel standing on its end in front of the screen. 'This is all you've got in case you need to take cover. Mike, take the one next to her.'

On top of each was a semiautomatic. 'They're real guns,' he said, 'but they've got soap cartridges inside. They're connected to the computer. You seen these yet, Mike?'

'Nope.'

'I'm going to run these films. Each one is three or four minutes long. You and Mike have answered a call to come to this apartment. Shots fired. Reports of a drug deal gone bad. Try aiming your gun, Alex. It should be a lot lighter than the one you just used.'

I lifted the gun and pointed it at the screen, lining it up with the sight. Not only was it dark, but I thought the quiet should make it easier to concentrate.

'Ready?'

'Yes.'

The clip began with the closing of the door of the patrol car behind me. I was viewing everything from the vantage point of the first officer on the scene. Voices in the tenement building I virtually entered were shouting that the cops had arrived. A man in a bright-colored shirt was racing up steps – several flights – as I tried to overtake him, and from behind me, Pete was barking out commands.

'Police! Drop your weapons! Stop! Police!' he shouted as though he were actually at the scene. 'C'mon, Alex, you're chasing the guy up the stairs. He's taking them two at a time. He's got you beat.'

The camera lens bounced up and down as I was turning corners after the fleeing suspect. An apartment door slammed shut somewhere above me and the camera lurched upward, toward the high-pitched sound of a child screaming for help.

'It's that one, Alex,' Pete yelled. 'You're going to kick on that door. You'd better tell them you're a cop.'

My virtual foot shoved the door and it opened onto a frenetic scene. A man whose Hawaiian print shirt resembled the clothing of the guy who had run up the stairs leaped over the back of a sofa. He was holding something but he moved so quickly I couldn't tell if the object in his hand was a gun or not.

'Is that your man in there? Are you sure? You better tell them to *freeze*, Alex. Let me hear you shout at him, okay? Where's your partner? Has he got you covered?'

It was all happening too fast. The slender woman seated on the edge of her chair had drug paraphernalia in front of her. I could make out the white powder and pipe, and as I looked to my right to see whether Mike had his gun poised to back me up, I caught a hand-lettered sign over the picture of a uniformed cop that said 'Kill the pigs.'

The man behind the sofa stuck his head up above the top of the cushion and called something out to his companion. I couldn't understand what he said. A baby started crying on the left side of the screen. As my eyes darted in that direction, the woman lifted the lid on the shoebox next to the cocaine and pulled a gun from it.

Before I could aim, she had fired at me. Mike squeezed off a round that nailed her in the throat, although in real time I couldn't have seen him do it. I would have been dead.

'Saved your skinny ass again, Coop.'

'I give up. I don't know how you guys do it, day in and day out.'

'Ready for another one, Alex?' Pete asked.

'I'm telling you this should be mandatory training for every prosecutor your office hires. Most of them have no idea what we're up against till they're chauffeured to a crime scene in an RMP at three o'clock in the morning,' Mike said, referring to the department's blue and white radio motor patrol cars, 'and they get an up close and personal sense of what the job is like.'

'I don't think I can do it, Pete. I need a nice still target like the thug – nobody shooting back at me – in a quiet room like this. Nothing interactive.'

The second tape started to play. It appeared to be a routine traffic accident. A dark green Toyota truck smashed into a silver Honda and spun the car around. The driver of the Honda was slumped against the steering wheel and the wailing siren announced the approach of a police car.

Mike moved into place behind one of the barrels. He didn't need instructions from Pete. I watched as the driver of the truck stepped out of its cab. A passenger in the Honda got out and opened the rear door, coming up with a tire iron.

'Stop right there! Put it down,' Mike said.

Instead of obeying Mike's command, the passenger continued walking toward the Toyota, cursing at the other driver, who was reaching into his rear pocket to remove his wallet. The second man returned the expletives with some ethnic slurs, as Mike yelled at them both to back off.

The Honda's passenger began to charge the truck, banging on the hood with the tire iron. As the camera sped in – representing Mike's dash toward the Toyota – the driver turned around and pulled a gun from his waistband, shooting at Mike before pivoting to kill the civilian.

Mike had been quick enough to duck behind the barrel but the shot he fired off was neither timely nor accurate.

'That's why you need a partner you can trust, Coop. There's barely time to think when things heat up on the street. It's like a combat zone.'

'I guess what you need, Alex, is the old-fashioned, basic indoor range. It's much calmer, and you'll be able to concentrate,' Pete said. 'Want to give that a try?'

'One more chance. Then it's back to the law library for me.'

Pete shut off the equipment and we walked out of the building, down the steps, in the direction of the huge visitors' parking lot. 'We've got to go past the gatehouse,' he said, 'beyond all the shooting ranges and bomb squad.'

The heat was escalating as the late-morning sun climbed higher. The three of us were sweating as we crossed behind the equipment trailers on the edge of the property to get to the new indoor range. There was no shade on the path, just ten feet from the border of scrubby brush that separated the facility from its nearest neighbors. And ever present was the sound of dozens of automatic weapons being fired by cop after cop, eager to plug the thug on the target.

Pete squared the corner at the entry checkpoint, just past the last RESTRICTED sign. Mike stopped short behind him and leaned over to massage a kink in the calf of his left leg. He was still recovering from a stress fracture he had suffered earlier in the year.

I kneeled to retie the laces on my sneakers. Just as I did, I heard the sharp repeat of a semiautomatic weapon fired from within the stand of trees closest to the entrance where dozens of police officers had parked their cars.

I fell to the ground as bullets dimpled the side of the gray shingled gatehouse. Mike thrust himself onto the dirt and crawled over to me, shielding my body with his own, screaming at me to stay down. I could barely breathe, between the fright of the close call and the pressure of his body on my chest.

16

Pete Acosta called for backup and ran off in the direction of the shooter. The uniformed cops at the checkpoint – at least four of them – took up chase with him. I lost sight of them in the dense shrubbery that edged the roadway near the entrance.

Four others answered Mike's call and formed a circle around us. Mike helped me to my feet and we brushed ourselves off, reassuring the men that we had not been hit.

'Take her into the gatehouse,' he said. 'I'll catch up with Pete.'

'Could you just stay here with me a minute?' I didn't want to be left with strangers while Mike exposed himself to whoever had been shooting at us.

Mike wasn't going to indulge my nerves. He walked away and inspected the holes in the side of the building. 'Might as well get Crime Scene out here. Let them dig these bullets out.

See what they are,' he said to one of the guys trailing behind him.

'You don't even know where Pete is,' I said. 'You don't know who's out there.'

'Inside for you, Blondie,' he said, grinning at me to try to ease my anxiety. 'Some nut's running around with worse aim than you have. Should make you feel better already.'

The fifteen-minute wait for Mike and Pete to return seemed like hours. All the windows in the little shack were open for ventilation, and I could hear the endless volleys of gunshots.

'What'd you get?' I asked, standing at the door as I saw the men coming back.

Their arms were covered in scratches, and Mike had a long, thin trail of blood down one cheek. The thick foliage had been hard for them to penetrate.

'What did we *get*? STDs, in all likelihood.'

'What?'

'This may be the first case where the Center for Disease Control can count poison ivy as a sexually transmitted disease,' Mike said, dabbing at his face with his handkerchief.

The other officers looked at me and Pete Acosta said, 'What?'

I could feel myself reddening.

'Only for the love of Coop would I take off into a briar patch. The rest of you must be dumber than I am. It's itchy already,' he said, rubbing the back of his neck, 'and you don't even know the broad. You got a hard line in there?'

'Yeah,' one of the cops said. 'There's no cell reception.'

'I noticed,' Mike said. He walked past me, patting me on the shoulder, and dialed his office. 'It's Chapman. Give me Lieutenant Peterson.'

'Will you tell—?'

He put his fingers to his lips. 'Sssssssssh. Anybody know you were coming here today?'

'No.'

'It wasn't in the gossip columns, was it? You didn't give it out to Liz Smith? Or the Social Diary?' he said, trying to defuse the tension in the group by poking fun at me. 'What blond prosecutor had a midmorning tryst with a thug on the old Pell's Point estate, once the private reserve of Samuel Rodman?'

'Somebody was shooting at us, Mike. Why is everything a joke to you?'

The cops were laughing.

'Hey, Loo. I'm up at the range. Just had an incident. I think you'd better call headquarters and let them know.'

Mike was going up the proper chain of command. He explained to his boss what had happened as we walked near the perimeter of the restricted area.

'No reason to take it personally,' Mike said. 'Coop? Other than eating a mouthful of Bronx dirt, she's fine. She's having an outer-boroughs experience this week.'

Peterson was asking all the questions.

'Pete Acosta – he's one of the instructors – he'll sit down when the CO comes on for a four to twelve. Pete's guess is that it's somebody on the job, a member of the department with a major problem. Better let the commissioner's office know. Check who's been put on the rubber gun squad lately,' Mike said, referring to cops ruled psycho who've had to surrender their service weapons.

'The shooter was aiming at *us*,' I said.

Mike held his finger to his lips again as he listened to Peterson.

'Hard to tell,' Mike said. 'You know how the range is set off from everything around it. If someone was hunkered down in a clearing, he'd have been completely hidden by the undergrowth. We trampled it pretty well when we went after him – or them – whoever it was. Crime scene'll have to go back into the area and look for spent shells. Of course, the whole damn place here is covered with cartridges, Loo.'

He ended the conversation.

'Maybe one of you wants to explain why you're ignoring me,' I said to Mike and Pete.

'I asked you if anyone knew you'd be here.'

'Just Mercer and Laura.'

'You see what I mean? Your pals, that's all. And by the way, did you get hit?'

'No. But the shooter didn't miss any of us by much.'

'I got more enemies just on the force than you'll ever have to worry about. Yours are all nicely tucked away in the Cooper wing up at Attica,' Mike said. 'Most of mine are out and about, and they all have toasters.'

That was the latest street name for handguns.

'Alex, we've got hundreds of cops coming here five days of the week – Sundays just for sport,' Pete said, 'and every one of them is armed. A service weapon, an off-duty gun or two. Thirty-seven thousand cops in the NYPD? C'mon, we've got some loose cannons. Here I am feeling guilty, thinking someone is taking a potshot at me, and you just happen to be along for the ride. What are you worried about?'

'Let's let these guys get back to work,' Mike said, still scratching his neck.

I didn't move from my seat. I wanted to reargue my case to Pete.

Mike pointed to the door and I hesitated. He was the only one who caught it. 'What is it with you? You need a bulletproof vest to get to the car?'

I wrote down my name and number on a slip of paper I ripped off the phone pad and gave it to Pete. 'I'd like to talk to your CO later, too.'

'Sure.'

Mike went out of the gatehouse first. I looked around as I stood on the top step, sweeping the trees and bushes on the far side of the paved parking lot, but saw no movement. Then I walked beside him to his car.

We drove out the road that led back to the small traffic circle that would take us to I-95.

'Hard to believe this is the Bronx,' I said.

Mike was driving slowly for a reason. Like me, he was scouring the trees for signs of intruders, although all of this forested land leading up to Rodman's Neck was public.

Within ten minutes, we were back on the highway, deep in weekend traffic headed to Manhattan and New Jersey. Housing projects and tenements stood cheek by jowl along the six-lane asphalt interstate.

'What will you do now?' I asked.

'After I drop you off, I'll go up to the office to make some calls. Check in with Dickie Draper. Pull up the old records on Amber Bristol's superintendent.'

'Who? The guy who let us into the apartment the other night? The one who said she was always attracting trouble?' I thought of his smile as he talked to us earlier in the week, cracking his thick knuckles as he commented on Amber's lifestyle. 'I knew you were going to run him, but you didn't tell me he had a sheet.'

'Came up blank the next day. Vargas Candera. The lieutenant had the brains to run it in reverse. Candera Vargas. Bingo! Two collars for using his girlfriend like a punching bag. Bronx County. He deserves another knock on the door.'

'Can't I—?'

'Peterson's on it. I'll let you know when you can be useful. I'll probably swing by the hospital and have a chat with Herb Ackerman.'

'Don't you want me to be there?'

'You've earned a pass.'

'Not with my shooting skills.'

'Your agility under fire. I'd hate to think you might have gotten shot on my watch. I'd never get another cigar from Battaglia,' Mike said. 'Ride out your conviction from yesterday. Enjoy the weekend. Let's see how I do with Herb. Maybe I can fill in some of the blanks.'

'Like what?'

'I think you were distracted when you spoke to him because you had to go to court.' I had told Mike about the conversation. 'You left out a few things, that's all I'm saying.'

'You think he's going to open up to you?'

'It would help to know whether Amber Bristol was a free agent or worked for an escort service, wouldn't it?'

'I forgot to ask. I guess I did feel rushed.'

'Did he pay her with cash, or by check, or with a credit card?'

'Don't know.'

'She couldn't have been the first woman he'd hired, you think? I doubt you grilled him about any of the others. Might be good to talk to them.'

Mike was right. I should have pressed Ackerman harder. If he'd actually succeeded in killing himself, Mike wouldn't have had this second chance.

'Then there's the big question.'

'What's that?'

'Cloth or paper or plastic.'

I smiled and leaned my head against the car window.

'Really, Coop. Imagine if Amber had been Pampered to death with plastic diapers. Open-and-shut case against Herb Ackerman. All the news that's fit to print,' Mike said. 'You'll be fine, kid. I'll get you home. You ought to take a nap.'

'I guess I need it.'

'Grab one of the girls and go to a movie tonight. Get your mind off this.'

'I've got a friend in from out of town. We're having dinner together.'

'You're not holding out on me, are you? It isn't Nina or Joan?'

My closest friends adored Mike. They liked his intelligence and his humor, his intolerance for bullshit and bureaucracy, the

tenacity and spirit with which he kept at one of the most difficult jobs imaginable.

'Keep them away from you if they were in town? Not a prayer,'
I said. I hadn't told Mercer or Mike about Luc. 'And you, are
you covering for anyone tonight?'

'You know me, I'm always looking for OT.' The overtime
money was good, and Mike was usually happy to double up on
his shifts.

Half an hour later, at two in the afternoon, Mike pulled in
front of my building and I thanked him again for getting me out
of harm's way.

'Will you call me if anything interesting turns up over the
weekend?'

'We don't want "interesting," Coop. No bones, no blowflies,
no bullets, no bodies.'

He pulled out of the driveway and the doorman handed me
an envelope. 'The messenger who delivered this asked me to tell
you it was urgent.'

17

The note inside the padded envelope was written in bold callig-raphy that I had come to recognize these past two months.

'Confirm package ordered to arrive Plaza Athénée, at the Bar Seine, at seven-thirty tonight. Needs food, wine immediately . . . and occasional affection. Driver will be downstairs to make pickup. Pack contents carefully to avoid melting in transit.'

The card was attached to a large brass key with a red ribbon.

I fanned myself with Luc Rouget's missive as I rode up in the elevator. We had met in June at the Martha's Vineyard wedding of one of my best friends, Joan Stanton. She had despaired of a string of broken relationships following the death of my fiancé, Adam Nyman, shortly after my graduation from law school. Luc and Joan's husband had known each other for years, and her plan to surprise me with an introduction made a romantic weekend even more emotionally charged.

Since the night we met, I had seen Luc three other times in New York. He was the son of a renowned French restaurateur, and although he lived in Mougins, a tiny village perched high in the Alps, he was making frequent trips to the city with the prospect of reestablishing his father's classic dining spot.

Inside my apartment, I turned up the air-conditioning and immediately began to fill the bathtub with warm water, adding scented potions to make loads of bubbles. I needed to create an artificial wall to distance both the horrors of the last week and this morning's scare from a personal life that too often took a backseat to my work.

There were three messages on the answering machine – all from Luc – and I played them as I undressed.

The first one was a fuzzy cell call from the international arrivals terminal at JFK, shortly before noon. The second, during his cab ride into the city, expressed his concern that he had spoken to Laura, who told him I wouldn't be in the office at all that day.

'Luc here, Alexandra. I'm beginning to worry now that one of your cases might change our plans,' he said on his third try. 'It's Friday afternoon, and I have to leave for DC in the morning. I'm in meetings all afternoon. Please call. I'm hoping I've found a way to unlock some of your secrets, *ma chère*.'

His French accent was always a turn-on.

On Martha's Vineyard I kept a collection of old keys on my desk – from flea markets and antique shops – to use as paper-weights. Luc must have seen them after Joan and Jim's wedding.

I left a voice mail for him at the hotel before I slipped into the tub.

I felt better after a long, soothing bath and an attempt at a nap. But I was too wired to sleep, excited by my feelings for Luc – feelings I hadn't experienced in more than a year.

Joan and my friend Nina were determined to help me find a balance between my private life and the intensity of the prosecutorial job. I liked the emotional involvement of my work, but it was difficult to translate how richly rewarding it could be to someone who'd had no experience with the dark world of sex crimes and homicides.

It was an admittedly odd juxtaposition. When I closed my eyes to think about kissing Luc, I had to force out thoughts of the two dead women whose killers we were trying to find. I could remember every word Luc had whispered to me that first night on the Vineyard, but the staccato sound of gunshots still reverberated in my ears, even in the quiet space of my home.

There was something so easy, so comfortable about spending time with friends who were prosecutors and detectives. There was no need to explain how we coped with the trauma that we witnessed almost every day, or to applaud our efforts to help put people's lives back together, or to question our often Sisyphean interest in bringing the guilty to justice.

I needed to leave some of that baggage at home when I walked out the door to meet Luc.

I wore a strapless sundress that always lightened my mood when I put it on. It was aqua silk, with a swing skirt that just touched the top of my knees. My legs were tanned and it was too hot for pantyhose, so I chose a pair of black patent sandals with thin straps and high heels. I carried a sequined throw over my shoulders, in the unlikely event it cooled down during the evening.

I took a last look at myself in the mirror, then pulled back my hair, sweeping it off my neck into a knot and clipping it in place with a beaded barrette.

'There's a car service waiting for you, Ms. Cooper,' the doorman said when I came downstairs.

'Thanks, Vinny.'

He held the door open and whistled for the driver to pull up. 'Glad you're taking the night off. That's a tough schedule you've been keeping.'

Even the doormen knew I needed to get a life.

It was a fast ride to the elegant hotel on Sixty-fourth Street and Madison Avenue. Bright red awnings and neatly trimmed topiary marked the entrance, and I stopped to reapply my lipstick before I went into the lobby.

Bar Seine was one of the most attractive rooms in the city. Dark wood paneling gave it a rich, warm look, and the low lighting and soft music added to its appeal. As soon as I stood in the doorway, Luc came forward to greet me.

'*Bon soir*, Alexandra,' he said, taking me in his arms and kissing both my cheeks several times. 'I've been looking forward to this for weeks. I'd have been – how do you say? *Désolé* – there's nothing in English that quite captures that expression. I don't know what I would have done if you'd thrown me over for another case.'

Luc guided me to a banquette in a corner of the room. Before we sat, he lifted my fingers in the air and twirled me once around. 'You look ravishing. I've kept the driver, so perhaps we'll go dancing after supper.'

'Lovely idea.'

'*Une coupe?*'

'*Oui, monsieur.*'

There was a bottle of champagne chilling in a cooler. The waiter saw us sit down and came over to pop the cork.

'That's the last thing I'm going to say in French.' Luc had made fun of my accent on our second date, despite years I spent studying the language in high school and college.

He raised his flute and tapped it against mine. 'Well, if you just say "*oui*" to everything I ask from this point on, we'll do fine. Here's to a splendid evening.'

There was something wonderfully seductive about Luc's manner. Although Nina had declared him GU – geographically undesirable – when she learned he was just visiting from France, she, too, had been taken by his charm and charisma.

'Are you hungry? Did you have any lunch?' he asked before the waiter left.

I had been too upset to eat anything after the episode at the range. 'Something light would be good.'

'*Huitres*?'

'Perfect.'

'Perhaps not as fresh as the oysters you get in Chilmark from Larsen's Fish Market or those fried clams at The Bite, but they should do,' Luc said, ordering two dozen for us. 'Now tell me about your day. What kept you out of the office?'

'Tell me about yours. You probably have more exciting news.'

Luc was forty-eight years old, divorced with two children who lived nearby in his hometown. He wasn't classically handsome, but he had strong features – blue gray eyes that reflected his enthusiasm, even behind wire-rimmed glasses, and a long, thin Roman nose. He was tall and lean, with hair just a few shades darker than my own, and his great style was evident in the way he dressed and carried himself.

'I think things are beginning to shape up well,' he said. 'This is the height of our season in Mougins. It's hard for me to get away in August, but the opportunity to duplicate my father's creation is quite thrilling for me.'

Luc smiled easily. He delighted in the pleasures of the culinary arts, and his energy was infectious. I couldn't imagine a professional world – certainly neither law nor medicine, with which I'd been surrounded since childhood – that didn't involve life-and-death decisions but simply enjoyment.

André Rouget had moved to New York from France in the 1960s and had built a remarkable career in a notoriously fickle business. One of the first celebrity chefs, he had opened a landmark restaurant in a town house on East Fiftieth Street. Lutèce became known for the finest French cuisine in America, maintaining its excellence as it passed from Rouget's leadership to that of the great André Soltner, until it closed its doors almost forty years later.

'Have you found a location?' I asked.

'I'm hoping to do this exactly in the manner of my father,' Luc said, explaining that his partner in the venture was scouting for a building very much like the original.

'And you'll call it Lutèce?'

'*Bien sûr*. There's a great history in that name. You know what it means?'

'Wasn't Lutetia the original name of Paris? Isn't that the Latin word, from the time of the Roman conquest?'

'Even more complicated, Alex. The Parisii were a Celtic tribe, living on the Ile de la Cité. The derivation of the word is Celtic – louk-teih, the place of the marshes.'

I didn't want to be thinking of Mike Chapman now, but the mention of a useful piece of trivia brought him to mind at once. The information would serve me well betting against him on *Jeopardy!* some night.

'But let's talk about you. Tell me why you aren't on the Vineyard this weekend.'

The oysters arrived on a bed of ice chips. They were cold and delicious, with a slightly briny taste that I especially liked.

'I couldn't plan anything because of the trial. I should be able to get up there for the long Labor Day weekend.'

'Such a beautiful island, especially where you are, in Chilmark. It must restore your spirit, when everything else about your work seems so harsh.'

'My own little piece of paradise, Luc. I love it there. What happens in Washington tomorrow?'

'My partner wants me to meet a guy who lives on the Eastern Shore – a potential backer for the restaurant. Then I fly directly home. Back to work. We have to feed all those American tourists, you know,' Luc said, refilling our glasses and touching the rim of his against mine again. 'Laura told me you had a big victory yesterday. Can you explain the case to me?'

I didn't want to bring Kerry Hastings's story into our

rendezvous. It was too somber to mix with champagne and Malpeques.

'It's a very long story. I'd so much rather talk about your summer and anything that has to do with getting you to New York more often.'

'I sent you that key for a reason, Alexandra. You know the Marches aux Puces in Paris? Clignancourt?'

'Of course. It's my favorite place for antiquing.'

'Then I shall add that to our list of things to do together when you come to France. That brass key is from the wine cellar of an old chateau in Bordeaux. You can add it to your collection, but you know I bargained hard for it. I'm trying to find a way to get into your heart. Open you up a bit. Perhaps one of those keys will be useful.'

Luc reached across the table for my hand.

'I don't think you need any help with that.'

'But I realize that I learned more about you from my conversation with Nina than I know from talking to you.'

The afternoon after Joan's wedding, I had been called back to the city for a break in a case I was working on. Luc had been fogged in on the island, and my college roommate had told him more of my personal history during that long evening than I probably would have revealed in the most intense cross-examination.

We finished the oysters and opened a second bottle of Cristal by ten o'clock. I didn't want any more to drink. My hair was coming loose from the barrette, wisps of blond ringlets curling around my brow and neck. By this time there seemed to be very little we didn't know about each other.

'You know, I had a reservation in the dining room for nine o'clock,' he said, laughing as he looked at his watch.

'I'm not the least bit hungry now.'

'Not for anything at all?'

'I didn't say that.'

Luc reached into his pocket and put the small gold room key on the table. I picked it up and closed my hand around it.

He stood up beside me. 'Dancing?'

'I think it's a waste of a lot of euros to keep that driver waiting.'

'But that dress looks so lovely when you move.'

'Then I'll move,' I said, slipping out of the banquette and leading Luc across the room. I looked at the number engraved into the key. Four seventeen.

I crossed through the lobby to the far side of the reception desk and called for the elevator while Luc went outside to dismiss the driver for the night. We got on and the doors closed.

Luc took my head between his hands, putting his lips to mine. I opened my mouth and we exchanged kisses, deep and long. He pressed my back against the gilded elevator wall. I started to laugh.

He lifted my chin and kissed my nose. 'Am I that funny?'

I closed my eyes so I wouldn't see the camera lens in the corner of the ceiling. I kept telling myself to stop being a prosecutor and pay no notice to the surveillance equipment that this hotel, like every other, had installed in public areas as a security measure.

'Somebody's watching us,' I said, pointing at the miniature device.

He held up one of his long arms as though to block the lens. 'Then let me take you to a more private place.'

Luc led me down the hallway to his suite. He stepped aside for me to unlock the door, and then I followed him in.

The first time we made love was slow and playful. I was comfortable with Luc, trusting him, giving myself to him with an excitement I hadn't thought possible.

We rested, talked, and made love again. Finally, at two o'clock, Luc said, 'We still haven't eaten any supper yet.' He nibbled at my stomach. 'Not enough there to feed me.'

'How can you even think of food now?'

'It's against my religion to skip a meal, Alexandra. You've got to get used to that. What will you have?'

'Whatever you order.' I went into the bathroom, wrapping myself in a thick white terrycloth robe.

'Suppose I give you a choice. Two things easy for the chef in the middle of the night. They don't have to do much to get some caviar up here. Or you might indulge one of my favorite childhood memories.'

'What's that?' There were bottles of sparkling water on the desk in the living room. I opened one and curled up in an armchair.

'A peanut butter and jelly sandwich,' he said, kissing the crown of my head as he walked to the phone to dial room service. 'I can't get peanut butter in Mougins. I usually come to the States with an empty suitcase and take home jars of it. That and Oreos and English muffins.'

'Hold the caviar. I'd much rather have a sandwich.' Luc's sophistication was irresistible, but so was his lack of pretension.

In the morning, the previous night's driver was standing beside his car at the curb in front of the hotel. 'We'll drop you on our way to La Guardia,' Luc said.

'I feel like I'm walking on air. I'll just stroll up Park Avenue and be home in no time. Just kiss me once more and tell me when you're returning.'

The driver was discreet enough to turn around while we said our good-byes, and Luc rode off with a wave, promising to call when he reached home the next afternoon.

It was another sultry day, but I cheerfully greeted dog walkers and people out to get their newspaper and coffee. I said hello to all the white-gloved doormen I passed and stopped for the men unloading furniture for the ongoing renovation at the massive brick structure of the Seventh Regiment Armory.

This would be the second week in a row that I missed my Saturday morning ballet class, but I was too tired and had no desire to concentrate on the drill of barre and floor exercises.

I was digging for my key chain in my small jeweled handbag as I heard a wolf whistle from behind me.

'You're either way too early for streetwalking or you're late for Cinderella's pumpkin.' A car door slammed and Mike Chapman's voice turned the heads of two of my elderly neighbors, gossiping on the sidewalk.

'I – uh – I'm just getting – I didn't – obviously, I've been out all night,' I stammered, suddenly embarrassed, with no idea how long Mike had been waiting for me.

'Sequins and sandals. I didn't know breakfast was going to be formal or I would have put on socks. What happened, the guy didn't think you were worth the cab fare home?'

'Look, I'm sorry I wasn't here if you needed me. Is something wrong?'

'There's another girl dead,' Mike said, running his fingers through his hair. 'You've got to help me, Coop. We've got a maniac on the loose.'

18

Forty-two minutes later, having traded in my evening clothes for sneakers, jeans, and a cotton sweater, I was waiting with Mike for Mercer at the Thirty-fourth Street heliport.

There were clouds moving in over the East River, and Mike kept glancing up at them. He was a nervous flier, especially in small planes and choppers.

'Fifty-five miles north of here,' Mike said to Joe Galiano, one of the Aviation Unit's crack pilots. 'How long is that going to take, Sarge?'

'I should have you down in twenty minutes.'

The craft was a brand-new Bell 412 – one of seven for which the NYPD paid ten million dollars each. In the aftermath of 9/11, the faster, more powerful equipment had been purchased to enable high-tech surveillance and serve as effective counterterrorism tools.

Today, it would be the fastest way to get up the Hudson to the place where the twenty-year-old victim's body had been discovered the previous afternoon.

'It's an island, Sarge. It's a piece of rock in the middle of the river. How the hell are you going to land?'

'I got six acres to work with, Chapman. And the local cops are trying to clear the weeds to give me a pad right now,' Galiano said, patting the side of his blue and white flying machine. 'I've put cops on project rooftops with this baby. Worse that happens is that I hover low and drop you three out.'

Mike was biting his lip. 'The weather going to hold?'

Aviation was an elite unit founded in 1929 as the world's first airborne division in law enforcement. Its officers, with good reason, had more than the usual cop swagger.

'I'd expect a little chop. But these things are more stable than fixed wing, so don't let your knuckles get too white,' Galiano said. 'Here's Wallace. Let's get her up.'

'What's the name of this place?' I asked.

'Pollepel Island.'

'I've never heard of it.'

'You've seen it.'

'What do you know that I don't?'

'When's the last time you took the train to Albany?' Mike asked, as Mercer shook hands with Galiano.

'In May.' There were frequent legislative meetings in the state capital, and Battaglia had appointed me to serve in his place on the review committee for sex crimes and domestic violence.

'Just beyond Cold Spring, there's a castle that sits out in the river. The Breakneck Ridge station stop on Metro North is right above it.'

'I know exactly where you mean. I've seen it dozens of times. It looks like an enormous old fortress. Who's the girl? What was she doing there?' I asked. 'And what does this have to do with us?'

Mike looked at his notepad. 'Connie Wade. Twenty years old, like I told you. African-American. She was about to start her third year at West Point.'

'She must have been a very talented kid. It's fiercely competitive to get in there.' I knew that candidates were evaluated not only on academic ability but on leadership potential and physical attributes. They needed a nomination from a member of Congress or the Department of the Army. I could only imagine the qualities and strengths that had commended Connie Wade for such an honor.

'Yeah. Another heartbreaker. Smart girl and a great athlete. Originally from Indiana. Had ten days' leave to go home for her sister's wedding last weekend. Disappeared on Wednesday, on her way back through the city. Never got to the Point.'

I settled into the backseat of the chopper, next to Mike. Mercer was in front with Sergeant Galiano. While Galiano checked the controls, Mike gave us the rest of the facts explaining why he was called.

'The island's deserted. Has been for thirty years. The castle's decayed and the whole place is supposed to look like an overgrown jungle. The state owns it now.'

'How would anybody get there?' Mercer asked.

'Boat's the only way. Kayaks, speedboats, canoes. Cops tell me tree huggers and paddle-pulling exercise nuts like to poke around out there, even though it's off-limits till the building can be restored. It's a thousand feet offshore.'

'It's not far from West Point either, then.'

'Spitting distance, upriver,' Mike said, putting his pad away as he fastened his seat belt. 'During the Revolution, soldiers used Pollepel as a base to try to stop the British from getting any farther north. They sunk a few hundred logs with iron spikes in their tips underwater to sabotage enemy ships. It was an old medieval defense. How's my French, Coop? *Chevaux-de-frise.*'

I did a double take, wondering if he had any way to know about Luc.

'So you've been there,' Mercer said.

'Nope. But the island's history is right up my alley. This is not quite the way I wanted to see it.'

'You're going to have to put your headsets on,' Galiano said. 'They're miked up, so you'll be able to hear and talk to each other.'

The rotors started to spin and the big bird vibrated as we prepared to take off.

'Two nature lovers were hiking around late in the day. They were looking for frigging snakes, if you can believe that. Found Wade's body, just outside the entrance to the main building, 'cause they saw one slithering over what turned out to be her foot. That's the only part of her skin that was visible.'

Mercer leaned forward. 'What makes them think—?'

'Blunt force trauma to the face and head. Start there. She was naked. Left at the scene at least twenty-four hours earlier. Wrapped in an old olive green blanket, just like Elise Huff,' Mike said. 'And there were handcuffs still on her wrists. They had to move her right out 'cause there's a lot of wildlife on the island.'

'Why'd the locals have the good sense to call New York?' I asked.

The helicopter rose off the pad, dipping its nose toward the water before lifting and turning to the north. Within seconds, we were directly over Roosevelt Island, about to clear the 59th Street Bridge, following the outline of Manhattan as it narrowed to Spuyten Duyvil, where the East River met the Hudson. Mercer pointed down at the remains of the deadhouse, the old smallpox hospital that had figured in one of our more challenging cases.

'They didn't,' Mike said, answering my question. 'But the commandant of the academy had the good sense to want to retrace the girl's steps. She was in Manhattan the day she went missing. Never showed up at Port Authority, so far as they could tell, for the bus ride back to school. Missing Persons routed the call over to us late last night.'

Mike was clutching the back of Mercer's seat, barely able to look out the sides of the chopper, which were all glass, as we continued our noisy ride along the Palisades.

'No clothes at the scene again?'

'Not a shred.'

'Anybody know how she was dressed?' I asked.

'She had to travel in uniform,' Mike said. 'Gray cadet jacket, white pants. Only way to get the military discount.'

I thought of Arthur Huff and his West Point ring.

'You know the ring that Elise Huff was supposed to have been wearing?' I said, reminding Mike about my conversation with Elise's father. 'That's a strange coincidence. I wonder if this victim had one of those, too.'

'You know I don't believe in coincidence, Coop,' Mike said. 'They've designated a colonel to be liaison to the investigation. Spoke to him this morning and asked him whether he thought there was any significance to Huff's ring. Says they stopped making them before this Wade kid was born, and she didn't have any relatives who'd gone to the school. Unlikely she had a ring like that.'

Twelve minutes later, Sergeant Galiano told us to look off to the left. 'The United States Military Academy. Damn impressive site.'

Mike braced himself and looked out at the magnificent campus below. I knew he had visited the Point countless times, out of his fascination with American history. Many of his heroes – Grant, Pershing, MacArthur, Eisenhower, Denman, and Patton – had been educated here, and occasional trips to its museum of military treasures added to his storehouse of knowledge.

'George Washington picked the spot himself,' Mike said. 'Considered it one of the most critical positions on the American continent.'

'Why?' I asked.

The Hudson took a sharp S-shaped curve just above the hilltop setting of the original fortifications.

' 'Cause you could control all the river traffic from this place. South to New York, north to New England, and west to the Great Lakes. The Brits would have split the colonies in half – right down there – if Benedict Arnold had succeeded in giving the Point away, like he tried.'

'Here's your rock,' Galiano said. 'Pollepel Island.'

On the right side of the river, not far above West Point, the turrets of an enormous castle rose above the dense green growth that covered the ground.

Galiano swooped his bird close in on the south side and started to circle to the west of the abandoned ruin.

Mike gripped the seat back even tighter. He looked out the window, and I knew he was trying to see where Galiano would put down the chopper. 'Hey, Sarge,' he said, 'I didn't bring the rosary beads.'

'I'd say it's a little bit like Walt Disney meets Stephen King. Give me a minute.'

As we hovered at the north end of the island I noted four or five more buildings, mostly roofless, smaller than the six-story castle that soared above the gray waters of the Hudson.

'There,' Mercer said, pointing down through the glass bubble of the helicopter's nose. 'Check it out. State police and army craft, off to the east.'

On the edge of the rocky shore, there was a small cluster of boats. Like the NYPD's emergency rescue craft, they had large initials on their tops and sides, for identification by other agencies approaching by air or sea.

Several men in windbreakers marked with orange neon sleeve reflectors were waving their arms at Galiano.

'Got it,' he said. 'There's a clearing on the southeast. That'll do me fine.'

Mike closed his eyes and pulled his seat belt tighter.

The chopper continued around the far side of the structures, banking as it made the final approach. It hovered again, swaying from side to side as Galiano took great care to avoid the surrounding trees and center on the only flat strip of land we had seen.

The big machine hit the ground with a thud, and we waited for the powerful rotors to come to a stop.

I could see the tops of the ruined castle and the thick tangle of weeds and vines that had swallowed the buildings' foundations.

'It looks like we've traveled back in time,' I said. 'To another century.'

'To a ghost island, Coop. That's what this place is,' Mike said. 'Maybe we got some new ghosts now.'

19

A tall, heavyset man a little older than I held out a hand to guide me down from the chopper. 'Step lively, miss. Snakes, spiders, ticks, and poison sumac.'

'We were with his cousin, poison ivy, yesterday. I'm Mike Chapman.' He introduced Mercer and me to our official greeter.

'Bart Hinson. State police.'

The brush that surrounded our landing pad was as tall as the trees behind it. Boulders and branches ringed the clearing that had been hacked out this morning for our arrival.

'Any developments?' Mike asked.

'Just trying to make sense of what we have here. Nothing much got done overnight. It's not easy terrain to search. Follow me,' Bart said.

We entered a trail about twenty feet long, ducking beneath

weathered limbs that had been intertwining, it appeared from their density, for many years. When we emerged, I faced the most unusual array of huge stone buildings – all with turrets and towers, elaborate carvings, and coats of arms.

The men waiting for us next to a crumbling entrance to the building complex were from a mix of agencies. There were six other troopers – two of whom specialized in crime scene work – four landscapers who'd been called in with chainsaws to make room for us to land, and a caretaker who lived on the mainland but supervised the property for the state.

Bart Hinson was the lead man. 'I thought we'd show you where the girl's body was discovered,' he said. 'Tell you a little bit about this place.'

I craned my neck to look up the side of one of the buildings that was about a city block long. It was covered in red paint that had faded over time. Written across it in chipped and mottled gold lettering were the words BANNERMAN ISLAND ARSENAL.

'You find the boat yet?' Mike asked. 'That must be how the killer got her here.'

Bart shook his head. 'Well, up this way, everybody and his uncle has a boat. More docks than you got subway platforms. Fancy name-brand little yachts, simple outboard motors, fishing boats – just about every size and shape. Then you got your kayaks and canoes.'

'I hear you.'

Bart pointed at the caretaker. 'He uses an aluminum rowboat to go back and forth. Wouldn't take much to slip over here and back even with someone else's boat and nobody ever know.'

'How about the currents?' Mercer asked.

'This part of the Hudson is an estuary, so the tide changes from north to south a couple of times a day,' Bart said. 'It's been pretty calm this week. A strong rower wouldn't have much trouble if he knew the tides.'

'I thought this was called Pollepel Island,' I said, pointing up at the writing on the wall. 'What's that sign about?'

'Pollepel was its name centuries ago. The Native Americans spun tales that this spot was haunted. Then along came the Dutch sailors, who had good cause to believe it was spooked, too,' Bart said. 'Thought it was the devil made the ships crash into the rocks and sink with all their goods aboard.'

'Was this fortress part of West Point? Did the army build it to defend the Hudson from the east?'

Mike dismissed me. 'It has nothing to do with the government.'

'But you said the state owns it.'

'That's only been the last thirty years,' Bart said. He swept his arm around the bizarre vista. 'This was all the folly of one man, Alex. A privately owned island, bought in 1900 by a complete eccentric named Frank Bannerman.'

'And he built this – this . . . ?'

'It's supposed to look like an ancestral family castle back in Scotland, complete with drawbridges and a moat. But you're right to call it a fortress. The arsenal – that's the second-largest building here – was one of the biggest munitions warehouses in America. Nations went to war a century ago outfitted entirely by Frank Bannerman, from his crazy island outpost.'

'You know about this guy, Mike?' Mercer asked.

'My aunt Eunice had a cellar full of Bannerman's catalogs. Probably still does. Uncle Brendan had been collecting them since he was a kid.'

Mike's military interests had been fueled by his father's oldest brother, who had landed at Normandy.

'What was Bannerman doing up here?' Mercer asked.

'The family emigrated from Scotland to New York in the 1850s, right after he was born,' said Bart. 'At the end of the Civil War, young Frank started buying up tons of military goods – surplus equipment – that the government was auctioning off. He purchased everything from scrap metal and bayonets to ships that the navy wanted to unload, figuring he could sell them to whatever government went to war next.'

'He had all the weapons and ammunition stored in offices downtown, on Broadway,' Mike said.

'Till after the Spanish-American War. Bannerman purchased 90 percent of all the military hardware and black powder when that conflict ended, but it was so dangerously explosive that the city demanded he move it out. In 1900, he bought this island and moved everything up our way,' Bart said. 'Designed all the buildings himself.'

'Did he live here?' I asked.

'That castle,' Bart said, pointing at the enormous structure with four rounded towers and crenellated peaks, 'was built to be a house for his family. See how there's not a right angle anywhere on it? The guy was a master of detail.'

'And people actually bought this stuff from a private individual?'

'He outfitted entire regiments in World War I – turning a handsome profit off our own government' Bart said. 'Sold something like a hundred thousand saddles, rifles, uniforms, and about twenty million cartridges to the Russians for their war against Japan a century ago.'

'Everybody from Buffalo Bill to the silent film directors bought their gear from Bannerman's,' Mike added. 'Bayonets and muskets, spurs and torpedoes – all straight out of the catalog. You know the commemorative cannons you see in town squares all over America? I bet more than half of them were sold right off this island.'

'There's got to be some kind of connection between Elise Huff, with her West Point ring, and Connie Wade, a cadet whose body was brought out to this arsenal, practically within sight of the academy. How come you and Bart know so much about Frank Bannerman and I never heard of him?'

' 'Cause little girls read Nancy Drew while little boys studied the pictures in these catalogs. They were still being published when I was a teenager.'

'Does he have any descendants? Anyone who still has access here?' I asked.

'Nope. End of the line.'

Mike was animated now, telling Bart and Mercer about his uncle Brendan's collections. 'He used to buy things from Bannerman's that came packed in their original crates, and my aunt Eunice saved them just that way. He had these kepis—'

'Kepis?' I asked.

'Hats. The kind soldiers wore in the Civil War. Paid something like seventy-five cents apiece for them.'

'Sounds like an army-navy store,' Mercer said.

'The very first one. Bannerman sold relics from Admiral Perry's Arctic expedition and weapons from the Battle of Yorktown. Put your hands on one of those catalogs, Coop, and I'll tell you what else you'll find,' Mike said, snapping his finger at me as an idea came to him.

'What?'

'Let's get that label from the olive green blanket that Elise Huff's body was wrapped in. See if there's anything like it on the one that was covering Connie Wade yesterday – or have the lab compare the fibers. Could be from the same stock. Could be our killer's a military buff gone AWOL.'

20

Bart Hinson asked one of the other troopers to lead the way, with Mercer behind him, minding the cracked stone paths that once connected the buildings.

I said to Mike, 'That doesn't account for Amber Bristol. There's nothing we know about her that has any military connection.'

'Full speed ahead, Coop. Two out of three with a West Point nexus. Let's work this one through.'

'We learned this morning that Cadet Wade was on the women's crew team,' Bart said. 'Every time they practiced it took her right past the island. Can't say she ever stopped here, but it would be hard to row by without becoming curious.'

Bart stopped beneath a small archway. The cracks in the structure overhead stretched out in all directions like an endless succession of spider webs.

'Here's where the body was when I got called in last night,' he said, pointing to a place just beyond the stone overhang. 'Her bare feet were right there, and the rest of her sort of that way, lengthwise, all covered up.'

The familiar chalk outline of urban policing wouldn't have worked in this setting. Bart pulled a Polaroid photo out of his pocket and handed it to Mike. 'Can you make it out?'

All the colors were muted. The dark material of the blanket blurred against the brush around it. Connie Wade's skin, lighter than Mercer's, was barely visible through the weeds.

Mike stooped to examine the ground around the site, pulling apart tall grasses to look for traces of anything that might be useful in the investigation. It was impossible to know whether this part of the scene had been trampled by the killer or by the troopers who'd been called in after the body was found.

'What's your bet? Killed somewhere else or right here?' Mercer asked.

'I'm thinking she was alive when she got to the island. Probably handcuffed and gagged, and forced to walk up here from the landing. I don't think a kid with all her smarts would volunteer to explore this place with a complete stranger,' Bart said. 'He'd have to be awfully strong to have carried her from a boat.'

'Facial trauma?'

The trooper took a deep breath before he answered. 'I can show you those pictures, too. The commandant from the academy couldn't even recognize her.'

Mike stood up, looking around the rough landscape. 'You got a guess at a weapon?'

'My men carted off a few dozen of these chunks of rock to the lab. Her face was probably crushed by one of them.'

'Were any of them around the body?'

'They're everywhere here. That's why the whole thing is off-limits. State officials have been worried about lawsuits if pieces fall on trespassers' heads. I never imagined one of Bannerman's building blocks might be used in a homicide.'

Weathered and worn, the castle towers looked like oversized chess pieces that had broken apart and shattered as they landed on the hard, rocky surface of the island.

'Blood?'

Bart shook his head. 'Nothing obvious. Nothing spattered around that we could see. But there's so much blood on the inside of the blanket that he may already have had the girl covered up when he finished her off.'

'I guess it's too early to know about DNA,' I said.

'The lab tech went over the body with a Wood's lamp before they bagged her. No external signs of seminal fluid,' he said, referring to the ultraviolet light used to reveal the presence of semen on skin. 'The autopsy will tell us more. How about your other cases?'

'No semen in either one,' I said.

Mike was walking away from us, shading his eyes from the glare. 'Is there a particular place for boats to land? Can you track a route to this spot?'

'The original dock Bannerman put in has been reinforced, just for caretaking purposes. The rest of the island is too rocky to risk. I'd say our man most likely came ashore there.'

Mike was off to the side of the trail. 'Something's been dragged through here.'

'I'm sorry to say we've made it tougher on ourselves – and for you,' Bart said, following him. 'Our crime scene guys brought their equipment in this way. Probably obliterated whatever marks the killer made getting the Wade girl from water's edge to where he left her.'

Indoor sites – the neat confines of a residential apartment or an office building – presented far fewer challenges to investigators. There were usually obvious perimeters to the start of the violence and the exit of the perpetrator. Here, nature and the elements seized control of the setting.

'Should we come with you?' I asked Mike.

Mercer had started off in the opposite direction.

Mike waved me on. 'Gotta keep her close, Bart. You could give Coop two canteens and a compass and it still might take her a week to find her way out of Central Park.'

They were twenty feet ahead of me and I traipsed off to catch up. To the left, my peripheral vision picked up something moving quickly out of my way in the brush. I froze in my tracks.

'Hurry up,' Mike said.

I couldn't move.

'What is it?' Mike asked, as Bart Hinson came back to escort me.

'Probably a black rat snake,' he said, offering his arm.

'They eat blonds?'

'Bullfrogs, mostly. That's why they like it here. They're diurnal. Great daylight hunters, and very fast.'

'And extremely long,' I said, still frightened by the appearance of the satiny black reptile slithering away.

'Poisonous?' Mike asked.

'No. But you'll see lots of them around. They'll come out to bask on the rocks if the sun gets stronger.'

Mike turned away and I grasped Bart's arm as I forced myself to keep moving. Birds circled overhead – harmless, I was sure, but now I imagined they were vultures. Everything on the island looked ominous.

From the river, I could hear the noise of motorboats and jet skis. It was the only sign that we were anywhere near civilization.

For more than an hour, the caretaker and several of the troopers stayed close to Mike, who was going over every foot of the trail from the old wooden dock back toward the castle. From time to time, he would bend to point out debris – pieces of candy wrapper impaled on the tip of a branch or an empty soda can that was wedged between rocks. He insisted that every item be picked up, tagged, vouchered, and sent to the lab. Odds were that none of this related to Wade's killer, but that was a chance Mike Chapman never took.

The clouds thickened, the humidity rose, and the mosquitoes proved themselves pros at getting underneath my clothing. When Mike was convinced that the painstaking work was being done to his standards by the troopers, he led us in search of Mercer.

I stood beside Mike in the doorway of the main entrance. The roof had long ago caved in, so although daylight revealed the baronial hall, the collapsed boulders and beams made it impossible to walk very far inside.

From the distance, I heard a sharp yell – and then Mercer calling Mike's name.

'Over there,' Bart said, as we went back. 'They're in the powder house.'

Beyond the six-story castle and the arsenal was one of the smaller structures. It appeared as though fire had ravaged it years earlier, and as we ran to the entrance, I could see what was left of the rear wall, blackened and charred at its fringes.

One of the young troopers had slipped through a piece of flooring. With a panicked expression on his face, he was struggling to keep a grip on Mercer's powerful arm and stop himself from plunging into whatever basement was below.

Mike and Bart rushed to the edge of the broken planks and helped lift the officer back up onto solid footing.

'You okay?' Mike asked.

'I'll be fine, but it's all rotted out,' the trooper said.

Bart stooped to examine the wood. 'This place was gutted ages ago. A whole load of ammo blew up inside. But I'm thinking these boards don't match the rest of the old planks in here.'

'Give us some light,' Mike said to the caretaker, who had run in at the sound of the commotion.

Mercer leaned over and peered in. 'Well, well. I think we've found ourselves a little bunker here.'

He held on to the surrounding planks and dangled one of his feet into the open space.

'Where the hell are you going?' Mike shouted.

'Some kind of makeshift steps,' Mercer said, counting them off for us as he moved slowly down. 'One, two, three, four of them. Now I'm standing on dirt. I'm in.'

Mike handed the flashlight to him and Mercer ducked down to examine the space. Seconds later, his head reappeared.

'All the comforts of home,' Mercer said. 'If you like living in a black hole.'

21

Mike handed me a pair of latex gloves and I stifled my intense claustrophobic fears to lower myself into the dungeonlike space.

'Don't touch anything, Coop. Bart's getting a team in here to tear it apart. Just look around and tell me if you get any brainstorms.'

I couldn't stand up all the way. Hunched over, I shined the light around the four-foot-square room. A ladder had been cobbled together from large tree branches, while smaller limbs – strung with strips of canvas – were hung as shelves, above an old army cot resting on rusted springs.

'Looks like he's moved out,' I said. 'No clothes, no fresh food. Not even water.'

'There's no potable drinking water on the island,' Bart said. 'You'd need to bring that along to live here.'

There were several cans of food and fruit stacked under the cot, and packages of MREs, the meals ready-to-eat used by our military. A large shovel lay beneath the rungs of the ladder, and next to the spade was the translucent skin of one of the island snakes.

Weapons of every variety were ranged on the floor and propped against the walls. Ropes of varying lengths and widths were stuck into the dirt walls with large nails. Hunting knives and revolvers, hand grenades and bayonets from another era, fierce-looking metal objects large enough to trap a bear – Bannerman's arsenal had inspired some modern-day madman to collect his own assortment of deadly toys.

'You see anything to suggest Connie Wade was down there?' Mike asked from above.

If the same man had killed all three victims, the impersonality of the crime scenes was the most solid link we had. He had left no signature at any of them, dumping women in remote locales without depositing a hint of his genetic profile – despite the obvious sexual overtones to the attacks.

'No.'

'Put yourself in her place.'

'I wouldn't have lasted an hour,' I said, my gloved hand on the ladder, ready to pull myself out. It was dark and dank, and the daddy longlegs that was scampering across the narrow cot seemed as anxious for me to leave his home as I was.

'Everything goes,' Mike said to Bart as I climbed out. 'Don't let anybody touch the handle of the shovel. Maybe we'll get his DNA on that or on the trigger of one of the guns.'

Bart nodded in agreement.

'Who's got the handcuffs?' I asked.

'They're already in Albany, at the state lab.'

Mike was writing Bart's phone number in his pad. 'If this killer was as organized as I think, he was wearing gloves. There won't be anything on the cuffs.'

'I'm talking about swabbing the *inside* of the cuffs,' I said.
Mike raised an eyebrow at me.

'In addition to Connie Wade's DNA, you might find Amber Bristol's. Link your cases to each other through the victims, even if you can't find any trace of the perp yet.'

'Every now and then you are useful, Coop.'

Mercer extended his hand and pulled me out of the hole. 'You've got to think that maybe our man never got Wade this far,' Mercer said. 'Maybe he was on his way to this spot with her when something interrupted him.'

'Could be,' Bart said. 'Hard as we try to keep people away from the island, it's impossible to stop them.'

'We'll need a news alert covering the killer's window of opportunity, see whether anyone can come up with a description, if that's the case,' Mike said. 'Maybe someone else passed our man on his way to the dock or on the other side of the shore, where he parked.'

'What else will you need from us?' Bart asked.

'Everything you've got, for starters.'

Mercer looked at Mike. 'RTCC?'

The most innovative new development was the NYPD's Real Time Crime Center, a state-of-the-art computer system designed to accelerate the analysis of data, interact instantaneously with field personnel, and connect the dots between law enforcement agencies all over the country. Discrete bits of information supplied from commands in any jurisdiction were fed into a 'brain' that coordinated them to enable patterns to emerge from seemingly unrelated facts.

'You bet. This guy's a poster child for Real Time Crime. I'll call the lieutenant on our way back. The chief of detectives will have us up and running by sundown,' Mike said. 'We'll enter every bit of detail you and your men have got into this think tank.'

Bart led us back through the maze of brush to get to the

clearing where Joe Galiano was waiting to return us to the city. It must have been the layer of haze and the storm clouds forming off to the west that had mercifully kept the serpents from sunbathing on the boulders.

We climbed into our seats and buckled up. Galiano had the rotors whirling within minutes, warning us that we would be flying through some rough weather.

Mike was as uncomfortable in this fast-moving glass-enclosed bubble as I had been underground. We lifted off over the river, climbing above the West Point campus on our bumpy ride back to Manhattan.

I thought he would kiss the ground when Galiano lowered us onto the landing pad at the heliport.

A uniformed cop was waiting for us at the security gate. 'Detective Chapman? You're to go directly to One PP,' he said. Police Plaza, the department headquarters, was farther downtown, three blocks south of the criminal courthouse. 'Commissioner Scully wants to see the three of you immediately.'

22

I had known Keith Scully for more than five years. He was the chief of detectives when we first worked together – the department's rising star – before the mayor appointed him to be top cop a couple of years ago.

If he was pleased to see me again, I wouldn't have known it from the expression on his face. He was an ex-marine, tall and sinewy, with close-cut hair that had whitened since his promotion, just as more creases had been etched in his face.

We were ushered into his office on the fourteenth floor shortly after two o'clock. With him were Guido Lentini, the deputy commissioner in charge of public information, and Mike's boss, Lieutenant Raymond Peterson. Scully was a stickler for protocol, and it was a sign of his respect for Peterson that the old-timer was allowed to smoke – maybe the only person in the department who was – in the headquarters building.

'Word travels fast, Loo,' Mike said to Peterson. 'Maybe too fast.'

'You can't sit on something like this, Mike. The public has to know.'

None of us thought the case was ready to present to the commissioner yet, and certainly not to the media. Mike would have liked the lieutenant to hold back until we had learned more about each of our victims and had some lab results in hand. But Peterson had apparently taken the story promptly to the PC after he got the morning's news from Pollepel Island. He hadn't even paused to ask me about the previous day's shooting at the range.

'You giving this out to the press, sir?' Mike asked.

'You tell me, Chapman,' Scully said, standing behind his great desk, not a paper out of place, although the hefty piles represented some sort of mayhem in each of the five boroughs of the city.

'We're just beginning to try to put it together.'

'Good. Keep it up. Use your time well. You've got all night. In the meantime, give Guido something to run with,' Scully said, hitting a number on his speed dial. 'I've got to let the mayor know you're here. He's hot to go on this.'

'No offense, Guido,' Mike said, cocking his thumb at the commissioner as he talked to the mayor's secretary. 'But who put the bug up his ass?'

Guido looked at Scully to make sure he hadn't heard Mike's comment. 'The governor called the mayor as soon as he heard you guys were flying up the river to consult with his troopers. Like we're supposed to keep our killers within city limits.'

'Is he talking press conference?'

'It's all politics, Mike. If we don't get out in front on this, then the governor will scoop the story and point his finger at City Hall.'

'Battaglia and his wife left for London last night with the kids. Family vacation,' I said. 'He won't like missing this one.'

'I always think of Scully as the strong, silent type. He was chief of d's during that museum caper the three of us handled. He almost took my head off over a harmless leak.'

'I hate to correct you, Mike, but it was *my* head that almost rolled on that one,' I said. Both Battaglia and Scully had jumped all over me when one of the facts we were sitting on appeared in a feature story.

'Yeah, 'cause you were dating that television news jerk.'

'Whatever happened to him – that Tyler guy?' Guido asked. 'I never see him on air anymore.'

'There's a whole graveyard full of Cooper's capons.'

'Capons?'

'Castrated roosters, Guido. They vanish into thin air when she's done with them. But that's all going to change now. Right, Mercer? I'm forming a committee of Coop's friends. We're going to pick her men for her.'

'And why would that be necessary?' Mercer asked, leading us into a conference room where sandwiches and drinks had been set out for us.

' 'Cause her picker's broke. That's been obvious for years,' Mike said, getting up to grab something to eat and smiling at me. 'Although I have to admit she started her day a hell of a lot better than I did.'

Through the open door we could hear Keith Scully arguing with the mayor against the idea of a press conference.

Guido looked stumped. 'Why? What did you do so early, Alex?'

'Finished the Saturday *Times* crossword puzzle before Mike rang my doorbell,' I said, hoping I had on my best poker face. 'It was an absolute bear to get done.'

Scully finally slammed down the phone and joined us. 'As much as I'd like to know what Alex was up to this morning, I think we'll all take a pass, okay? I'd like to tell you exactly why there's a bug up my ass, Chapman. Keep eating. Yeah, I heard you. You'll need the stamina for all the OT I'm going to authorize.'

The commissioner hadn't missed a thing, although he had lost his point with the mayor.

'Sorry, boss. I didn't mean—'

Scully picked up a sheaf of DD5s – the detective division reports, legal-size pages filled from top to bottom with single-spaced narratives of all the work that had been done on every case. He flipped through them as he recited details of Amber's and Elise's autopsy reports.

'I've been holding the lid all week on Amber Bristol's "quirks" – to quote from your creative paperwork,' he said, tapping Mike's DD5s with the back of his hand. 'I got Dickie Draper dragging his heels in Brooklyn 'cause he'd rather sit in the squad room and wait for an informant to drop the killer's name in his lap than do a day's worth of work. And now, we've got a West Point cadet murdered on state property and the governor's story is going to be that the NYPD didn't warn the public that there's a psycho on the loose.'

Peterson was the only person who still referred to the commissioner by his first name. 'Keith, they can't stick you with—'

'This is Saturday, Ray. This is when kids go clubbing and bar-hopping. Suppose another girl goes missing tonight? Who else is there to blame but the cops? You can't be a politician if you're just willing to suck it up. It's much easier to stick someone else in the line of fire.'

Scully walked toward the enormous map of the city that hung on the wall and stared at it, then swiveled when Peterson starting talking.

'You've handled worse, Keith. You'll survive it.'

'The mayor thinks that he and I have got our own little town, and that we run it side by side. Only I have all the same problems he's got – plus a few more of my own – and I'm the one who gets none of the ribbon cutting.' His ice blue eyes were fiery and his short hair seemed to bristle.

'Every one of my employees has a gun. Every one of them. I've even got to worry that a few may have – what's the politically correct jargon? – "emotional issues." That one of mine might have been the guy taking potshots up at the range yesterday,' Scully said. 'Yes, Alex, I know all about it. We're checking into our loose cannons and the ones who've been discharged or sent out to pasture.'

'I didn't mean to make—'

'There are union reps at all of my job sites. You think that doesn't add to my aggravation? And within my patrol territory I'm responsible for airports and churches, schools and opera houses, crack dens and sports arenas, housing projects and penthouse palaces.'

He poked his chest with his forefinger. 'When people feel threatened, when they think their loved ones aren't safe, then it's *my* problem, Ray. Then *I* own it, all by myself, 24/7.'

None of us spoke. Scully's direction was clear.

Peterson lit another cigarette. 'You're just feeding the beast, you know. They devour the headlines, Keith. You study these guys, the serial killers who wind up in prison, and they've all got scrapbooks. They like making news. They get off on reading their own ink.'

'So does Coop. Doesn't make her a bad person.'

'That's always the balance, isn't it, Ray?' Scully said, ignoring Mike's shot. 'We've been lucky that Bristol and Huff didn't get much attention. That all changes with Connie Wade. The governor's going public at six o'clock tonight. He's got the perfect victim and he wants to take the lead.'

'So what did the mayor say?'

Scully laughed in spite of himself. 'He wants me in the blue room at five.'

'Whatever happened to the old "wait and see" attitude?'

Peterson asked. 'Used to be a valued principle in policing, back in the day. Don't rile the public. Figure the killer will get tired of the high cost of living in the big city and move on. Become someone else's headache. Seems like this character's already moving upstate.'

'And there's a gubernatorial primary the second week in September,' Scully said. 'Nobody wants to sit on a political hot potato.'

Peterson opened the foil on a turkey sandwich and handed me half. 'Give the man what he needs, Mike. You two have anything to contribute,' he said to Mercer and me, 'feel free to jump in.'

'What do we know about Connie Wade?' Scully asked.

Mike read her physical description from the notes he'd taken in his first phone conversation and our meeting with Bart Hinson. He outlined what he knew about her background and family, where she had traveled from and when she had last contacted relatives and friends. He described the injuries and the manner in which they were similar to Amber and Elise's.

'Elise Huff,' Scully said, scanning the police reports. 'Have you made any progress finding this guy she was supposed to meet?'

'No, sir. The bar car's going to give me some help this evening,' Mike said, referring to the detectives assigned to check on all the establishments that sell liquor and are licensed by the SLA. 'I hit a few clubs near the Pioneer last night but came up empty.'

'I don't need another disappearing act tonight. I want every young lady who goes out on the town for a cocktail to come home safe. Troopers still waiting on confirmation about what Connie Wade was wearing?'

'They're thinking uniform. Fits in with the whole military fixation this guy has.'

Scully was back to Elise Huff. 'And Huff, in this airline outfit, you think it could have fooled a guy who knows his stuff?'

Mike scoffed at the suggestion. 'What? Like it was real military gear? No way. I'm assuming he knows better. She had on a neat white blouse, wings on the collar, and navy pants with a crease up the leg. But our killer wouldn't be thinking wild blue yonder.'

'Don't forget she had that ring of her grandmother's she always wore,' Mercer said. 'Her best friend claims she's a storyteller, commissioner. Maybe our perv recognized the ring and knew what it meant. If the perp makes his pickup in a bar, maybe she told him she had a West Point connection.'

'I'm willing to buy that,' Peterson said. 'But Amber Bristol, I don't see how she fits with these other two girls. I like the manner of death and the cuffs and the remote dump, but there's nothing military about her.'

'What's Herb Ackerman's condition?' Scully asked. 'Maybe he can establish a connection.'

'They wouldn't let me back at him yesterday,' Mike said. 'Still too groggy from the overdose. Mercer and I will put him on our list for tomorrow. I gotta be honest with you, sir, he doesn't strike me as recruit material for Parris Island.'

'I've met the man, Chapman. I don't see him rowing a body out in the middle of the Hudson, either—'

'Not without really shitting in his pants, sir.'

'Let's see how long it takes these investigative journalists to sniff out their own. I'll be leaving his involvement out of the news bulletin. But Ackerman was a war correspondent in Vietnam. Read his columns sometime. He knows as much about our armed forces – and weaponry – as anybody in the media. I'm just looking for connections here,' Scully said, listing commands for us to follow. 'Find out who does Ackerman's research, who edits his copy. What led him to write about the ferry terminal. Maybe he's got a young buff on staff – somebody who knows his secret. We don't even have Amber's client list. Don't even know if this freak is in her little black book. And how about that bar owner? Amber's boyfriend.'

'Jim Dylan. That's still a work in progress. He looked good

to me before we found Huff's body. I haven't given up the idea that he hired someone to get rid of Amber.'

With us all trailing, Keith Scully went back to his office and stacked the Bristol and Huff case reports next to each other on his desk, then began a third pile with his pages of notes about Connie Wade. He pursed his lips and shook his head. 'Yeah, well he's damn unlucky if the guy he hired can't turn off the faucet when he's in the mood to kill.'

'I haven't mentioned Amber Bristol's superintendent, Keith,' Peterson said. 'He's dirty. Has a couple of assaults he got walked out of court on. Beats his woman.'

'Bring him back in,' Scully said, then pointed to Guido Lentini. 'Be sure to get details on the old cases for the mayor.'

'Commissioner Scully,' I said, replaying in my mind each conversation I'd had about these women, 'do you have the report Mike wrote up based on my interview with Herb Ackerman? It was Wednesday morning, before I went to court.'

He licked his thumb and looked through the dates on the top of each page. The image Herb Ackerman painted came back to me faster than the police commissioner could pull it up on paper.

'Amber Bristol,' I said. 'The night she walked out of Ackerman's office she was wearing a new outfit. She looked just like the captain of a ship, he told me. White cotton, double-breasted jacket. It was trimmed with gold buttons and epaulets, with some gold braid on the shoulders.'

'That doesn't make her an admiral,' Mike said, blowing me off.

Ray Peterson crushed his cigarette against the sole of his shoe. 'I see where you're going.'

'Could be what turns the perp on, Commissioner, is women in uniform,' I said. 'Not authentic, not armed services for real, but just the look of it. He's a sexual psychopath, guys. Maybe all it takes to trigger his sadistic urge is the sight of a woman in uniform.'

23

'What you know about serial killers couldn't fill a thimble, Chapman.' Dickie Draper had arrived twenty minutes later and joined us in the conference room.

We'd been ordered to marshal all the case evidence for the mayor's presentation. The long wooden table with elegantly carved legs that had once been the centerpiece of Teddy Roosevelt's office in his time as New York City's police commissioner was covered with DD5s and crime scene photographs.

Scully and Peterson were scrambling to notify their borough commanders. By 5:00 p.m., when the mayor would make his announcement, he would have to be able to say that he had assembled a task force to search for the killer. Officers would be pulled from squads and foot patrol to give the community the illusion of safety when the frenzy started.

'What I do know, Dickie, is that while you were daydreaming about your next meal, Elise Huff's killer struck again.'

'What can I say? The odds were against it.' The mustard from his ham and provolone sandwich was smeared on Dickie's jowls.

'We're at three and counting. That's the FBI's magic number to go serial.'

'Pulp fiction. A broad can't go to the supermarket or the hairdresser without getting snatched by a lunatic if you're looking for box office dollars or best sellers,' Dickie said, wiping his chin with the back of his hand. 'C'mon, can you name a serial killer who's worked this city in the last five years?'

I couldn't think of a single one.

'Rapists, sure. Serial sex offenders, you probably have fifteen, twenty patterns a year in Manhattan, just like we got. Queens and the Bronx, too. I'm right about that, aren't I, Alex?'

'Yes.'

It was an indisputable fact. There was never a month when the NYPD's Special Victims Units weren't looking for recidivist rapists – usually several of them at any given time. There were a hundred Floyd Warrens in this country for every serial killer, who are far more common in the pages of crime novels than in real life.

'What are we supposed to be doing here?' Dickie asked, walking around the table to look at the exhibits that had been laid out.

'Give the commissioner the answers to all the questions he'll be asked by the reporters,' Mike said.

'What questions?'

'Do a full Battaglia,' I said. On dozens of occasions, I had gone in with Mike and Mercer to brief the district attorney on every aspect and detail of an investigation. Before I could pause for breath, Paul Battaglia would cross-examine us about factors we had never considered. 'Think of all the questions the best reporters will ask and arm him with the answers before he gets on the platform.'

'Where and how have serial killers hit in this city before? Is there anything useful in the facts of those cases to help us put this one together?' Mercer asked. 'Give Scully some ready answers. Separate facts from fairy tales.'

Dickie grabbed the bag of chips and sat across from me. Mike's chair was at the far end, and he leaned it back and put his feet up on the table.

'Son of Sam,' Mike said. 'In this town, it all starts with David Berkowitz, 1976.'

'No disrespect to Ted Bundy,' Dickie said. 'Ted just never got to Gotham, but his numbers make Berkowitz look like a piker. He put up some numbers, that Bundy kid.'

'We're not talking NFL stats,' Mike said. 'Son of Sam.'

'Your father work the case?' Mercer asked.

'The great Joe Borelli ran the show. Sure, my dad and every cop they could mobilize. One pathetic whack job and it took the department more than a year and two hundred detectives to bring Son of Sam down,' Mike said. 'You taking notes, Coop? Operation Omega, that's what they called it. Scully needs to give this task force a name. Something strong. That always placates people.'

The Son of Sam story was a law enforcement legend. Berkowitz had been a quiet misfit who stalked and shot his victims, some on city streets and some in parked cars, killing six and wounding many others. Most were young women, either alone or caught in compromising positions on isolated lovers' lanes.

'Everybody knows the expression *Son of Sam* but I don't remember much about him, other than photographs in the press,' I said.

Like many cops, Mike and Dickie knew the details of department cases as if they had worked the jobs themselves.

'Berkowitz had a neighbor with a black lab named Sam. Claimed it was a devil dog, possessed by Satan. When Sam howled,' Mike said, 'it was a message to Berkowitz to go out and kill women. All a bullshit story he admitted making up so he could use an insanity defense if he got caught.'

'But they weren't sexual crimes, were they?' I asked. I didn't think Berkowitz had ever molested the women he killed.

'He didn't rape them, if that's what you mean. He and Ted Bundy were the first two serial killers ever interviewed by the FBI. Berkowitz claimed he became aroused by the act of stalking women. After he shot them, he'd often go back to the scene and masturbate. Tried to find his victims' graves for the same reason. That's got sexual sadist stamped all over it.'

Dysfunction was a problem for many assailants attempting to rape or sodomize. If our killer hadn't consummated any sexual acts with our victims, the lack of DNA might be explained by his physical inability to complete the assault.

'Any other sexual history?'

'Best the shrinks could tell, Berkowitz had sex one time in his life. Got a venereal disease from a prostitute his first time out, when he was in the army.'

'He had a military record?' I recalled the letters he'd written to the press, taunting them to capture him. Berkowitz had called himself 'Beelzebub, the chubby behemoth.' 'He didn't look the type.'

'Three years. Tell Scully to keep that in mind. That flabby lunatic Berkowitz – nothing personal, Dickie – didn't fit the physical stereotype. And yes, he learned all he needed to know about guns in the army.'

'You believe in the MacDonald triad?' Dickie asked Mike.

'MacDonald – the researcher who says there are three traits that are childhood predictors of a serial?'

'Pyromaniac, zoosadism, bedwetting beyond an appropriate age.'

'Berkowitz set fires in the hood all the time when he was growing up.' Mike and Dickie were in their own killer zone, trading perpetrator pedigree information like most boys would banter baseball batting averages. 'Cruelty to animals? All his life. He even shot Sam, the dog. And bedwetting? It's still a problem for him in state prison. There's a helpful hint. Check Herb Ackerman, Coop. Maybe that's what the diapers are about.'

'How'd they finally catch him, guys?' I asked. 'That's the detail we need.'

'Dumb luck. They had the task force working round the clock for a year, going nowhere. Then the schmuck ends up getting a parking ticket when he steps out of his car to murder somebody,' Mike said. 'Put a star next to that one. Our guy has to have a car or a van to move these bodies. We need scrips of vehicles, checks of E-ZPass before and after the girls were found in Queens and upstate, and parking violations. Check it all out.'

'Give me another one, Chapman,' Dickie said. The crumbs from the bag of chips were scattered on his tie and the shelf created by his stomach when he sat. 'Who else you got?'

'The Zodiac.'

'Very good, Mikey. Eddie Seda, 1989. I worked that one myself. Seven years till we got the bastard.'

'I thought the Zodiac was a serial killer on the West Coast, in the Bay Area,' I said.

'That's the original Zodiac,' Dickie said. 'Never caught that one. Brooklyn, we had the copycat. East New York, Highland Park. Ambidextrous, he was.'

'Ambidextrous?'

'Whatever they call it. Killed men, killed women. I think he had some sexual identity problems. Sent a letter to the cops with all the zodiac symbols and a note – "Orion is the one who can stop Zodiac." Mailed it with one of those LOVE stamps. Then began belting out bodies like clockwork. Libra, Taurus, Virgo, like that.'

'Did you nail him, Dickie?'

'Eddie shot his sister in the ass with a zip gun 'cause he could hear her making love in the next room. Dumb luck again. Precinct guys show up at the house, take him in for questioning. While they're talking to him about the domestic, his palm prints match up to some of the case evidence. He killed more people than Berkowitz,' Dickie said, licking the salt off his fingertips. 'I did Rifkin, too.'

'Who?' I asked.

'Joel Rifkin, 1989 to 1993. Another outer boroughs boy. Eighteen murders. Picked up his girls in the city but dumped them out by us. Hookers, mostly. Had sex with them, then strangled them to death. This one's your classic – not guns like the other two. He was the Ted Bundy kind – real hands-on stuff, strangulation, not shooting. And by the way, always after he had sex with them.'

'There's the prostitute angle again,' Mercer said.

'That might work for Amber Bristol, but not for the others,' Mike said. 'Elise Huff and Connie Wade weren't pros.'

'Rifkin liked to snap their necks, those hookers,' Dickie said, brushing the crumbs off his tie.

It was a sickening thought. 'Why?'

Dickie looked at me as though I had two heads. 'Why? I told you why. He just liked doing it, I guess. Liked the noise it made. How the hell do I know? He said he liked it.'

'Your squad make the arrest?' I asked.

'State troopers.'

'Now that's the last thing Scully wants to hear,' Mercer said. 'Troopers getting credit for the collar. The press'll jump all over that one.'

'Once again, dumb luck. Routine traffic stop. Rifkin didn't have a front plate on his van. Troopers chased him and he crashed into a lamppost,' Dickie said, taking a swig of his soda. 'There's your sexual sadist, Alex. That's the kind of creep you're looking for.'

'Kenneth Kimes. Sante Kimes,' Mike said, trying to play perp catch-up with Dickie. 'Manhattan, 1998.'

'Mother-son grifter team. Doesn't count, Mikey. Yeah, they killed people from California to the Big Apple, but it was all about larceny. They were poking each other, that sick broad and her mama's boy. They weren't interested in sex with anybody else, just each other. Like you can't count your mutt drug dealers and your gang shoot-'em-ups. They're not serials. You got your Malvo-Muhammad nuts, too. Beltway snipers. They're spree killers, not serials. You got your mass murderers—'

'We're looking for a type like James Jones,' Mercer said. 'I worked that one.'

'Never heard of him. He make the papers? The news never got as far as the BQE,' Dickie said, referring to the Brooklyn-Queens Expressway. 'How many'd he do?'

'Strangled five, but only two of them died. Nine-month rampage, 1995. They were all prostitutes, too.'

'There you go. That's why he didn't get any press attention. I'm telling you, if this guy had just done your girl Amber, nobody would have cared. It worked for Jack the Ripper. It doesn't work anymore. They had that series of murders out near San Francisco, remember? Cops closed them all with a code: NHI.'

The unsolved crimes had been back-burnered until a reporter revealed that the letters stamped on the police files were shorthand for No Human Involved. Serial killers who picked underclass victims often got a pass when there was no one in the community to pay much attention to their disappearance or ultimate fate.

'Your man Jones,' Dickie asked, 'he shoot 'em or what?'

'No, he used a rope.'

'See? Hands-on. Just like Rifkin and Bundy. The real deal – hard to come by.'

'Picked them up, took them to cheap hotel rooms,' Mercer said, looking over at me. 'Bound and gagged them. I mean they *let* him do that to them. All of the survivors admitted it. Told them he said he couldn't get off unless he did.'

'You're thinking maybe Amber allowed herself to be bound?' I asked.

Mercer shrugged his shoulders. 'Scully's got to consider that.'

'Then he yoked the rope, this Jones guy?' Dickie asked, reaching for another sandwich.

'Last thing he did was make them each point their toes. Like a ballerina, he said. Made them point their toes, and then he killed them.'

'Wasn't he the guy who worked at that lawyer's organization on Forty-fourth Street?' Mike asked.

Mercer nodded. 'Yeah, Jones was smart, with a good job, actually. He was in charge of all the audiovisual programs for the Association of the Bar.'

'Was there a task force?' Dickie asked.

Mercer smiled. 'You know better. Not for those victims. Word was out on the street, working girls looking out for each other, like they usually do. They figured they'd find him before we would. One of the surviving vics saw him a few months after she was attacked, flagged down the RMP, and pointed him out to the two rookies in a patrol car.'

'I'll be damned. Dumb luck again,' Dickie said.

I could remember only one serial sadistic sex murderer who had been prosecuted since I joined the office more than a decade ago. Both Mercer and Mike had been assigned to the investigation in its later years, and I had gone to the courtroom often to watch two of my colleagues – Rich Plansky and John Irwin – try the case.

'Arohn Kee,' I said.

'Worst case I ever worked,' Mercer said.

Kee's attacks began with the sexual assault and murder of a thirteen-year-old girl in East Harlem in 1991. For the next eight years, his own reign of terror in that neighborhood went unchecked, and more than six other teenage girls were raped and attacked – some strangled and stabbed to death, one burned beyond recognition on the rooftop of her building – before he was identified and charged.

'He killed kids?' Dickie asked. 'All kids? How come that one didn't make the news?'

' 'Cause they were black and Hispanic,' Mike said. Mercer nodded in agreement. 'Twenty blocks farther south, on the Upper East Side, somebody burned a white girl to death on the top of a Madison Avenue condo, every cop in the city would have been pulled out to solve it.'

'That's the last serial killer we've had in Manhattan,' Mercer said. 'Nobody much cared at the time, 'cause the victims all lived in projects, all poor kids.'

'Don't tell me you solved that one by detective work?'

'Came pretty close. Old-fashioned legwork almost paid off.'

Mike interrupted Mercer's story. 'Yeah. Mercer and Rob Mooney figured out who it was. Before they could get his DNA, Kee walked into a computer store with a stolen hard drive. The clerk just went to the back and called 911 and turned the kid in for some lousy misdemeanor theft charge.'

'Dumbass luck, one more time,' Dickie said, finally using a napkin to clean his face. 'Bottom line – tell Scully to save himself the trouble of a task force. Let the troopers upstate catch the bum. Operation Dumb Luck.'

'What's the trigger?' I asked. 'Where does this guy come from?'

'We got SOMU working on this as soon as Elise Huff was reported missing,' Mercer said.

The Sex Offender Monitoring Unit was responsible for tracking rapists who had served their time and were released to parole. New laws in every state required them to register with police agencies set up to monitor their whereabouts and alert communities where the most dangerous felons relocated.

'No one with this kind of m.o.?' Dickie asked. 'Maybe he's just out of the military. Back from combat. There'll be a couple of dozen more bodies before you pry any records away from the feds, that's for sure.'

'Amen to that,' Mercer said. 'Takes forever. And Scully's got to be prepared to deal with the question of why there isn't DNA.'

'Organized serial,' Mike said. 'Intelligent, methodical, knowledge of forensics, keeps control of the crime scene. Abducts in one location and dumps in another.'

The FBI characterized these murderers as either organized or disorganized, the latter having less intelligence and acting more impulsively.

'How about Coop's theory that our guy may be into women with uniforms?' Mike said.

'Tell it to the profilers,' Dickie Draper said. 'They'll have us staking out waitresses in coffee shops and Girl Scout troops and bus drivers in drag. Hold that thought, Alex, will you?'

'Here's one fact that doesn't make sense,' Mercer said. 'Amber Bristol's apartment – that was cleaned out. Am I right, Mike? Sanitized. All of her personal stuff gone.'

Dickie shook his head. 'Gives new meaning to an organized serial. They're not into housekeeping. Trophies and souvenirs, yeah, but not housekeeping.'

'Maybe he had an accomplice on the first kill,' Mike said. 'Then he spun out on his own.'

'The other vics didn't live alone,' Mercer said. 'Could have been his only chance to get in one of their homes.'

'I'm telling you,' Dickie said. 'You can't go serial too early.'

'What the hell do we tell Scully?' Mike said.

'Assurances. People like assurances.' Dickie started to count off traits on his fingers. 'The guy is young, okay? Eighteen to thirty-five, tops. Takes a lot of energy to do this shit.'

I thought again about Floyd Warren, who seemed to have aged out of his serial rapist pastime.

'White,' he said, holding his left forefinger with his right hand.

'Kee and Jones were black.'

'Yeah, but that's unusual, Mercer. Mostly a white boy's game. Besides, gets the commish into all that ugly racial profiling stuff. Safer to say white till you know different.'

He was on the third trait, double chins jiggling as he said, 'And they're never Jewish. Safe bet on that, too. Not your people, Ms. Cooper.'

'Berkowitz,' Mike said. 'Rifkin.'

'Do your homework, Mikey. Berkowitz was adopted. Born Falco. Got it? Rifkin's adopted, too.'

Guido Lentini opened the door and lifted his glasses to the top of his head. 'Chapman, the commissioner wants to know more about the Amber Bristol scene. The old Battery Maritime Building.'

Mike took his feet off the table and sat up. 'What does he need?'

'Wants to know about the ferry slip. When the boats run. Where they go.'

'To Governors Island.'

'That's the only place, right?'

'Right. And only during the day. They don't run at night,' Mike said.

'They used to go from that terminal to some piers in Brooklyn, didn't they?'

'Yeah, but not in my lifetime.'

'Governors Island. It was a military post, right?'

'For two hundred years, yeah.'

'What's it named for, Chapman? Governor who? They're likely to ask that, too.'

'When the British took New Amsterdam from the Dutch,' Mike said, 'they used the island as a retreat for the royal governors. Should have stayed in school, Guido.'

'You did a search over there, didn't you?'

Mike frowned and brushed his hair off his forehead. 'Did I? Like personally?'

'Yes, you – Mike Chapman. The homicide squad. Somebody the commissioner can rely on.'

'Bristol's body was found on this side of the water, Guido.

Detectives from Night Watch went over to the island to check it out. The killer never got her there, trust me. The fire department took them all around the place.'

'Scully won't like that,' Guido said.

The schism between New York's Bravest, the NYFD, and New York's Finest, the NYPD, had widened after their heroic actions on 9/11. The tension between the two commissioners had intensified in the aftermath, as operative responses were more carefully defined for each of the services.

'The frigging place hasn't been inhabited since the coast guard gave it up in '96. Even an amateur would know if someone had been on the island. People work there during the day – groundskeepers and the ferry crew. But the only two guys who live on the island – I mean overnight – are firemen, for the protection of the historic buildings.'

'This is going to be ugly,' Guido said.

'What now?' I asked.

'You know who owns Governors Island?'

I shook my head from side to side.

'The city *and* the state. They've both got jurisdiction. The governor will have the place swarming with troopers by morning, and the mayor'll get to announce that the NYPD hasn't really investigated there yet,' Guido said.

Mike started pacing behind my seat. 'Just to add to your agita, Guido. The feds will jump in, too. The old fortress is still their property. It's a national monument.'

'Then if I were you, Chapman,' Guido said, checking his watch. 'I'd get your ass over there on the next boat. Make the commissioner an honest man when he goes on the air at five o'clock to tell them his department is doing a thorough investigation. There's got to be something to that idea of a military nexus to the murders.'

'We're moving,' Mike said, looking down to meet my eyes when he spoke. 'I know what's over there, Guido. It's another ghost island.'

24

An RMP with lights and sirens made our trip from Police Plaza to the old terminal building in less than two minutes.

We left Dickie Draper behind at headquarters, to help Guido triage the data in the police reports that would be the subject of media scrutiny.

Mike got out and handed the driver a slip of paper with a Brooklyn address on it. 'Eunice Chapman, she's expecting you. Bay Ridge. She's going to give you a box full of old catalogs. Take them to – your apartment okay, Coop? Drop them with Ms. Cooper's doorman,' he said, adding my address to the note.

Mercer walked to the entrance of the northernmost ferry slip. It was the place through which Mike and I had entered to climb up to the grim room in which Amber Bristol's body had been found. Now, a twelve-foot wire mesh fence blocked the way, with a sign that warned: ACTIVE DRIVEWAY – NO PARKING. And in smaller letters below: 'Watch for vehicles entering or leaving the site.'

'Yo. Anybody home?' Mercer shouted.

Mike came up behind him and called again. 'Would have been nice if someone actually had been looking for vehicles leaving the site the night Amber was dumped.'

A man in a blue jumpsuit came from behind the interior building. 'Yeah? Whaddaya want?'

Mercer flashed his badge. 'Police. We need a lift to Governors Island.'

'Next service run is at four o'clock. You make arrangements with anyone?'

The *Lt. Samuel L. Coursen* was berthed at the dock, just thirty feet ahead of us. It was three fifteen and Mike was impatient. 'The captain's expecting me.'

'He is? He didn't say nothin' to me.'

'Hurry up. We're trying to beat the rain.'

The man looked confused but unlocked the gate, and before he could close it again Mike was leading us to the ramp of the old motor vessel.

'That's where Amber's body was,' he said to Mercer, pointing up behind us to the landing at the top of the building's rust-encrusted staircase.

'Good place to leave it. Looks pretty uninviting to me.'

There was bright red lettering on the door that said: DANGER – HIGH VOLTAGE. Everything around the space was so filthy and dilapidated that it didn't seem surprising that no one had ventured in to find the missing woman until the stench became over-whelming.

Mike stepped over the railing that separated the aft platform of the ferry from the landing bay and held out his hand to help me over.

Two men came running down the staircase from the bridge

of the boat. Mike explained to them why we needed to cross as quickly as possible.

'C'mon. You can drop us off and be back here in twenty minutes.'

They reluctantly led us up to the wheelhouse, called over to tell the crew on Governors Island to expect them, and fired up the engine.

'Any of you ever been over here before?' the captain asked.

Only Mike answered. 'Yes. Twenty years ago, when it was the largest coast guard base in the world.'

'I thought you said it was an army post,' I said.

'That's why it was built in 1776, when George Washington sent the first garrison there. By 1966, it was turned over to the coast guard.'

I covered my ears as the copilot blasted the ferry horn to announce our departure to the boats around us on the river.

'How long's the ride?' Mercer asked.

'Six minutes. It's just eight hundred yards from Manhattan.'

'Ferries are open to the public?'

The captain answered with a firm 'No.'

'But that's all about to change,' Mike said. 'This is the year they announce a plan for the island's future, isn't it?'

We pulled out into the swirling gray water. Landing off to our right, dwarfing us, was one of the Staten Island ferries, and ahead on the river was a lively mix of pleasure craft, small yachts, water taxis, sailboats, and Circle Line tour ships.

'What future?' I asked.

'One hundred seventy-two acres of prime New York City real estate,' the captain said. 'The city and state have to figure out how to use it – jointly. It's all in the planning stage now, for re-development as civic space, with an arts center and recreational activities. The island's a pretty spectacular place.'

'I had no idea it was so large,' I said.

'The historic district is only twenty-two acres,' Mike said. 'The

National Park Service still owns it. That piece will be restored and maintained while the rest is developed.'

'There's a national park on Governors Island?'

I looked across at the massive stone fortification on the southern tip of the island.

'Any private boats go there?' Mercer asked.

I knew he was thinking of the short, easy ride from the mainland to the dock at Bannerman Island.

'The forty-two seats on this old reliable is all you've got, at the moment,' the captain said, gesturing to the pier ahead. 'Trying to land there is worse than threading a needle when you're drunk. See those two slips? They run perpendicular to the current, which is always trying to drive you away. Pretty rough. And on either side of them, you got a brick seawall that could smash a small vessel to smithereens.'

'And who rides with you?'

A sloping manicured lawn topped by a series of two-story colonial brick buildings ran down to the water's edge.

'We got some park rangers who patrol the area from ten to five. Then we get a few developers and government types who come back and forth for planning and surveying. Occasionally retired army personnel who were stationed here years ago request permission to come back, show their families around.'

'Anyone keep track of their names?' Mercer asked.

'I don't know. Check with the rangers. They've been holding events here from time to time during the summer. Real pain in the neck for us. We've had pretty slow going for so long.'

'What kind of events?'

'Rock concerts, dance recitals, ball games on the old polo grounds—'

'Polo?' I asked.

'Yeah, while it was an army base for a couple of centuries, the cavalry trained here. There's a big polo field,' the captain said. 'July and August are the worst.'

'Why?'

'Last couple of years, GIPEC's been holding—'

'GIPEC?'

'Governors Island Preservation and Education Corporation. They run the place,' the captain said, navigating around a long barge headed slowly upriver. 'They've been using the parade grounds and the old fort to stage Civil War battle reenactments on Sundays.'

'What kind of battles?' Mike asked. 'Who shows up?'

'It takes all types, Detective. You get these history buffs who like to dress up in old uniforms and chase each other around. Military nuts.'

'But who watches them? How do people get here?'

'There's always a crowd. We don't have much capacity on this sweet thing, so GIPEC rents some of the water taxis to get people on and off for the day.'

'Is there an event tomorrow?' Mercer asked.

'Next big one is Labor Day weekend. But there'll be a rehearsal tomorrow. There's one every Sunday. Fifty or so guys, in the old blue and gray. A few gawkers come along for the ride. We'll make a couple of extra runs, use our freight boat as backup, and get them all over. It's only the big displays I need help transporting the sightseers.'

'Weapons?' Mike asked.

'The Park Service has that old stuff stored away here. Cannonballs and muskets spread all over the place. These boys are just out to amuse each other. Nobody gets hurt.'

Mike flipped open his cell phone and dialed Peterson's number.

'Talk fast,' the captain said. 'You won't get any reception on the island.'

He was steering the nose of the boat toward the landing dock, patiently trying to control it as the aft end fishtailed in the strong current.

'Loo. You still in Scully's office?' Mike asked, then repeated the story about the battle reenactments to his boss. 'You're going to need a detail here tomorrow if the mayor stays on course. The press will be all over the place by morning. Have someone checking IDs at the old ferry terminal, okay? Slip number seven. The last thing we need is our killer walking around the battlefield with live ammo. Talk to you later.'

The stern of the ferry bounced off the pilings in the pier and we swayed from side to side as the shore crew stabilized her.

'Gives me more reason to think this may have been where our guy was headed with Amber Bristol – maybe even while she was still alive,' Mercer said.

'I'm surprised Battaglia didn't push me on coming over when Amber's body was found at the terminal,' I said.

'He doesn't have any constituents on Governors Island, Coop. Nobody to vote for him. High anxiety but low priority.'

The shore crew – three men and a young woman in dark blue jumpsuits – secured the boat before they took the chain off to let us disembark. At the end of the ramp was a tall man in a khaki uniform, arms crossed and unsmiling.

'I'm Russell Leamer,' he said. 'Park Service. Commissioner Scully's office called. I understand we haven't satisfied your curiosity.'

At the top of the landing was an enormous black cannon, mounted in a cement surround, made to appear more benign by the field of red impatiens that had been planted around it.

'It's more than curiosity, Mr. Leamer,' Mike said. 'Three women are dead, and the killer has some fixation with the U.S. military service. One of his victims was dumped right on top of your ferry terminal.'

'We let some of your men poke around, Detective. They were here the very next day.'

'That was before we knew what we were looking for, Mr. Leamer.'

'And exactly what are you looking for now?' Leamer asked, his arms locked in place across his chest.

Mike looked from Mercer to me. We had very little time before the mayor made his announcement and the media would attempt to swarm over all of the places directly or indirectly connected to the disappearances and deaths of our three victims.

'You'll hear the news shortly anyway,' Mike said. 'The guy who killed the girl in the abandoned offices over the terminal – well, he probably murdered two others. He might have been trying to get here with his victim. Maybe had a place to hide her on the island.'

Leamer's expression didn't change. 'Hard to get lost in a crowd over here. We know everything that goes on.'

Mike started to walk around Leamer, who stretched out an arm to stop him.

'Look, the mayor and the police commissioner want this done, and we're going to do it.'

'You're standing on federal property, Detective. You want to swim around to the part of the island the city owns? Be my guest. Otherwise, the three of you need to sit on one of those benches and wait for the agents.'

'What agents? FBI? You've called in the feebies?'

'Yeah. I've asked for a detail to come over from the city. You want a guided tour, they can take you.'

'C'mon, Coop. Stick with Mercer,' Mike said, as he continued to charge up the incline and called back to Leamer. 'By the time the feds figure out what's going on around here, there'll be more bodies than they can count.'

25

I was trying to keep up with Mercer, who was trailing behind Mike. He had turned right at the top of the hill and was leading us on the uneven cobblestone path that paralleled the seawall along the edge of the island.

'Think military, Mercer. I'll tell you everything I remember about this place and see if that gives you any ideas, okay?'

A light drizzle began to fall. Off to our right, the river's water darkened and swirled. To our left was a low brick building more than a city block long.

'What's that?' Mercer asked.

'Built as an arsenal.'

'Like Bannerman?' I asked.

'This one was done by the government in the early 1800s. Held all the arms and ammo for army posts on the entire Atlantic coast,' Mike said, jogging up to the building to peek in several windows. 'Closed up pretty tight. When the army shut down, this became administrative offices. Looks like it's still in use and too near the ferry landing to be a viable hiding place.'

The three of us kept up our fast-paced march, moving out into a wide open space with stunning views of Staten Island and New Jersey that made the strategic setting of this forgotten island crystal clear to me. The wind gusted and I held on to the metal fence that bordered the water, just below my feet.

'Can you see why this island was so coveted by every military leader who saw it?' Mike asked, sweeping his arm in a large semicircle across the vista. 'It's the single most important vantage point for the protection of New York Harbor.'

'We're below Manhattan,' I said, looking back at the most perfect view of the mist-covered skyline. 'We're south of it.'

'Get yourself a map, Coop,' Mike said, shaking his head. 'The Lower Bay is beyond Brooklyn. This is the world's busiest harbor and Governors Island controls the access to the entire thing. And to New Jersey's coastline as well. The Dutch practically stole this from the Indians to build a fort here to keep all comers away, even before they settled on the mainland. Fort Amsterdam. Henry Hudson and his *Half Moon* were the first Europeans to discover it, in 1609. It was Pagganck to the Indians, Nooten Island to the Dutch. Full of nut trees – that's what the Indians had going for them. Quiet little place before the Europeans arrived.'

'Then the Dutch lost it to the British?' Mercer asked.

'In 1664. The Big Apple became New York, and this island wound up as the home of His Majesty's governors, till the British military had the brainstorm to use it as a base during the French and Indian Wars.

'Like I said, it was Washington who sent the first thousand men here, under General Israel Putnam, 1776. But the British army whipped George's troops in the Battle of Brooklyn – the earliest engagement of the American army with British forces. Most war theorists think if their navy had attacked this little island, the British could have ended the Revolution right then. But the tides were too strong and the weather was too nasty for an invasion here. So Washington's men destroyed their own cannons and retreated, leaving this place to the British, till their occupation of New York City ended in 1783.'

I lifted my collar against the wind and light rain and started to turn away.

Mike stepped behind me and put his hands on my shoulders, pointing off in the distance. 'But by 1800, Washington had convinced the government to take control of this harbor, along with Bedloe's Island – see it over there? That's where the Statue of Liberty is now, and that's Ellis Island, off in the distance. Over there is Castle Clinton, on the Battery. His plan was to use each of these points around this critically important harbor to build a defense system to protect against foreign invasion.'

Mercer got it now. 'So there were forts on every one of them.'

'Exactly. At the base of Liberty was Fort Hood, and Ellis Island used to be Fort Gibson.'

My eyes followed his finger. 'Then there's Castle Clinton, on the Battery, named for one of New York's governors, DeWitt Clinton. See, only one story tall? The government ran out of money, so they never completed it. Now turn around.'

Behind us was a massive red sandstone fortress, a great circular watchtower looming over the bay from the northwest corner of the island, three stories high with a huge parapet at the top.

'The jewel in the coastal defense crown,' Mike said. 'Castle Williams.'

'Who was Williams?' I asked. 'Who's it named for?'

'Jonathan Williams. The guy who designed this fort. He was also the first superintendent of West Point.'

'Add that to your list. Another little West Point factoid that might play into the others.' Mercer walked away and was standing at the entrance to Castle Williams. 'The gate is open,' he said to us, and we followed after him.

The grounds of the building were trim and well kept. At regular intervals around the seemingly impenetrable sandstone walls, there were three columns of casement windows, twenty-six rows of them ringing the building. The largest ones were nearest to the ground, getting smaller toward the top. Each had been fitted with cannons, the tips of some still visible as we approached.

Mercer entered the castle first and led us through its thick, dank walls into the middle of the fort, which had no roof. It was shaped like a giant horseshoe, with its solid front facing the rocky shoal and a small opening to its rear. I turned in place, looking up at the three tiers of galleries and the parapet above them, which housed a cluster of giant black cannons, still poised over the waters of the bay.

Mercer spotted the iron bars in the doorways of the rooms that fronted the courtyard. He went over to one and pulled on the modern padlock that was looped around the old metal hinge.

'Looks more like a jailhouse,' he said.

There were at least a dozen such doors, and we took turns testing the locks on each as we moved around the large interior space.

'You got that right,' Mike said. 'By the middle of the nineteenth century, these fixed cannon positions had become pretty obsolete. There were all kinds of artillery that was more mobile and had longer range, even on the ships. That's when the army set up the arsenal here and invented other uses for the island. Bet you didn't know that General Winfield Scott made this the headquarters of the entire U.S. Army in the 1840s before the Mexican War.'

'I count on you for all things military,' Mercer said.

'Well, during the Civil War, this fortress became a prison for Confederate soldiers. Some fifteen hundred of them crammed into these makeshift cells at a time, many of them awaiting execution on espionage charges. Executions that took place right in this very courtyard, so the other prisoners could watch. Our own little Devil's Island.'

'Why here?' I asked.

' 'Cause there's no way out of this place, Coop. The walls are forty feet high and eight feet thick. The only exit is that once-barred gatehouse we came in through. If the rebels were successful at firing into Castle Williams from the water, the people that would be killed were their own comrades.'

'Awfully bleak place,' Mercer said, continuing to test each lock.

'After the Civil War it became a military stockade.'

'So this was to the East Coast what Leavenworth and Alcatraz were to the rest of the country? Right here in New York?' Mercer asked. 'I never knew it.'

'Where's your list, Coop?' Mike said.

I took a notepad and pen out of my pocket.

'We've got to find out who has the keys to these locks,' he said. 'What's kept in here and when's the last time anyone's been in these cells.'

Mercer had found the staircase that led to the upper tiers. I watched him climb and walk to the door of each pen, checking that the locks were secured.

'Anything open?' Mike asked. 'Any sign of life?'

'Nope.'

'You know, seeing these cells reminds me that somewhere on this island there was a black hole,' Mike said.

'What do you mean? Like Pablo Posano's cell?' I said, thinking of my gang leader rapist, confined upstate with no outside communications allowed.

'Yeah. And like that bunker under the floorboards at Bannerman's house.'

'Why do you call it a black hole?'

' 'Cause that's what the expression came from – long before astronomers figured that there were great voids in space, Coop.

The black hole of Calcutta? In 1756, the nawab of Bengal threw hundreds of British soldiers in a dungeon, and half of them died there. I'm telling you, during the War of 1812, the most dangerous prisoners were kept in solitary confinement here on Governors Island, in what the troops called a black hole. Now we just have to find it.'

Mercer emerged from the stairwell. 'Every one of the cells is closed up tight. Let's move on.'

We passed out through the thick walls of the entryway and onto a smooth black asphalt road that led away from the water, to the interior part of the island. There was still no sign of Russell Leamer or any of his reinforcements.

We were all conscious that the time was near for the mayor's press conference and that any information we might gather would come too late to be useful.

'On the right, that's the post hospital,' Mike said.

We approached it together, climbing the imposing double staircase that led up to the front door of the elegant four-story brick building, so incongruous beside the old fortress just a couple of hundred yards away.

Mercer reached the top first and pulled repeatedly on the large brass door handles. 'Locked. No give at all.'

We were back down the steps in seconds and split up – I followed Mercer in a jog around the building – to check for broken windows or signs of entry, but there were none.

The main roadway veered to the left, and suddenly we were facing a magnificent tree-lined block of elegant brick mansions that could have been lifted out of Main Street in any prosperous small town in America. A beautiful grassy area and promenade surrounded the private homes. Elms and ginkgo trees bordered the structures like silent sentries.

'Colonels' Row,' Mike said. 'Built a century ago to improve the quality of life for the officers and their families who were stationed here.'

The drizzle was steady now, and Mike ran up and down the paths and front steps of the first couple of houses while Mercer and I waited on the road for him.

'Damn it,' he said. 'I forgot how many of these homes were here. We'll have to get some uniformed backup to get into every one of them during the next week.'

'You don't think the guys from Night Watch checked this out, the morning after Amber's body was found?' I asked.

Mike looked at Mercer and shook his head. 'I'm sure they gave it the once-over, but at that point there was no reason to think that the Battery Maritime Building was anything but an abandoned dumping ground for a dead girl.'

While not pristine and certainly not lived in, the homes were fairly well maintained. It looked like with a fresh coat of paint and some basic landscaping, families could move back in and set up housekeeping almost at once.

'Why did they continue to build military housing here, even after the fortress was obsolete?' I asked, as Mike picked up his pace.

'Because this little island played a part in every single war America fought until the army closed the place down. The Revolution, the Seminole War, the war with Mexico, the Civil War, the Spanish-American War.' He was spitting out the names faster than he could walk. 'It was a major embarkation point of American troops during World War I, and even the most important New York induction center in World War II.'

Opposite the far end of Colonels' Row was another massive brick building, fronting on the south end of the historic property.

'Liggett Hall,' Mike said. 'Designed by one of New York's most famous architectural firms – McKim, Mead and White. Built to house an entire regiment – more than a thousand troops.'

The dead quiet of the island was broken by the sound of a siren wailing in the distance. 'Where's that coming from, do you think?'

Mike laughed dismissively. 'Maybe the feds ferried over in full force. C'mon. Let's get a sense of what's got to be done before they get in my face.'

He cut across the roadway, beginning to huff a bit as we jogged up a slight incline.

Then he stopped to get his bearings, leaning on the vertical bars of a tremendous old navigation buoy about twenty feet high.

'Down there is the South Battery. It faces on the narrow waterway that separates Governors Island from Brooklyn. Its bell was meant to keep enemy ships out of Buttermilk Channel, on the back side of the island.'

The sound of the siren seemed to be getting closer.

'Come this way,' Mike said, waving me off the roadway.

Adjacent to the buoy, I passed the entrance to a small white shingled building, a Roman Catholic church named Our Lady Star of the Sea. This island outpost had all the makings of a small village.

But across the way was an entirely jarring structure. It was of more recent vintage, and the dilapidated sign on top of the structure said SUPER 8 MOTEL.

Mike and Mercer loped straight past the eyesore, and seconds later I was standing at the edge of another beautifully laid-out park, with a huge central green. Around it were a dozen wood houses, much older than the brick mansions of Colonels' Row. Each of them was painted a pale yellow with white trim, and each had a yard dotted with horse chestnut and maple trees.

'Nolan Park,' Mike said. 'The oldest houses on the island. These are where the generals were quartered. Ulysses S. Grant himself. And what they called the Governor's House is right up there, too.'

The sirens were drowning out Mike's voice.

'The highest point,' he said, lifting his arm to show us, 'that's Fort Jay, the original island fortress, built starting in the late eighteenth century, complete with a moat.'

As we started to climb the hill, a shiny red fire truck barreled off the roadway and blocked our ascent. From behind our position, two black vans pulled up and eight men in dark suits and sunglasses – agents, no doubt – spilled out and walked toward us.

'Who's Chapman?' the lead man asked.

Mike raised his hands in the air. 'Got me, man. Walking on National Park grass, right? Felony or misdemeanor? But I swear we haven't picked any flowers.'

The two firemen – the island's only permanent residents – laughed as they watched the encounter from the cab of their truck.

'I'm Avery. Steve Avery, FBI. You seen enough?'

'Actually, I was hoping to buy a ticket for the twilight tour,' Mike said. 'The one that gets us inside the buildings before sunset. I think the mayor would kind of like us to.'

'Well, the U.S. attorney for the Southern District hasn't put them on sale yet. Tell Battaglia to get in line. Besides, there really won't be much of a sunset tonight.'

'The federal prosecutor is—?'

'National Park. National Monument up there,' Avery said, pointing at Fort Jay. The dark clouds overhead were thickening. 'One West Point cadet dead. And you guys haven't been able to figure it out, have you? So we're gonna put the three of you back on that boat, sail you over to America, and let you get on with your work, Detective Chapman. We'll check out the island and spare everybody any hysteria before tomorrow's event. It's a big fund-raising day for the island restoration project, and nobody wants to spoil that.'

'My tax dollars at work with you guys in charge of security. I feel better already.'

'Now why don't you get yourselves into one of the vans and we'll give you a proper send-off at the ferry?'

Mike turned and whispered to me out of the side of his mouth.

'Give him your beautiful whites, Coop. Shake those blond curls. Lay on the charm.'

I stepped forward and put on my best smile. 'I'm Alexandra Cooper. I work for Paul Battaglia. It would make so much more sense if we put a team together and got this done before there's any more trouble. It's not crazy to think our perp may have been on Governors Island, at some point. That there may be something to help us identify him – maybe something that he left behind – if he was using this place around the time he killed Amber Bristol. Why don't we do it that way?'

'Because the sandbox isn't big enough to hold Battaglia this time. Your boss has grabbed too many cases from the U.S. attorney, and he doesn't seem to like anybody else sharing the spotlight with him.'

'We really have a jump start on you guys, so you might as well let us help,' I said, pushing a damp clump of hair out of my eyes, as drops of rain rolled down my neck.

'I hate to tell you you're all wet, Ms. Cooper,' Avery said, returning my smile. 'But you really are all wet.'

26

We stopped at headquarters so that Mike could tell Lieutenant Peterson what needed to be done on Governors Island to coordinate with the feds. In addition to coverage of the next day's muster, Peterson planned to work with the FBI to allow uniformed cops to search the buildings.

Guido Lentini's assistant had taped the press conference, so we watched the replay for twenty minutes. The mayor and Commissioner Scully had taken a sober approach in their short remarks, warning about the possible connection between the deaths of the three women but urging New Yorkers to remain calm.

They downplayed the idea of a military connection – because of the lack of evidence in Amber Bristol's case – and, as was customary, withheld certain facts, like the cat-o'-nine-tails, Elise's heirloom West Point ring, and the green blankets in which two of the bodies were wrapped.

It was after eight when we reached my apartment, and I was aching with exhaustion. The exhilaration of my night with Luc was losing its juice, and I needed some rest before thinking about what tomorrow might entail.

The doorman gave Mike the old cardboard boxes that the cops had delivered from his aunt Eunice's home in Brooklyn, and he and Mercer carried them onto the elevator.

'What's the story with that Super 8 Motel?' I asked.

'In the 1960s, when the coast guard took over the island from the army, they put in a motel and a bowling alley and a movie theater. Stuff to make it easier for guys stationed there to have their families visit.'

'How come you went there?' Mercer asked Mike.

'You remember my uncle Brendan. His army buddies from the Second World War used to meet on Governors Island for reunions. Ex-military guys and their relatives were allowed to use the place, even after the coast guard inherited it. Brendan took me there now and then on a Sunday morning to see a polo match.'

'Polo?' Mercer said, laughing. 'You and the sport of kings?'

I opened the apartment door and they put the boxes inside. 'Just leave your wet jackets on the back of the chairs to dry off. I'm starving. Let me order something in.'

'They must have had a bunch of army and coast guard brats running all over the island,' Mercer said. 'They'd know every nook and cranny. Who do we call to get a list of everyone stationed there, working backwards from the nineties?'

'That's the feds again,' I said. 'That'll take forever.'

'Alex, can I use your computer? I'll bet they've got a Web site. Everybody does.'

'Sure. The one in my office is a mess, with all the papers from my trial. Use the one in the bedroom.'

Mercer went inside while Mike filled the ice bucket and headed straight for the bar. I grabbed a towel from the powder room to dry off my hair and stretched out on the sofa with the portable phone.

'What do you want to eat?' I asked, as Mike handed me a Scotch.

'Call Patroon. Ask Ken to send over three of the biggest New York strips he's got. Black and blue. Mashed potatoes, onion rings, sautéed spinach. Caesar salad. Pronto.'

I dialed the number of the best steak house in town and ordered our dinner while Mike carried over the cardboard boxes and sat in the chair beside me as he opened the first one.

'You've got three messages on your machine, Alex,' Mercer called from the bedroom.

'Play 'em back for her. Could be important,' Mike said.

'Just leave them, Mercer. I'll deal with them later.' I knew that at least one of them must be from Luc. I wanted to savor that in private. 'Anything urgent would be on my cell, and I checked that five minutes ago.'

Mike winked. 'Burning the candle at both ends leaves a lot of melted wax in the middle. You look like you're fading. I'll set the table. Why don't you rest until the food gets here?'

'Let me know if you find anything interesting, okay? I just need a catnap.' I took a sip of the Dewar's, then rolled on my side and closed my eyes.

The insistent ring of the house phone, announcing the delivery, awakened me at nine o'clock.

I signed for the order and plated the food in the kitchen. Mike and Mercer had set out the china and opened one of my better bottles of red wine. The velvet voice of Smokey Robinson sang softly from the CD player in the den.

Mercer came to the table with papers printed from the computer, and Mike got up from the living room floor, where he was searching Bannerman's catalogs.

My stomach had been growling for hours. I sliced into the tender steak and began to eat.

'Here's one way around the feds,' Mercer said, patting his pile of papers.

'What's that?' Mike asked, chewing on some rings.

'I just used the search engine to check Governors Island plus military plus brats – and got to a site immediately. Looks like there are a few others, too.'

'What did you find?' Mike asked.

'It's angelfire.com. Adults discussing about what it was like to live there when they were kids. They talk about the buildings and the schools and playing inside the forts. I sent out a few questions – let's see what comes back.'

'How about asking was anybody frigging nuts? Anybody locked up? Anybody like to play inside the prison cells? Anybody freaking out the little girl brats?'

'I hear you. I'm on it.'

'What's the matter?' Mike said, turning to me. 'You're eating like you haven't had a meal in days. The guy didn't feed you?'

'Lay off her, Mike. She doesn't want to go there. What'd you find?'

'Nothing, yet. When we're done with dinner, you can give me a hand before we head home.'

I cleared the table and washed the dishes before resuming my position on the sofa. Mike and Mercer were on the floor at my feet.

'Go to bed, Coop. We'll let ourselves out,' Mike said.

I don't know how long I had been dozing before I heard Mike's yelp.

'Show me,' Mercer said.

I sat bolt upright.

'Bannerman's. Winter 1938. Look at the photograph,' Mike said, leaning over to show Mercer. 'Blankets. Dark olive green, it says. Surplus World War I stock, made for the U.S. Army of 'pure Scottish wool. Even the stitching on the edges is the same.'

'Got a manufacturer?'

'Yeah, McCallan Brothers. You saw the tag, Coop, didn't you? The one Dickie Draper found on the blanket? The last three letters were L-A-N. Eureka!'

Mike and Mercer exchanged high fives.

'Well, there's not going to be anyone around who can trace a sale from that year with a company that's been out of business half a century,' I said. 'I don't know what you're so excited about.'

'Where's your sense of adventure? You know what this does? It opens up the possibility that the killer's link to Bannerman Island wasn't a coincidence. Maybe his old man was as wacky as Uncle Brendan. Maybe instead of keeping useless magazines, he had a cellar full of blankets and weapons and things he actually bought from the catalog. Things somebody might know about and that could lead us to this sicko.'

'Mike's right. Both Elise Huff and Connie Wade were wrapped in blankets like this.'

'And Amber Bristol wasn't. I'm just saying you shouldn't get too excited.'

Mike's cell phone buzzed on the coffee table. He reached for it and flipped it open. 'Chapman,' he said, getting to his feet, catalog in hand.

He listened as the caller gave him some news.

'It's not even eleven o'clock yet. Make sure you keep an eye on him. Mercer and I will be there in half an hour.'

'Where to?' Mercer asked. 'What's happening?'

'It's the guys from the bar car, Manhattan South. Looks like with all the gin mills in the world, they finally stumbled into the right one.'

I stood up. 'Where?'

'A couple of blocks from the Pioneer,' he said. 'Ever hear of Ruffles?'

'No.'

'It's a pretty new joint on Prince Street, off Lafayette.'

'What's there?'

'The owner is a kid named Kiernan,' Mike said. 'He's tending bar tonight.'

Barbara told us that Elise had been hoping to hook up with a guy named Kevin or Kiernan. The latter wasn't very common, so maybe things were beginning to break our way.

'Nice going,' I said, stretching as I got up.

'I know, Coop. But wait until I tell you the rest of it.'

'What?'

'Think Jimmy Dylan, okay. Amber's boyfriend. The owner of the Brazen Head.'

Mercer and I both nodded.

'This is his number-two son, set up downtown with a place of his own. The bar is called Ruffles, and the owner's name on the license is Kiernan Dylan. You want to join me for a nightcap?'

27

I squeezed in between two twenty-somethings and took the last stool at the bar. Mike planted himself behind me and threw down a fifty-dollar bill – mine, of course – to get the attention of one of the bartenders. The scene was too white and too young for an over-forty African-American, so Mercer waited in the car across the street.

'I'm surprised there was no line to get in,' I said.

'It's not midnight yet, and that rain has to dampen the enthusiasm of even the most desperate broads looking to get lucky.'

The downtown scene picked up between twelve o'clock and four on weekends. Velvet ropes blocked access to the hottest doors in town, and bouncers were usually on hand to dispatch the unruly as well as to select the sexiest to jump ahead of the crowd.

'Welcome to Ruffles,' a short, stocky guy with sandy hair said, squaring off opposite me. 'What are you drinking, sweetheart?'

'Sweetheart's starting with a club soda,' Mike said. 'She got hammered last night, so we'll tune her up a bit later. What have you got in single malts?'

'If this stuff is too heavy for you, I do a wicked watermelon martini.' The bartender was talking to me as he handed over a small Lucite stand framing a list of drinks. Printed on one side were microbrews and wines by the glass; on the other was the assortment of fine Scotch.

As Mike looked over my shoulder, I pointed at the logo and message written in italics across the bottom of the page: *Ruffle: To create a disturbance (Webster's Dictionary). Kiernan Dylan, Proprietor.*

'Make a decision?'

'I'll take a Lagavulin. Neat,' Mike said.

'Intense, man.' The bartender turned to the well-stocked shelves behind him and brought over a full bottle of the smoky, amber-colored Scotch.

I swiveled on the stool and took in the scene. After Mike got the call about Ruffles, I had put my hair in a ponytail to affect my most youthful look and dressed in a tank top and tight jeans.

Fresh-faced young women continued to arrive in twos and threes. Guys at the bar looked them over, some moving in on the groups before they had even settled at one of the small round tables against the wall. The place was filling up, and while young men chatted up girls on their first and second drinks, those anxious to hook up with someone before last call would begin a more frantic pursuit as the hours wound down.

Waitresses in white ruffle-trimmed blouses and black cotton slacks worked the floor from the service bar, not far from where I sat.

'Dylan's Law,' Mike said, pointing as new arrivals stood in the doorway. One looked poised for a walk down a Seventh

Avenue runway, while the other had thick makeup troweled on and enough dark eyeliner to resemble a raccoon.

'What law would that be?'

'For every pretty girl, there's an ugly roommate.'

'Jimmy Dylan?'

'You got it. I told you he was a pig. He'd stroll through the Brazen Head watching all his kids' friends getting their load on, passing judgment on the crowd.'

The bartender was keeping an eye out for glasses that needed a refill.

'You Kiernan?' Mike asked.

'Nah. Wouldn't be working back here like an ordinary stiff if I was one of Dylan's kids,' he said, wiping the water marks off the wood. 'I'm Charlie.'

'Good to meet you, Charlie. I'm Mike. I thought Kiernan takes a turn every now and then.'

'Sure he does. Covers for us while we take our breaks, when he's here. For him, though, it's just amusement. He walks away when he's got something better to do and leaves me with all the drunks. You looking for Kiernan?'

'Nah,' Mike said, 'I know his big brother. Just thought I'd say hello.'

'Junior? You a friend of Junior's?'

'Yeah, you could say that. I know him from uptown. From the Head. How long has Kiernan had this place?'

'His father set him up over the winter. Six, seven months now.'

A girl who couldn't have been more than sixteen wedged herself between me and Mike, extending her arm and putting her empty glass on the bar top.

'What can I do for you, love?'

'Whatever that last one was you gave me? It was delicious. You know, that sort of blue thing with the vodka in it?' She was giggling and flirting with Charlie.

'Coming right up.'

'That guy over there in the corner, with the navy blue T-shirt,' she said. 'He said to put it on his tab.'

While Charlie stepped away to mix a concoction for the kid, Mike chatted her up. 'I know I've seen you somewhere before. Do you go to Nightingale? I've got a little sister. Maybe you've been to a party at our apartment.'

'Like, who's your sister?' she said, shaking her head. 'I go to Spence, but I hang with a lot of girls from there. What's her name?'

Mike had made his point. He pretended he had a sister at one of the city's premier private schools and got the teenager to admit she was still a high school student.

'Ava. Ava Gardner,' Mike said, knowing the kid wouldn't have a clue that he'd named his nonexistent sister for one of his favorite movie stars.

'I don't think I know who she is,' the girl said with a pained expression, as if he had asked her to determine the square root of 327. She used Mike's arm to pivot away from the bar with a full glass of blue liquid, then sipped from it and giggled again. 'Don't tell Ava, but I'm a senior at Princeton for the night. I've got an older sister, and she'd kill me if she caught me here. It's so fun, isn't it?'

She headed back to Mr. Navy Blue T-Shirt, who was surrounded by three other teenagers.

'I'd say we got Kiernan for serving minors, in case he turns uncooperative,' Mike said to me. 'It must be in his genes.'

Charlie was at the service counter, filling an order for one of the waitresses, before he turned back to us. 'Ready for something else?'

'Actually,' Mike said, 'I was hoping to talk to Kiernan. Is he still around?'

'What do you mean "still"?'

'One of my buddies was in earlier tonight. A guy who knows him. Said he was here.'

'You looking for a job? I'll give you a number to call.'

'Nope. It's kind of a personal thing.'

The bartender had braced his arms against the wooden counter, glancing from time to time at the narrow hallway at the rear of the room. 'Then give him a personal call. This here's his business.'

'Well, if I knew how to reach him, I might do that.'

'If it's personal you should know how to reach him.' His genial manner had turned cool.

A second girl, as young-looking as the first, wobbling on four-inch heels, stood behind Mike and asked for another margarita.

'Let me see that ID, will you?'

'C'mon, Charlie. It's still just me,' she said, fumbling in her pants pocket for a driver's license that was undoubtedly fake.

I guessed that the bartender's sudden attention to the rules meant that he had figured Mike for a cop.

'Lucky for you,' Mike said, 'I'm a patient man. Don't you think if I wait long enough, Kiernan will come around?'

Charlie looked to his left again. There was something besides the rest rooms down that hallway.

'Lucky for me is that any minute now my two bouncers will show up and remind you where the door is.'

'Even if I haven't ruffled anything? Caused any disturbance?'

'Hold my spot, will you, Mike? I need the ladies' room.' I slipped off the stool and started for the hallway.

Charlie seemed to think about abandoning his busy post to follow me, but a tall, well-dressed young man moved in next to Mike, put down some bills, and ordered a Jack Daniel's and a Cosmopolitan.

The dark passageway had four marked doors. The first two had symbols for men and women posted above them. The one after them was tagged with a metal sign for the basement, and at the far end, I could read the word *Office* in the dim light from the overhead bulb.

Mike got off the stool as I approached and started to sit down.

'Look,' Charlie said to me, 'if you're not drinking, love, I've got people who'll be glad to give me the business. I can use your seat.'

'I'm not feeling all that well,' I said to Mike, so that Charlie could hear. 'I think I'm going to be sick. Would you walk me back to the ladies' room?'

I took Mike by the hand and started to lead him through the groups of drinkers, while Charlie called after us. 'Take it outside, okay? Don't be messing up in here.'

A couple claimed our seats as soon as we were out of the way. Charlie looked around desperately for someone to give him a hand. He called out to one of the waitresses, but she couldn't hear him over the music and laughter.

As we disappeared into the hallway, I looked back and saw Charlie reach under the bar and come up with a telephone receiver.

'You really overdid it last—'

'I'm fine, Mike. I was just scouting for a place where Kiernan might be holed up,' I said, pointing to the sign on the last door. 'You want a shot at him? If he didn't see tonight's news, we're way ahead of the game.'

Mike brushed past me and opened the door. There was a staircase going up a flight, but no lights. He went up the steps as quickly as possible and I followed behind him.

At the top was another door, and the sound of scuffling behind it. I could hear voices, two people talking to each other. Mike jiggled the handle but the door was locked, so he pounded on it.

'Whaddaya want? Who is it?'

'Police. Open up. C'mon – right now.'

'Police? What are you, crazy?' a male voice called out. 'You got a warrant or something? I'm gonna make a phone call.'

'I don't need a warrant, Kiernan. I'm not here to search anything,' Mike said. 'Calm down. You don't make a call and I won't make a call.'

'Whaddaya mean? Whaddaya mean you won't make a call?'

'Walk to the front of the room and look out the window. You're gonna see a black Crown Vic. We've got the place staked out, up and down the block. Take a look, Kiernan. I'll wait that long. One call from me to my crew, they come marching in the front door of Ruffles and all those cute little twinkies whose blood alcohol level is higher than their SAT scores? The next time you see any of them – or a liquor license – you'll be too old to know what to do with them.'

There was no noise for a minute, and then I could hear the man's footsteps march away, toward the window facing the street. Slowly, he made his way back and cracked open the door.

'Chapman, Mike Chapman. NYPD.' Mike left out the homicide reference. It was often the fastest way to end a conversation. 'This is Alex Cooper. She's with the DA's office.'

'Kiernan Dylan.' He said his name but blocked the entrance with his large body.

'We'd like to come in.'

'This isn't a really good time. I've got somebody with me. If you just want to talk, we can do it this way.'

'I'm afraid of the dark,' Mike said, pushing the door open and walking past Kiernan. 'I'd prefer it in here.'

I took a few steps in and heard a sniffling noise from someone huddled in an armchair in the corner.

Mike found a floor lamp and turned it on. 'You okay, young lady?'

The black-haired teenager wiped her nose with the back of her hand and looked up at Kiernan before answering. 'Uh-huh. Yeah.'

I saw him cover his crotch and heard the sound of his fly zipping up. In addition to the desk and several file cabinets on the side of the room, there was a large futon under the window. I assumed from the disarray of the sheets that we had interrupted an intimate encounter.

'Can I go?' she asked. Her eyes were red and her nose was running. Hard to know whether she had been crying or snorting cocaine, until I saw the razor blade on the glass-topped table. A bottle of tequila and two paper cups were on the floor beside it.

'What's your name?' Mike asked, kneeling to make eye contact with her.

Again, she looked at Kiernan before speaking. 'Sally. Sally Anton.'

'How old are you?'

Kiernan started to answer for her but Mike held out his arm and he stopped. 'I'm twenty – um. I'm twenty-two.'

'Let's see your ID.'

'Look, Chapman. Everybody gets carded here, okay? The SLA has no beef with me. I don't know why you cops think you can barge in—'

Mike looked at the license. 'What year were you born?'

Sally looked at the ceiling and sucked on her lower lip, trying to do the math. 'Like, um, nineteen eighty um . . .'

Mike snapped his fingers a few times as he stood up. 'You got to get that down, Sally. Next ID you buy,' he said, pocketing her fake license, 'you've got to learn to memorize the date of birth, not just your age.'

Tears rolled down her cheeks as she pulled up her strapless halter top.

'How are you going to get home?' I asked her.

'Well, he was going to go with me.'

Kiernan took twenty dollars from his pocket and handed it to her. 'Tell Charlie to have one of the guys put you in a cab, babe.'

'What guys?' Mike asked.

'The ones who work the door,' Kiernan said, looking at his watch. 'They'll be on any minute. Take a cab, Sally. I'll call you later.'

The young woman collected her belongings – pocketbook, cell

phone, and a thong that was on the futon, tangled up in the wires of her iPod – before closing the door behind her.

'Have a seat,' Mike said to Kiernan. We pulled three chairs in a circle.

'What's this about?'

Kiernan Dylan was built like a fullback. He was taller than Mike – at least six three – and looked like he weighed more than 240 pounds. His eyes were set too close and his nose appeared to have been broken several times.

'How old are you?'

'Twenty-eight,' he said, leaning back so that the two front legs of the chair tipped off the floor.

'Ever hear of statutory rape?'

The chair thudded down and Kiernan slammed his hand on the desk. '*What?* You must be crazy, man. I don't have to rape anybody. I got girls – never mind.'

'I know Sally isn't twenty-two. Here's hoping she's at least hit eighteen.'

'That's what this is? You policing my social life? Not even my mother does that, Chapman.'

'You go to college, Kiernan?'

'Yeah. Boston University.'

'Any military service?'

'ROTC. I was ROTC at school.'

'Did you like it?'

'Yeah, yeah, I liked it. My father wanted me to go into the marines – like him – but I didn't do it.'

Mike was stone-faced. 'Did you listen to any news tonight?'

'What news?'

'Some people, they're interested in world affairs or local politics. Sports. Weather and traffic. Winning lottery numbers. Sound familiar? The news, Kiernan, you watch any?'

'Not lately.'

'How about last week?'

'I'm asking you, what news?'

'Your friend Elise Huff. Anybody tell you she's missing?'

'My friend *who*?' Dylan's heavy eyebrows vibrated like a thick caterpillar across the center of his forehead.

'Elise Huff. The girl who was supposed to meet with you two weeks ago at the Pioneer.'

'I don't know who you're talking about. Why would I go to the Pioneer when I've got my own place?'

' 'Cause a lot of your friends still party there,' I said. ' 'Cause maybe you didn't want to bring another girl in here, when so many others are waiting to play with you.'

'Elise Huff,' Mike said again. 'From Tennessee. Worked for an airline.'

'Oh, yeah,' Kiernan said, his mouth agape. 'The stewardess. I didn't even know her last name.'

Or the sales agent who told people she was a stewardess.

'How many times did you see her?' Mike asked.

'Why?' he asked, his large hand grabbing a rubber band from the desk and stretching it as he talked. 'She's got no gripe against me. I never touched her.'

'I asked you how many times you saw her.'

'I met her one night. Once.'

'Where?'

'At the house of a girlfriend of hers. I was just along for the ride with one of my college buddies. Just hanging out, is all. She was like a stalker, you know what I mean? Followed me around all night like a puppy dog. Kept calling me all the time after that. Trying to get together with me. Really annoying, she was.'

'Nothing sexual that first night?' I asked.

'Maybe we made out and stuff. If she thinks that entitled her to anything else, then she's dumber than I thought she was.'

'She had your cell number? How'd she get that?'

Kiernan stared at Mike. 'Okay, so I gave it to her. Is that a big deal? I got lots of friends. I'm always trying to get people to come downtown, show them the bar. I give it out a lot – maybe more than I should. Look, I don't know what you're after but you're wasting your time.'

Kiernan stood up and kicked the chair back behind him.

'Sit down.'

'Finish up, Detective. I've got work to do.' He put his hands on his hips and seemed to puff up his solid chest.

Mike stood and faced off with Kiernan. 'You see Elise Huff a second time? On a Saturday night, two weeks ago?'

'I told you I never went to the Pioneer to meet her.'

'And I didn't ask, this time, if you went to the Pioneer, did I? Did she show up at Ruffles? Did you meet her somewhere else? Did you return her calls that night? Sit down, take it easy, and let's go over my questions one by one. There'll still be some talent waiting for you downstairs when I'm done.'

'I don't even remember what the girl looks like. I don't think I ever saw her again, to be quite honest with you. You'd have to show me a picture.'

'You come to the office with me, it just so happens I can do that,' Mike said. 'Which would you rather see? Her college year-book or the autopsy photographs?'

Kiernan Dylan exhaled. His voice was quiet now, and his cheeks reddened. 'What autopsy photos? What happened to her?'

'She stayed out pretty late one night, looking for you. That's an answer I figured you had for us.'

The rubber band snapped, hitting Kiernan on the chin. He picked up a stapler from the desktop and heaved it against the wall. It ricocheted and smashed several wine glasses that were lined up on a side table.

'There's that Dylan temper,' Mike said. 'A chip off the old block. You must make your old man proud.'

'Shit! You leave my father out of this. You didn't tell me you knew him. What the hell are you looking to do? Shut me down? For what?'

'Just take a minute and pretend that you feel bad about the fact that the girl is dead. Can you do that for me?'

The phone rang.

'Ignore it, kid.'

'It's only the intercom. It's Charlie, wanting to know if everything's okay up here.'

Mike nodded and Kiernan picked up the receiver. 'No problem. I don't need anybody. Take care of Sally for me.'

Kiernan lowered his big body back onto the chair. 'Where were we?'

'You were going to tell me how bad you feel about Elise.'

'Sick to my stomach bad.'

'Pleased to hear it. For her or for you?'

'I'm telling you I met her one time.'

'Quite an impression you made.'

'Everybody was talking about Ruffles that night. The place is doing really well. Kids that used to be all over the Brazen Head are coming downtown now. She wanted to be part of the mix, I guess. She wanted to meet guys, she wanted to have a good time.'

'That first night you met Elise,' I said, 'where was the party?'

'I'm not exactly sure of the address. I went with friends. It was the house of some girl they knew. Her mother and father were away, out of town.'

'East Side? West? Downtown? C'mon. Help us with this.'

Kiernan looked at me, surprised that I didn't know the basic facts. 'It wasn't in Manhattan. I was out at my parents' place for the weekend.'

'Where's that?'

'Breezy Point.'

I didn't know much about the beach community on the far western Rockaway peninsula of Long Island, in Queens, but Mike would fill me in later.

'So you met Elise out at the beach?' Mike said, picking up the thread. I knew he must be thinking, as I was, of the olive green blanket in which her body had been wrapped, and the sand that Dickie Draper had found in it.

'I met her at somebody's house, okay?'

'A warm summer night, a few cocktails, a walk along the ocean, a little action. No wonder she was chasing you after that. You call her the next day?'

'She called me. Monday.' He had picked up another rubber band and was twisting it around his fingers.

'To make a date?'

'I guess.'

'Well, isn't that what Elise wanted?'

'She wanted passes to Ruffles. I was handing them out to friends, so they could drink for free the first time they came. And VIP cards to get past the lines.'

'But she was interested in you, wasn't she?'

Kiernan shrugged his huge shoulders. The rubber band was twisted so tight around the ends of his fingers that the tips were turning white.

'When did you go to Breezy Point next?' Mike asked.

'I'm back and forth all the time. My folks have had the place since I was a kid. I've always spent summers there.'

'You take Elise out with you?'

'No way. She was nothing to me. I told you, I saw her once and that was it.'

'Gets crowded out there in the summer, doesn't it?'

'The Point? Yeah.'

'I was thinking about your family's house, in particular.'

Kiernan didn't know where Mike was going with this. He cocked his head and squinted, his eyebrows rolling into the shape of a fuzzy V.

'What with all those brothers and sisters of yours, your mother—'

'She spends the month in Ireland, with my grandparents.'

'Your father, too. But I guess he's had a playmate to keep him company while your mom's gone, then. What's his friend's name? Amber? Isn't it Amber Bristol?'

Kiernan Dylan opened his clenched fists and spread his fingers wide, snapping the band off as he did. He stood up and kicked the drawer of the heavy old oak desk, moving it back almost a foot.

'That bitch has nothing to do with him anymore. You understand that, Detective? Amber won't be back, so you can just leave Jimmy Dylan out of my business. You coming after me? Then leave my father alone.'

28

'What do you mean Amber won't be back?' Mike asked.

'We're talking about Elise Huff, I thought.'

Kiernan had seated himself in the armchair in the corner after Mike calmed him down. If he had read a paper or heard a newscast in the last few weeks, he had missed all of the crime stories or was playing a good game.

'And I thought you didn't know anything else about her. I'll get back to Elise. Maybe when you listen to the cell phone messages you left her, it'll tweak your memory,' Mike said, trying to completely unhinge his subject, jumping around from one sensitive topic to the other.

Elise's cell phone had never been recovered, but from the way Kiernan's legs started bouncing, he didn't want to be reminded of their exchanges.

'How long have you known Amber?'

He was caught between the proverbial rock and hard place. He had no reason to think we knew anything about Amber and was clearly blindsided by Mike's reference to her.

'I've met her a couple of times.'

'Where?'

'The Head. I helped my dad run it before we opened down here.'

'How long have you known about their relationship?'

Kiernan closed his eyes and thought for almost a minute. 'What relationship would that be? She was a friend. Everybody likes my dad. Everybody. Then we opened Ruffles, and she'd drop in to say hello sometimes when she was downtown.'

Mike rolled the desk chair over to sit face-to-face with Kiernan. 'Did Amber get booted from the Head?'

'Did she tell you that?'

Mike kept staring at Kiernan.

'Okay, okay. You're asking me. Maybe she did. She couldn't hold her liquor. Kept saying a lot of stupid things. Embarrassing things.'

'What did you mean when you said she isn't coming back?'

'She went home. Amber comes from some Podunk town out west. My dad told me – no, no, forget my dad. I guess I heard from my brother Danny or one of the guys who works at the Head that she finally figured out she had no frigging future hanging around waiting for some married man to give it up for her. That totally wasn't happening, get it? It was over.'

'Did you see her before she left?'

'She came in here a couple of times this summer. I'm easy with the free drinks,' Kiernan said, forcing a smile. 'Look, why are you asking me about Amber?'

The music from downstairs was louder now. So was the crowd, shouting over the noise from the jukebox. The buzz from the sidewalk in front of the bar was also heavier.

'Nobody's seen her in a few weeks.'

'I'm telling you, she's gone home.'

'Convince me. How do you know that for sure?'

Kiernan Dylan's feet were tapping on the floor. He bit the inside of his cheek and looked up at the ceiling. ' 'Cause I packed up some stuff for her, okay? 'Cause she asked me to throw out some of her weird, freaky – her stuff, okay? 'Cause she was never coming back to use it – she told me that herself.'

I tried not to react as Kiernan admitted that he had been the person – or one of the people – who had so carefully sanitized Amber Bristol's tiny apartment.

Then he leaned in and looked at Mike. 'And she sure as hell didn't want that pervert superintendent who was always looking to jump her bones to make any trouble for her after she was gone.'

Vargas Candera. The guy who had a penchant for beating his girlfriend.

'So you were just being a Good Samaritan,' Mike said. 'You weren't trespassing or, say, breaking into Amber's pad, were you?'

'You're looking to screw me, aren't you? You don't get me one way, you try to do it the next. Maybe I need to call a lawyer.'

'Maybe so. Your old man must have a hotline to some jerk for every time he gets a summons in his place. You got a car, Kiernan?'

'What?'

'A car. To get back and forth to Breezy Point. To get rid of the things Amber asked you to.'

'Yeah. I need it for business. For picking up liquor and supplies. Sure I got one.'

'What do you drive?'

'A minivan, 2005 Ford.'

Mike was thinking the same thing I was. The perfect vehicle for moving a body or two from one place to another.

'Where do you keep it?'

'On the street. I park on the street.'

'What's the tag?' Mike said, taking out his notepad to write down the plate number.

Kiernan put his head back again and recited the letters and digits. He swallowed hard and looked at Mike again.

'It's nearby? You mind if we look at it tonight?'

'I – uh – I don't have it anymore.'

'You just lost me,' Mike said, lowering his head and rubbing his eyes.

'It was stolen. It was stolen about ten days ago.'

'Your van was stolen? From where?'

'Not far from here. Near the Bowery, a few blocks away.'

'You got a copy of the police report?'

'That's the thing. I haven't made one yet.'

'You what?'

'I haven't had time. It's been crazy busy here at work.'

'You run a bar, Kiernan, not a hedge fund. Once you've made sure the place is stocked with booze and you got somebody who can pour the damn stuff, what the hell else do you have to do? Tell me the *real* reason you haven't called the police, that's what I want to know. 'Cause you didn't want to open this whole can of worms, right? Big, fat, juicy, lying, cheating Dylan worms.'

The young man's anxiety was mounting. He was wiggling in his seat, looking at the telephone as though deciding whom he should call before he got himself in any deeper.

'How much longer are you two gonna be here? I'm through answering your questions. I need to use the bathroom, okay?'

'Coop, check it out.'

I walked to the door Kiernan pointed at, near the entrance. Mike wanted me to make sure it wasn't another staircase or exit, that there was no telephone inside and nothing Kiernan could use to hurt himself.

There was only a toilet and a sink. When I said it was okay, the young man practically mowed me down getting inside and latching the door.

Mike was on his feet. 'I'm taking him in.'

'You're going to collar him now?'

'Got to.'

'Don't do it. He's giving you all kinds of stuff, hoping you leave his father alone, I guess. It's all good – he's tying himself up in knots. He'll clam up faster than lightning the minute you arrest him.'

'He's giving us bullshit,' Mike said, running his fingers through his hair. He was beginning to look as weary as I felt.

'That's fine. Don't you want to keep it coming? Why shut it off?' I tried to get Mike to look at me but he paced around me.

' 'Cause we can turn him, that's why. Have some leverage. If he's protecting someone else, he won't have the balls to stick with it. Lock him up and—'

'For?'

'For serving alcohol to minors. For burglarizing Amber Bristol's apartment.'

'Prove that.'

'He just admitted it.'

'No, he didn't, Mike. He denied it. He said Amber asked him to do it for her. How the hell do I prove she didn't, now that she's dead?'

'You're the lawyer. You're so goddamn smart you can find me a crime.'

'I like it this way. He's spinning in circles. He'll dig himself a little deeper, and I can use each and every contradiction, each and every inconsistency, in front of a jury. You put him in cuffs and we'll have to read him his rights. End of story.'

'Ever been to Breezy Point?'

'No.'

Mike was talking fast and Kiernan seemed in no rush to leave the bathroom. 'It's a private community.'

'That can't be. It's part of New York City.'

'Thirty-five hundred homes. The whole damn neighborhood is a privately owned cooperative. The houses, the streets, the beaches – every inch of the place is private. It's got the highest concentration of Irish-Americans in the United States. More than 60 percent. Boozy Point, as they say about themselves. You'll get no help out there. They'll circle the wagons around Jimmy Dylan and his boys, I can guarantee you that.'

'Then we can—'

'You don't even know how to get there, do you?'

'What difference does that make?'

'Take the Belt Parkway for starters. Very close to where Elise Huff's body was dumped.'

'Mike, I agree the kid looks good for this,' I said, pulling on his arm to hold him in place. 'But let's slow down and try to build a case.'

'What? Leave him out so he can destroy evidence? So he can skip town, like that doctor you didn't fight to put behind bars? Half the Dylan family is still in Ireland. They'll take Kiernan in with open arms. C'mon, Coop. You've fallen for that crap before.'

'Lock him up for a couple of misdemeanors and he'll still be out of jail before you finish your paperwork on the arrest. It's been a long day. Let's get some rest and look at it fresh in the morning.'

'I don't want to argue the point with you. You don't like it? Take a hike. I'm not half as tired as you are.' Mike was peeved at me, perhaps for personal reasons, and ready to dismiss me.

'You ought to lay off him and let me go at him for a while. Different style.'

'Bottom line is, I'm bringing him in.'

'Not for murder.'

'Of course not. But I just can't take the chance that we leave him out here when three women are dead and he's got a clear connection to two of them. At least we can shut this place down and have the SLA pull the license so nobody else gets hurt.'

The bathroom door opened and Kiernan Dylan slowly walked over to us.

'I'm not answering any more of your questions, okay? I'd like you to get out of here.'

I put out my hand to grab Mike's arm but he pulled away.

'We're leaving, Kiernan. But you're coming with us.'

'What the fuck does that mean?' He was fired up now.

Mike flipped open his cell phone and hit the speed dial for Mercer. 'C'mon inside. Ask for Charlie, the bartender, and tell him Kiernan wants you to come upstairs.'

There was nothing close enough for the young man to throw or kick this time. 'What'd I do?'

'Let's start with your liquor license. We'll worry about the dead girl later.'

'You arresting me? Is that what you're telling me?'

'You act like a gent and I won't cuff you in front of all your friends. You're going to leave here and come back to my office to talk to us.'

'I want to make a phone call.'

'You'll get your call,' Mike said, 'as soon as we get up to the squad.'

The door opened and Mercer entered the room. The fact that he was bigger and taller than Kiernan Dylan was comforting to me, and surprising to the angry young man.

'Coop, you go on ahead. Call Peterson and tell him we're on the way. The precinct needs to send a squad car to come by and keep things quiet,' Mike said. 'And get the bar car back ASAP to get as many names and identifications as they can.

'Mercer, you and I will flank Mr. Dylan here as we walk through the crowd of his admirers. No cuffs as long as he behaves. And you, sir, you can tell your man Charlie to make it last call in about ten minutes, once we're out of the way. You think your pit bulls are guarding the door?'

Dylan was speechless now. He nodded his head.

'Well, just tell them to be cool with this while we leave here and the rest will go down easy.'

I worked my way through the bar area and out onto the street. I crossed to the curb on the far side of Mercer's car and made the call to Lieutenant Peterson.

Minutes later, the front door of Ruffles opened and Mercer stepped out, followed by Dylan and Mike. Kiernan told the two rough-looking men in black on either side of the entrance that he was going off with the police.

The line of patrons waiting to get in was almost a block long. Several kids recognized Kiernan and shouted out his name. Near the front of the group were four guys who seemed to be friends of his. One called out, saying they had come to meet him and asking where he was going. Kiernan hesitated, and Mike and Mercer paused with him.

The dark-skinned bouncer told the group to shut up. 'Back off,' he said. 'They're cops.'

The most vocal of the foursome took his cell phone from his pocket and aimed its little camera lens at the departing trio, framing them under the Ruffles sign as his flash went off.

'Get ready to hit the gas, Mercer. Coop, you're riding in front.' Mike opened the rear door of the car and got into the backseat with Kiernan. 'The last thing I meant to do tonight was stage a perp walk.'

29

'Where's my kid, Chapman? I want to see my kid.'

Five o'clock on a Sunday morning and the Manhattan North Homicide Squad room was as quiet as the morgue. Jimmy Dylan's basso voice shattered the silence as the heavy door swung shut behind him.

'Jeez, Mr. Dylan. I got a funny feeling you're the last guy in the world he wants to talk to right now.'

Mike, Mercer, and I were chewing on the remains of egg sandwiches that Mercer had picked up at one of the greasiest spoons in all of Harlem, a block away from the station house.

'Your father used to look the other way now and then. Decent people, hardworking people – he gave them a break first time out,' Dylan said, his green eyes aflame with rage. He was about Mike's height but much stockier, with red hair and sideburns tinged with gray. 'You're a disgrace to his name.'

'Fortunately for you, Kiernan didn't fall too far from the tree.'

Mike had predicted that Jimmy Dylan would show up before daybreak. Kiernan must have had second thoughts about calling one of his father's business lawyers, hoping he could skate through the ABC violations – Alcoholic Beverage Control laws – and be out of court before he was missed.

Instead, he had phoned one of his high school friends – a defense attorney – who was driving in from his vacation at an inn in Montauk, almost three hours away. But Charlie the bartender must have gotten the news to Kiernan's brothers and given them the choice of telling their father.

'Where's my boy, Chapman? What the fuck do you mean bringing him here to a homicide squad office?'

'Temper, temper, Mr. D. Can't you see there's a lady here?'

Dylan's ruddy complexion deepened in color, as the flush streaked down his neck and disappeared beneath his blue and white striped oxford cloth shirt.

'I wouldn't give a damn if she was Mother Mary. Where's Kiernan?'

Two uniformed cops came pounding up the staircase and pushed open the door behind Dylan. Mike got to his feet and held out his arm. Mercer stood up next to him.

'Game's up for the moment, Mr. D. We're talking to Kiernan. You can see him when we're done.'

'He's got rights, dammit. He's got the right to see me.'

'I'm the prosecutor working with the detectives. Your son actually didn't want us to contact you. He was very firm about that. Kiernan's called a lawyer,' I said, standing behind Mercer. 'They can meet as soon as he arrives. Meanwhile, he's comfortable and having something to eat.'

Dylan took a step in my direction, wagging his finger at me.

'He's . . . he's just a kid, missy. You keep me away from him and there'll be hell to pay. You'll never set your ass in a courtroom again.'

'I'm handling this, Coop, okay?' Mike gave me his most exasperated look before he turned back to Dylan. 'Trust me, Mr. D., you got no more control over where that skinny ass goes than the rest of us do. No more threats, got it?'

'Kiernan's got rights.'

'Jeez, you sound like all the lowlife morons I take off the streets. Everybody and his mother's got rights. Don't know what they are or how to use 'em but slap the cuffs on any scumbag around and bam! He's got rights. Kiernan may be your son but he's a grown man. Only kids that have a right to be questioned in the presence of a parent are minors, under the age of sixteen.'

'I want to be with him. I want to make sure he knows what he's doing,' Jimmy Dylan said, wiping the sweat off his neck with the cuff of his shirt. 'What's with this homicide bullshit?'

'Cool your heels for a while. We finish up with Kiernan, there'll be plenty of time to chat with you.'

Dylan grabbed Mike by the shoulder. 'Don't play God with me, Chapman. This here's my son and there's something bigger than a lawnmower chewing up my guts from the minute Junior called to tell me about this. If it's *my* problem you want to know about, then deal with me and let go of my kid.'

'What problem would that be, Jimmy?' Mike brushed his hand away.

Dylan nodded in my direction. 'Where can we go to talk?'

'Right here. Right now. You think this is gonna be a secret, backroom conversation?'

'It's personal. It's confidential.'

'I got news for you. It's not confidential anymore. Even Kiernan had a few things to say about it.'

'He *what*?' Dylan said, pounding a tight fist into the open palm of his left hand.

The door opened again and a young man in a sweatshirt and chinos came into the room. One of the cops tried to stop him as he pulled out a business card to identify himself.

'Mr. Dylan. Frankie Shea,' he said, approaching to shake hands. 'Kiernan called you?'

'Yeah.'

'I got a stable of lawyers. I got guys who do all the licensing for me with the SLA, deal with all the nuisances and aggravation. Why the hell did he reach out for you?'

Shea lowered his voice. 'My office does a lot of – um – like violent crime stuff. My boss is on the panel for homicide assignments. Kiernan was just a little nervous about these guys who brought him in. One of you Chapman?'

'Mike Chapman, Mr. Shea. This is Detective Mercer Wallace and Alexandra Cooper, from the Manhattan DA's office.'

Shea was short and wiry, with chiseled good looks and the edgy air of a lightweight boxer.

'You holding my client?'

'Yeah. He just had some chow. He wanted to take a nap till you got here.'

'Want to tell me what this is about?'

'Sure. We'll step into the lieutenant's office.'

Dylan roared again. 'For me you had no place to talk, Chapman? You got a mouthpiece still green behind the ears – look at him – and you're going to tell him what's going on before you tell me?'

'Hey, Mr. D. He's got rights, you know what I mean?'

'Frankie, tell him I can sit in on this.'

'Sorry, Mr. Dylan,' Shea said, scratching his head to think of a way to say what he needed to without further infuriating his friend's father. 'There could, you know, be some kind of conflict down the road. I mean, if you and Kiernan – well, I just can't let you do it.'

Mike and Frankie Shea spent about fifteen minutes together

in Peterson's small office before coming back to us.

'You fellows want to escort Mr. Dylan downstairs to wait for a bit longer?' Mike said to the two cops. 'When Mr. Shea tells you he's ready, you'll get your shot.'

Jimmy Dylan was fuming. He stood his ground until Shea urged him to make things easier by moving along.

Kiernan had been held in an interview room down the hall. Mike and I walked Shea to the door, and as we opened it Kiernan picked his head up from the table, where it had rested next to the debris from the sandwich and soda Mercer had given him.

Shea stepped in and patted Kiernan on the back a few times, before asking us to close the door and leave.

Jimmy Dylan had gotten no farther than the top of the steps. When he heard Mike's voice, Dylan asked to come back into the room. He was sweating profusely now, and the veins in his neck looked like they were pumping up to an explosion that would blow off the top of his head.

'If this is about that whore, Chapman, just let my boy go, okay?'

'Grab a chair, Mr. D.' He waved the cops off and pointed to the door. 'Which whore would that be?'

Dylan looked over at me.

'Now's not the time to worry about Ms. Cooper's sensibilities. She knows more whores than the Queen, I promise you. Give me a name.'

'Amber Bristol.'

Mike knew as well as I did that there was little chance we would get another word out of Kiernan Dylan after Frankie Shea finished his sit-down. He would chide his friend – his client now – for having talked too much already. He would advise him to take the hit on the ABC violation and walk out of court with no other formal charges held over his head.

The kid would carry with him just the ugly label that Mike had wanted to pin on him like a scarlet letter – person of interest in a homicide investigation. Maybe that would be enough to bring someone – a witness, a cohort, a conspirator – out of the woodwork to head us in the right direction.

'He didn't do anything to Amber. My Kiernan's a decent kid.'

'You know what happened to her?'

'I know she's dead, Chapman.'

'Murdered.'

'Yeah, I heard that.' Dylan reached for one of the napkins and wiped his sweaty face. 'Kiernan had nothing to do with her. I mean, maybe he met her a couple of times. Stupid of me to let her into the Brazen Head to begin with, but I got rid of her on my own.'

'You what?'

Dylan realized Mike thought he meant something more dramatic. 'Told her to get lost, get out of my life. That's what I mean.'

'Why is that?'

'Look, Chapman, you probably know more than I do. The newspaper articles, they just talk about the temp job she worked. Maybe you and your investigators don't know what else she did to pay the rent.' Dylan paused to test the waters. 'You know how crazy that girl was?'

'Just crazy enough to keep you interested in her, apparently.'

'Yeah, well, I lost interest, okay? I wasn't into any rough stuff, you know what I mean? It was getting too far-out for me, Amber's shenanigans. And her big mouth, talking to some of these men about – well, about me and her relationships. She was getting to be a loose cannon.'

'She didn't take the breakup very well, did she?'

Dylan didn't answer.

'You must have been scared shitless when she went off the radar screen.'

'I didn't notice. It's exactly what I wanted, that she head back home to Idaho.'

'Then why'd you bother to clean out her apartment?'

'Clean out her apartment? Talk to the Neanderthal superintendent who used to drool over her. You can't pin me with that.'

'Why not? You didn't let Kiernan do it alone, did you?'

Dylan's eyes widened again and he shouted an answer. 'Leave the kid out of this, for chrissakes. He's never been to her apartment. He wouldn't even know how the hell to find it.'

Mike put his forefinger in his ear and shook it up and down. 'Must be something wrong with my hearing. Coop, didn't Kiernan tell us something a little different?'

'What'd he say? What did he tell you? I do everything possible to give that kid every chance I can and now he steps in his own shit? What did he say?'

'Excuse me, Mr. D., but I think it was yours he stepped in.'

'Where is he? Let me talk to him.'

'See, it's a bit late, 'cause Kiernan's already given us some important information, so maybe you should just tell us what you know. Put it in perspective for us. If it makes things go easier for your kid, all the better.'

Jimmy Dylan heard a door close in the hallway and Frankie Shea's footsteps coming toward us.

'Your man ready for us?' Mike asked the young lawyer.

'Look, Detective Chapman. Of course Kiernan wants to do everything possible to cooperate with you in your investigation. What are you charging him with this morning?'

'We're waiting on word from the local precinct about the results of the canvass. Violations for serving alcohol to minors – how many counts and all.'

'So the sign on the door, that's all for show?' Frankie pointed to the gold lettering of the word HOMICIDE.

'Three dead girls, and Kiernan Dylan knew two of them.'

Jimmy Dylan took a deep breath. 'Two? Who's the other one?'

Frankie Shea ignored Dylan. 'I'm afraid your long ride uptown and the effort at intimidating my client did wonders for all of our sleep deprivation but very little for your case. He's got nothing more to say to you. From now on, you get the idea that you want to talk to Kiernan Dylan, you call me.'

'He's coming home with me?' Jimmy Dylan asked, smiling for the first time since he arrived at the station house.

'No, sir. They'll take him downtown to be arraigned, but he'll be out by the end of the day,' Shea said. 'They've got nothing on Kiernan.'

'Can I see him now, before you take him out of here?'

Mike walked away from us to get his prisoner. I knew he didn't want to see an "I told you so" expression on my face, so I stifled my annoyance at having wasted the opportunity for a more careful interrogation.

Kiernan entered the squad room in front of Mike.

'Pick up your head, boy,' Jimmy Dylan said. 'You got nothing to be ashamed of. You've done nothing wrong. You own a joint that sells liquor, and all this crap goes with the territory. Cops like to throw their authority around when they should have better things to do.'

The young man's eyes were bright red. He had obviously broken down while talking with Frankie Shea, perhaps becoming even more embarrassed when he learned from Shea that his father had inserted himself into the middle of the investigation.

Kiernan headed straight for his father. I assumed the emotional older man would embrace his son and wait until later, when they were home, to chide him for talking to us.

'I'm really sorry, Dad. I didn't mean to involve you in this.'

'Do what Frankie says, kid. We'll—'

'Tell me it's okay, what I said to them, Dad,' Kiernan said, starting to blubber as he looked his father in the eye.

I gathered up my notes, trying to glance away from the painful encounter, while Frankie Shea urged his client to stop talking and get the arrest process under way.

'Say something, Dad. I couldn't help what I said about her. I didn't know—'

Jimmy Dylan reached out to grab Kiernan's arm with his left hand, and with his strong right fist he hauled back and punched his number-two son squarely on the jaw.

Kiernan Dylan's knees gave out and he fell backwards, smacking his head against the corner of a metal file cabinet.

30

Mercer was on top of Jimmy Dylan, slamming his body across a desk and pinning him in place while Mike and Frankie checked on Kiernan. I could see that a gash had been opened on the back of his head, and I called down to the patrol sergeant to send someone upstairs with paper towels and Band-Aids.

'Get Jimmy out of here, Mercer,' Mike said. 'Make sure they know not to let him back in.'

Now the father was trying to apologize to Kiernan.

Mike was having none of it. 'I treat your son with kid gloves, Dylan. Don't put him in cuffs, don't stick him in the holding pen behind bars, feed him, and make him comfortable. I hear one question from the judge about whether the hole in his head is a result of police brutality, you'll all be sorry we've ever met.'

'Save it for later, Mr. Dylan,' Frankie said. 'I'm a witness, Chapman. Let it go.'

'If I were you, Mr. D.,' Mike said, 'I'd be calling that legal hotline so you can give me someone to talk to on your behalf. 1–800–SHYSTER. That's one of your rights, too, pal. Spend as much money as you'd like for the tackiest lawyer you can find. Be sure and tell him you took a whack at your own flesh and blood.'

Mercer steered Dylan out the door, while Frankie Shea made an effort at cleaning up his client's head wound and getting him to his feet.

When Mercer came back upstairs, he told me that two of the cops were standing by to drive me home.

'What about you?'

'Mike's got the collar to deal with. And I'll sleep here on one of the cots. I've got to cover that muster on Governors Island in a few hours. It's Sunday, remember?'

'I feel awful that you have to work today. There's nothing I'm up to doing except going to sleep.'

'Rest up, Alex. The papers will be full of stories about the murders. This may be the only day off you'll have for a while. The pressure will really be on to solve this.'

He walked me downstairs to the front desk, where one of the officers was waiting for me. I got in the backseat of the car and leaned my head against the window, telling the driver where I lived. The night with Luc had been so full of tender exchanges that it was hard to absorb the brutal events of the last few hours.

It was after six thirty in the morning, and although the sky was lightening, there was still a gray mist falling across the city. We followed Broadway downtown under the elevated tracks from 133rd Street and turned east on Ninety-sixth Street, crossing through Central Park.

At the entrance to my apartment, Vinny opened the car door for me and I thanked the cops for the ride.

'Don't you get a night off this weekend?'

'Nah. Covering for Oscar. He's got a cold. How about you, Ms. Cooper? You almost beat the newspaper delivery.'

'The papers go upstairs yet?'

'Yeah. Yours is in front of your door. I got a *Post*, if you want to see it,' Vinny said, heading for his marble-topped stand in the middle of the lobby. 'Here I thought you were out having a good time the other night, and instead you're chasing a serial killer.'

He handed the paper to me – a thick Sunday edition, full of extra ads and inserts. The large graphic was a map, with red arrows pointing to the locations at which each of the three bodies had been found.

I didn't know whether Commissioner Scully had come up with a compelling name for his task force, but the tabloids were starting a frenzy about the mysterious military connection of this sexual sadist: SEARCH FOR SERIAL KILLER: SON OF *UNCLE* SAM?

31

I fell asleep the minute I got into bed. I didn't awaken until three thirty in the afternoon, when Luc called from his home in Mougins, anxious to know why he hadn't been able to reach me the night before.

Now I regretted telling him so little about the case when we were together on Friday evening. I'd never imagined the developments would be so dramatic in the short time since we said good-bye in front of the Plaza Athénée. He renewed his offer for me to come to visit him at the end of the investigation, and I accepted, feeling an easing of the tension that had gripped me all weekend.

I showered and dressed and spent the last hours of the afternoon doing ordinary chores, routine things that would ground me after the intensity of the previous day. I rinsed out some lingerie in the bathroom sink, paid a stack of bills that had mounted on my desk, toasted an English muffin to snack on, and called my parents to let them know I was fine.

At six o'clock, Mercer called. He had finished the day at Governors Island, watching the reenactment rehearsal of the Civil War muster.

'All quiet on the military buff front.'

'Many people show up?'

'More than seven hundred.'

'I had no idea they'd draw that size. Any way to keep track of them?'

'This time, everyone had to sign in and show ID getting on the ferries to come over. There was a bit of a stampede getting folks off between four and five, but it looks like all the sightseers signed out.'

'You hear anything from Mike?'

'I'm stopping by the squad now, on my way home. Peterson's setting up a daily briefing meeting, starting tonight at seven. I can stop for you on my way uptown.'

'I'd like to be there.' The door might not be open to me long. I worked well with the lieutenant and his team, but once the other borough commanders and trooper supervisors stepped into bigger roles during the coming weeks, I was likely to be shut out of daily police meetings. It was commonplace for many prosecutors in other offices to be a step behind the investigators, but Battaglia counted on our senior staff to partner with the NYPD as closely as possible.

On the ride uptown, Mercer told me about his day. He described the dozens of men, young and old, who dressed in antique military garb, armed with weapons from the Civil War period, and staged mock battles all over the historic grounds of the island.

'Any structure to it?' I asked.

'It's run by an arts foundation, so they know who the players are and what they're up to. But it's very chaotic, and no one has a clue about the spectators. They're just people who see ads in the paper or read about it online.'

'And the costumes?'

'Everybody brings their own. Not my idea of a hobby, but it clearly drives a lot of these buffs. They were skirmishing everywhere, with bugle brigades and drum corps.'

'No women?'

'Plenty of them. I'm not sure if General Hooker's followers were onboard, but there were some ladies in uniform and others doing quilting bees, handing out rations,' Mercer said, shaking his head at the odd experience. 'Just glad that nobody went AWOL.'

The homicide squad room was a much busier place than when I had left it twelve hours earlier. There had been two murders in northern Manhattan during the night. A man who had slit his wife's throat with a machete because, he told the cops, she had burned his chicken wings was sleeping like a baby on the narrow wooden bench in the cell. Another guy, who had shot a rival drug dealer, was handcuffed to the handle of a desk drawer over against the window, fidgeting jumpily as though his last hit of crack cocaine was still coursing through his body.

Peterson waved us into his office when he saw Mercer and me. Mike was there, along with two of the best detectives from the Special Victims Unit, Ned Tacchi and Alan Vandomir, who had been added to the task force because of their expertise on serial rapists.

We greeted one another and took seats in the cramped room.

Mercer handed a sheaf of papers to Peterson. 'Maybe you can have some copies made. You got a junior man on this, let him go through and do record checks on some of the names. It's the list of people who came over on the water taxis and ferries this morning.'

Peterson laid the pile to the side of his desk and checked his watch. 'I'll get somebody on it tomorrow, so long as nothing of interest happened today. Could you tell if the feds were paying any attention to a search of Governors Island? They say anything?'

'The feds were on to it big time. Must have had fifty guys – excuse me, Alex – men and women. They started as a grid up at the highest point, Fort Jay, at daybreak. Then they spread out and claimed to be searching every building. Had all they could do to keep the civil warriors from storming each of the structures they opened up. There was still a crew of them there when I left.'

'Talk about the blind leading the blind – and the inept. If the feds found anything useful, they'd have to wait till a memo went up to the attorney general and back before they could get clearance to show it to us. They should have let us stay,' Mike said. 'And, Loo, Dickie Draper should be here any minute.'

'Did you get any rest?' I asked him.

'Yup. I delivered Kiernan to Central Booking and went home for the afternoon. You miss me?'

'I just want to make sure you don't lose your edge. It's those constant jabs in my back that keep my spine so straight. Anything new?'

'Nope. Unless you count the phone calls. The tip line is ringing off the hook.'

'Nothing useful?'

The cigarette dangled from Peterson's lips as he looked at a list on top of his in-box. 'Fifty-three calls and three confessions. One from a guy in San Francisco who says he time travels to kill women. So far, the fruitcakes are in the lead.'

Every one of these would be followed up in some fashion. It was rare that any of them proved to be of help, but the risk of ignoring them was too great for the department to take.

'I got a long shot for you, Loo,' Mercer said.

'Throw it on the table.'

'Tomorrow morning is the sentencing for Floyd Warren, the cold-case conviction that Alex got last week.'

'Yeah, I saw the clips on that.'

'I'm just thinking out loud – Alex, don't jump all over me, okay? Maybe we ask the judge to put that off a few days, so I can talk to Warren. Maybe make a deal to take some time off the top, if he cooperates.'

'Now what do you possibly hope to get from Floyd Warren?'

'It's just coming to me. Hear me out. All that talk yesterday about serial killers? They really are rare – compared to the guys Ned and Alan and I lock up every month. Here you got a serial rapist responsible for more than fifty crimes.'

'Exactly. He should never see daylight again.'

'But he never escalated to murder, did he?' Mercer continued. 'He had that opportunity, over and over again. Vulnerable women, alone in their homes or cars – some of them, like Kerry Hastings, who struggled with him. He was armed with a weapon every single time. And yet he never killed one of them. No evidence was ever found to connect him to a homicide.'

'Way to go,' Mike said. 'Ask him why. Work it from this end, Alex. What's the piece that's missing? What are we looking for in our guy that separates the thousands of violent sex offenders from the ones that move on to rape, and to torture, and then to murder their victims.'

'Why not let me go forward with the sentence? Talk to him an hour later,' I said. 'You know you won't get anything from him. He's so hard-boiled.'

Mercer leaned forward and put his hand on my knee. 'Alex, there's nothing to lose. Suppose he's got a nugget to give us? Even the smallest hint of a reason? That's more than we have right now. I'm not talking about letting him walk. The real deal is that the man's going to be in jail for the rest of his life. Change the numbers a bit, shave off a few months, give him the illusion of a bargain.'

I shook my head from side to side. 'You think I'm going to suggest that to Kerry, after all she's been through for thirty-five years?'

'I'll deal with Kerry. I bet she'll understand it better than you do.'

I looked from Ned to Alan, who spoke for both of them. 'Give it a crack. The old guy was a pro. Mercer's right.'

'If it's what you all think we should do, then I'm certainly not going to be stubborn.'

'Bottle that for me, will you, guys?' Mike said. 'I've known mules that were easier to coax than Coop.'

'I'm picking up Kerry at her hotel in the morning, bringing her down by taxi,' I said to Mercer. 'Will you meet us at my office? Talk to her?'

The door opened as Mercer told me that he would. Dickie Draper entered sideways and tried to wedge himself behind Mercer's chair.

'Sorry I'm late, Loo. Got the beep while I was at the movies. Wasn't a breeze in the house, so I took the wife. Air-conditioning and Sharon Stone. Hard to beat.'

'Hope you took a pass on the buttered popcorn,' Mike said.

'Figured you'd have this all cleaned up by now, Chapman.' Draper wiped the sweat off his jowls with his handkerchief.

'We've made a little progress, Dickie,' Peterson said. 'Tell him about your night at Ruffle Bar.'

'Ruffle Bar? You should have called me. Now you're back in my territory.'

Mike scratched his head. 'You knew about it?'

'Sure.'

'You didn't say anything? You didn't make the connection?'

'What connection?'

'Kiernan Dylan. Jimmy Dylan. Ruffle Bar. To your case, Dickie,' Mike said, snapping his fingers in the fat detective's face. 'Elise Huff.'

'Jimmy Dylan? The barkeep? The Brazen Head?' Dickie said, referring to the information he'd been given in the meeting at One Police Plaza yesterday. 'What's the clue I'm missing?'

There were puzzled expressions all around the room.

'Tell him what you did, Mike,' Peterson said again.

'So, late last night we get a call from the First. Mercer, Coop, and I headed to the bar around midnight.'

Draper laughed and interrupted Mike's narrative. 'Somebody pulling your leg? It's been deserted for years.'

'It's actually only been there a few months.' Mike's annoyance was growing. He ran his fingers through his hair and frowned at Dickie. 'Are we talking about the same thing?'

Dickie held out both hands, palms up, and slowly repeated the words, exaggerating the pronunciation. 'Did you hear me good, Chapman? You said Ruffle Bar, am I right?'

'Yeah.'

'You're asking me why I didn't tell you anything that I knew, and I'm just as stumped about why you didn't call me. You thinking someone was trying to get Huff's body to Ruffle Bar?' Dickie laughed again.

'She never got there.'

'Well, of course she never got there. But thanks a lot if you can prove any link to the case. Sorry, Loo, but maybe I should have stayed for the second feature. You call me in for this?'

The lieutenant took over. 'Jimmy Dylan's joint is uptown. Now he's opened one for his kid downtown. And to put this right in your territory, the Dylans own a house in Breezy Point. Dylan's son Kiernan – turns out he knew the Huff girl.'

'She was trying to hook up with him the night she went missing,' Mike said.

Draper paused for a moment. 'I know Breezy Point real good. I'm thinking—'

'Let's get a sample of sand from the beach at Breezy,' Peterson said. 'Compare it to the sample you got from the blanket Huff was wrapped in. There must be a geologist at the Museum of Natural History who'll do that.'

'The feebs have guys at Quantico who can analyze it – all the mineral deposits and stuff. They're good at that, Loo.'

'Screw the feebs, Dickie. We'll get it done right in New York.'

'I'm thinking what kind of screwball we got here,' Draper said. 'After all, maybe if he used a boat to get to Bannerman Island with that cadet's body – I mean, maybe he really was trying to take Elise Huff to Ruffle Bar. Maybe he's got a fishing boat on the water he was planning to use to get there. It's dead in the middle, between Breezy Point and where her body was found.'

'What's in the middle?' Mike asked.

'Who's on first, Chapman?' Draper said, holding his forefinger in the air and moving it back and forth in front of his eyes. 'Am I thinking too fast for you? I'm talking about Ruffle Bar.'

'Dickie, it's in Manhattan. We were there last night.'

'Then you oughta take a look out from Brooklyn with me, to Jamaica Bay.'

'What have you got to show us?'

'Ruffle Bar, Chapman. You can see it from the bridge that connects the Belt Parkway over to Breezy Point. It's an abandoned island, not far from where Elise Huff got dumped.'

32

'So you think Kiernan Dylan's Ruffles might actually be named for this spit of sand out in the bay?' Peterson asked. 'That would put the noose a little tighter around the kid's neck.'

'You'd have to have roots in the Rockaways – like the Dylans do – to even be aware the island existed, I guess,' Draper said. 'None of you knew what I was talking about, did you?'

'Sorry,' I said. 'After last night, we were all putting ourselves in a pub, not out on a sandbar. What is the place?'

'There was a time in the 1880s that Ruffle Bar was a resort, a little community with about fifty homes, a boat club, and a fancy hotel, the Skidmore House. Kids who lived there had to row back to the Rockaways to go to school every day, so I know it's doable. The locals did a thriving business in oystering.'

'What happened to it?'

'High tide, Alex. High tide and a couple of fierce hurricanes. There are a lot of little islets in the bay – Ruffle Bar, Hog Island, maybe a dozen others. What with erosion they all lost the battle with nature. By the 1940s, there were just some fishing shacks and squatters. Loo, you got a city map?'

Peterson stepped out and returned with a map that Draper unfolded and spread out on the desk. Directly south of Manhattan, just off the shore of Brooklyn, was Governors Island. The double red line of the Belt Parkway circled the borough, and shooting off it was a single artery – a highway and a bridge over the bay waters – to the Rockaways, the peninsula that ended in the village of Breezy Point.

Beyond that bridge, in the large body of water bounded by JFK airport on the east and Floyd Bennett Field on the west, were more than a dozen islands.

I ran my fingers over the unnamed pieces that looked like parts of a jigsaw puzzle floating on the blue background of the bay.

'Sandbars, like Ruffle. The bigger ones are a wildlife refuge now. They're all deserted. This one here,' he said, pointing to the one closest to Breezy Point, 'it's Ruffle Bar.'

'Give me a hypothetical,' Peterson said, using his cigarette stub to light another one. 'Say Kiernan Dylan meets up with Huff.'

'Where?' Mercer asked. 'What's your idea of where?'

'Who cares where? His joint, another joint. They wind up in his van. He comes on to her and she says no.'

'I hate to tell you, Loo,' Mike said, 'but Elise was the one chasing after his ass.'

'That doesn't mean they didn't fight,' I said. 'Maybe she wasn't interested in a sexual encounter in the back of the van. Maybe he wanted to do it one way and she wanted something else. Maybe her idea of hooking up was different than his.'

'And I've already got them at the beach,' Peterson said. 'Something goes wrong out there. She gets hurt and then he panics.'

Peterson was tracing his finger from the end of Breezy Point back to the highway and around the bay to where Huff's body was discovered in the marsh along the water's edge.

'None of this explains Amber Bristol,' Mercer said. 'Or Connie Wade. We've got to get this down and figure out our next move, before he makes his.'

'I never thought I'd see the day I had to apologize to Dickie Draper,' Mike said. 'I'll give you your props, my man. If I had known about the real Ruffle Bar when I was talking to Kiernan Dylan, I might have spooked him into a little bit more conversation.'

Mike picked up the receiver on Peterson's desk.

'Now what?' the lieutenant asked.

'Central Booking. If he hasn't been arraigned yet, maybe I can take another shot at the kid on his way out.'

Behind Mike's back, I held up my hands in frustration and mouthed an emphatic no to Peterson.

'He's got a lawyer now, Mike.' I let the lieutenant do the talking. I knew Mike would take it better from him.

'Yeah, but the only thing he's been charged with is the ABC violations. Maybe Shea will want to play with me. Just keeping my options open.'

Mike talked into the phone. 'Chapman. Manhattan North Homicide. Checking on a prisoner named Kiernan Dylan.'

He listened to the answer, thanked the officer, and replaced the receiver in the cradle. 'He's docketed and all. But the cut on the back of his head split open so they took him up to Bellevue to be stitched. He jumps to the front of the line when he gets back.'

'You still dumb enough to do turban jobs, Chapman?' Draper said. 'Smack a guy around and have him in bandages before he sees the judge?'

'His father did it for me.'

'You got no class.'

'Look,' Peterson said, 'Shea told you to call him, Mike. That's the way we have to work it. We'll take it step by step. The interview room is open now. Why don't you lay out all the stuff we've got and split up the assignments for the week. If I have to ask the commissioner to put a tail on Kiernan 24/7, I'll do that.'

We spent the next two hours in the small windowless room, trying to make sense of the facts we had and dividing tasks. I made a list of items that needed to be subpoenaed – documents to be prepared by me and signed by the foreman of the grand jury – that included cell phone and Internet records for Kiernan Dylan. It grew longer with every idea the detectives had.

'You ever do a sand analysis before?' Mercer asked. He would be the contact person for the museum's expert.

'Yeah,' Draper said. 'We got miles of beaches.'

'Does it take long? Is it reliable?'

'Piece of cake. The color varies, the texture can be smooth or grainy, sometimes it's got rock or coral or particular shells in it. You know how sometimes it sticks to your body, while in other places the sand brushes off real easy?' Draper went on to detail the distinctive features that would allow our witness to compare the samples.

'Spare me the thought of Dickie sitting on the beach with sand sticking to his crotch,' Mike whispered to me as he stood to stretch.

Shortly before nine, when we were wrapping up the session, Peterson came back to the room, bracing his back against the doorjamb.

'Score one for the troopers,' he said, taking a long drag on his cigarette. 'They just found Dylan's white van.'

'Where at?' Draper asked.

'Hudson Highlands State Park, not far from Bannerman Island. Ditched in the woods. License plate stripped off, but the VIN number's a match.'

'Damn it,' Mike said, cracking his pencil in half. 'I apologized to Draper, I might as well eat it all and apologize to you, too, Coop. I never should have jumped the gun collaring that kid.'

'Apology accepted,' I said. 'As soon as we get some forensics back from the lab, we'll make that call to Frankie Shea.'

'That'll be the state lab in Albany, Alex,' the lieutenant said. 'They get to do the workup on the van. Even the olive green blanket that was balled up on the floor behind the rear seat.'

The news that another blanket had been found in Dylan's vehicle galvanized all of us.

'Get a check on the arraignment, Mike,' Peterson went on. 'Tacchi, Vandomir – you guys okay to start to tail the kid from the courthouse tonight? I'll have relief for you in the morning and we'll keep on it till we see if there are prints or hair or whatever in the van.'

Mike had flipped open his cell and was talking to the officer at Central Booking again. 'Chapman here. That Dylan kid, how long till he sees the judge?'

He didn't like the answer he got. He pocketed the phone and repeated it to us.

'Walked out the door forty-five minutes ago. ROR'd,' Mike said. The judge had released him on his own recognizance, denying the prosecutor's request to set bail. 'Lock your doors, ladies. Mr. Dylan's on the loose.'

33

Mike drove me home on his way to his place, a cramped walkup apartment not far from my high-rise that he nicknamed 'the coffin.'

I went upstairs alone and used the deadbolt and chain to lock up, even though I had the luxury of two doormen on each of the three shifts. Every twist in this case seemed creepier and creepier, and the idea of a serial killer at large – spreading his victims' bodies beyond the city like a growing cancer – was chilling.

I slept fitfully, leaving home later than usual because there was no need to get Kerry Hastings to the courthouse much earlier than her ten o'clock appearance before Judge Lamont. Before I left my apartment to hail a cab, I called to tell her I was on my way and would wait right in front of her hotel.

Mercer was going to meet us in my office. He had put too much into this case not to see Floyd Warren through to his sentence. And now he would try to pitch Kerry on the idea of using her rapist to help us understand our killer's motive. It seemed senseless to me, especially as the evidence against Dylan seemed to be mounting.

I could see Kerry under the awning of her hotel when my taxi pulled up at nine fifteen, and I slid across behind the driver's seat to let her in.

'Good morning. I guess I don't have to ask about your weekend. The newspapers and television are full of it. I don't know how you do it, Alex. Doesn't it ever get to you, all this violence and pain?'

'Sure it does. But it's an awfully good feeling to be able to try to do something about it, try to put people's lives back together. Were you able to relax at all?'

'It's beginning to sink in now. I'm starting to feel like there *is* life after Floyd Warren – that we've turned the tables on him at last.'

I shifted in my seat and stared out the window as the driver went back to the FDR Drive for the ride downtown. Kerry Hastings wasn't a vindictive woman, but I didn't think she'd like the idea that Mercer was about to propose.

'Do I need to tell you what I'm going to say to Judge Lamont?'

'Only if you want to,' I said. Impact statements were a relatively new phenomenon, a result of the advocacy movement of the 1980s, which expanded the rights of crime victims. I didn't have to try to articulate what effect Kerry's night of terror had had on the rest of her life – she would address Lamont directly, expressing her own thoughts and emotions.

'I wrote it out. I'm sort of worried about breaking down.'

I smiled at her. 'This part is so much easier. You'll do fine.'

She handed me a copy of the words she intended to say and I skimmed it as we cruised down the highway. 'I ceased to be human during the rape,' she wrote, after detailing the facts. The thoughts she had during the occurrence of the crime were things she was never allowed to speak at either trial. 'I became prey to Floyd Warren, who attacked me like a rabid beast.'

'Too strong?'

The cab veered from side to side as a livery driver cut into our lane. 'Take it easy,' I said to the driver. 'We're not in a hurry, okay?'

'Is it too much?'

'It's great. If I'd been half as descriptive to the jury, the verdict would be overturned on appeal. People who don't understand these crimes need to hear this.'

The driver made the turn off the highway under the Brooklyn Bridge and began to wind through the streets of Chinatown that would bring him behind the courthouse, around to the DA's office at One Hogan Place.

We came to a full stop at the intersection of Baxter Street and Hogan. I waved at a couple of colleagues crossing in front of us. One of them spotted me through the open window and gave me a thumbs-up, shouting out, 'Nice win on that Warren case.'

The block was unusually short and narrow for the city. The avenues on either end of it were restricted to one-way traffic, but the only two doors on Hogan Place were the entrances to our office – the south end of the vast criminal courthouse that fronted on Centre Street – and the rear door of our satellite building across the way.

The driver stopped the cab as I directed, and I leaned forward to hand him the fare. Kerry unbuckled her seat belt and started to get out.

She had one foot on the pavement and the other still in the cab when we were rear-ended with enormous force. The taxi lurched forward and my head slammed against the partition. Kerry screamed as she fell out onto the ground and was dragged along for almost fifteen feet, hanging on to the door, as the driver's foot hit the gas instead of the brake.

34

Cops came running from every direction, in uniform and plain-clothes, throwing cardboard coffee cups and brown paper bags filled with doughnuts and bagels to the sidewalk as they dashed to Kerry Hastings's side. On any given day, hundreds of officers were scheduled to appear in the DA's office – to testify in old cases, to participate in trial prep of new matters, to transport prisoners or bring them to be arraigned, and to kibbitz with courthouse friends.

The cabdriver, sobbing, had stepped out and raised his hands over his head. He was mumbling some kind of prayer in an unintelligible dialect.

'It's fine,' I told him. 'It's just an accident.'

I unbuckled my belt and got out on my side to check on Kerry, who'd been surrounded by detectives, two of whom were squatting, reassuring her and checking her vital signs. Before I could get around the tail of the cab, I realized that several cops had set out to chase after the occupants of the car that had smashed into us.

Their guns were drawn and they were yelling at two young men and one woman to stop. On the asphalt park behind the office, scores of Asian children in a summer school gym class scattered as the cops ran among them and dashed between their kickballs.

I got to my knees beside Kerry. The men who were comforting her recognized me and moved back.

'I'll be fine,' she said, closing her eyes as she winced in pain. 'I've been through worse.'

'We got a bus on the way, Miss Cooper,' one of the men said to me. 'I just called for an ambulance.'

There was blood all over Kerry's arm, and a large stain growing on the fringes of her pants leg, which had ripped apart from her thigh down to her ankle. She tried to put her scraped hands down on the ground to boost herself up.

'Don't try to move, miss. Something may be broken.'

She looked up at the cop. 'I think it's just a lot of cuts and bruises. I didn't let go of the door because I was afraid I'd wind up under the wheels.'

'I'll wait with her,' I said. 'Would you go into the lobby and tell the security officer to call my secretary? Ask her to send Mercer Wallace down here, please.'

A crowd had gathered along the length of the block – prosecutors, defense attorneys, civilian witnesses, support staff. I could see that the front end of the old green Plymouth that had hit us was completely crumpled, and beyond the car, I could hear the commotion of all the onlookers watching the chase.

I felt a strong hand on my shoulder, and then a familiar voice spoke to me. 'I never thought I'd be offering myself as a witness for the prosecution, Alex. The kid that hit you must have been going forty miles an hour. How's your head?'

Justin Feldman was one of the best lawyers in New York. We had crossed swords occasionally, but most of his work was in the federal courthouse one block away, with corporate clients who relied on his great expertise in securities litigation.

'I'm fine, Justin. Lucky I was belted in. That car came out of nowhere.'

'Actually, it didn't,' he said, pointing to the empty parking space at the corner of the street, where our cabbie had made the turn into the block. 'I was on my way down Baxter Street, coming from federal court. Those kids picked a pretty dumb place to pull a stunt like this, but your cab passed by, made a full stop right in front of them – it would have been hard to miss you – when the driver floored it and crashed right into you.'

It sounded like sirens were close by. Within seconds, an ambulance pulled in the wrong way, stopping nose to nose against the cab.

The attendants jogged over to Kerry's side as I stood up and we all moved back so they could make an initial determination about her condition.

Mercer came through the revolving door of the building and greeted Justin and me. 'What's happening?'

'An accident. They're checking Kerry out now.'

'She's being generous,' Justin said, as Mercer got close to the EMTs so that Kerry could see he was there. She smiled when he caught her eye.

A cheer went up from the crowd. The five or six cops who had taken off after the occupants of the car were coming back in our direction. Two of them had someone by the arm. I could see only the dark hair – heads bowed – of the male and female who were being pulled along by the officers.

The courthouse crowd, including defendants on their way to calendar dates and hearings, was boisterous, and a handful of uniformed court officers were trying to clear a path for the cops.

I turned back to Kerry. The medics were helping her to her feet, telling Mercer that it didn't appear anything was broken.

'We're going to take you over to the hospital, okay?' one of them asked her. 'Let the docs clean you up, maybe give you a tetanus shot in case any of these scrapes came from the metal on the cab.'

'I'll come for the ride,' I said. 'I'd like to keep her company.'

Mercer took Kerry's hand. 'I've got her. You get to work.'

'What's everyone shouting about?' Kerry asked. 'Haven't they ever seen an accident before?'

'The driver fled the scene,' Mercer said. 'It's not only stupid, it's against the law.'

'Please don't make me testify at another trial,' Kerry said, looking at me as she started to limp toward the ambulance. 'And don't start that sentencing till we get back here. I want the judge to listen to me.'

Justin Feldman steered my elbow toward the entrance as Kerry and Mercer walked away. 'Why don't you get out of this crush? Go on up to your office,' he said, his quiet elegance a sharp contrast to the rowdiness of the spectators lingering on Hogan Place.

I climbed the three steps and stopped to look back.

A heavyset black teenager wrapped in a layered chain collar of bling with matching gold caps on his front teeth called out to the young woman who was being marched to the building between two cops. 'Hey, shortie! I'll see your ass after court. I'll teach you how to run, mama! I'll teach you good.'

Half of the onlookers cheered again, while the girl shouted a stream of obscenities at him in Spanish.

Her cohort was a few paces behind her, being pulled along by two other plainclothes officers. I was about to push the revolving door to go inside, when he picked up his head – clearly angered by the situation and the fact that she was rising to the bait – to tell her to keep her mouth shut.

'*Callate la boca, puta!*'

We locked eyes and a wave of nausea bubbled in my stomach. The young man threw his head back and laughed, exposing the tattoo on his neck.

He was a Latin Prince, one of the leaders who had disrupted the courtroom during Kerry Hastings's trial.

35

I was sitting at my desk at one o'clock that afternoon when Mercer came back from the hospital. Laura had instructions not to let anyone else in to see me after I returned from Judge Lamont's chambers, having adjourned Floyd Warren's sentencing till the next day.

'What's the matter, Alex? Does your head hurt?' Mercer closed the door behind him and walked to my desk, opening a bag with sandwiches and coffee for each of us.

I wasn't even aware that I was rubbing a small knot on my temple, where it had smacked against the cab's partition. 'I can't remember whether there was a time before last week when my head *didn't* ache. How's Kerry?'

'She's going to give new meaning to the colors black and blue by the time her bruises are in full bloom tonight. Everything checked out fine, but she's hurting. I took her back to the hotel. I assume you postponed the case?'

'Yes. No problem, of course.'

'Well, Kerry just wants to get on a plane and go back home.'

'I don't blame her. Did you bring up the subject of talking to Warren?'

'I did. She's okay with it, Alex. Anything that might prevent someone else from becoming a victim. He's sixty-one years old, and Lamont is threatening to hit him with the full fifty. Half of that will be fine, if he gives us anything.'

'It's not the time behind bars. It's the symbolism. It's a statement on behalf of what he took from Kerry's life and all the other women who were attacked.'

'Call Gene Grassley now,' Mercer said. 'Let's give this a go.'

He was unwrapping the foil on our sandwiches when Laura buzzed me on the intercom. 'Ryan Blackmer's here, Alex. It's about this morning's accident. The Latin Prince from court last week who crashed into your cab.'

'Let him in.'

Ryan was one of my favorite colleagues, smart and creative and always willing to go the full nine yards with any cop who brought him an interesting case.

'Hey, Mercer. Alex. I didn't know you were at the vortex of a Dominican jihad. I always figured you for getting trampled to death at a sample sale of designer dresses. This rocks.'

'And what's "this"?'

'*Tu amigo* Antonio Lucido, *carida*. I'm supervising in ECAB today,' Ryan said, referring to the intake section through which every arrest passed for processing – the early case assessment bureau. 'Laura told me this guy and his buddies were stalking you in court last week. I went up to Lamont to get a statement from him before coming here.'

'He was in the car, this Lucido kid?' Mercer asked. I had left a message on his cell shortly after I came upstairs, telling him about the involvement of the Latin Princes in the crash.

'Yeah. The guys brought him in for leaving the scene. He was in the passenger seat, according to one of the cops who made the grab.'

'Is he talking?'

'You know Alex likes the strong, silent type. Not a word. Turns out the car is stolen, too. Taken out of long-term parking at Newark Airport just after midnight, so that adds a little heat to the charges.'

'Will you keep this yourself?' I asked.

'Absolutely. And then there's the matter of the gun under the front seat. Fully loaded semiautomatic.'

'Damn,' Mercer said. 'You got raps back on him yet?'

'Waiting on that now. You want to tell me what happened?'

'I didn't see anything. I really didn't,' I said. 'If that street was a bit wider so the Plymouth could have gotten around us, I would have thought we'd been rear-ended accidentally and they just ran off scared.'

But I knew it was no coincidence that Posano's posse had been waiting for me outside my office with a loaded gun.

'We've got a lot of witnesses, Alex.'

'Add Justin Feldman to the list. He thinks maybe they could have seen me inside the cab, through the open window.'

There was a sharp rap on the door and before I could ask who was there, Mike opened it and came in. 'You're like a frigging heat-seeking missile, Blondie. What is it with you?'

I frowned as I glanced at Mercer.

'I had to call him, Alex.'

'You didn't take me away from anything important. Yes, the troopers found human hair in the back of Dylan's van. Yes, they found his fingerprints – as well as prints that don't match his. Yes, they've swabbed it for DNA. Be patient and we'll have comparisons in the next forty-eight. And – oh, yeah, you'll like this one 'cause it was your idea. They got results back from the swabs of the inside of the handcuffs they found on Saturday. Turns out they were used on both Amber Bristol and Elise Huff. Like you said, link the cases by the vics if you can't do it by the perp. Otherwise, I had nothing to do today but worry about you.'

'I thought you were going with Dickie Draper, out to see what the story is on Ruffle Bar. The real one.'

'Turns out Special Ops uses that place once a month for drills. Peterson asked their CO to send men to look it over. They keep a chopper on standby.'

'What do they use the island for?' I asked. I knew that Special Ops was a high-powered training division of the NYPD, made up of members of the Harbor, Aviation, and Emergency Services units.

'They stage disasters, Coop, so they can prepare for the response. Terrorist attacks, plane crashes, boat accidents. The bodies – well, the mannequins – wind up on Ruffle Bar, and Special Ops has to swim in or fly in to triage the victims. If there's anything of interest on that sandbar – including a sample of the sand – they'll get it for us. What's new, Ryan?'

Ryan and Mike shook hands, and Mike listened to details of the morning's arrest.

'You really don't need to be here,' I said. 'Who's tailing Kiernan Dylan?'

'It's tough to tail a guy when you don't know where he is.'

'Didn't he go home after he got out of court last night?'

Mike put both hands in his pants pockets and looked down at the floor. 'Peterson's got somebody sitting on his apartment, his father's place, the house at Breezy Point. No sign of him anywhere.'

'How about the bar?'

'Some jerk,' Mike said, making the sign of the cross on his chest, 'was stupid enough to want to shut that place down. Nobody home.'

'Let me get back downstairs,' Ryan said. 'I just wanted to

know if you saw anything, heard anything. Sounds like you didn't. I'll draw this up with the cops who witnessed it. No injuries to you, right? Just your victim?'

'Exactly. You think you can keep him in?'

'Shouldn't be difficult. Throw in a reckless assault, too. Got myself a real case in the middle of the off-season. I can't imagine Antonio got to this level in the Latin Princes without a few visits to the can. If we don't have enough to hold him on this, I'm sure he's got a rap sheet that will help. I'll let you know as soon as it comes back.'

'Any idea who the driver was?' Mercer asked.

'Not yet. And Senor Lucido isn't saying nada. The car's being towed. They'll actually dust it for prints. Helps to have a victim with juice, Ms. Cooper.'

'Who's the girl?'

Ryan looked at the arrest papers folded in his rear pocket. 'She's been playing games with us. No ID on her, so we're waiting on her prints, too. The first thing she told the cops was that her name is Clarita Munoz. Then about five minutes later she changed it to Clarita Cruz. Then she clammed up completely. Had a pocket-size canister of Mace in her jeans. Love to know where she was going with that.'

'Thanks, Ryan. When you find out, let me know,' I said, as he walked out of the room. 'See you later.'

'Why does that name sound familiar to me?' Mercer asked.

Mike was at my desk, helping himself to half of my turkey sandwich. 'Probably because you've been watching too much Tele-mundo, my pal.'

Mercer called out to Laura, who came to the door. 'Help me with this. You got Alex's book there?'

Laura turned to her desk and picked up my red appointment diary. 'Sure.'

'What's the name of the girl who was scheduled to come in at eleven today? Alex and I were standing right next to you while you were on the phone with Ed, in Witness Aid, making the date when we came down from court last Thursday.'

Laura found the entry. 'Clarita Munoz.'

I was rubbing my forehead again but nothing registered.

Mike was chewing while he puzzled this out. 'You were supposed to meet with this girl today? And she's sitting in a car, waiting for you to show up at the building, with a can of Mace, a loaded gun, and two Latin Princes? *Que pasa*, Coop?'

'They couldn't possibly have known I was coming to work in a cab. That I'd be squaring the block from Baxter Street,' I said. 'That's not my usual route.'

Mercer was pacing the room. 'Like everyone says, it's a stupid place to stage an accident. So suppose that crash was just a spur-of-the-moment idea. The guys were there to accompany Clarita, who had an actual appointment to walk right in this door. Set her up for whatever she was going to do and be her getaway car – if she was getting anywhere. The cab pulled up, they see your platinum head in the window, and the driver makes a command decision, on the spot, to lock fenders. Just to shake you up, like they were doing last week.'

'Okay, so they certainly weren't trying to kill me,' I said, wanting to believe that. 'Not inside One Hogan Place.'

'But if Clarita is Posano's shortie, maybe she's trying to make her bones with him. Imagine she gets up here – right to the main floor of Battaglia's center of power – and sprays you with Mace. How much more in your face does it get?' Mercer said. 'Imagine her status when word gets up to state prison. Meantime, she hasn't caused you any serious injury. She'd hardly get more than a slap on the wrist.'

'I like your thinking, Detective,' Mike said.

'And you need to call Rodman's Neck,' he went on, wagging a finger at Mike. 'See what happened to those cartridges they were going to analyze from Friday morning's shooting.'

'The range?' Mike put down the sandwich and brushed the

crumbs off his hands. 'What's this babe got to do with that?'

'You and Alex didn't think anyone knew you were going to be at the range on Friday morning. Didn't think that shooting had anything to do with her, right?' Mercer said. 'Well, when Laura was on the phone with Ed she was talking him through Alex's schedule.'

Laura's hand flew up to cover her mouth.

'I heard her tell Ed that she was checking Alex's availability, that if the jury came back as fast as expected, she'd be at the police range the next morning.'

Laura removed her hand and nodded. 'Maybe she heard me. Or Ed said it out loud. I know I could understand the girl perfectly well when I asked Ed to get me her name. She didn't wait for him to repeat my question. She said she was Clarita Munoz. I'd guess she could hear me just as well as I could hear her.'

36

'There's a lawyer named Frankie Shea on line one,' Laura said about an hour later, after I had gotten Gene Grassley's permission for Mercer to talk to Floyd Warren and met with Judge Lamont to tell him about Antonio Lucido and Clarita Munoz.

I picked up the receiver, not expecting the harangue that he began to unload.

'Slow down, Mr. Shea. I don't know what you're talking about.'

'You told the press you were going into Ruffles the other night? That sure as hell changes the complexion of any information you got out of my client.'

'What? There was no press involved. Neither Chapman nor I went in there expecting to make an arrest.'

'So much for your credibility, Ms. Cooper. You suckered my

client right into a photo op just to top off the five o'clock news conference about the serial killer.'

'Listen to me, Shea. Nobody called the media. Nobody set Dylan up.'

'You know how my client's family is being harassed today? They can't open the door of their apartment, his father can't get into his business, his brothers—'

'Why? What's that got to do with us?'

'The newspapers. He's all over the newspapers.'

I covered the mouthpiece and asked Mercer to get the papers off Laura's desk. 'I haven't seen them yet. But I swear I haven't even had a chance to tell the public relations team what happened. Battaglia's out of the country and I'm waiting to update them now, for the first time. You have my word that the release couldn't have come from our end.'

'You did a perp walk in front of Ruffles. Admit it, okay? Kiernan's photo, his face – it's splattered all over the place.'

Mercer opened both tabloids to the pages with the grainy black-and-white photograph of Kiernan Dylan, flanked by Mercer and Mike, frozen under the sign that said Ruffles Bar.

'I don't have much else of value in this business except my word, Mr. Shea,' I said. 'I'm looking at the picture right now. It was actually taken by a friend of your client's, with a cell phone.'

'Right. And it just found its way into the papers.'

'The sad truth is that there are a lot of people out to make a buck who sell photos, information, evidence – all of that – to whatever media outlet will buy it. They do it without a second thought of giving it to the police. Every local news broadcast ends with some version of "If you see news happening, call us." It's a nightmare for law enforcement that there are people who would rather score the money than make themselves available as witnesses.'

Shea didn't speak.

'Last year, two weeks after I finished a murder trial, one of the perp's friends sold a videotape he'd made of my defendant telling jokes about how he'd killed the victim. He was high on coke and entertaining his buddies at a party. We never knew the tape existed, but a reality TV show bought it for twenty-five grand. So don't point your finger at me, Mr. Shea. Ask Kiernan who the schmuck with the camera was.'

'Well, your pal Chapman seems to have gone out of his way to make this as unpleasant as he can for the Dylans.'

'You want to sit down with us, talk about cooperating?'

'Now that you've driven Kiernan under a rock? Who knows when he'll come out.'

'Where is your client, Mr. Shea?' There was no harm in asking.

'He's got a court date, Ms. Cooper. He'll be there. In the meantime, you might as well call off your dogs.'

Mike took one of the newspapers from my desk to look at the photograph. It had been blown up to fill a quarter of a page buried pretty far back in the tabloid, opposite one of the gossip columns. But the text made no connection to the serial killer cases. It appeared under the headline RUFFLED FEATHERS, with a two-line description of the police, flanked by the unsmiling bouncers, taking Kiernan Dylan out of the bar – a 'popular nightspot for hot chicks in cool plumage' – which was being closed for underage beverage service. It only made news at all because of the history Jimmy Dylan had had over the years at the Brazen Head.

'Surprised my mother didn't call yet,' Mike said, examining his own image before closing the paper and dropping it on my desk. 'Tell me I need a haircut.'

'Will you check with Peterson?' I asked. 'Am I still invited to tonight's briefing? I assume we'll be going over some of the stuff the troopers found in the van.'

'I spoke to him this morning. You're good to go until some other agency boots you out. Has Battaglia tried driving this train from London yet? How long's he supposed to be away?'

'The family's on vacation until Labor Day. Don't worry, he's left messages for me three times today and I'm to keep Tim Spindlis informed of every detail,' I said. 'I stopped in to see him on my way down from Lamont. I asked if Marisa, Catherine, and Nan could work with us on the case.'

Spindlis was the chief assistant district attorney, in charge of the office during Battaglia's absence, and he would be responsible for oversight of the investigation while the boss was away. My three senior lawyers had proven themselves over and over, and I was certain Spindlis would have no objections to bringing them into the case.

'You're in luck. He left Spineless in charge? That guy couldn't make an important decision to save his life.'

'I'd rather deal with a jellyfish than have my usual head butting with Pat McKinney.' Spindlis was the yes man to Battaglia's strong personality, which is why I often skirted him and went straight to the district attorney with matters of great importance. To those on the staff below his position, Spindlis procrastinated endlessly and never had the backbone to take a forceful stance in support of the young lawyers in the office.

McKinney, on the other hand, was head of the trial division and looked to cut my legs out from under me every chance he could.

'He's on vacation, too?'

'For the moment. But he's got no life, with his girlfriend back in Texas and his wife not on speaking terms with him at the moment. It's a break for all of us that he's still away. No chance to second-guess my every move or sabotage it. The only person he detests more than me is you, Mike. Everybody wants a piece of this case. That's why I had Laura hold all my calls this morning. The less interference the better.'

'Is there a time set for you to conversate with Floyd Warren?' Mike asked Mercer.

'Alex said that Gene Grassley asked for four o'clock, when he finishes the hearing he's got in front of Judge Wetzel.'

The three of us discussed the plan for Mercer's interrogation of Warren, and I took notes on the issues they raised.

Laura stuck her head in again and told me Ned Tacchi was on the phone.

I took the call. 'What's up? You find Kiernan Dylan?'

'Not happening. Peterson's got me on the tip line in the meantime. You won't believe the crap that comes in on this thing. But I got a lady who just called. I think you better talk to her. She's completely freaked out.'

'Is she making sense?'

'Not to me. But you guys know the case. Besides that, she only wants to talk to a lawyer.'

I grabbed a pen. 'What's her name?'

'She wouldn't give it to me. She just kept saying she knows who the killer is. It's a Jersey number, 201 area code.'

I took down the other digits. 'So why'd you single this call out? Why do you think it's any more worth pursuing than all the others?'

'Hey, we're getting back to every damn one of these dial-ins, call by call. But this woman's talking about the picture in the newspapers today. The one of the Dylan kid,' Ned said. 'I saw it this morning, Alex. It doesn't even mention the murders. She put that together herself.'

'I'll do it right now. Mike and Mercer are with me.'

I flopped into my chair, threw back my head, and exhaled loudly, then reached for the newspaper so that I had the photo in front of me when I spoke to the woman.

'Get ready for the next wild goose chase,' I said. 'Ned's got me calling someone from the tips hotline.'

'What's the reward money for information up to?' Mike asked.

'Twenty-five grand if it leads to the arrest,' Mercer said.

'The higher it goes, the more nuts come out of the woodwork. Make like you're the Home Shopping Network, Coop. Chat her up nice and offer her two front row seats at the trial.'

I dialed the number, and a woman answered on the second ring. 'Hello?'

'Hello. I'm Alexandra Cooper. I'm a prosecutor in the Manhattan District Attorney's Office. Detective Tacchi gave me your number and asked me to call.'

There was no response.

'Hello? Can you hear me? I'm working with the police on the investigation of the murders of—'

The conversation ended abruptly as the woman hung up the phone.

'She disconnected me.' I hung up, too, and exhaled again.

'Uneasy lies the head that wears the tiara, Coop. Give it a rest.'

'We'll check out that number in the reverse directory,' Mercer said.

Laura buzzed me. 'The switchboard has a caller on the main line. Wants to put it through. Says she was just talking to you.'

I picked up the receiver again. 'Hello, this is Alex Cooper.'

'I'm sorry I cut you off, Ms. Cooper. I wanted to make sure you were really calling from the DA's office. I wanted to be certain you are who you claim to be. I called information and got the number. I know it sounds rude, but I'm – well – I'm terribly nervous.'

'I understand completely,' I said. The woman's voice was soft and she spoke with some hesitation. There was no point in asking her name until she was ready to identify herself.

'I'm calling from my home, Ms. Cooper. I suppose you can figure that out pretty quickly yourselves, with all your sophisticated surveillance information. I had to leave my office, you see. This call could cost me my job.'

'Is that what you're nervous about?'

She paused for fifteen seconds. 'That, of course. But I'm also terrified of becoming a target. A target of the killer.'

'Is there something we can do right now – I've got two detectives here with me – something to make you feel safe?'

'I told the man who answered the hotline that I wanted to speak to a lawyer.'

'Yes, and I'm a lawyer.'

'Obviously. But you can't be *my* lawyer, can you? I may lose my livelihood if – if the fact of this phone call gets out.'

'I have no reason to betray your confidence, Miss—?'

'Not now, maybe. But I know the system, Ms. Cooper. I know I'm putting myself in the eye of the storm. I know you'll have to use me at some point in the court proceedings. I need some legal guidance about privilege.'

I rolled my eyes at Mike and Mercer. My caller was intelligent, but she was clearly conflicted about talking with me and I couldn't make a judgment about her credibility.

'If you need to talk to a legal adviser before you tell us what you know, then I would urge you to do that as quickly as possible. But if your personal safety is your concern as well, I just want you to understand the need for speed. That's help we can give you.'

Again, silence.

'If you're assuming that Kiernan Dylan is still in custody because the photograph you saw – the one that you called the hotline about – showed him being taken away by police, I just want you to know that he was released by the court.' I hesitated before I told her what I hoped would be the tipping point to put herself in our care. 'We have no idea where Dylan is today, but he's not been seen anywhere in the city.'

'I don't give a damn where he is, Ms. Cooper.'

I took my pen and drew a large X through the caller's phone number. This was turning out to be a waste of my time.

'Well, you have my office number, and of course the hotline that you first called, if there's something you want to get back to us about. Thank you—'

'Would your detectives come to my house, Ms. Cooper? I live in New Jersey, in Harrison. It's not far from Newark.'

'For what reason, ma'am? Come to your house to protect you, is that what you mean? I'm sure we could arrange for the local police to do that if it's necessary.'

'I mean that I can't talk at my office. I've brought some of the records home with me, but I couldn't take everything. You need to see them, to understand that this should never have happened.'

I tried to remain patient but the woman's flat affect and her ability to draw me back in when I thought the conversation had ended were annoying me.

'I don't know what records you're talking about, and I don't know where you work. When you think you can help us, I trust you'll call again. Now I've got to hang up and—'

'I work at the Department of Corrections, in New Jersey. In Kearny, at the Northern Regional Unit. Do you know what that is?'

The woman had my complete attention now. 'I do. Yes, I do. It's the maximum security psychiatric center, isn't it? Where the sexual predators are held. Won't you tell me, please, what this has to do with Kiernan Dylan?'

I knew that Dylan had no criminal record. What could possibly connect him to one of the most violent collection of criminals in the country?

'Nothing at all, Ms. Cooper. I told you that.'

'But you called the police because of the photograph in today's newspapers, didn't you?'

'I called because the man – see the black man standing on the far right, over the detective's shoulder? He's Troy Rasheed, a prisoner here for more than twenty years. He was released from this facility six weeks ago, despite my testimony at his hearing,' the woman said, clearing her throat before she spoke again. 'I don't know what he's doing in that photograph, but you want to talk to that guy. My name is Nelly Kallin. I supervise the unit at Kearny.'

I stared at the face in the photograph. The man Kallin was talking about was standing on the top step as the three of us walked out of Ruffles. We paid him no attention, and left him behind to deal with the crowd when we took the Dylan kid away. He was tall and powerfully built, with a shaved head and tattoos up and down his well-muscled arms.

'Mr. Rasheed was working at that bar,' I said. 'He's a bouncer.'

'He's a convicted predator, Ms. Cooper. He raped women – three that he got caught for and dozens more the prosecution couldn't prove, back in the days before DNA. Rasheed tortured them all, too,' Kallin said. 'It's what he's good at. It's what he likes to do.'

37

'You can't work in a licensed bar if you're a convicted felon,' I said, as Mike turned the corner onto the street where Nelly Kallin lived. The ride from my office, through the Holland Tunnel and down the Jersey Turnpike, had taken less than forty minutes.

'Yeah, Coop. And jail rehabilitates perverts. What kind of fairyland are you living in? Mercer, you see any numbers?'

Neat-looking yellow brick houses stood side by side, separated from each other by narrow garages and rows of hedges, some clipped and others overgrown.

'Should be the third one on the right.'

While Mike drove, Mercer and I had worked our phones, alerting Peterson and Spindlis about the call, getting a team poised to move if Kallin's information was legitimate.

'I mean that it's illegal to hire a felon to work in a place that serves booze.'

'I know, I know. You think creeps like the Dylans care about that? And don't bother saying that if I hadn't insisted on shutting the bar down Saturday night, you'd be able to get the names of all the employees,' Mike said, turning off the engine.

I called the listed number for Ruffles during the drive, but no one answered the phone. I left an urgent message at Frank Shea's office and hoped that he would get back to me sooner rather than later.

'We don't know if this guy gave a phony name when he applied for the job,' Mercer said, trying – as always – to make peace between Mike and me. 'Don't know if the Dylans did a proper record check on him. Don't know if he was being paid off the books. You want to hire a bouncer for a rowdy bar, wouldn't you think you're pretty much looking for a thug? Stay cool, Alex. We'll find him.'

As the three of us started up the flagstone path, the front door of the house opened. 'You're in the right place. I'm Nelly Kallin.'

She was in her midsixties, I guessed, short and heavyset, with frizzy gray hair that was cropped just below her ears. She was wearing a lightweight pants suit with a shapeless jacket that was meant to mask the extra weight around her solid middle.

'Thank you for calling,' I said. 'We're racing against the clock with this case, hoping we can identify the killer and stop him before he hits again. Any help you can give us will be critical.'

Kallin ushered us through the living room into a well-furbished kitchen with a large table on which she had spread out the files she had taken home from her office.

'Why don't you sit down?' she said, pulling out one of the chairs for herself. 'I'll give you whatever I can.'

She had the newspaper clipping in the middle of the table and turned it around so that Mercer and Mike, sitting opposite her, could look at it again. Then she opened a manila folder and removed a handful of photographs.

'Here's Troy Rasheed,' Kallin said. 'This was his release picture, taken in early July.'

I leaned in to look at the 8 × 10 color photo of Rasheed dressed in his orange prison jumpsuit and compared it with the man in the grainy black-and-white newsprint. A long, thick scar ran from the lower side of his left cheek down his neck like a tiny railroad track, disappearing into his collar. There was no question that he was one of the bouncers manning the door at Ruffles on Saturday night.

'Are you his shrink?' Mike asked.

'He wouldn't be on the street if I were. No, Mr. Chapman. I'm on the administrative end,' Kallin said. 'I've been fascinated by psychiatry all my life. Had my heart set on going to med school, but in those days it wasn't easy for women to be admitted.'

That was true of the law as well, as I knew from the handful of prosecutors who had pioneered the work I did today.

'So I settled for a master's in behavioral psychology, and a PhD in Prison Administration. I've been in the department almost thirty years.' She spread an array of Rasheed's older photographs across the table, like a deck of playing cards.

'But you must know where he is now, don't you? You have an address for him?' Mercer asked. 'So we can get our guys looking for him – to question him – while you fill us in.'

'You said you were in the Special Victims Unit right?

'Yes.'

Kallin reached behind her on the kitchen counter for a pack of Marlboros and lighted a cigarette. 'Then you ought to know the problem. Troy had to register as a sex offender, of course. He did, as soon as he was cut loose from Kearny. He got himself an apartment in Jersey City.'

She rearranged the manila folders and pulled out the one that had his registry information. 'Showed up the first two weeks, which endeared him to the local cops and got them off his back. But like in every other state, the overload these monitoring units carry is appalling. They scheduled his next appointment for mid-August, and Troy failed to keep the date.'

'Has anybody checked the Jersey City address?' Mercer asked.

'Sure they did. He was out of there by August first, Detective. You know how it goes. I guess they haven't had any cases on this side of the Hudson that fit his m.o., so his file goes in the hopper with all the other flimflam artists. Troy Rasheed has no known address, like thousands of other sex offenders who've been released. Most of them are homeless. I can promise you that no one in the system will be able to tell you where he is today.'

One of the most shocking problems with the sex offender registration laws that had been passed in the 1990s was the lack of resources in every state to track the dangerous felons who had completed their prison sentences – and the number of these predators who were homeless.

'Tell us about him,' Mike said. 'Every detail that might be useful. Tell us why you think he's capable of this – that it isn't just a coincidence that Rasheed's working at the bar that one of the victims wanted to visit.'

Among the details Commissioner Scully had held back from the media was the connection between Amber Bristol and the Dylan family. Nelly Kallin was only going on the fact that the story she read had mentioned Elise Huff's downtown bar-hopping.

Like a three-card monte dealer, Kallin put her forefinger on an old mug shot – upside down to her – and swept it smoothly around the table so each of us could look at it. 'Troy Rasheed. Age twenty-two.'

The dark-skinned, rail-thin young man sneered at the camera. He was wearing a T-shirt and tight jeans, with close-cropped black hair that was shaved on the sides of his head.

'How long ago was that?' I asked.

'He's forty-six now.'

'And in prison all this time?'

'Every minute of it,' she said, targeting another photo with her finger and moving it in a circle to display for us. 'Bulking up, working out, lifting weights. We build better perps in the jail yard, Ms. Cooper. We give them sharper tools for another shot at their victims when they leave us. Troy earned himself the *mas macho* reputation when he survived a throat slashing by some Hoboken gang members he dissed in the cafeteria one day. Spent a long time decorating his remade body with prison art. He must have been dreaming for decades about the day his pumped-up persona would have a brand-new chance to torment another woman.'

The lean face and wiry body of the young Troy Rasheed had aged into a solid, hardened adult. His arms and chest reflected years of bodybuilding, and some of the sequential photographs, showing him in short-sleeved prison garb, recorded the annual addition of tattoos above his wrist and on the side of his neck, where they highlighted his thick scar.

I lifted two of the pictures to study the markings. 'Not the usual, are they?'

Most jails had strict rules against inmates tattooing one another. But with homemade tattoo guns, the artists who violated the prohibitions were among the most popular prisoners. The standard swastikas, guns, and spider webs often masked gang affiliation symbols, but Troy's arms were lined with two-inch-high initials elaborately drawn in a flourish of script letters.

'His victims' names, Ms. Cooper. The big ones on his biceps are the women he was convicted of raping. So he'd never forget them, he said. The smaller ones seem to be the vics for whom he didn't get nailed.' Nelly Kallin stood up to crush her cigarette. 'I'm only sorry you can't see the serpents.'

'Serpents?' I was thinking of the body of Connie Wade and the many snakes that inhabited desolate Bannerman Island.

'He's got several on his chest. And one large constrictor that's wrapped around his penis. That made Troy a hero to most of the creeps with rap sheets like his. I only hope to God it was as painful for him to get it as I like to think it was.'

'Tattoos are the new T-shirts,' Mike said.

'What?'

'When we were kids, Coop, people went someplace they bought postcards. Collected 'em or sent 'em to relatives to show where they'd been. Then ten, fifteen years ago, you take a trip and suddenly big fat Middle America comes home with their vacation hot spots plastered across their chests instead of on a picture postcard. "Virginia Is for Lovers." "Bubba's BBQ." "Stonehenge Rocks." Your friends – excuse me – it's St. Bart's and Aspen and those tasteful little logos that scream some designer spa you have to go to in order to recognize the secret symbol. Now, you been somewhere, done something, raped somebody – just friggin' engrave it on your body.'

'That's Troy, Detective. He wears his life story.'

'How come you know so much about his tattoos?'

'Part of my business. Like you say, every time one of these inmates defies our orders, it's to make a point. His T-shirt of the moment. And it's my job to know what that point is – what gang, what faction, what message, what hate group. They're all documented by the department, whenever these guys have a physical.'

'Twenty-two. That was the age of his first arrest?' Mike asked.

'No, sir,' Kallin said, leaning against her kitchen sink. 'Started with a juvenile record. Nothing remarkable. Mostly burglaries and thefts. Arson, too. Didn't appear to move into sexual abuse until he was about seventeen, from what anyone could tell. Beat the first couple of cases but then was convicted for a series of rapes that occurred in the north Jersey suburbs, near the Palisades.'

'You mentioned DNA on the phone,' I said. 'But this conviction was before DNA was being used in the courts. Before 1989.'

'Yes, Troy was caught by fingerprint identification and then line-up IDs. Abducted each of the women after they parked their cars on their way into their apartments. Forced them into his van, raped them, then dumped them out – alive, in those days – in deserted places along the highway. There were prints at the last scene, on the victim's leather handbag. By the time his final appeal was perfected seven years later, the defense attorney made an ill-advised motion to have the DNA analyzed. It all matched.'

'What do you know about his victims?'

'Whatever is in the presentence reports,' Kallin said, returning to the table and leafing through that folder. 'The women were each young – in their early twenties. All strangers. They seemed to be random choices, just girls in the wrong place at the right time for him to cross their paths.'

'Nothing to connect them to one another?' Mercer asked.

'Not that the prosecutor ever figured, I don't think,' she said, shaking her head. 'One was a nurse coming off the night shift at a community hospital. The second one—'

'How was she dressed?' Mike asked.

'The nurse? I don't know. You can look through the police reports for a description. The second one was a grad student who worked evenings as a security guard at a mall. Not armed or anything. Just sitting there making sure no one came out of the dressing room with stolen clothes stuffed in her shopping bag.'

'But in uniform?' Mike interrupted Kallin again and she seemed annoyed.

'I don't remember. The third one was a stewardess, on her way home from Newark after a flight from Spain.'

Three for three possibly in some kind of uniformed dress.

'The crimes, Miss Kallin,' I said. 'Can you tell us what Rasheed did to these women?'

'Would any of you like a drink?'

'No, thanks.'

She walked to her refrigerator and opened it, removing a half-full bottle of white wine. She took a glass from a cabinet above the sink and uncorked the bottle.

'I had to look at him almost every day,' she said. 'I had to be civil to this animal, knowing what he'd done. Hard to believe it wasn't enough to keep him away from society for the rest of his life.'

'His m.o., Ms. Kallin,' I said. 'It's important for us to know.'

She poured the wine to the rim of the glass and sipped at it before she returned to the table. 'Troy had been doing burglaries in the area. Out of work, breaking into apartments to steal stuff that he could sell. Electronic equipment, jewelry, silverware – whatever he could get his hands on. The first girl in this pattern – those initials on his left arm? Her name is Jocelyn. She said she was tired after a long evening at work. Got out of her car and was walking to her condo, oblivious to everything because she was home. Know what I mean? You get that safe feeling that you've got the day behind you when you've reached familiar territory?'

'Exactly.' We'd each heard it from scores of victims.

'Jocelyn saw Troy get out of the van and walk toward her building. Calm, easy, not in a hurry. She could see his face in the streetlight overhead. He nodded and gave her a big smile. She gave one right back at him,' Kallin said, pausing to look at Mercer before she went on. 'Said there weren't a lot of blacks living in her complex, so she had a moment of concern, but chastised herself for having such a racist thought once he smiled at her.'

I knew that reaction wasn't a first for Mercer, either.

'He got behind her and in a flash had his arm around her neck and a knife to her ear. Told her he'd kill her if she screamed, that he just wanted her cash and her jewelry. Dragged her out of the light to his van. The rear door was open – just waiting for her – and he pushed her down inside, banging her head against the floor of it to stun her.'

That gave him time, no doubt, to get in and close the door.

'Troy must have had a sock in the van, ready to gag her. That's what he used in his first couple of cases, too – the ones he got away with. Jocelyn said he shoved the sock in her mouth, while he straddled her. Then he put the knife down so that he could bind her hands together.'

'Bound her with what?' Mike asked.

'Duct tape. Also in the van, like he'd done this before. She testified that he was swift and sure about what he was doing. Tied her feet with rope, too. Then he drove off.'

'Where to?'

'Jocelyn testified that she didn't have any idea. A wooded area, dark and isolated. There's miles of it all along the Palisades. He pulled over and climbed into the back with her. That's when the torture began.'

Nelly Kallin lit another cigarette and swallowed her wine like it was water.

'What did Troy do to her?'

'First he played with the knife, Ms. Cooper. He traced the tip of it around her eyes and down the side of her nose. He scraped the surface of her face until she bled at the corner of her lips, so that she could taste the blood as it ran into her mouth and was absorbed by the cotton sock. Then he used it to cut her clothing off, ripping her skin as he did. Nothing life-threatening, not stabbing her, but leaving lacerations the length of her body. He cut the rope off her ankles so that he could penetrate. You can read the rest if you can't figure it out,' she said, patting the thick folder that held the detailed police reports.

'And that's where he dumped her?' Mike asked.

'No, no. He abused Jocelyn for hours, for most of the night. Then he retied her legs, drove away, and left her just before dawn at another point off the highway. Threw the handbag out, too. Never bothered to take her money. That's how the cops got his fingerprints.'

'Who found her?'

'A sanitation worker. The patent leather from her pocketbook

279

reflected the sun's rays. The guy walked a few feet into the woods to explore it.'

'Was the body wrapped – I mean, was Jocelyn naked when he left her there?'

Nelly Kallin licked her thumb and paged through the file. 'I don't think she was. I'm pretty sure each of the women was covered up with something. Here it is. Old blankets, the same kind in each case.'

'Green,' Mike said. 'Drab olive green, I'm betting. The scumbag must have cornered the market in those.'

She handed him the report that confirmed what we already knew.

'In each of these instances, Ms. Kallin,' I asked, 'did Rasheed ejaculate?'

'Yes. Those were the semen samples that ultimately led to the postconviction DNA match. But you won't be so lucky.'

'What do you mean?'

'You haven't got DNA in any of these cases, have you?'

Another fact that hadn't been made public by the commissioner. I shouldn't have answered her question but I was fascinated that she was so confident. 'No, no, we don't.'

'Troy Rasheed has been chemically castrated.'

'Jesus,' Mike said, as always put off more by sexually explicit conversation than by the cold clinical facts of murder. 'You could do that in New Jersey? By the boa constrictor on his penis or by the docs?'

'He volunteered for it, Mr. Chapman. He was smart enough to think it would make it easier for him to get out of prison. They didn't chop it off, you know. He just took ten months' worth of injections of a drug called Depo-Provera.'

'So what are you saying, ma'am? That Troy Rasheed couldn't be a sexual predator? On the one hand, you're telling us he's our man, and on the other hand, you're saying he's been castrated.'

Nelly Kallin's impatience with Mike was growing. 'You think

these crimes are only about sex? You don't think binding and torturing women has something to do with power and physical domination?'

And anger and lust, and sometimes pure pleasure.

'So we've got a serial killer who's impotent.'

'It's not these bastards' gonads that drive them to assault their victims, Detective. It's their twisted heads.'

38

'Well, then, Nelly,' Mike said, one arm on the kitchen table and the other brushing back his hair, trying to work his charm on her. 'Why don't you take us inside Troy Rasheed's head?'

Mercer was on the phone to Lieutenant Peterson suggesting an all-points bulletin for the released prisoner. He was reading a date of birth from the prison records and the inmate number so that New Jersey's Department of Corrections could e-mail a copy of the photograph to go out on the wire services.

'He was paroled in July, Loo. We can always pick him up on a violation.'

Kallin turned to look at Mercer and wagged a finger at him. 'That's wrong. There's no parole hold. You can't get him for that.'

Mercer put his hand over the receiver. 'What do you mean?'

'Rasheed served all his time. Maxed out after twenty-one. The last three years of incarceration have been a civil commitment.'

'Sweet,' Mike said. 'A state that allows chemical castration *and* civil commitment. Get used to me, Nelly. I may pack my bags and take up residence in New Jersey.'

There were few issues more controversial in the criminal justice system than the new laws, passed in fewer than twenty states, that allowed the government to authorize the involuntary commitment of convicted sex offenders who have completed their entire prison terms. The acknowledgment of the high recidivist rate of rapes – and murders – by these predators, all over America, led to this radical form of preventive detention, in which the prisoners are transferred to psychiatric lockups at the end of their terms and held for as long as they are deemed a risk to society.

'Politicians love this kind of hot-button fix, Mr. Chapman.'

'Put away the bad with the mad and everybody on the street cheers. We're just revving up for it at home,' Mike said. The legislature had defeated proposals to introduce the law in New York, until the governor was successful in pushing it through just months earlier.

'The defense lobby fought it pretty hard in New York,' I said. I hadn't yet participated in any case that had gone forward. 'Is that why you were so worried about your role in telling us about Rasheed's release? This commitment proceeding is a very hush-hush event, isn't it? I've only heard rumors from my counterpart in Bergen County.'

Mercer hung up the phone and joined us at the table.

Nelly Kallin pushed her glass away. 'The whole thing gives new meaning to the word *secret*. If you knew how many men have been sent to Kearny and how many have come out, you'd understand why. We've got close to three hundred prisoners being held there. The state wins 95 percent of the cases, and the hearings are closed.'

'How can they be closed? Who attends them?' Mercer asked.

'New Jersey, unlike the few other states that have done this, seals the commitment process. We don't use a jury system, on the theory that we're protecting the patient's confidentiality. So Troy Rasheed's name has never entered any public record since he finished serving his sentence.'

'Nowhere? There's no record of this?'

'No. Two Superior Court judges handle all of these matters, and then the cases are sealed. If you don't hear the facts from me, I doubt there's any way you could find out any of them. And once I tell you, I'll probably be planning an early retirement.'

'Nelly, you point me in the right direction and I'll take it the rest of the way. If you go, I go with you. Coop won't let them can you,' Mike said.

She looked at me for reassurance that I couldn't give her. This wasn't the normal whistle-blower situation.

'How did it work?' Mercer asked, his deep voice and earnest expression helping to calm the nervous woman. 'Rasheed's hearing.'

'Like every other uncomfortable mix of law and psychiatry,' she said. 'The SVPA – the Sexually Violent Predator Act was passed in 1998, sort of designed along the lines of commitments for the mentally ill. But there's a major distinction.'

'What's that?'

'In a proceeding for a mental patient, the focus is on the patient's state of mind, his current condition. Things he did in the past, even in those cases in which crimes were committed, they're not usually relevant. But at Kearny – and for Troy – they use the prior crimes as critical evidence of his thinking, his behavior, his probability of offending again in the future. The law lets us keep these monsters confined for their thoughts, not just their actions.'

'Count me in,' Mike said, standing and starting to pace the old wooden floorboards of Kallin's kitchen. 'Thought police – my kind of department. I'd love to make collars just for what the bad guys are thinking, before they pull the trigger.'

'So the patient's state of mind is at issue,' I said. 'I guess that lets in just about everything, right? Hearsay, old psych evaluations from the pretrial exams, statements he made in treatment, while incarcerated?'

'That just scratches the surface. The shrinks testify about the prisoners' sexual tastes and their fantasies – what are supposed to be their fantasies. Prosecutors are able to shop around for psychiatric opinions. Well, the state can almost always find some reason to keep these guys behind bars.'

'Then why did Rasheed get out this time?' I asked.

'Because he learned how to beat us. Troy copied the handful of guys who made it out before him. And I'm convinced that you'll find he didn't pounce on these victims – these women who were murdered – like he did on Jocelyn and the others. I'm sure of that. Something put them in his path and this time he thought he knew how to get them to come along with him, without even having to show a knife.'

There seemed little prospect at the moment of reconstructing the last hours – or minutes – of the lives of Amber Bristol, Elise Huff, and Connie Wade.

'So how did it go for Rasheed?' Mercer asked again.

'Almost four years ago,' Kallin said, 'just a few days from the end of his jail time, he was told he was being transferred to Kearny. That's how it always begins. A secret process, with a surprise notification.'

'But who picks which prisoner goes?'

'My colleagues – the administrators at DOC. No written guidelines.'

'That's part of the reason these commitments are being challenged in federal court,' I said. 'The inmates claim they're unconstitutionally arbitrary.'

Kallin hesitated and looked out the window. I followed her line of vision and saw only the hedges between her small yard and the house next door.

'Did you see someone? Something?'

She went back to twiddling her thumbs. 'Probably just the neighbors.'

Mike stood behind her and kept his eye on the narrow alleyway.

'After that, the attorney general's office screens the cases. They usually support us in about half the applications. Troy was no different from any other inmate when he got here. He'd spent almost half his life in prison, was just days from walking out, but then got smacked in the face with the news that he wasn't going anywhere.'

'So the first hearing was three years ago,' Mercer said.

'Yes. And there aren't many perps who make it through that initial one. They're so angry about the transfer, all the state has to do is present its diagnosis and tack on the fact that the guy has bad control of his impulses. What they really have to show – and it was easy in Troy's case – is that he has serious difficulty in controlling his behavior.'

'What was his diagnosis?' I asked.

'Personality disorder, NOS, Ms. Cooper,' Nelly Kallin said.

'NOS?'

'Not otherwise specified. It's the same diagnosis that got him discharged from the army when he was twenty-one years old.'

39

Son of Uncle Sam.

'When was Troy Rasheed in the army?' Mercer asked.

'He enlisted when he was nineteen and was thrown out less than two years later,' Kallin said.

'Where did he serve? Why was he tossed?'

'For the six months before his discharge, he was in Germany. There was an incident with a woman on the base. He wasn't the only one involved – there were three or four guys from his command. Sort of a date rape – a lot of alcohol and some not very clear allegations.'

'Was there a trial?' I asked, wondering if that young woman, too, had been in uniform when the drinking began.

'Way back then? No way. You probably know what it's like trying to get records out of the military. Everything disappears.

And a drunken female claiming sexual assault? The army still doesn't do so well with that today. I can't believe the girl was taken too seriously. Troy must have had a stack of other offenses leading up to that incident.'

Kallin stretched her neck and looked out the window again.

'Personality disorder, NOS,' Mike said. 'That sounds pretty mild for a serial rapist.'

She turned to look at him and loosened up for the first time. 'You'd fit that diagnosis for sure, Mr. Chapman. Anybody interesting would. Troy's really an ASPD but the shrinks didn't have to create a stir by going that far. The defense team couldn't rebut this one. He'd been tagged with it before he even encountered the legal system.'

Anti-Social Personality Disorder was one of the hallmarks of serial killers in the *DSM-IV*, or *Diagnostic and Statistical Manual*, the bible of the forensic psychiatric community.

I started to tick off the traits of this psychopathic behavior as listed in the *DSM*. 'Failure to conform to social norms, limited range of human emotions, lack of empathy for the suffering of others—'

'Which leads to risk-seeking behavior,' Kallin said. 'Deceitful, impulsive, aggressive. Repeated lying, use of aliases.'

There would have been no reason for Troy Rasheed to use his real name in applying for a job with Kiernan Dylan. How easy it must have been for him to slip away from New Jersey after he had complied with the need to register his name with the state's monitors.

'Do you have his military records here?' I asked, pointing at her stack of folders.

'No. The prosecutor was never able to get them – just the discharge summary.'

'What do you know about his family background?'

Some movement in the corner of my eye drew my attention to the window. I looked out but saw nothing.

'You're jumpier than I am,' Kallin said to me.

Mercer eased himself out of the chair. 'I left my cell phone in the car. I'd better get it. Don't want to miss the lieutenant's call-back. Mind if I use this door?'

I knew that Mercer was going to check around the outside of the house. It wasn't likely that anyone could have followed us, but I'd been even more on edge since Kerry Hastings had been injured simply by virtue of her proximity to me.

Nelly got up, too, removed the chain, and unlocked the kitchen door, which led onto a deck. I watched as Mercer disappeared down the path alongside the house.

'Troy's mother died more than ten years ago. Before that, she came to see him once a week, every single week. A sister who's married with three kids, but she lives in Texas. His father's still alive. I called him after the hearing in July.'

'To give him the good news about junior coming home?' Mike said.

'Oh, no. When Troy was transferred to my facility, Mr. Rasheed made an appointment with me. He hadn't visited his son, never even attended a day of the trial. Troy was the great disappointment of his life and, unlike his wife, he just cut himself off from the kid.'

'You mean when Troy was arrested?'

'Before that, actually. When he was discharged from the army. The father, Wilson Rasheed, had always dreamed of a military career for himself, except that he has a congenital heart defect,' Kallin said. 'Whatever it is, it disqualified him from service. But he was a civilian contractor for a long time, building facilities on some bases up and down the East Coast. Noninstitutional structures – housing and such. And Mr. Rasheed didn't want anything to do with his son after the kid's discharge.'

'That's a pretty severe reaction, considering Troy was only twenty-one at the time,' Mike said.

'I think some of the son's personality traits were inherited.'

Mercer came back into sight and waved his cell phone over his head as he climbed the steps and opened the door. I knew it had been in his pocket since we left the car, but he was signaling to me that no one was lurking around Kallin's house.

'The father's a real loner,' Nelly went on. 'Retired and reclusive. Still has the apartment in Newark that Troy was raised in but spends most of his time in a cabin up in the mountains, near Sussex. I don't think he's got heat or electricity. Just his guns.'

Nelly Kallin got up again and opened her pocketbook, which was on the kitchen counter. She removed a piece of paper from her wallet and unfolded it.

'Handguns? Shotguns?' Mike asked. 'Has the father got a record, too?'

'He's a hunter, Detective. Never been in trouble with the law. I don't know much about guns, but he's got some kind of collection of old military stuff. Spent all his spare time hoarding it away.'

The three of us exchanged glances, and Mike let out a soft whistle. 'Whoa, Nelly.'

'How do you know that, Ms. Kallin? If Troy and his father had no contact?'

'Some of the background is from the family history in our documents and some is what his father told me when I met him last month.' She held the creased paper out to Mike. 'This isn't anywhere in the prison records, do you understand? That's the way Mr. Rasheed wants it, and that's what I agreed to do.'

'Why?'

'Troy tried to call him at the apartment when he got the news of his release. First time in all those years the son even made an attempt to reach him. But Wilson Rasheed had changed his number, unlisted the phone. He knows even more than we do, Mr. Chapman. He doesn't ever want to see his son again.

'The guards reported a flurry of calls by Troy that same day – trying to find his sister out west, old neighbors in Newark, any link to the outside world,' Kallin went on. 'But he's been away an awfully long time. People moved on and most of them were happy to have left Troy Rasheed behind.'

Mike reached out for the paper. 'You have the father's new number?'

Nelly nodded. 'I called him right after I phoned Ms. Cooper today. It just rang and rang. I doubt he's at the apartment. He wasn't planning to wait around for Troy to knock on his door.'

'So this first address is Wilson's place in Newark, right?' Mike said. 'And the other one is his cabin in the mountains?'

'Exactly. He wanted me to have both, but he insisted that neither be part of the official record.'

'Why?' I asked.

'Because, Ms. Cooper,' Nelly said, 'Wilson Rasheed had nothing but contempt for the psychiatrists who tried to treat Troy over the years. He didn't want to hear from them, and he never wanted to see his son again. I promised to let him know when the release was imminent, and that's the last I expect to hear from him.'

'How come this whole commitment proceeding gets cloaked in so much secrecy?' Mike asked.

'No one will talk about it,' Nelly said. 'Not prison officials, not the AG, not the public defenders.'

'Troy was turned down for release twice, you said.'

'Right before his second hearing, he had a flare-up. He was on his way to his therapy session and he brushed up against a guard. A woman guard. His lawyer claimed it was an accident and that it wasn't sexually motivated.'

One more lady in uniform, even when Troy was behind bars.

'The state shrink testified that he must have had some kind of sexual arousal by engineering such close contact – the prisoner's hand touching the genitals of a female guard. Sent him to solitary confinement, which triggered a hunger strike and a refusal by Troy to speak to staff.

'At the second hearing, the AG made a big deal of it. He

argued that the prisoner's reaction spoke to his egocentric view of the world, showed his complete lack of self-control. And the judge agreed, saying that Troy was once again asserting his entitlement, acting against his best interest.'

'And Troy never admitted anything about it, did he?' Mike said.

Nelly Kallin just laughed.

'So back into jail for another year,' I said.

'That's when he must have found a mentor in the inmate population. Some other sicko who took Troy under his wing,' Kallin said, tapping her finger on the pile of folders.

'What changed?'

'He'd been known for very recalcitrant behavior. Denials, rationalizations, blame shifting. Years of it. Now he became an active participant in treatment sessions for the first time. For a realistic chance at release, an inmate has to show he's deeply committed to changing his life.'

'And Troy Rasheed did?' I asked.

'He stopped fighting the conclusions the shrinks had made in the past. He told them he'd wear a security bracelet, a chip with a GPS tracking device. He offered to urinate in a jar any time they wanted him to. He submitted to a penile plethysmograph for the first time since arriving at Kearny.'

'A what?' Mike asked.

'They use it here like a lie detector for rapists.'

'Shit. A peter meter?'

Kallin tilted her head toward Mike and suppressed a smile. 'It's a tubular ring filled with mercury that's placed around the prisoner's penis. They show him photographs – provocative ones, like women in bondage, images of things that have traditionally excited him. Then the doctors measure any changes in circumference that reflect the magnitude of his erections.'

'And that kind of witch doctoring is enough to let a serial rapist walk out the door?'

'Not in my book. But that and his voluntary submission to chemical castration – even though that's only a temporary fix – put Troy at the head of the class. This last year, he became the therapeutic community's idealized vision of the rehabilitated sex offender.'

'No such animal,' Mercer said.

'Despite the dreadful criminal history and the years of predatory behavior and fantasies,' I said, 'the AG's shrinks didn't consider him a grave risk for reoffending?'

'The expert who testified for the state this summer only met Troy Rasheed for the first time a few weeks before the hearing.'

'That's absurd. What about the docs who'd been treating him for years?'

'Another catch-22, Ms. Cooper. Therapists who've actually treated the prisoner don't normally testify, since that might interfere with the actual treatment sessions.'

'So these docs only see his current conduct, hear his recent statements,' I said. 'They don't know a fraction of what others who've had contact with the inmate would know, except from what's in the cold written reports.'

'And since the records of the previous hearings are sealed, there isn't anyone else who's going to tell you what Troy said to me when he learned that he was coming to this facility instead of being released three years ago.'

'What's that, Nelly?' Mike asked.

'It's a blueprint for his future, Detective. It's the reason I told the psychiatrists from the outset that his next victims weren't likely to survive their encounters with Troy Rasheed,' Nelly Kallin said. 'The day he was admitted to Kearny, he asked me whether there was any such thing as civil commitment for murderers.'

She reached for her wine glass and clenched the stem of it in her hand.

'No, I told him. No, there wasn't. A kid Troy's age would probably have been paroled long before now, even for homicide.

We both figured out that piece of irony. He just looked at me when I answered him, and laughed.

' "I'd be better off if I'd killed those girls, wouldn't I?" he said to me.' Nelly Kallin closed her eyes and sighed. 'He was right about that, you know.'

40

'You mind if we take these files with us, Nelly?' Mike asked. 'Make copies and return them to you? It would give the task force a great head start to get all this background.'

'I've gone this far. You might as well have them.'

'How about you? Wouldn't you be more comfortable staying with a friend or relative till we find Troy?'

'I'm more worried about my supervisor reacting to the fact that I've gone off the reservation than I am about him,' she said. 'I've decided to spend the week at my sister's house in Princeton. It will keep me out of reach of the department so I won't have to dodge phone calls.'

Mercer was flipping through one of the many manila folders. 'Why do you think Rasheed's rapes won't be blitz attacks anymore?'

'He didn't make it through all these years, especially navigating a release, without learning how to become a manipulator. He's been rewarded for learning that behavior.'

'The classic sex offender motivational attributes – power, anger, lust – you put any stock in that?'

'Not very much,' Nelly said. 'Sure, these perpetrators are angry, but if it was all about that, then any kind of physical assault would work. Clinical studies make it pretty clear that anger inhibits sexual arousal. Along with anxiety, it's a major cause of dysfunction.'

Nelly Kallin was intelligent and direct. Mike was listening to her intently, with clear respect for her observations.

'There's a reason that a sexual act is the weapon these men use. Perhaps because it's the ultimate humiliation, the most intimate kind of act they can impose on another human being.'

'Does it mean anything to you if I tell you that each of his victims—'

'Mr. Wallace, I'm not a shrink,' Kallin said, shaking a finger at him. 'Just a wannabe.'

'You're smart, Nelly,' Mike said, pacing again. 'You've seen Troy Rasheed – if he's our man – day after day for more than three years now. We want your perspective.'

'If every one of these victims had some kind of uniform on when she was attacked, would that surprise you?' Mercer asked.

Nelly Kallin stopped to think. 'Not really. Get your hands on his military records. He's been frustrated by that experience all his life. His father's ambitions for him, his own discharge, the fact that it ostensibly had to do with an assault on a female member of the service. Maybe he blames her for all his problems. He's had a few decades to chew on that.'

I could hear shouting outside the house. It distracted Nelly and she glanced around at the windows once more. Mercer looked up from the files.

'Control,' she said. 'I'd say that control and having someone weaker than he was, someone he could think of as inferior to himself, that probably had something to do with Troy's crimes.'

'You mean the way he bound the women, tortured them for a period of time?' I asked.

'Sure. You've probably worked with as many sexual sadists as I have, Ms. Cooper. Don't you think there's something else going on here?'

The intense humidity had wilted my clothes and created blond curls around my forehead. I pushed them back. 'I do,' I said. 'Of course I do.'

'The docs have known about all this for more than a century,' Kallin said. 'Krafft-Ebing and his definition of sadism.'

'The experience of sexually pleasurable sensations, including orgasm, produced by acts of cruelty,' I said. 'The *DSM* hasn't done any better than that definition, all these years later.'

Mike was running his hand through his hair.

'I think Troy Rasheed *likes* hurting women,' Kallin said. 'It may be as simple as that, Detective. It's one of the few things in life that has given him pleasure, and he's had a long time to look forward to enjoying that sensation again.'

She stood up and walked out of the room, returning with a notebook. 'I've collected my own "who's who," Ms. Cooper. Sometimes the young shrinks aren't even aware of the history of these crimes, they've got so many new perps to study. Gilles de Rais – ever hear of him?'

'A fifteenth-century French nobleman who kidnapped, tortured, and murdered children,' I said. Like Kallin, I had researched these crimes for more than a decade, trying to under-stand the motivations of these monsters and crimes that made no sense at all.

'Hundreds of children. Entirely for his own pleasure and phys-ical delight, is how he described it. His "inexpressible" pleasure, to quote him exactly,' she said, turning several pages. 'Vincenz Verzeni?'

I shook my head. 'No.'

'Italian, nineteenth century. I'm surprised you missed him. Raped and mutilated his victims. Described his unspeakable delight in strangling women, experiencing erections while he did so.'

Nelly Kallin closed the looseleaf book and stacked it on top of one of the piles. 'Shrinks spend a disproportionate amount of their time analyzing motivation, grasping at reasons "why" these men commit such heinous crimes. You don't need to look much beyond the fact that many of them simply like to do it – something the rest of us can't begin to fathom. It's what gives these sadists pleasure.'

Voices outside the window were closer now, voices of people who seemed to be arguing with each other as they ran up the path next to the house.

Mercer got to his feet as Nelly Kallin grabbed his arm to hold him back.

'It's not a problem, Mr. Wallace,' she said.

But something crashed through one of the panes of the kitchen window at that moment and I jumped as glass shattered onto the floor behind me.

41

Nelly Kallin wasn't the least bit upset by the baseball that flew into the room like a missile. The thirteen-year-old twins who lived on the other side of the hedge had returned home from summer camp over the weekend, and she explained good-naturedly that it wasn't the first time she would have to replace a window that faced their walkway.

Mercer opened the door for the kids, who came to apologize for the accident.

Mike turned me around to make sure no bits of glass had landed on my head or back. He rubbed my shoulders with both hands. 'You're shaking, Coop. You're really strung out.'

'Overtired. Worried about Kerry. Scared to death that the killer is out there.'

Mike's fingers massaged my shoulders and neck. 'Crabby can't be far behind. This is when you take it out on my hide.'

'Well, you're stuck with me till you find Troy Rasheed. And Kiernan Dylan.'

Nelly Kallin dismissed the two boys and Mike told her we had to get back to work with her files. She took ten minutes to go upstairs and pack a bag, and we all drove away at the same time.

'You want to try the Newark address for Wilson Rasheed?' Mike asked Mercer.

'Yeah,' Mercer said, looking at the paper that Mike handed to him. 'You know the street? It's not far from the Amtrak station.'

There were so many Manhattan perpetrators who commuted from New Jersey to commit their felonies that most cops in each jurisdiction were familiar with the other. It was less than a fifteen-minute ride to the three-story row of attached houses in an as yet ungentrified part of the old city that seemed continually to fight a losing battle with violent crime.

Mike and I waited in the car while Mercer entered the vestibule, presumably to look for the doorbell or some way to identify Rasheed's home. Ten minutes later he emerged to tell us that when he got no answer he gained entry by ringing a neighbor's buzzer. The man knew Wilson but hadn't seen him in more than two weeks. Mercer slipped a card with his name and phone number under the door.

'How about a ride up to Sussex County?' Mike asked Mercer.

'It's after six,' I said from the backseat behind Mike. 'We won't get there till at least eight o'clock.'

'It's going to be eight o'clock no matter where you are, Blondie. Might as well make yourself useful. Close your eyes and enjoy the ride.'

Mercer got on his cell to call the sheriff's office in the small village of Colesville, near the spot where Wilson Rasheed's hunting cabin was located. He asked the sergeant he was connected to if anyone there knew the man. There was a pause, then he gave

Mike and me a thumbs-up. We listened as he persuaded the sergeant to lead us up the mountainous area to the property.

'They won't go in without us,' Mercer said when he was off. 'Says Rasheed's a real oddball. Doesn't like people trespassing on his property. They don't exactly want to drop in on him without a reason. He's been known to take a few potshots with a rifle and claim later that he thought he was shooting at a black bear.'

'Damn. You better stay in the car when we get there, pal. Hate for the guy to get you in his sights.'

I must have fallen asleep once Mike reached the interstate. The smooth road and the light rain tapping on the windshield put me out.

I awakened when Mike got off the highway and stopped at a gas station. He filled the tank and bought coffee and sandwiches, which we ate in the car. The attendant directed us to the small building on the outskirts of town that housed the sheriff's office, where the diminutive Sergeant Edenton was waiting to lead us up to Rasheed's hideaway.

'I'll stop at the property line,' he said. 'It's a dark, winding drive up. Then you'll have to walk a bit longer.'

'I understand he doesn't have a phone,' Mike said.

'The man don't believe in creature comforts at all. It's better if he can't see me, 'cause I only show my face when we get complaints about him.'

'You know his son?'

'Troy? Haven't seen that troublemaker since he was a teenager. Heard what he got locked up for and just glad it didn't happen around here. You have flashlights?'

'One,' Mercer said, holding it up for Edenton to see.

'Let me get you two more,' he said, going back into the building and returning with two lantern-sized beams. 'You need to stay on the main path. Wilson's got it all booby-trapped up there. Step in the wrong place, you'll find yourself in a bear trap or a hole in the ground.'

'Wouldn't it make sense to come back in the morning, in daylight, with an Emergency Services team?' I asked.

'The guy's not a criminal,' Mike said. 'He's a kook. We don't have time to waste, Coop.'

'You're fine on the main path,' Edenton said, laughing at me. 'Just announce yourselves when you get close to the house. Maybe you send her in first, saying she's the Avon lady.'

'We always send her in first. That's how come Mercer and I have lived so long.'

Once we followed Sergeant Edenton off the paved town road and up the dirt drive that wound around the small mountain, a blanket of fog descended. Dense evergreens towered over us on both sides, and deep ruts bounced the department car, which had already surrendered its shock absorbers to the potholes of city streets.

Mike had given up air-conditioning in favor of opening all the windows so that we could hear noise, if there was any. Moths attached themselves to the headlights and mosquitoes searched for landing places on my face and hands.

The SUV Edenton was driving tracked the familiar course faster than we did, and he repeatedly stopped to let Mike catch up.

We drove for more than a mile, but the fog made it impossible to tell whether there were any occupied buildings set back from the road. When Edenton finally turned off his engine and got out of his car, his flashlight focused on the red and white metallic surface of the NO TRESPASSING signs that lined the path.

'You got a plan, Mike?' the sergeant asked.

'Mercer'll back me up. I suppose I'll shout when I get close enough to see the cottage,' Mike said. He took his gold shield from his pants pocket and held it up in his palm. 'Shine your light on it, Sarge. Does it gleam?'

From a distance of five feet, the rays danced off the metallic badge. But the mist would obscure it from any farther away.

'There should be an old jeep next to the place if he's home. And I'm telling you guys, watch your step,' Edenton said.

'Will do. Light a fire and Coop'll roast you some marshmallows. It's one of the few culinary chores I think she can handle.'

Mike saluted the sergeant and started off slowly, walking on the right tire track. Mercer was just a few steps behind him.

Edenton seemed embarrassed by his decision to stay back with me. A minute or two later, he opened the rear of his SUV and took out a shotgun, checking to make sure it was loaded. 'I'd better give them a hand. You want to sit in the car and lock the doors?'

There was an eerie stillness in the woods around me. 'I'll follow you.'

We walked for at least five minutes, and although Mike and Mercer could not have been more than fifty yards in front of us, it was impossible to see them.

I stopped short when I heard Mike's voice call out Wilson Rasheed's name.

'Are we close to the cabin?' I asked Edenton.

He swept his light around the foliage. 'Should be. I can't pick up any reflectors from the back of the jeep.'

'Mr. Rasheed. My name is Chapman. NYPD,' Mike was shouting now, and I pressed Edenton's back to move him ahead. 'I'm here with some other detectives. We've come to help you, sir, so I'm going to approach your door and knock on it.'

I could see Mercer's large frame outlined in the haze by the sergeant's flashlight. Edenton stepped over the hump in the middle of the roadway to the left track, and I advanced closer behind Mercer.

'Where's Mike? Did you lose him?'

'Right up ahead,' he said, lifting the light. 'See the door?'

I added the beam of my flashlight to the others and could make out the shape of a primitive log cabin. There was no sign of a car close to the place. Mike was standing on the porch, to the side of the front door. There were no lights from within the small structure and no sound except the buzzing of mosquitoes and black flies around my head.

Mike rapped on the door several times. No noise, no response.

He turned around so that his back was against the building. He pocketed the flashlight and drew his gun in his right hand, reaching out to lift the latch with his left. The door opened and swung in, banging several times against an interior wall.

'Give me some light.'

Mercer took two steps forward.

Mike swiveled around, and as his right foot landed squarely in front of the door the plank beneath him cracked in half. His foot disappeared into the hole it made, and his gun bounced off the steps as he dropped it in order to grab on to the jamb to keep from falling into the crevice.

Mercer was there with three giant steps, crossing over the hole into the entrance of the shack, supporting Mike under the armpit with one of his enormous hands.

Mike clung to Mercer with both arms and disappeared from my sight into the blackness of the entryway. I started forward before Edenton could, letting my light guide me behind Mercer and taking a big step to avoid the hole Mike had almost fallen into.

Mercer stopped me, bracing me at arm's length. 'Stay back, Alex. It's bad.'

Edenton came up behind me and shone his flashlight into the room. 'My God,' he said. 'It's Wilson.'

The body was laid out on the floor on its back, spread-eagle, the skull crushed, probably by the large rock that rested next to one ear.

The blade of a foot-long bayonet pierced the heart and was impaled in the floorboard beneath the decomposing corpse of Troy Rasheed's father.

42

'Wait outside, Coop,' Mike said.

'It's raining. I'm better off with you.'

'Sarge, how fast can you get some men up here?'

'I have to drive back to town and call them in. The coroner, too. No cell reception on the mountain. How long you figure he's been dead?'

'Days,' Mike said. 'Maybe a week or more.'

'Don't touch nothing. I'll get my investigators on it.'

'Right.' Mike rolled his eyes as Edenton gave instructions. He saw more homicide scenes in a slow month than this sheriff's office probably handled in several years. 'You're in charge.'

Edenton's stubby legs could barely make it over the hole on the porch. 'Told you the damn place would be booby-trapped.'

He bent over to pick up Mike's revolver and pass it back to him.

Mike reholstered it on his belt and stooped to examine the flooring with his flashlight. He blew on the end of one of the boards and sawdust flew up and mixed with the falling rain.

'What's in the hole?' I asked.

Both Mike and Edenton directed their beams. 'Bear traps, like I figured,' the sergeant said proudly. 'Lucky it stays so much cooler up at this altitude. Wilson don't smell so bad as I'd expect.'

'Want to get a move on it, Sarge? And put out a stolen-vehicle report on the jeep, will you? My boss'll want everybody in North America looking for that one.'

Mike waited until Edenton was far enough out of range before he turned his flashlight back into the room. Mercer was already walking around the living area, gingerly testing each plank with the ball of his foot before moving forward.

'Remind you of anything?' Mercer asked.

'The trap door on that little black hole up on Bannerman Island,' Mike said. 'Looks like a trick our boy learned from Papa. Then he hoisted him on his own petard.'

Mike took a pair of latex gloves from his pants pocket. They were part of his routine gear and he was always ready with them. He tossed his spares to Mercer, then kneeled next to Wilson Rasheed's body to do a superficial examination.

'I'm guessing that Troy came up here for some reason. He'd known the place from his childhood. Maybe he wanted to see his father, confront him about something. Maybe he wanted things that were stored or hidden here.'

'Or had things he planned to hide,' Mercer said. 'And maybe he stole his father's jeep, but then how did he get to this part of the world?'

'Think of the geography, Mercer,' Mike said. 'If it was Troy who killed Connie Wade and dumped her on Bannerman Island, then it was Troy who used Kiernan's van to get her upstate. With Kiernan or without him.'

'That's another question.'

'So he – or they – ditched the van in the woods, right? Troy's known this spot since childhood. It's north Jersey, almost directly across the river from where the van was dropped. He could have hitched a ride, taken a bus, gotten himself to Colesville, and just walked up the hill to pay a call on Dad.'

The entire time he talked, he was looking at Rasheed's injuries – examining the man's head, pushing aside his bloodstained shirt to expose the gaping wound in his chest.

'This is a beauty. Check it out, Mercer. Coop, stay where you are, okay? You don't need to get any closer. And try not to look at the guy either. It's bad for your health.'

Mercer stood on the other side of Rasheed's body. Mike had obviously satisfied himself that there was nothing he could do about his murder victim, but he was fascinated with the weapon that protruded from the dead man's chest.

'What is it?' Mercer asked.

'See the markings? Prussian Army, 1890s, I'd say.'

'Hard to come by?'

'Exactly the kind of thing you could buy from a Bannerman's catalog.'

Mike was pointing to the place where the handle of the deadly sharp sword fitted into the socket of the gun barrel. 'When peasants in a little town engaged in a battle ran out of powder and shot, they rammed their hunting knives into the muzzles of their muskets to turn them into spears. A complete accident that changed the course of warfare for hundreds of years,' Mike said. 'Bayonne, it was.'

'New Jersey?' I asked, thinking he meant the American Revolution.

'Bayonne, France, kid. Bayonet.'

Mercer crossed the threshold into a second room and Mike called after him. 'What's in there?'

'Bedroom, sort of. Guy slept on a cot. Like an army cot.' He paused for several seconds. 'Come on in here.'

Mike took a few steps toward Mercer and I went after him. From beside Mike, I could see clearly when he lifted his light. A drab olive green blanket covered the narrow military bed on which Wilson Rasheed once slept.

Mike ran his gloved hand around two corners of it until he found the old McCallan Brothers label. 'It doesn't get much better than this, if you want to link Troy Rasheed to the bodies of Elise Huff and Connie Wade. Let's just hope CSI Colesville doesn't screw this scene up before we send reinforcements.'

Next to the cot was a stand that held a kerosene lamp. Mercer stopped to light it. My eyes adjusted to the illumination and the three of us took in the array of military gear that decorated the walls and homemade pine shelves. Almost every inch of space had photographs stuck in the wood with thumbtacks. Most of them showed troops dressed and armed for combat in old wars. Also hanging were medals of every sort, with torn and faded ribbons like those I had seen at flea markets – the kind that always made me wonder why relatives had ceased to care about some ancestral hero.

Mercer opened the only other door in the room. It was a small closet with a single rod. The few items of clothing in it were khaki-colored shirts and pants and a camouflage jacket that had fallen off its hanger. It had come to rest on a pile of green blankets – maybe eight or ten – neatly folded and stacked on the floor. Next to them, there must have been ten long guns – rifles and other bayonets, standing on end against each other.

'There's got to be a kitchen,' Mike said, backtracking out of the room. Mercer poked through the closet before he and I went off after Mike.

On the far wall opposite the entrance to the cabin, another

opening led to a room at the back of the building. Mike had lighted a second kerosene lamp and was exploring the equipment.

'He's only got a two-burner hot plate in here,' Mike said, showing us Rasheed's collection of beat-up pots and pans and a cabinet that held canned goods – soups, vegetables, fruits – and tins of crackers. Six-packs of beer were stacked against the wall and packages of black licorice were on the countertop. There was a small picnic table at which he must have taken his meals, and here again the walls were covered with scenes of men in combat gear.

Mike pulled open drawers but there was nothing of interest in any of them. Behind the table was a door with a window, and when he held up the lamp we could see that it led to a yard behind the house. He pushed it out.

Ten yards away was a tiny wooden structure. 'That answers that question,' Mike said. 'Must be the outhouse.'

Mercer stood in the doorway and held one lamp overhead while Mike checked out the footpath. He walked to the door and peered in. 'No surprises. A one-holer, with a flashlight on the floor next to it. The body smells better than this place does.'

Mike let go of the door and, holding the lamp in front of him, started off slowly circling the outhouse. The rain had picked up and a strong wind was now blowing.

I heard something creaking and we all looked around. In the limbs of one of the sturdy old trees farther away from us was a tree house, like something made for a kid. Mike went toward the tree and rested the light on the ground, reaching hand over hand on the rope ladder. He got as far as the fourth rung when he called out that the next two were missing, so he climbed down, leaving the tree house to the men who would come after us.

Mike turned back to where Mercer and I were standing and, with the light shining in our direction, stopped again. He crouched and lifted the lamp, moving it back and forth in front of him.

'What do you see?' Mercer asked.

'The ground's not even. Must be some of Wilson's games.'

'Go slow, Mike.'

Mike got on all fours, standing the lamp beside him, while Mercer held his light overhead. Inching forward, Mike began clearing away a small mound of rocks and dirt. When he had uncovered the edge of a hole in the ground, he looked around for one of the fallen pine branches. He stuck a foot's length of it downward and we each heard the jaws of a steel trap snap at the wooden decoy.

Mike crawled a few feet to his left, cleared a second mound and secured another pine bough. Again the fierce bite of a trap's teeth.

Mike raised one knee and started to get up. 'If Troy's papa laid all these in around the property, the old boy was a real whack job.'

Mercer's gaze was fixed on one of the dark holes as he took a step closer. 'What color's the trap, Mike? Hold your light up over it.'

'It's black, man. It's—'

Now I could see something else shining from inside the hole.

'Quick, Coop. The guy's got soup cans up to the ceiling,' Mike said. 'Find me a ladle in the kitchen. Find me something with a long handle.'

I pointed my flashlight inside and went over to open a drawer, but there were no utensils in it bigger than a tablespoon. I pulled on the handle of a cupboard and beside the filthy mop and ragged broom stood three long swords. It was too late to worry about fingerprints at this point, and I yanked at the grip of one so hard that the others fell to the floor.

'The best I could do,' I said, slipping past Mercer to kneel beside Mike.

He lowered the sword practically to its hilt and brought up a white cotton jacket with epaulets and shiny gold buttons that had caught Mercer's light just moments ago.

'Amber Bristol,' I said. 'The outfit she was wearing the night she disappeared.'

43

Within an hour, Edenton had assembled four of his deputies and the county coroner on Wilson Rasheed's property. By the time they got there, Mike had used the tip of the sword to hook and retrieve more than a dozen articles of clothing and a cache of sex toys wrapped inside them that we presumed belonged to Amber Bristol.

Then Edenton led us down the mountain, stopping at his office so that Mike could call Lieutenant Peterson before we got on the road. Commissioner Scully, Peterson told Mike, had gone public that evening with a statement about Troy Rasheed's being sought as a 'person of interest' in the murders of three women. The morning papers would lead with that story, by which time Peterson expected the superintendent at Kearny would be forced to give out the most current photograph taken of the now-homeless prisoner before his release.

Edenton accepted Peterson's offer to send an NYPD crime scene team familiar with the evidence in the earlier murder cases to process the bizarre little home and its surroundings. Rasheed's body would be removed to the morgue that night, the cabin would be secured by the deputies, tarps would cover the holes Mike had discovered, and a complete search of the property by experienced investigators would begin at daybreak.

I made my calls from the backseat of the car as we headed to the highway, fueled with fresh cups of coffee from the sheriff's kitchenette. I left a message for Frank Shea, telling him it was urgent I meet with him on Tuesday about Kiernan Dylan. And I gave a complete update to Tim Spindlis.

'Spineless giving you a hard time?' Mike asked. 'Sounded like a cross-examination.'

'Tim's trying to get himself up to speed. Battaglia's going to make a decision about whether to cut his vacation short and come back from England on Wednesday. I'm to be in Tim's office at two for a conference call – with all the facts, if not the suspect in tow.'

'I didn't think this was an election year. I guess headlines is headlines and if you're the DA you gotta get 'em when you can. It isn't every day a serial killer rips through town. The PC has his mug in front of every camera, so I guess Battaglia wants to stick his great big Roman nose in, too.'

'What are you going to do about Frank Shea?' Mercer asked. 'He's not going to want to come to the table, Alex. Saturday night's fiasco with Kiernan, the closing of the bar, Jimmy Dylan's affair with Amber Bristol – and now it's all over the news that the bouncer at Ruffles is a sexual predator?'

I rubbed my eyes. 'I'll think more clearly tomorrow. I've got to be able to convince Shea that we need Troy Rasheed's employment application – what name he used, what address he gave.'

'Coop, we don't even know what the relationship is between

Kiernan and Troy. Kiernan admitted to us that he cleaned out Amber's apartment himself. And now we find some of her things at Rasheed's father's house,' Mike said. 'If the Dylans have been paying him off the books, chances are they never bothered with the State Liquor Authority and a proper record check. I bet they just hoped that strong, scary-looking creep would show up at the right time every night to keep the rowdy twerps in line.'

I remembered the look of disgust on Kiernan's face when he claimed to us he had thrown out some of Amber's 'weird, freaky stuff.' He and Rasheed appeared to have nothing in common on the surface, but something had linked them both to the deaths of two young women who disappeared on a single weekend in August.

The late hour and steady downpour seemed to lighten the traffic, and it was close to midnight when I saw the first signs for the George Washington Bridge. Mike was cruising at eighty now, southbound on the Jersey Turnpike.

'Aren't you taking the bridge?' It would be a faster way to get to my apartment than either of the tunnels that crossed into Midtown and Lower Manhattan.

'No backseat driving, Coop. We've got one more stop. That last java wired me up.'

'Have mercy, man. Vickee's going to board me in the hound hotel before this case is over.' Mercer tried to straighten out his arms, stretching to wake himself up, but there wasn't enough room in the car. 'Where to?'

'It's summertime, isn't it? And you guys have hardly been to the beach.'

'Slow down and let me out,' I said. 'I'd rather walk. I want to go home. Why do I have the feeling I'm not going to enjoy this?'

'Anything I offer you is better than going home to an empty bed. There'll be no pleasant dreams with that image of Mr. Rasheed dancing in your brain.'

'I take it you're planning to rap on Jimmy Dylan's door,' Mercer said. 'You've got the address?'

'It's the one Kiernan gave me when I booked him.'

'Seriously, Mike. I'm out of this car the minute you slow down. He's got a lawyer, damn it,' I said.

'He's also got a father and lots of little siblings.'

We had left the turnpike and were on the Goethals Bridge, about to cut across Staten Island and over the massive Verrazano to loop onto the Belt Parkway.

'Mike's not wrong,' Mercer said, turning his head to talk to me. 'Jimmy Dylan's got more problems than he can handle. You think he lost control at the squad the other night. He opens his paper tomorrow and reads that his boy is linked to a convicted rapist? To the murders of three women?'

'A convicted rapist who happens to be a black man? He'll thank me for coming to tell him myself.'

'What do you mean by that?' I asked.

'Breezy Point is not only private, it's also lily-white. I don't think social diversity is Jimmy Dylan's strong suit.'

'I'll be waiting in the car with you, Alex,' Mercer said. 'I'd probably be about as welcome as one of Wilson Rasheed's black bears.'

Thirty-five minutes later, we went through the toll plaza on the Marine Parkway Bridge, the gateway to Rockaway Beach.

Mike drove slowly, pausing at each corner in the quiet community, looking for street names. There were small groups of teenagers walking along the roadway, talking and laughing, oblivious to the rain, and several locals out with their dogs. It was shortly after midnight and lights were still on in many of the homes.

We turned off at Beach 221st Street, near the Surf Club, and Mike looked for numbers on the houses.

'That's it,' he said. 'That big old rambling job, right on the water.'

Three houses stood side by side, facing the ocean. Two of

them were well lighted, upstairs and down, including the one in the middle of the cluster, to which Mike was pointing.

He got out of the car and walked down a path bordered by huge hydrangeas. I couldn't see or hear anything, but Mercer and I figured that when Mike didn't return he'd been admitted to the house.

'The water looks mighty rough,' Mercer said, turning on the radio to check the track of the rainstorm that had been predicted for the next day. 'Hope that damn thing blows out to sea instead of hitting us.'

'They downgraded it from a hurricane, didn't they?'

'That's the last I heard.'

We were talking through the case with each other when a screen door slammed on the back porch. Two girls who appeared to be teenagers came out together, and a man's voice called after them.

'Shauna? Damn it, girl, get back in here.'

'I'm just walking Erin home, Dad. I'll be right back.'

Mercer and I watched as they passed in front of our parked car. The one called Erin removed a joint from her pants pocket, lighted it, and then passed it to Shauna, who took a few drags before they resumed their walk.

They continued on their way until they were out of sight, but the distinctive sweet smell of the marijuana wafted through the car window in the heavy night air.

A few minutes later, Shauna came back down the street by herself, the hood of her rain jacket drawn tightly around her face. She stopped in the driveway behind her house for a few more tokes before going back in.

'Take a shot at her, Alex. You've got nothing to lose.'

I hesitated for several seconds, then opened the car door. When I shut it behind me, the girl turned her head to check me out and threw her cigarette to the ground.

'Shauna Dylan?'

She didn't move, but she didn't answer either.

'Are you Shauna Dylan?'

'Yeah. And you're the police, aren't you?' She wiped her eyes with the back of her hand and I could see that she had been crying.

'I'm not a cop. I'm with the DA's office. And yes, I'm here with Detective Chapman.'

'Well, Kiernan's not home, if that's what you've come for.'

'I'm glad to hear that, actually.'

'Right,' she said. She was steadying herself with the handrail on the steps, twisting her body to look at me, as though she was stoned or had been drinking too much. 'You're totally full of shit. You've wrecked Kiernan's life, you know. You've wrecked his life over what? My father's mad as all hell at him, he won't let my mother come back from Ireland till all this stuff in the newspapers calms down, and everything they've both put into Ruffles will be gone. Completely gone.'

She was crying now, reaching down with one hand to lower herself onto the top step of the porch, beneath the roof that shielded her from the rain. I took a couple of steps in her direction.

'Stay away from me, okay? I don't even have a family anymore. The detective thinks Kiernan's a murderer and now my mother's threatening to leave my father because she's so mortified about that – that whore. We're all sick over this, and Frank Shea won't even tell my dad where Kiernan's gone. Now I'm glad. I don't want him to come back here so you can try to make a fool out of him again.'

Shauna pulled herself up to walk to the back door of the house.

'You reek of marijuana, Shauna. Unless your father doesn't mind that.'

She stopped in place, swaying a bit from side to side. She sniffed a few times, first the air and then her hands. 'You gonna lock me up, too? You gonna lock me up 'cause I'm wasted – 'cause my whole family is falling apart?'

'I didn't want my friend to arrest your brother on Saturday. We had a big fight about it, too.'

She eyed me warily now.

'We really didn't come here to talk to Kiernan tonight. Mike Chapman wanted to tell your father some things we found out today. About somebody else. About a man Kiernan knows who may have killed the three women who've disappeared.'

Shauna smiled despite herself. 'Like he wants to apologize, this detective?'

There was no need to tell her that Mike didn't view it quite that way.

'He wants to explain what's going on to your father,' I said. 'Would you mind sitting with me on the steps for a couple of minutes, till they're done? Let me get out of the rain?'

She sniffed her fingers again and then sat down beside me.

'How old are you, Shauna?'

'Nineteen. What's the difference?'

'What do you do?'

'I'm gonna be a sophomore at college. Going back next week, after Labor Day, if my father lets me with all this going on.'

'Have you spent much time at Ruffles?' I asked.

'My father won't hear of it. I'd catch hell for it, 'cause of my age. The boys do it all right, but somehow it's different with my sisters and me.'

I got it. Let everybody else's kids get loaded. Take their money and send them out into the night with any guy who'll pay the tab. But keep your own child out of harm's way.

'Are you and Kiernan close?'

'Sure we are. We're all close.'

'I want you to tell him something, Shauna. I want you to—'

'I don't know where he is. None of us do.'

'He's got a cell phone, hasn't he? Or you can tell Frank Shea to get a message to him.'

She stared straight ahead, listening to me but not making any promises.

'He didn't kill those girls, Shauna. I know that and Detective Chapman knows that. We weren't sure about it on Saturday night, but we're certain now,' I said. 'You've got to tell him that before he does something foolish.'

'Like what?'

Desperate people, Mike liked to remind me, did desperate things. 'Like go to Ireland, where you've got family, instead of resolving these things with the police. Like hurt himself, even accidentally.'

Shauna closed her eyes and took a deep breath.

'When I asked you if you've spent any time at Ruffles, you told me your father doesn't let you go there. That's not exactly an answer to my question, is it?' I asked. 'You've been there, haven't you?'

She looked away from me.

'Do you know the guys who work there?'

She wouldn't even meet me halfway.

'Charlie. You know Charlie, don't you?'

'Yeah.' There was a slight inflection in her voice, as though she was surprised I knew the bartender's name.

'How about Troy?'

No answer.

'Have you met a guy named Troy, Shauna? He's one of the bouncers.'

'That's how much you know. You cops think you know everything about Kiernan 'cause you went to Ruffles once. It's such a joke. There's nobody called Troy, okay?'

'He'd be new. Started this summer, maybe the end of July or the beginning of this month.'

'You can tell my father I've been to Ruffles, okay? I don't care what he does to me. It can't get any worse than this. But I'm telling you I was at the bar last week, with my brother Danny and my friend Erin,' Shauna said, pointing down the street. 'There isn't any Troy. I'd know if there was.'

'Did you see the picture of Kiernan in the paper this morning?' I said reluctantly, knowing the perp walk image would revive her hostility.

'Did I see it? Hello? I mean everyone we know saw it.'

'There's a man standing behind Kiernan, over the shoulder of one of the detectives. He was working the door on Saturday night,' I said. 'He's in his forties, a tall black man with a thick scar on the side of his neck, and tattoos – tattoos with initials all up and down his arms.'

Shauna was dripping with sarcasm now, pleased to show that she knew more than Mike and I did. 'Why? The detective wants to apologize to *him*, too? For thinking he's Troy somebody or other? Well, he's not Troy. There is no Troy at Ruffles. His name is Wilson.'

'Wilson.' I thought of the body we had discovered tonight. Wilson Rasheed. 'You've met him?'

'That's who my friends had to ask for to get in. I mean, I've seen him there the last couple of weeks. It's not like he's my buddy. Wilson and Hank. They're the guys on the door. You ask for them, you show them one of Kiernan's cards, and you get in.'

'Wilson – that's his first name or last?'

'Now why would I know that? Just Wilson is all anybody called him.'

A perfect alias to adopt, whether Troy's father was dead or alive when he first borrowed the name. Wilson was unlikely to come down from his cabin any time soon, had no way to be contacted by authorities while he was holed up, and had no criminal record if anyone were to do a name check.

'Tomorrow morning, Shauna, there'll be pictures of Wilson in the newspaper. Only his real name is Troy Rasheed, and he's the guy we're looking for. We just came from the place his father lives – his name was Wilson – and he's been killed, too.'

The girl was listening now, looking at my face.

'You can wait till the morning and read it in the newspapers or check it out online, or you can believe what I'm telling you and try to call Frank Shea – or Kiernan – right now. We need Kiernan's help. We need any little bit of information he has about Troy – the complete name he was using, where he said he was living, whether he had access to a car of any kind, all—'

'What's in it for my brother?'

'I'm handling one of the murder cases. I can work a deal on the problems he's facing about Ruffles. I can probably—'

'Probably? Well, that really sucks. You expect Kiernan to help you and *maybe* you're going to do something for him? Maybe?'

'It's not entirely up to me, Shauna. There's a judge, of course,' I said, and there was also the fact that I couldn't get a handle on why Kiernan Dylan had admitted cleaning out Amber Bristol's apartment. There'd be no guarantees until he explained that fact to us.

We both started at the sound of a door slamming. Mike was walking along the hydrangea-lined path toward the car, and from within the house I could hear Jimmy Dylan shouting. 'Shauna? You upstairs already?'

'In a minute, Dad.'

She got to her feet and I did, too. I took a card from the pocket of my pants and handed it to her. 'Don't wait until morning, I'm begging you. Kiernan's best chance to help himself is in the next few hours, before everybody sees Troy's picture.'

Shauna took the card with my cell number as well as my office phone and read my name aloud. 'Alexandra Cooper.'

'There's no reason for Kiernan to be protecting this guy. Troy's killed at least four people these last few weeks, including his own father. He's in too much of a frenzy to stop himself. It's likely to be someone just like you he'll hurt – a young woman with her whole life ahead of her.'

'Now you're blaming Kiernan for protecting a man he hardly

knows?' she said, stuck on my first sentence, turning toward the back door of the house. 'That's so stupid.'

'Kiernan told us about my victim, Shauna. Connected himself to her after she disappeared. If he's been covering something up for Troy Rasheed, it'll go better for him if he explains that to us sooner rather than later.'

'You don't get it, Alexandra, do you?' Shauna Dylan said, pulling at the handle on the screen door as she burst into tears again. 'You don't get why my whole family is broken up.'

'I understand how painful it must be, how—'

'You understand nothing,' Shauna said, letting the door close behind her and turning out the overhead light on the porch. 'Kiernan thinks it's my father who killed that whore. Accused him of it when he came home from court yesterday. It's our own father he's been trying to protect.'

44

'I got squat from Jimmy Dylan,' Mike said. 'What the hell were you doing out in the rain?'

'Chatting up one of his daughters.'

Mike made a U-turn and headed back to the Belt Parkway.

'I know it's a bad simile in light of poor Wilson Rasheed's demise, but I practically fell on my sword in there to get some help from Dylan.'

'Metaphor.'

'Whatever. The girl know anything?'

'I keep going back to your interrogation of Kiernan. If Troy murdered all three women, why did Kiernan admit packing up Amber Bristol's belongings? And why did we find them in Rasheed's house?'

'You think they're a team, Kiernan and Troy?'

'I can't imagine that. But the girl says there was a big blow-up when Kiernan came home after his arraignment.'

'About?'

'He accused his father of killing Amber Bristol. Look at it from Kiernan's perspective.'

'Good job, Alex,' Mercer said, thinking it through slowly. 'Suppose Amber came to Ruffles, maybe after her Friday night session with Herb Ackerman, at his office. She'd been fighting with Jimmy for weeks 'cause he was trying to break things up.'

'And he'd booted her out of the Brazen Head,' Mike said.

'We need to get to Kiernan as soon as possible,' Mercer said.

'I've got his sister working on it – well, thinking about it, at least.'

'If Amber was a nuisance to Kiernan, he might have put her right in the hands of a deadly predator hungry for his first kill. What if he told the bouncer to get rid of her,' Mike said. 'Figuratively speaking – or is that a metaphor for something, too?'

'Could have done that without even knowing the guy was a freak,' I said. 'And Shauna Dylan also told me Troy was using his father's name. He goes by Wilson.'

Mercer reached his arm over the seat back and high-fived me. 'She going to call her brother?'

'No promises. I told her it had to happen before morning if it's to be of any use. She's got my cell number.'

'Where's your car, Mercer?' Mike asked.

'Seems like a few days ago, but I have a vague memory of parking down at the courthouse this morning. Alex, you mind if I use your dining room table for a few hours?'

'I don't need—'

'I know you don't. I just don't feel like taking the extra time to drive all the way home and back into Manhattan at the crack of dawn. Wake Vickee up just to aggravate her and not even get to see the baby. Might as well start going through the files Nelly Kallin gave us till my eyes give out.'

Mike's apartment, not far from my own, was too small for even a sofa. Mercer had crashed at my place many times over the years, and this way he would get a jump on reading the information that Commissioner Scully – and Battaglia – would want by midday.

Mike dropped us in front of the door and we each carried a bundle of folders to the elevator.

'I can't even begin to help you tonight,' I said to Mercer. 'I've got to get a few hours of sleep. The guest room is all made up, when you're ready.'

'I don't like the fact that he's out there, Alex. We're losing this race.'

'I'll see you in the morning,' I said, closing the door to my bedroom after spreading out the files on the long formal table where Mercer liked to work.

I took a steaming hot shower, slipped on a nightgown, and got into bed. As exhausted as I was, Mike was right. When I closed my eyes, I watched either a replay of Kerry Hastings being dragged along the street when the taxicab was rear-ended or saw the body of Wilson Rasheed pinned to the floor of his cabin.

I tossed and turned until shortly after six thirty, when I was sure I heard voices in my living room. I got up, wrapped a robe around me, and went out to look.

Mike was standing over Mercer's shoulder, and both were drinking coffee.

'How did you get in here? Did I sleep through the bell?'

'I called Mercer on his cell. He opened the door.'

'What's wrong?'

'There's another girl gone missing, Coop. A twenty-year-old named Pam Lear.'

'Twenty,' I said, cringing at the thought of another victim in the hands of this monster. 'What do you know?'

'It happened sometime between Sunday evening and yesterday morning. Her roommate on Long Island reported her missing when she didn't come home again last night. The Suffolk County cops are on their way in with the roommate now. We were just waiting for you to wake up so we can have a go at her.'

'Where was Pam last seen?'

'At her job, Coop. On Sunday,' Mike said, hitching his thumb on his belt. 'She was a summer intern, a guide with the National Park Service.'

'Does that mean a uniform?'

'Light brown shirt and dark brown trousers. Smokey Bear hat.'

'What park?' I asked. 'Where?'

'Fort Tilden. An abandoned army post.'

'Not quite as dramatic as Governors Island,' Mercer said, 'but another military ghost town.'

'Where is it?' I asked, turning back to the bedroom to throw on some clothes.

'You were a stone's throw from it last night, when we were in Queens,' Mike said. 'The kids in Breezy use the place like it was a playground, Coop. It's less than a mile from the Dylans' house.'

45

'It's as dark now as it was in the middle of the night,' I said, looking at the clouds overhead as I climbed the steps of Joe Galiano's Bell 412 shortly after 7:00 a.m. for the short chopper ride to Fort Tilden. The rain had let up for the moment, but the sky was threatening.

'Good to see you again, Alex. Yeah, they've got storm warnings posted for the whole region. The damn thing is moving up the coast awfully fast. We're trying to evacuate folks from Beach Channel Drive before it hits,' Galiano said. 'Air is the only way to go.'

Mercer and Mike came in behind me and belted themselves in as the pilot readied for liftoff. This time, as he hovered before thrusting out over the river, the heavy machine lurched when caught by a fierce gust of wind.

Galiano cleared the Manhattan Bridge and then set a course straight through the middle of Brooklyn. There was no point trying to talk to Mike. The turbulence had him braced in his seat, silently staring down at the apartment rooftops for the ten-minute ride to Queens.

'Where can you put her down?' Mercer asked. The ocean was churning below us, and the small islands that still dotted Jamaica Bay – pinheads among the swells – looked likely to meet the fate of their one-time neighbor Ruffle Bar.

'You don't know Tilden?'

Mercer shook his head. 'I've only seen it on a map.'

Mike mumbled without picking up his head. 'During the cold war in the 1950s, Fort Tilden was the first place in New York City to house a Nike missile base, to defend against nuclear attack from the Soviet Union.'

'Nike missiles, in the Rockaways?' Mercer asked.

'Makes a sweet little landing strip for me, now that the base has been mothballed,' Galiano said. 'Those Nike Hercules that were deployed at Tilden were forty feet long, with nuclear warheads that could destroy an entire formation of bombers.'

He circled over the area again and found his target, swinging in the wind as he aimed for a cracked stretch of cement in the middle of the deserted beach.

Two park rangers came running in our direction from beyond a fence that seemed to cordon off the old missile site from the rest of the facility.

'Detective Chapman?' one asked. 'The young lady is just a short ride away from here – the roommate of the missing girl. The police are on the bridge now, and Detective Draper is here already, sir, if you'll follow me.'

I had dressed for the foul weather. I expected it would be a long and unpleasant day. The navy rain jacket I wore was a gift from a friend in the Hostage Negotiation Unit. It had an NYPD logo on the front, and the words TALK TO ME on the back.

It was as though we had landed on the dunes of the Vineyard's South Beach. There was a wide swath of sand rising to crests covered with beach grass and bayberry bushes. Gulls patrolled the choppy shoreline, picking at empty shells that had washed up among the strands of seaweed.

A ranger led us up over the dunes on one of the many trails that bordered a small maritime forest of gnarled pines and cottonwoods. I paused on the incline, and as I looked off in every direction there were footprints in the sand – far too many footprints to be of any value in an investigation.

The second ranger brought up the rear.

'This is a public park now?' I asked.

'Yes, ma'am. Seven miles of beach. Not usually empty like this, but we've cleared it of all the birdwatchers and bathers 'cause of the storm.'

The entire skyline of Manhattan unfolded to the northwest, under a mantle of dark clouds. I'd never seen the sight from a beach, and it was one more painful reminder to look over at the great hole where the twin towers used to stand.

Mike and Mercer were standing still on the highest point of the dune, atop a sun-bleached wooden staircase, trying to get their bearings as they scoped the area. I joined them.

Ranger Barrett was answering their questions. 'It's operated as a seasonal park only. Pam just had a summer job with us. In fact, Sunday was her last day.'

'She was here?'

'Yes, sir. Came here Sunday morning. She signed in.'

'And left when?' Mike asked, cupping his hand to his ear. The wind was carrying away our words.

'I have no idea, I'm sorry to say.'

'Why not?'

'Well, it was actually an unusual situation, Detective. We don't have a very big staff, and the Park Service pulled some of them out for a special program they were running at another facility.'

'Governors Island,' Mercer said. 'Had to be the muster.'

'That's exactly right, sir,' Barrett said. 'Since it was Pam's last day and all, I don't think there was anyone around to care whether she signed out or not.'

'But she was assigned right here?'

'Yes, yes, she was.'

Men were scrambling up and down the dunes, moving in and out of a dozen or so structures, most without windows or roofs.

'Who are they?' Mike asked.

'All the civilians are gone, sir. Those are rangers that have been called in for the search. And a number of your men from the local precinct.'

Mike took a single latex glove from his rear pocket. He walked onto the beach and scooped a handful of sand, filling two fingers of the glove and knotting its top. 'Elise Huff. The sand in the green blanket around her body. Could be the guy had her out here. They can compare this to Dickie's sample.'

A small caravan of black Crown Vics approached in the distance, undoubtedly carrying Dickie Draper and our new witness.

'Where can we do this interview?' Mike asked, starting to walk down the far side of the dunes.

'Can you see that gazebo?' Ranger Barrett said. 'The long building behind it was the old officers' club. There are still some benches in there. It's all I've got for shelter.'

'Don't trip, Coop,' Mike said.

There were Virginia creepers and bayberry bushes criss-crossing the paths, concealing huge blocks of cement that were visible in the sand every few feet.

'Cannon casements,' the ranger said. 'The fort was active from 1917 until it was decommissioned in 1974.'

'Local kids play here?' Mike asked.

'That's one of our biggest problems,' he said. 'Talk about an attractive nuisance.'

Barrett sidestepped the trail and kicked some sand off a rusting metal door that was set into a cement block. There was a large red X sprayed onto the door.

'These bunkers are everywhere. Kids in the neighborhood know their positions better than my rangers do.'

'Why the X?' I asked.

'That means someone has checked inside this morning, made sure there's – well, no body. No evidence.'

At the base of the sandy hill off to my right was an enormous concrete arc the size of a Greek amphitheater, its open side facing the ocean. Two uniformed cops were walking up and down its many layered façade, also looking for clues.

'What's that?' Mike asked.

'When this place boasted antiaircraft guns and giant cannons, here and in Sandy Hook, New Jersey, that were supposed to make New York impregnable to attack by sea, the batteries were all right there where you stood, on the highest dunes. If the enemy overran the fort, the thick arc meant the guns couldn't be turned around and used against the city.'

'And inside?'

'A metal gate shuts off the interior space in case of attack. It's got a warren full of empty rooms dug underground that used to hold the gunpowder and artillery shells.'

Mike shook his head and started to walk more briskly toward the black cars. 'Get as many man as you can in there. I want every crevice of this place turned inside out, Mr. Barrett.'

'We're short on personnel, sir. With the storm coming so fast—'

'And we're short one girl, Barrett. I'll get you all the cops you need, but you'd better show them every possible hiding place. You sift every grain of sand before you even think about getting off this beach.'

'You believe Pam was abducted from here, Detective? You think something happened to her before she left?'

'I'm thinking nothing good, pal,' Mike called over his shoulder. Then he put his head down and one hand on top of it to hold his thick black hair out of his eyes. 'Don't know if she's here or in the deep blue yonder or in a better place. But we've got a maniac on the loose – or two.'

He turned to Mercer and me. 'We're looking for a serial rapist who likes to torture his victims and thinks he's safer by killing them. And a despondent Dylan – or his old man – who probably used this park as a playground.'

I could see Dickie Draper through the open side of the former officers' club. His weight served him well today. He was anchored upright to the ground despite the wind, while the rest of us were fighting it head-on.

Before I could reach the covered building, there was a huge clap of thunder and a streak of lightning off in the distance. The cloud overhead burst and the rain poured down in torrents. I dashed the rest of the way for cover.

In the far corner of the windowless room, a thin young woman sat alone on a bench, wrapped in a trenchcoat. A policewoman wearing a Suffolk County uniform stood behind her.

'You and me will have to share this one,' Draper said. 'No need to bring in someone from the Queens DA's office till we know what we got.'

'I'd be happy for help, Dickie. But we might as well get right on it.'

Mike turned to Ranger Barrett as I approached the girl. 'Nobody stops. I don't care if they're soaked to the bone. The search goes on until your men find every underground bunker and whatever else is hiding in the sand. I want this girl alive.'

Mercer was on the phone to Peterson to demand more backup.

'I'm Alex Cooper,' I said. 'I'm with the Manhattan District Attorney's Office.'

'This here's Lydia,' Draper said.

I sat opposite her, on another old bench with wobbly legs.

She kept looking at Draper as though he had a second head, less than charmed by his manner.

'She's been telling me about Pam. She says that—'

'I think it's better if we back up a bit.' I wanted this information from Lydia, not filtered through Draper in the retelling.

Lydia's eyes darted back and forth between the two of us.

'Do you understand what this is all about?'

'I'm beginning to, I think.'

'There's no detail too insignificant for what the detectives need to do. Every word, every description, every fact you know about Pam might be useful,' I said. I needed the most critical information first, but I also needed to know something about Pam – her judgment, her strengths, and her vulnerability.

'I don't know her well,' Lydia said. 'She's a student at Stony Brook. She had an ad on MySpace for an apartment rental for the summer. I – um – I answered the ad. I had to make up some classes at summer school.'

The two had gotten along well as casual acquaintances but were not close friends. Pam was a serious student, majoring in history, who loved her internship with the Park Service because it combined her interest in American history with her desire to spend time outdoors.

'Tell me about this weekend. About Sunday,' I said. 'Did you see Pam?'

'No. No, I didn't. She had to be at the park – I mean here – by eight o'clock. I had dinner with her on Saturday. But then I went out for a while, so I slept in on Sunday morning.'

Lydia's long brown hair hung on her shoulders. Her hands were in the pockets of her coat. Every time a roll of thunder sounded in the distance, she seemed to get more agitated.

'Did you speak to her after that?'

'Yeah, yeah, I told Mr. Draper that I did.'

'How many times?'

'Twice. Twice more.'

'When?'

'I guess the first time was around noon. She was supposed to turn in a bunch of things that the NPS had given her to use during the summer, for orientation. Pamphlets and stuff. She also had to return her ID and her uniforms,' Lydia said. 'But she accidentally left her backpack somewhere, so she called to ask me if it was in the kitchen, 'cause if not she was afraid she had lost it on the bus.'

'How long was the conversation?'

'Like a minute or two. I went to look around the apartment, and the backpack was still on the floor, near the front door. Pam told me she was relieved – she could always turn the stuff in on Monday. She asked if I wanted to go out for dinner, you know, to celebrate the end of her job. I told her I had to study for a final exam on Monday morning and I wasn't in the mood to celebrate. That I'd let her know if I changed my mind.'

'Did she say anything else in that first phone call? Anything about who she was with or what she was doing?'

Lydia shrugged. 'No.'

'The second call, did you make that one or did she?'

'It was Pam who called me again.'

'What time? Why?'

Lydia looked past me at the roiling surf. 'I'm not sure. Maybe two thirty. Maybe three. I was curled up in my bedroom with the door closed,' she said plaintively, trying to explain what now seemed like indifference to Pam's situation. 'I was cramming for a chemistry test. I resented every interruption, every phone call.'

'Why did Pam call?'

'I don't know that either.' Lydia's fingers were nervously scratching the inside pockets of her trenchcoat.

'What did she say, exactly?'

'She was all hyper, like excited. Sort of talking fast. Some of it making no sense.'

'About what?'

'The first thing she asked me was what time did she have to be home for dinner. I told her I didn't know what she was talking about, that I'd already told her I couldn't go out with her. But she repeated something about our dinner date – looking forward to it and all. Then she said for sure she'd be home by eight.'

'Do you know what Pam meant?' I asked.

'I thought she was showing off for someone, pretending she had a date. That's why I was kind of annoyed with her. I asked her what was going on, and that's when she told me she was with a guy.'

'What guy? Did she tell you anything about him?'

The men had formed a semicircle behind me. Lydia looked around at their faces and hunched her shoulders as the thunder boomed again. 'You're all staring at me like I'm supposed to solve this for you,' she said. 'I barely know the girl, and I have no idea who she was talking to. I didn't know anything about a serial killer when she was on the phone.'

Lydia removed her hands from her pocket. I took them between mine, clasped them together, and tried to keep her engaged and cooperative.

'We understand you had no reason to connect any of this to Pam. Please keep talking, Lydia. Please tell us everything she said to you. What did she tell you about the guy?'

'Weird. I even asked her, "What guy? "Twice she said to me, "You know, the one who comes to the fort every week."'

'That's great, Lydia. Pam had talked to you about this young man before Sunday.'

'That's what's so odd, Miss Cooper. She had never mentioned him to me. Pam talked about her job, about the other interns. She loved anything that had to do with history. But she didn't have a single date these two months, much less say anything about a guy she met at work.'

'You're certain? You just didn't miss something while you were studying?'

'Pam never talked about a guy. Not once the entire summer. I mean, she was hoping to meet someone interesting, but it didn't happen.'

Either Lydia had been too deeply immersed in her periodic table of elements to listen to the earlier references or Pam was trying to make a point during that second phone call.

'What did she say?'

'I told you. She was with somebody, like I was supposed to know about who she meant,' Lydia said. 'Only I didn't.'

'What were her words, her exact words?'

Lydia took her hands from mine and tucked her feet under the bench. She seemed to be trying to think.

I pushed her. 'The words Pam used, tell me those.'

' "I haven't forgotten about dinner. I'll for sure be home by eight." That's how she started. I told her I didn't know what she was talking about. Then she said. "You know that guy I told you about? The one who comes here every week? Knows all these hidden places in the old fort?" "What the hell are you talking about?" I asked. Then it was something about history. That he wanted to show her something historical. Like a family place.'

'Family place?' I turned my head and looked at Mike. Whose family, I wondered, and what kind of place.

'I think what she said was where his family went for holidays.'

The rain was teeming now and the tide was rising on the beach.

I couldn't imagine Troy Rasheed and his family on a holiday outing, but I had visions of the Dylans at their vacation house a few miles away. I was as confused as Lydia.

'What holidays?'

Her words were clipped and firm. 'I don't know. If I hadn't been so annoyed about the interruption, maybe I'd have asked more questions. It was just so unlike Pam. Then she said she was going and that she'd call me again when they got there.'

'Got where?'

'Wherever the hell she agreed to go. Look, Miss Cooper,' Lydia said, standing up, 'at the time she called, I thought she was just showing off for this guy, pretending she had something else to do that night. I studied, I went to sleep and got up early. Pam wasn't there. Great. I figured she and her history pal hit it off. Nothing strange about that. I took my exam, went out with a bunch of friends from school, spent the evening at the library, and when I came home late last night I realized Pam's backpack was still by the door.'

'Did you try to reach her?'

'Yeah. Sure. I called her cell but it didn't even go to voice mail. I called five times. It just isn't like her not to follow the rules, you know? Not to turn in the park uniforms and stuff,' Lydia said, laughing a bit. 'She's such a nerdy kind of good girl.'

Lydia walked to the end of the bench, facing out to the rough sea, and sat down. 'I had no one to call, didn't know the people she worked with. Then I was watching the late news, and the story about these girls who'd been killed came on. It didn't seem possible that it could have anything to do with Pam. But I kept watching, and there was a local news story that showed one of the bodies was found in Brooklyn, not too far from here.'

Elise Huff, wrapped in the green blanket, was dumped in the marsh off Belt Parkway, right across Jamaica Bay from where we stood.

'That's when you called the Suffolk police?'

'Yes, ma'am. Just a few hours ago.' Lydia dug her hands back into her pockets. 'I'm kicking myself now 'cause I think maybe Pam was trying to signal me.'

'How do you mean?' I asked.

'She was so wound up, I guess she was really excited about whatever she thought she was going to see. But at the same time she was making a point to whoever was with her, if he was listening, that she had to be somewhere, with someone, by eight o'clock. Pam was obviously trying to let *him* know that she had talked about him before, even though she hadn't, I swear it. Like maybe she was a little bit afraid and wanted to warn him someone knew she was with him.'

'You're doing very well, Lydia. Everything you know, every idea you put together – it all helps us,' I said. 'Has anyone asked you, did Pam say where she was when she called that second time?'

'Oh, yeah. She was right here.'

'On her post, at Fort Tilden?'

'Yes, she and her friend – well, this guy – they were driving around the beach.'

'I got them working the Lear girl's cell phone already, Alex. Looking for pings. Seeing if we can trace where she's gone. Getting nothing from it so far. Could be he ditched it,' Dickie Draper said, waddling closer to me. Then he looked at Lydia. 'Must be wrong about where Pam said she was. Think harder. They don't let anybody drive on the beach here. The only vehicles these park personnel are allowed to use going over the sand are dune buggies.'

Lydia pursed her lips. 'I'm telling you what Pam said, Detective. That he was driving her all over the beach, showing her things she'd never seen before. In his jeep. I'm pretty sure she said he had an old army jeep.'

46

'An old army jeep,' I said, as I watched the Suffolk officer lead Lydia to the patrol car to get her back to the mainland before travel became impossible. 'What's the description of Wilson Rasheed's jeep that Edenton put out on the APB?'

'Willy MB, 1944,' Mercer said. 'Manufactured for the Department of the Army. Those little workhorses that could handle any terrain.'

Mike was giving Dickie Draper directions to Jimmy Dylan's Breezy Point house. 'It's a five-minute drive from here. See who's at home. We need to reel Kiernan in.'

'Whoa, whoa, whoa, Mikey. Who died and made you the commanding officer? This frigging breeze is turning into a hurricane. I'm outta here.'

'Don't panic just because they don't make life rafts big enough to hold you, Dickie. I didn't happen to come by car, so I'm counting on you to check it out.'

The thunder and lightning were getting closer. It was almost high tide and the surf was raging. Joe Galiano came trotting over from the broken-up concrete pad on which we had landed. 'We've got to get out of here now. It's going to be dicey. Winds are up to fifty miles an hour.'

Mike didn't need to be told a second time. 'Let's go, Coop.'

'One call. Give me one minute.' I held up a finger and backed into a corner of the long room so that I could hear once I dialed the number.

'You can fly in this?' Mike asked Galiano, as his hair whipped across his face.

'Seventy-four miles per hour makes it an actual hurricane. I'll get you home before that happens.'

'If Coop moves her ass,' Mike said, starting off behind Galiano. 'Mercer, she'll listen to you.'

'Who you calling?'

'Nelly Kallin,' I said. 'On her cell.'

Mercer tugged at my arm. I plugged one finger in my ear and held the phone to my other ear.

'Ms. Kallin? It's Alex Cooper. Are you okay?'

'I'm fine, thanks.'

'Still with your sister?'

'Yes, yes, I am. And I heard the news about Wilson Rasheed this morning.'

'I'm sorry we didn't call you about that. I don't mean to be rude, but I have to make this short, Ms. Kallin, because there's another girl who's been abducted.'

I heard a noise competing with the sound of the wind and waves and turned to see that Galiano had started the rotors of the chopper. Behind him, the city lights glittered as though it were midnight, powered up because of the darkness that had descended with the storm.

'It's got to be Troy, Ms. Kallin. It's another old military facility where the victim worked, and he was probably driving his father's jeep. She was a park ranger, wearing a uniform.'

'Oh, God.'

'You were right about his m.o., too. It wasn't a blitz attack. He somehow managed to convince her – convince Pam – to go with him.'

Mercer took my arm and started to walk me toward the door frame of the old building entrance.

'Those therapists taught him well,' she said.

'We didn't get through all your files yet. And you know so much more about him than anyone else. The man who kidnapped Pam told her he wanted to show her where his family went for the holidays. Does that mean anything to you? Did Troy talk about that at all?'

'What holiday?'

'I don't know which one. That's why I'm calling you. We may break up, Ms. Kallin. Call me back if you have any ideas. You seem to know things it will take us days to figure out.'

'I have good reason to, Alex,' Nelly Kallin said. 'If you look at those photos I gave you, you'll see a small set of initials tattooed on Troy's right arm, up near his shoulder. PW, for the name of one of the young women he savaged, who couldn't identify him.'

I was moving from the cover of the officers' club out into the rain.

'She's the daughter of my best friend. She never got her day in court, and she never really recovered from the trauma of the attack. I made it my business to try to see that Troy Rasheed never got a chance to hurt anyone else again. I've failed miserably.'

'We wouldn't have a shot at this without you,' I said, trying to pick up speed across the sand. It made sense that Nelly Kallin had been so interested in every detail of this prisoner's life. 'I had no idea you had any connection to one of his victims.'

'No one does, Alex. I've never told anyone.'

'Easter. Fourth of July. Labor Day,' I said, thinking that we were just days away from that holiday weekend. 'Thanksgiving. Christmas. Was there a time the Rasheed family did anything functional together?'

'I can barely hear you.'

'Those holidays, can you think of any significance to any of them?'

Nelly Kallin sounded dejected. 'I don't know where they went. I hate to disappoint you. Thanksgiving was Troy's favorite holiday. They went away every year, but I just don't know where. He talked about it in therapy because it's the place he had his first sexual experience – a consensual one, he claims.'

'The family traveled?' I asked, ducking beneath the rotors to follow Mercer up the steps of the sleek-looking helicopter.

'Not far from home. They used to go to one of the bases in the area for Thanksgiving weekend. They were able to stay for free because the base had a motel that Mr. Rasheed's company built for military families. I don't know if it was the turkey or the sex,' Nelly Kallin said, 'but the place made quite an impression on Troy.'

A base with a motel. Didn't we see an old abandoned one on Governors Island? I was trying to remember what Mike had said about it.

'The name of it, Ms. Kallin. Do you remember the name of the motel?'

'What did Detective Chapman say about tattoos being the new postcards? Like I told you, Troy identified it with some kind of sexual experience, a pleasurable one. He's got the number eight tattooed in the small of his back. It was a Super 8 Motel.'

47

Joe Galiano was poised to take off the moment Mercer closed the door and belted up.

'We've got to go to Governors Island, Joe. We've got to search there.'

'Have you lost it, Coop?'

'Call Peterson, Mike. Tell him to get a crew over as fast as humanly possible. Tell him to call the Park Service and—'

Lightning sliced the sky ahead of us and thunder boomed over the sound of the chopper's engines.

'Pay no attention to her, Joe. Let's get this buggy home.'

'That was Nelly Kallin I called. Forget Kiernan Dylan. Troy Rasheed has taken that girl to Governors Island. Don't fight me on this one, Mike. That's where they went on Sunday. That's where she is,' I said, not speaking the words *dead or alive*.

Mercer had flipped open his cell to make the call. 'She's right. And I bet we find that jeep parked in a lot not far from the Battery Maritime Building, if Troy hasn't skipped town.'

The chopper rocked from side to side as the winds pounded it.

'What's the verdict, gentlemen? We pass right over the island on our way home,' Galiano said.

Mike was clutching the edge of his seat as he argued with Mercer. 'You said they were checking everyone going on and off the island on Sunday.'

'And Pam Lear had Park Service ID. She had a uniform, too. According to the timeline that Lydia just gave us, they wouldn't have arrived till late in the day, when all the feebs were monitoring departures. I doubt she and Troy had any problem getting *on* the island, blending into the crowd. She would have looked more like she belonged there than anyone else. It's good, Mike.'

'You know the island, Joe?' Mike's fear of flying was justified in the storm. 'I guess if the Wright Brothers could take off and land there, you'll figure it out.'

'We once had a mayor named La Guardia,' Galiano said. 'He wanted to make the place the city's first airport. Been there dozens of times for training exercises. There's a nice flat spot in the middle of Colonels' Row.'

The chopper bounced its way back across Brooklyn as we sat riveted in our seats, contemplating Pam Lear's fate.

'Hang on,' Galiano said, clearing the rooftops of the old buildings as he aimed for a level space in the middle of the lawn.

The chopper's struts slammed into the ground and we rocked into place. The thunder rolled over us, louder and closer than it had been just minutes ago.

I picked my head up to look over Mercer's shoulder, and as I did, the entire Manhattan skyline faded to black.

48

The freak storm ripping through the city had sparked a massive power outage, a blackout that left Manhattan in late-morning darkness.

'So much for backup,' Mike said.

'Doesn't change what we've got to do,' Mercer said, opening the chopper door and climbing down. 'What was that guy's name – the one from the Park Service who took us around?'

'Leamer,' Mike said. 'Russell Leamer.'

'Let's make a dash for the ferry terminal. That's where his office is. Joe?'

'I've got to stay with my machine, guys. Double back if you need me.'

Cell phones didn't work on Governors Island. I remembered that the ferry captain told us that. No wonder Pam Lear couldn't make good on her promise to call Lydia when she reached her destination.

I followed Mike and Mercer as they jogged the cobblestone path past Castle Williams to the office that bordered the ferry dock.

We saw no workers or rangers on our run, just the empty old barracks and the fortress that stood sentinel over the angry seas of the harbor.

By the time we reached Leamer's office, scattered lights began to dot the cityscape. Buildings with their own generators came to life – police headquarters, huge medical centers that fronted the East River – and several office towers glowed again beneath the ominous clouds.

Leamer hadn't seen the helicopter land. He was seated at a desk, on a landline phone, when the three of us surprised him by walking in, soaked to the bone despite our windbreakers and jackets.

Mercer took the lead in explaining why we had come back to the island.

Leamer got to his feet, gesturing wildly with the receiver still in his hand. 'There can't be anyone hiding here, damn it. The feds searched everywhere.'

'They searched on Sunday,' Mercer said, knowing that they had finished their effort before Pam Lear decided to leave Fort Tilden. 'They started early in the morning and were done by midday, before this girl even disappeared.'

'How many men have you got working with you today?' Mike asked.

'I'm alone.'

'Where are the others?'

'They went back to Manhattan an hour ago, with the last ferry.'

'The last ferry?'

Leamer pointed out the window. 'The surge from the harbor

breached the seawall next to the dock. The tide is so high that the ramp has been lifted too steeply to meet the ferry. They can't make any trips until this passes, and there's no telling how much flooding there'll be.'

The sight was terrifying. The low-lying walkway that led away from the dock was full of water, and the river had risen almost as high as the landing slip.

'We need the phone,' Mercer said.

'I need it, too, Detective,' Leamer said, becoming more frantic with the news that we were looking for our fourth victim. 'I've got a disaster to manage here.'

Mercer calmed the man and took over the phone, calling the lieutenant and asking him to send men to the Battery Maritime Building, to get them to Governors Island the moment the storm blew through. The expression on his face changed at the end of the call – tightened – with some piece of news Peterson had told him, something he didn't want to hear. 'I understand, Loo.'

'Aren't there a couple of firemen posted here? How do you reach them?' Mike asked Leamer.

'They were evacuated with the ranger staff. The entire power grid for the metropolitan area was knocked out, Detective. Lightning hit one of the main transformer stations.'

'Shit,' Mike said, ready to tear the place apart to look for Pam Lear. 'Are you armed?'

'No, sir.'

'Lock this door and don't open it until you see us again, okay?'

'But the water – I've got to get up to higher ground. There are government documents I've got to save and—'

'Documents? We're looking for a human being. We're hoping to find her alive, okay? You wait right here by the phone until the last possible moment – unless you're going to help with this. And if anybody from the police department calls in with information for us, you stand up by that cannon out there and scream your lungs out till one of us gets back to you.'

Leamer's jaw dropped as we walked out the door.

More thunder boomed overhead, like giant bowling balls banging against each other, as we ran from Leamer's tiny office, across the roadway, onto the porch of one of the barracks that lined the waterfront.

Then a loud noise jolted me, coming even closer to us, as Joe Galiano's chopper rose into the sky over the surging river, heading away from the island.

49

'Galiano going for a joy ride?' Mike asked. He was tense and wired. I could read it in the way he tapped his foot and played with the zipper on his jacket.

'Apparently his communication system was still working on board the bird – a little more high-tech than the rest of this place,' Mercer said. 'Commissioner Scully ordered him back. Wants to be able to get a SWAT team in here, in the event we find anything, the moment he can assemble them. That's what Peterson said.'

'You know this place,' I said to Mike. 'Where do we start?'

He squatted beside me, drawing lines in the rain that covered the gray floor paint. 'Here's where we are, right next to the ferry slip. This is the route we took the other day, remember? Gotta go with Nelly's instinct and start at the Super 8.'

'Does the time frame fit with the dates Rasheed might have been here?' I asked.

'Yeah, the motel was built in the early eighties, along with a bowling alley and theater, when the coast guard had charge of the island.'

Mike pointed in the opposite direction from which we'd come. 'It's off that way. You need a break, want to stop, we just pull in on the porch of any of those houses in Nolan Park.'

There was a slight grade in the road as we doubled back past the enormous British cannon at the top of the ferry landing and ran up the roadway. The handsome row of yellow houses, once fancy homes to the generals, looked like the empty set of a horror movie. The tree-lined park that had been lush with foliage just days ago had been stripped bare of its leaves in the last few hours. Old screen doors torn off their hinges by the wind flapped against the hollow buildings, and broken glass from fragile windows lay scattered about on porches and steps.

At the end of the park, Mike hooked a turn. The Super 8 stood out from the rest of the elegant architecture like a dreadful anachronism.

Mike got to the office door first and opened it. The room was bare except for the original counter, where I imagined Wilson Rasheed once stood to register his odd little family.

'Check out over there,' Mike said to Mercer, pointing to the two-story wing on the far side of the office.

Door after door opened without resistance. There was nothing left inside, no furniture at all, but the men went into every one of the dozens of rooms, looking for signs of habitation in any of the spaces. I waited in front of the motel, under cover of the entrance, scouring the grounds that spread in either direction.

Mike's frustration was obvious. 'Hurry up, Mercer. Let's go into each of these houses,' he said, retracing our steps to Nolan Park. 'Can't tell if the windows were broken in the storm or by vandals before it. You do the ones on the west side and I'll take the east. Coop, plant yourself on a front porch right in the middle and don't move.'

There were almost twenty of the old buildings framing the park. The men disappeared into the two houses that formed a V at the highest point in the row, and I took shelter six doors down, hanging on to a pillar to stabilize myself against the strong gusts.

Windows rattled behind me, and as Mike and Mercer made their way from basements to attics down the row of houses, I could hear doors slamming and heavy footsteps pounding the floorboards.

The men were fifty feet beyond me now, and Mike waved for me to catch up with them. They were headed back in the direction of Russell Leamer's office. I ran behind them, slowed by the water that squished out of my sneakers as though I were jogging on a treadmill made of sponge.

Leamer opened the door and we pushed one another inside.

'Any calls from my boss?' Mike asked.

'None.'

'You got word on the storm? On getting the ferry back?'

'The eye just seems to be stalled right off the coast, Detective.'

'We were here on Saturday, Mr. Leamer. There were locked doors inside Castle Williams. We need your keys for those padlocks.'

'I – uh – I can't. There's nothing in those cells.'

'Give me the keys,' Mike said. He raised his voice and he jabbed his finger at Leamer's chest.

Leamer turned to his desk. He fingered a key in his hand but hesitated to open the drawer. 'If I've got the only keys to these locked spaces, then how could anyone else—'

'We're dealing with a killer who's got a history of burglary, okay? Don't ask me to explain things, just do whatever I tell you. You're coming with me, and I want to know why the cells are kept locked.'

'In Castle Williams?'

'Yeah.'

'Because they're in such bad shape it would be dangerous to let visitors in. There's just junk inside. Old furniture, folding chairs for events that we hold here. Nothing of value.'

'C'mon. First stop,' Mike said to Leamer.

'Troy Rasheed is so used to prison, so comfortable behind bars, it's a good idea he might be in one,' Mercer said. 'Go ahead. Take Alex with you. I'll stay near the office.'

I didn't want us to split up. 'Let's just leave the phone, okay?'

'I need you with us, Coop. Mercer's fine.'

I shook off the rain, ready to go out into the storm with Mike and Russell Leamer, who was slowly putting on his slicker and large hat.

'The walkway's flooded,' Leamer said. 'We've got to take the road.'

The river had continued to surge over the old seawall and the only way we could get back to the fortress was on higher ground.

Mike and I jogged along in tandem while Leamer, slowed by his long raincoat, lagged behind.

When we reached the deep archway that led into the prison, Mike waited for Leamer to take us inside. Now, in complete darkness, the three circular tiers of cells looked like the hellholes they were refitted to be during the Civil War.

'Where?' Mike shouted at Leamer.

We had tried these cell doors on Saturday. Now Mike was ready to tear through the entire prison again.

Leamer held out two keys on a chain. 'These open everything in here.'

Mike unhooked one from the chain.

'Coop, you take him and start on the top. Anything locked, open it up and look.'

I couldn't move. Huge waves were pounding against the lowest row of casement openings. Water was pouring onto the earthen ground floor of the dank building, and it looked like it wouldn't be long until it was partially submerged.

'Upstairs, kid,' Mike shouted at me. 'The faster you move, the faster we're out of here.'

I followed Leamer into the staircase and up to the third tier. He opened the doors that were locked and shone a flashlight, but there was nothing at all inside.

I could hear Mike clanging each of the cell doors below us and I yelled to him. 'All clear on three.'

Back down the steps to the middle tier, where the only locked cubicles had a few piled-up chairs stored in them.

Leamer shone his light into each of the others as we made our way around the perimeter.

'Stop!' I shouted abruptly. 'What's in there?'

It was one of the open cells, one that Mercer had examined on Saturday.

'Looks like – like,' Leamer pulled on the heavy iron door and we walked in. 'Like old canteens.'

The two canteens looked like something out of Frank Bannerman's military catalog. Beneath one of them was a knife – an open switchblade with six inches of rusty steel forming its sharp point.

I picked up the items and ran past Leamer, down the staircase to where Mike was completing his search of the ground floor.

He took the knife from me and closed it. Then shook the canteens, one at a time, turning them upside down. The first was bone dry, but a bit of water trickled from the second one.

'Park Service use anything like these?' Mike asked.

'No, no, we don't. There's no potable water on this island,' Leamer said. 'We bring it in by bottles.'

'So anybody planning an overnight visit might come prepared with some of them?'

'We don't allow overnights.'

'Troy Rasheed's a guy who specializes in what isn't allowed,' Mike said, turning slowly in place as he eyed the tiers around him once more. 'There must be a basement here, isn't there?'

Russell Leamer was watching the waves wash through the casements, as uneasy as I was about them.

'Not in Castle Williams, Detective. It's too low, too close to the water level.'

'But I thought there was a dungeon on the island. Most of the military accounts from that period said there was a black hole.'

Leamer took the other sets of keys from his pocket and jangled them, searching for one to hand to Mike.

'That's in the Governor's House, Detective, on the eastern side of the island. There's a dungeon where prisoners were kept in the basement of the post headquarters. That's the black hole.'

50

'How fast can you move?' Mike asked the ranger.

The cobblestones had been made slippery by the rain. The three of us took the back way along Colonels' Row, slowed by the slick road surface, to get to the ivy-covered brick house that stood separate from the officers' quarters.

Leamer was puffing as he walked, trying to explain what we were going to find. 'It was called the Governor's House when the British held the island but not used by our military as a residence. It was actually the place in which court-martials were held.'

Mike was trying to move the older man along. 'And now?'

'It's in better shape than many of the buildings, furnished – for ceremonial purposes – but nothing much has been done with it since the coast guard left.'

'And the dungeon? Is it accessible?'

'I don't think so. I mean, I can't imagine anyone has tried to use it. I've never seen it myself,' Leamer said. 'You know, there was also a tunnel below that building, according to legend.'

'For what?' Mike asked, impatient for Leamer to keep pace with him.

'It was sealed up years ago. But when the British controlled the island, the first governors in residence here built a tunnel below Buttermilk Channel large enough for horses and a carriage so that they could make their escape if war threatened.'

I had reached the hedges in front of the imposing mansion. 'Buttermilk Channel?'

'The spit of water that separates the island from Brooklyn,' Mike said, waving his hand toward the rear of the house.

'So there's a way to get on and off this place without a ferry?' I asked.

'So I'm told,' Leamer said. He mounted the staircase between two white Romanesque columns and we waited behind him as he put one of his keys in the lock.

I heard the click of the release and saw Leamer push on the door, but it didn't open. He stepped away, fumbled with another key, and tried again. No click. He was back to the first key. Again, a click, but the door didn't budge.

Mike took the keys from Leamer's hand. He unlocked the door and leaned his shoulder in to shove it, but there was no give.

'Something must be blocking it,' Leamer said.

'From the inside,' Mike said, finishing the ranger's sentence.

Lightning lit up the sky and thunder growled at us. I hoped I wasn't imagining that it was beginning to move away from overhead.

Mike handed me the knife and one of the canteens, then vaulted over the wrought-iron porch gate and raised his hand in front of one of the double-hung windows, smashing the other canteen through the glass. He broke a second and a third pane, reaching through the hole and up to the latch that secured the window in place.

The old frame was swollen from the heat and humidity, so Mike had to play with it for several minutes to raise it up. He brushed away the chunks of glass and raised himself onto the sash, through the opening. I watched as I put the switchblade in the rear pocket of my jeans. When I looked up again, Mike had vanished inside the Governor's House.

Russell Leamer was backing off the porch. He wasn't sure what was happening, but he didn't want to be a party to it. It sounded like Mike was moving something heavy out of the way. I could hear it scraping across the floor.

When he opened the door to let us in, he had his gun in his hand.

Leamer groaned.

'Give her your flashlight,' Mike said to the ranger. 'Go back to your office and send Mercer up here as fast as you can possibly go. Ask him to call the lieutenant first and tell him we've got a situation on the island, got it? Get somebody airborne.'

'What kind of situation?' Leamer whined.

'He'll understand me. And you, Coop, glue yourself to my ass, okay?'

Leamer took off immediately. I stepped over the threshold, around the massive mahogany table that someone had put in place to block the door.

'Hold that light up,' Mike said.

He started to walk from the entrance through a formal parlor, the walls of which were decorated with an assortment of antique military weapons. Portraits of bearded officers from another age were hung over the fireplace between the windows, and heavy gold drapes, faded from decades of exposure, still framed most of the windows.

Mike held out his arm to slow me down while he turned the

corner into the next room. He motioned for me to join him. I had the same nerve-wracked feeling I had experienced at the shooting range, that someone would dart out from behind a door and fire at Mike before he could defend himself – and me.

But there was only a succession of musty office suites, handsomely furnished and all seemingly undisturbed. At the very rear of the house, overlooking the narrow channel that separated the island from Brooklyn, the interior silence was broken as Mike's foot crunched down onto more shards of glass.

He didn't have to speak. I could see, too, that the pane closest to the handle of the back door had been broken and that someone had knocked it in, as if to gain entry from this side of the mansion. When the break-in had occurred, and whether the burglar was still anywhere around, was impossible to tell.

Mike and I crossed the small room, emerging into a larger office, clearly the centerpiece of the house. An enormous colored map of the island as it looked in colonial times hung over the mantel.

Mike was looking for doors now, for a way to get into the basement of the old building. We found the central staircase that led up to the second floor, but that was of little interest to him. He wanted to go belowground.

He tapped the wooden boards behind the staircase, rapping every ten or twelve inches, until we both heard a hollow noise. There was an elaborate panel in the wainscoting that ran through the entire house, and Mike played with the raised carvings on it until he found what he was looking for. A piece of wood lifted up, revealing a keyhole.

I tried to steady the light on his hand as he sorted the keys. There were three – one for the front door and two others that were marked with the initials for Governor's House.

On his second attempt, the door opened. We both stood perfectly still for almost a minute, waiting to hear if there was any noise below. Nothing.

Mike turned to me and whispered, 'Stay up here.'

'I can't.'

'What do you mean, you can't, Coop? Stay here.'

Thunder clapped outside the house. The storm hadn't moved as far as I thought.

'Glue, Detective Chapman. It's hopeless. I'm with you.'

One side of Mike's mouth twitched, but he wouldn't give me a full smile. 'Hold the light over my shoulder.'

He grabbed the banister with his left hand and tested each plank before he put his weight down on the old wooden steps. One at a time, I descended behind him – first one flight, then around a landing that twisted to the basement.

Halfway to the bottom, I could see that the fetid room was partially flooded. It wasn't surprising, since it was so far below the level of the house, adjacent to the channel.

Mike stopped a step or two above the floor. It was obvious in the flashlight's beam that the surging water had come through a small pair of windows that were set into the floor, probably the only source of light and ventilation in this dreadful room.

'Raise your light,' Mike said.

All around the blackened cellar were the remnants of a primitive prison. *Dungeon* – Russell Leamer's phrase – seemed like a much more appropriate word.

Thick bars formed a barrier between the open area around the foot of the staircase and the four walls of the room. Behind them were tiny cells, each barely large enough to hold a single individual. Neither a cot nor a mattress could have fit in such a confined space. It was clearly meant to be a barbaric form of punishment.

I moved the light up and down along the bars, around the circumference of the room. I did it a second time, sweeping the monochromatic walls horizontally.

'Too good for Troy Rasheed,' Mike said, taking a step back up toward me. 'I hate being wrong.'

I clung to the banister as he went by me. Sitting on the lowest dry step, I took one last look, aiming the flash lower than my first two efforts.

Lightning backlit several of the cells through the two small windows as I guided my own beam over the surface of the water.

'Pam?' I screamed, grabbing at the leg of Mike's trousers to pull him back down.

In a far corner of the room, curled on its side, was the naked body of a young woman who was hogtied with legs and arms behind her – the only way someone could have fitted her in the space of one of the cells. A third of her body seemed to be submerged in the rising water lapping at her lips and nose.

A piece of cloth gagged her mouth. Her eyes were open, staring back at me, and Pam Lear was still alive.

51

Mike jumped from the steps onto the floor of the basement and sloshed through the muddy water to Pam's side.

'I'm a cop, Pam. You're all right. You're going to be fine.'

I had never seen anyone's eyes opened wider, still full of fear and overflowing with tears that began to run into the water under her head.

Mike pulled the filthy piece of cloth out of the girl's mouth and she began to gasp for air, breathing and sobbing, unable to form or speak any words. Before I could remove my jacket, Mike had taken his off and put it over her body. The dirt that was caked all over her from head to toe didn't conceal the lacerations on her torso or her goose bumps from the chilly dampness of her cell.

I lifted my leg to step over Pam, so that I could help Mike

cut her bindings. Her chest was still heaving wildly and her eyes followed me with understandable distrust.

Mike was used to dealing with corpses. He liked every aspect of the cold, clinical procedures of a homicide investigator. It was with living, breathing, emotionally scarred victims that he was most uncomfortable.

But this time he was giving it all he had. He was kneeling in the water, talking to Pam and explaining what he was doing, in an effort to comfort her.

'You'll be fine,' Mike said, stroking the hair that was clotted to her head. 'We're going to get you out right now, get you safe and warm.'

Thunder clapped again and her body shook.

'You're alive and we're here to help you and—'

Just don't tell her that nobody's going to hurt her before we know where her torturer is, I thought.

She was still trying to control her breathing – how long had she been gagged? – and still couldn't find her voice. The only thing that came out of her mouth was guttural, choking sounds.

'My name is Alex. I'm going to touch you, Pam. I'm going to help Mike get these ropes off your hands and feet.' She had been manhandled and abused and assaulted by a stranger, and we needed to reassure her that our contact was meant to be helpful to her.

'You've got that knife?' Mike asked.

Her eyes popped again. She looked at us as though we were her abductors. 'No,' she said, gulping in more of the muggy air. 'No, no, no knife.'

'It's okay, Pam. I won't hurt you,' I said. 'That's the only way we can get you out of these ties.'

Mike was dabbing at her face with his handkerchief. He held Pam's chin in his hand and gave her his classic Chapman grin. 'You wouldn't want my friend Alex to cook for you, but she's got long, skinny fingers that are going to get you undone much faster than I can. Just stay with me, Pam. Trust me.'

I took the switchblade out of my pocket and opened it. On the blade, on top of the rust, there were dark stains, probably Pam Lear's blood.

Mike kept her focused on his face, telling her how happy he was to find her, talking to her about school and history and her summer job. He knew that more highly charged words – family and friends, who they were and where they might be – were the wrong connection to make at this moment. Too likely to result in more of a meltdown.

I leaned in over Pam's hands, which were tightly bound against her lower back. 'I'm going to lift your arms a little bit, to get them away from your body,' I said. 'Is that okay?'

'Yes,' she said, the breaths coming more regularly now. 'Yes.'

'If it feels too tight, you tell me and I'll ease it back down.' I raised her left arm – the one beneath her body – and rested the tip of her elbow on top of my knee, to give myself a bit of room to maneuver. I didn't want her to feel the back edge of the knife's blade against her skin.

Slowly and carefully, I began to saw at the rope in an upward direction. It took longer than I expected to cut through the dense material, and twice Pam's hands jerked away from me, pulling her ankles up behind her.

All the while, Mike tried to soothe her with banter and charm, tried to keep her attention away from me and the knife. There was no point in asking her questions until we were all out of this dungeon.

'I'm just about there, Pam,' I said. 'Your hands are almost free.'

A blast of thunder rolled over us. Pam's eyes blinked rapidly and she looked up the staircase to the landing. 'It's the storm,' Mike said. 'There's no one there and I'm not going to leave you. We're almost done.'

'There you go,' I said.

Her right arm dropped limply to her side. Mike took it between his hands and began to knead her slim wrist, massaging it to get the circulation back.

'Thank you, thank you, thank you,' Pam said, saying the words over and over, barely understandable through the sobs. She was hoarse from the gag that had absorbed all the moisture in her mouth.

I was able to slice through the bindings around her ankles more quickly, but her limbs were so numb she didn't seem to feel the moment of release.

'We're going to sit you up,' I said. 'Mike's going to turn his head for a minute while I put his jacket on you, okay?'

Explain everything you're doing to the victim. Give her back the feeling that she can help control her situation, take part in decisions that are being made.

Mike stood up while I took his nylon windbreaker, helping Pam guide each of her arms into a sleeve. I moved in front of her and zipped the jacket up.

'We're going to try to get you to your feet,' I said.

Mike leaned down and put his hands under the arms of the petite young woman. He tried to raise her slowly, and it was obvious she was struggling to control her tears. 'I can't,' Pam said. 'Can't. Can't.'

'You don't have to do a thing,' Mike said. 'I'm going to carry you upstairs. I'm going to put you over my shoulder, Pam. You've seen firemen do it, right? You just hang on to—'

'I can't,' she said again, looking at her hands.

'I'll be behind you. Let Mike do all the work,' I said, reassuring her.

Mike lifted Pam off the ground, out of the water, and, as gently as he could, hoisted her over his shoulder.

I pointed the flashlight at the bottom of the tall staircase, and as Mike started to walk, I took hold of one of Pam's hands that was dangling behind his back. Holding the jacket in place over

Pam's lower body, Mike marched us up to the landing and around again to the door that led back into the house.

He carried the dazed young woman into the room I figured must have been the commanding officer's suite – the largest one we had come through earlier – and lowered her onto an old upholstered divan along the wall.

I went to the window and yanked at a panel of the heavy gold curtain that sagged from its rod.

'What the hell are you doing?' Mike asked.

'It worked for Scarlett O'Hara.'

'What did?'

'Making a dress out of her mother's moss green velvet po'teers, Mike. Her old drapes.'

I dragged a chair close to the window, climbed up, and took the wooden rod down. The two panels fell to the floor.

I swept them up and took them back to Pam. 'They're just dusty. But I'd like to cover you with them till we get some dry clothes.'

'And I'm going to get some water for you,' Mike said. 'How long since you've had a drink?'

She lifted her hand and held it to her throat, as if that would make the words come out more easily. 'Not sure. What day is it?'

'It's Tuesday, Pam,' I said.

'Yesterday,' she said, as Mike walked to the front door of the house. He went outside and, when he returned, he was carrying the canteen he had thrown to break the window. Pam's eyes locked on it and she started to quiver again.

'Rainwater,' Mike said. 'I've filled it with rainwater. You've got to drink slowly, though.'

'It's his,' she said, recoiling from the canteen. 'No.'

Mike got to his knees again, in front of her. 'There's no fresh water on this island, Pam. This is all we can give you. You need to sip at it. C'mon.'

She shook her head violently from side to side.

Mike poured some of the water onto his handkerchief and dabbed at the girl's lips. 'This will feel good, Pam. You're dehydrated. You need water.'

She breathed in deeply and reacted instinctively to the moisture, putting her tongue out to taste it, then swallowing hard.

'I've wiped the canteen, Pam. Don't be afraid to use it.'

I took it from Mike. 'I'm going to hold your neck. I'd like you to lean your head back and take a drink.'

'It's his,' she repeated. 'Don't want it.'

'Whose is it?' Mike asked. 'Tell me who brought you here.'

'Wilson,' Pam said, dropping her head forward as she dissolved in tears again. 'He told me his name is Wilson.'

52

'Where the hell is Mercer?' Mike said, walking to the front door of the Governor's House. 'Where did Leamer tell him we were?'

'What if he looked for us while we were in the basement? Figured he was mistaken about the building?'

'I'd have heard him.'

'Over the thunder?'

Mike was walking back and forth impatiently. I could tell that he wanted to move out of this macabre setting and resume the search for our killer.

Pam had described her captor perfectly. It was Troy Rasheed, using the name he had taken, along with his father's life. She had not seen the tattoos on his arms and body until he had tied her up and removed his lightweight rain jacket. But in the hours that he spent torturing her, she had memorized most of the initials – the prison art – that constituted his personal rap sheet.

'The storm's passing, Coop. I want to go to the office and get that chopper airborne. Get Pam to a hospital.'

We both knew we couldn't take her out of the building yet. I rubbed her ankles as I talked to her, but I didn't know when she would be able to stand, much less walk.

'I was stupid,' Pam said. 'I was stupid to believe him.'

'You're alive,' I said, working her lower legs with my hands. 'You did something right. This isn't your fault.'

'He was friendly to me,' she said. 'Not just Sunday, but the other times he'd been at Fort Tilden during the month.'

'You don't have to go through it now. Don't upset yourself.'

Mike walked over and sat on the arm of the sofa. Pam wanted to talk now. He gave her more water, and in a hoarse voice she went on.

'I came with him because I'd never been here. I know all about this island but I'd never seen how beautiful it is.'

'I understand,' I said.

'I mean, it wasn't because I was attracted to him, really. He was kind and all that, but it wasn't about him.' She was looking at me for a sign that I believed her.

Nelly Kallin was right. Troy Rasheed had learned how to catch his flies with honey this time around.

'You're going to tell Alex everything that happened, Pam,' Mike said to her. 'There'll be lots of time for that when we get you taken care of, but it's more important that we start at the end of the story. I want you to tell me when Wilson left you, what he said to you, where you think he went from here.'

Mike had all the facts he needed from Pam for his purposes. He knew she'd been picked up by Rasheed, accompanied him voluntarily – as the other three woman may have done – and then been betrayed and assaulted. There was nothing more to know at the moment except how to find him and stop him.

'I don't know when he left me,' she said. 'I have no sense of what time it is. I – I guess it was last night – no, maybe in the afternoon. It's been dark for two days – no light in that – that prison.'

'How did you come to the island?' I asked.

'The ferry. Of course the ferry.'

'On Sunday?'

'Yes. Yes, he convinced me to leave my job early. It was my last day, and nobody from the intern program was around. He told me there was this event going on, this Civil War reenactment. I'd heard about them. And it was a Park Service program, so I didn't think it would be a bad thing to do.'

Mike caught my attention and rolled his eyes. He wanted to fast-forward the story so we could make decisions about what to do next.

'When he tied you up – Wilson, this man,' I said. 'Did he say anything about where he was going?'

'Did I tell you he was in the army?' she asked. 'That he was a veteran, back less than a year from Iraq? I mean, that's another reason I trusted him. I really respected all his years of service.'

'You don't need to justify anything, Pam,' I said.

Mike was on his feet again. I didn't need him to tell her that her abductor was a veteran of a different kind of system. She would blame herself for another error in judgment – an almost fatal one – when she learned that news.

I held a finger up in Mike's direction, warning him to hold his tongue.

'What did Wilson say, Pam? What did he say when he left you downstairs? Did he say he'd be back?'

'He left me several times. He came and he went – I don't know. I don't know what he did when he wasn't here.'

Mike was pacing like a caged tiger. 'Pam, did he say anything about what he was going to do to you?'

'There was nothing left for him to do, Detective,' she said, hanging her head. 'He was going to kill me.'

'Did he say that? Did he ever say those words?'

'When he was – was raping me – I don't know – the second time, maybe the third time,' she said, trying not to break down again.

So much for the short-lived effectiveness of chemical castration. I couldn't begin to imagine what had happened during her ordeal. After her medical treatment, the rest of her day – and mine – would be spent in an excruciating retelling of these events.

'He kept asking me how I wanted to die. That's what he said to me. "How do you want to die?" Then he took his knife and ran it all over my body,' she said in her hoarse whisper, dragging out each of the words, as I suspected Troy Rasheed had done. ' "I could stab you in the heart. I could carve you in pieces. I could tie the rope around your neck. Or maybe you'd like to starve to death?" Then, when the storm started getting really bad – was that last night? He said he could just leave me here to drown. I figured that's what he had done.'

How would Pam Lear ever sleep again? How would she get these memories, these images, out of her mind's eye?

'The island, Pam,' Mike said. 'Did he say anything at all about how he was going to leave the island? The storm's letting up. I've got to go meet up with my partner at the ferry office, to look for Wilson, figure out if he got off here before the boat stopped running. We need to lock him up so this never happens again.'

Fear overtook the girl's exhaustion. She grasped Mike's hand. 'What do you mean he isn't locked up yet? How did you find me? He must have told you I was here,' she said. I didn't think she had enough fluid in her body to form more tears, but they were running down her cheeks. 'I can't believe he's gotten away.'

'We'll get him,' Mike said. 'That's what I'm here for.'

He tried to pull away but her small hand, with rope burns creasing her wrist, dug tightly into him. She was trembling from head to toe as she pleaded.

'I beg you not to leave me here. I don't want to die. I don't want him to come back and kill me.'

53

'I'll go for Mercer,' I said.

'Not happening, kid.'

I started to walk to the door, after tucking the drapes around Pam's body. It wasn't a conversation I wanted to have in her presence.

I lowered my voice. 'Something's holding Mercer up. The only phone is in Russell Leamer's office and—'

Mike followed after me. 'Don't do this.'

'If Rasheed were still around, we'd all be locked in that dungeon by now. He had his moment. And he doesn't carry a gun.'

'How do you know?' asked Mike.

'Because he didn't threaten to shoot Pam, did he?'

Mike glanced over his shoulder at her.

'And I run faster than you can, so you do some hand-holding for a change,' I said.

'I'm going to stand right here in this doorway.'

'And what do I do, fire the cannon when I reach the office, just to give you a heads-up?'

'I can see you most of the way there,' he said. 'Get going, Blondie.'

I was off the porch and jogging down the rain-soaked path that bordered Nolan Park. In less than three minutes I reached the side of the rangers' office and turned the corner to get to the door.

Governor's House was out of sight at this point. The river was still churning, but the flooding seemed to have crested. The little ferry was nested below the terminal on the Manhattan side, and I guessed it would be some time before boats made the passage again.

I went up the steps and pushed open the door.

I could see Russell Leamer's back. He was leaning over the desk, his Smokey Bear hat and oversized slicker outlined against the cloudy harbor.

The door slammed closed behind me.

'Ranger Leamer,' I said. 'Mercer never got to the Governor's House. Where did you send him? Is it possible he went to the wrong building?'

He stood up straight and turned around, pointing a gun at my chest.

It was Troy Rasheed, wearing Leamer's outfit. He smirked as he studied the NYPD hostage squad logo embroidered on my jacket, taking a step in my direction. With his left hand, he stroked the long thick scar that ran down that side of his neck.

'Well, well, Detective, why don't you talk to *me*? I have to say I really like your uniform.'

54

I recognized Mercer's gun.

'Where's Mercer? The man whose gun that is.'

'What's that old saying about the bigger they are and how hard they drop?'

I needed to stay calm. I was no use to any of us if I let this monster outsmart me. I needed a way for Mike to know that Mercer was down and that Rasheed was now armed with a semi-automatic weapon. I needed to keep her attacker away from Pam Lear.

'Mercer!' I screamed out. Maybe one of the cloudbursts I thought was thunder had been gunshots. I took a deep breath.

'Now that's a stupid thing to do, Detective.'

I didn't think Rasheed would shoot me so quickly. He would torture me first, like he had the others, if time and the elements favored him. That scared me far worse than the thought of a single bullet.

'I'm not alone. There are other officers here,' I said.

'That's a pity, isn't it? You all get shipwrecked or something?' He laughed at what he must have figured was his own joke. 'The whole island seems pretty damn quiet to me. Your friends hiding? You think they'd like to watch?'

I glared back at him, willing myself not to tremble like Pam Lear.

'Now where is it you keep your gun? You got no hips, girl.'

'I – I – uh – I didn't have my gun with me last night. I do U/C work. No guns. They pulled me off a detail to come out in the middle of the tour.' This was hardly the moment to deny that I was a cop. He was going by the clothes I had on, and I knew he'd understand the lingo.

'An undercover police lady. Undercover what?'

'Narcotics.'

'Not in Harlem you haven't been no undercover. Nobody stupid enough to sell horse to you,' he said.

'Cocaine's my thing. Coke and Ecstasy. Upper West Side. Yuppies.'

'You bring any along?' Rasheed asked, still stroking his scar. From under the cuff of the jacket, I could see the letters tattooed on his left hand, the initials of one of his victims. 'What's your name, girl? Just hold on to your jeans with one hand, right there on the thigh. Pull on it and let me see what you've got.'

I kept my eye on the gun while I obeyed his command.

'Now the other one.'

He seemed satisfied that I wasn't wearing an ankle holster.

'Where's Mercer?' My beloved friend had been through one shooting on the job not too long ago. I couldn't bear to think he had been hurt again. 'That's his gun.'

'Fine piece.'

'Sig-Sauer. Nine millimeter.' I figured I might as well use the little bit of knowledge I'd picked up at the range the previous week. Maybe he'd think he'd be better off if he kept the gun away from me. Maybe he'd think I'd know how to use it if I got my hands on it. 'Same as mine.'

'I guess I'd better find out where that's at then. They'd make a pretty pair,' he said. As he moved toward me, I took a step back.

'In my locker,' I said. I lifted my windbreaker up and showed him the waistband of my jeans. 'No Sig.'

I started to reach into the pockets to turn them inside out.

'Hold it, bitch. I'll be doing that myself.'

I knew the door was just inches behind me. I didn't want Troy Rasheed's hands anywhere on me.

'You're not leaving yet,' he said, thrusting an arm over my shoulder to hold the door in place.

My back was flush against it. He was practically leaning his body on mine, and the handle of the knife he'd abandoned – the one I'd found with the canteens – was pressing into my spine. I didn't mind the discomfort. I just didn't want him to find it.

Rasheed put his left hand into my deep jacket pocket and pressed it in place, rubbing up and down slowly, then from side to side. He may have been looking for a gun or a waist holster, but he was also delighting in repulsing me with his touch.

He leaned back so he could reach his arm between our bodies to check my other pockets – jacket and jeans on my left side – raising the gun above my head with his right hand.

'You're sweating, girl,' he said.

'It's August.'

He laughed.

The warm moisture from my pores was mixing with the cool dampness of the rainwater that had saturated me.

He found something in my jeans pocket and slowly pulled it out. 'A Yankee fan. I like that in my women.'

It was the ticket stub from a game I had been to earlier in the month. While he read the small print, I looked out at the river, but not a single boat was plying the choppy water yet.

'Who'd they play?'

'Boston. We crushed them.'

Troy Rasheed was so close to me I could smell his stale breath and foul body odor. I couldn't take the chance of closing my eyes for a second, so I focused on a door to the side of the desk that opened into a second room. Maybe Mercer and Russell Leamer had been forced in there.

'Now I think it's time for the seventh-inning stretch. You and me, we're going to—'

'I need water,' I said, putting my hand to my throat. 'Is there any water inside?'

His head whipped around in the direction I'd been looking and back at me. He placed the Sig in the front of his waistband.

'I'll be deciding what you need for the time being,' Troy said, holding his lower lip between his thumb and forefinger. 'Shit, I don't even know your name. You didn't answer my question.'

I didn't speak.

'Now why don't you just tell me your name?'

'You don't need to know my name.'

His right hand smacked the side of my face faster than I could blink, and he laughed again. 'I told you, I'll be deciding what you need, and I'm certainly deciding what *I* need. I always do.'

Then he placed a finger on my jacket, directly above my left breast, and pressed into my chest as he drew an imaginary line across it, a couple of inches long.

'Now, if you weren't working undercover, Miss Detective, you'd have a shiny gold plate right here and I could just read your name.'

I swatted his hand away. 'Alex Cooper.'

'Alex Cooper,' he repeated, nodding his head up and down. Maybe he was visualizing how the initials would look on his forearm.

Troy Rasheed slipped out of the Park Service uniform rain-coat that he must have taken from Leamer and let it drop beside him on the floor.

He was wearing a plain white T-shirt, and now I could see the flourishes of the monograms up and down both arms, each one marking the heartbreaking experience of a woman who had crossed his path.

I needed to keep him talking. It would be only minutes before Mike figured a way to come check on me. There wasn't any room for an 'AC' to be added to his skin museum.

'The first thing you're going to do for me, Alex, is take off—'

The desk phone rang and Troy Rasheed was as startled as I.

'Well, you can't be quite so tough as you're acting, Detective Cooper, can you? Get all out of breath just 'cause the telephone rings?'

He took a step toward the desk but didn't answer, waiting out the sixth, seventh, and eighth rings, before the insistent caller gave up.

'You're gonna take off your shoes first, Alex. Those sneakers is not sexy,' he said, pulling on his lip again, extending it away from his teeth, as though it hurt him.

There was another noise – behind Rasheed – from within the second room. He didn't act as though he'd heard it. Thank God someone was alive in there.

'Get them off, sugar.'

I bent down to untie the laces of my sneakers. He was too far away from me, for the moment, for me to try to surprise him with the knife.

The ringing started again. Rasheed picked up the receiver and slammed it back down, then took it off again and rested it on the desk. In seconds, a shrill busy signal was bleeping at us, rendering the phone useless.

Another noise behind Rasheed. Not a voice but some kind of movement. He jerked his head in that direction.

'Let me see my friend Mercer. Let me see what you've done to him.'

He picked up an object from the desk and turned to face me. Troy Rasheed was holding a grenade.

'I'm gonna save the show-and-tell for later, Detective Cooper, when he's feeling a little better. But we'll take another one of these with us.'

'Take it where?' I raised my voice. I wanted Mercer and Leamer to know I was just a room away. 'That's how you got Mercer's gun. You used a stinger on them. Let me see him, please.'

'Now you've been well-trained, girl, if you've been playing with one of these. I hope you've never thrown this son of a bitch at any of your perps, Detective Cooper. That would make me very angry at you.'

Stingers, or Hornet's Nests, are less-than-lethal grenades made up of small rubber balls inside two spheres of hard rubber, instead of shrapnel in metal casing. Law enforcement agents use them to break up prison riots, and I had seen a SWAT team clear a small room with several of them, incapacitating their targets, dropping men to the ground, by the blunt force of the projectiles.

'Can I sit down for a minute?' I said. 'I – uh – I feel dizzy. I think I'm going to be sick.'

I knew women who had put off their assailants by becoming physically ill.

Troy tugged at his lower lip. 'I think the best thing for that is a little fresh air, Alex.'

I imagined Mercer and Leamer, bound and gagged like Pam Lear, on the floor of the adjacent room. I didn't want to leave them to go off with this maniac.

He grabbed my elbow and pulled me toward the door. There was a chain around his neck, hanging down under his T-shirt. Something dangling from it made an impression against the cotton in the shape of a dog tag.

He stopped in front of me and started to give orders.

'We're going for a walk, Detective, like I told you. And I'm gonna go nice and slow out there 'cause I know you're barefoot. I know that's why you can't exactly run fast, either. So you remember that, too. Oh, and did I tell you that you might want to be very careful where you walk?' he said, stroking my cheek with the back of his hand. 'You must be good at following orders, aren't you?'

I didn't answer.

'I asked you a question, girl, and I expect you to answer me. And the answer would be "Yes, sir."'

'Yes, sir,' I said, with hesitation.

' 'Cause if you walk off without me, I'd just hate to think of something fragging you into so many pieces I wouldn't be able to have any fun later.'

I'd seen more than enough news reports of soldiers 'fragged out' by the deployment of grenades. Rasheed had used his time well. He'd learned the deadly art of setting booby traps from his father, and in the hours since he'd tortured and deserted Pam Lear in the dungeon, he wanted me to believe, he had concealed fragmentation grenades around the island.

'And what do you say to that, Detective? You want me to have fun with you, don't you?'

There was no way to suppress the tremors that were rippling through me.

'Where is it, Alex? Where's the answer I want to hear? What do I want?'

I knew what I wanted. I wanted Mike to come running down from Nolan Park. I wanted Pam Lear to release him from her side so he could help me. I wanted Mercer to get himself loose and get back on his feet.

'Yes,' I said, quietly. 'Yes, sir.'

Gripping my elbow with his right hand, he opened the door with his left and led me out onto the steps and down to the cobblestone walk, where the pebbles blown around by the storm dug into the soles of my feet.

I prayed that he would turn left and take the path back to Governor's House. But instead, he pointed ahead to the large hill, to the great star-shaped landmark in the center of the island. It was Fort Jay, the place we'd been on our way to see when the feds kicked us off the island on Saturday.

'We're going to higher ground, girl. Don't want anybody to mess with you till we've gotten to know each other.'

I walked as slowly as I could, listening for sounds that boats or choppers were back in the water and air. I pretended the rocky roadway made walking painful.

'You can do better than that, Detective,' he said, pulling on my arm.

The rain was falling gently, and there an eerie silence now that the thunder had rolled off to the east.

Troy Rasheed toyed with his silver chain while I bent down to remove a small rock that had wedged between my toes. I was playing for time. He hadn't recognized me from the night at Ruffles. There was no reason for him to have done so, since he would have seen only my back as I left behind Mike and Kiernan Dylan. He didn't know I was aware of his criminal history – and of the fate that awaited me if I didn't escape.

'Get up, sugar. Time to go.'

I looked back over my shoulder and he jerked my arm to make me keep up with him. He lifted the chain and put the army dog tag to his mouth, biting nervously on the edge of it.

There was something else hanging from the chain. Something gold. It was the West Point ring, a gold band with a citrine stone and the USMA emblem, that Elise Huff had worn every day since her grandmother's death. It was the trophy that Troy Rasheed had taken from her body, a reminder of his resolve to leave none of his prey alive.

55

I felt like I was on a forced march back in time, to quarters like I'd just seen in the more primitive structures that surrounded this imposing centerpiece of Governors Island.

Behind me was the dark, silent city, just beginning to come to life, with scattered lights and the sound of aircraft somewhere overhead. Looming in front of me, on top of the hill, was the enormous mass of an eighteenth-century fort, far more complex than Castle Williams. I had no idea what remained behind its walls, but I feared that Troy Rasheed knew every crevice in it.

We had crossed the cobblestone path and roadway. Now we were on grass, and my captor broke into a run. His left hand held Mercer's gun in place in his waistband, while his right kept a tight grip on my upper arm.

'Too fast,' I said, pretending to stumble, but he wasn't having any of it.

'Run, damn it,' he told me, squeezing me with his big hand.

He was moving as though we were on an obstacle course, zigzagging so that I thought – or was meant to think – that he had rigged the muddy field with explosive devices.

I looked at the giant stone counterscarp, the side of the fort that seemed impenetrable. We'd flown over it as we landed this morning, and I'd seen its great five-sided star shape from the air. Now we were approaching an actual drawbridge that led into a covered entry, a forbidding separation from the rest of the island.

Rasheed apparently heard a noise overhead, too. He looked up, never letting go of me, to see whether whatever machine was flying in the pea-soup sky above was coming in to land, but the droning sound faded away.

'Almost there, girl. I'm gonna show you some sights.'

The switchblade was still in the rear pocket of my jeans, which were so tight that it hardly jiggled when I moved. Maybe this was the moment to try to slice at Rasheed's arm, before we crossed over into the fortress.

I was feeling dizzy. The view directly ahead of me shifted. We were sprinting toward the drawbridge but suddenly the ground to the left and right of the gate opened wide below me. A gaping hole appeared, twenty feet wide, stretching the length of the entire visible side of the fort.

'I can't,' I screamed at Rasheed, hoping Mike would hear me, hoping my voice would carry from the island's peak.

I stopped in place, terrified by the sight. It was a moat, a dry moat, and if I made a misstep, I would fall off the bridge to its bottom.

Rasheed confronted me, holding my shoulders with both hands, shaking me fiercely. 'You ain't gonna miss a minute of this, sugar. You come to your senses, okay?'

I was out of breath and frightened. I couldn't get any words out.

Then he removed Mercer's gun from his waistband and held it to the side of my head. 'Welcome to *my* house, Detective Cooper.'

He moved aside but picked up my arm again and kept the gun in his other hand.

We emerged from beneath the cover of the bridge, into a small village. Around a central courtyard were rows of brick buildings two stories in height. They were more elegant than the crude barracks that lined the waterfront, but just as deserted.

There was no way to see beyond the high walls of the fortress. I wouldn't know whether the river was calming enough for boats to be launched again, and I doubted that the tide would recede fast enough to let the ferry make the trip across.

But I could hear noises from above, and I was silently begging Commissioner Scully to get our chopper airborne.

'Now this here is where the officers lived,' Rasheed said, dragging me toward a building on the east side of the grounds. 'So I figured it was a fine place for me.'

Not exactly what the Sex Offender Monitoring Unit had in mind when they asked him to register his address.

'No, no, no, girl. Not up there,' he said, as I scanned the second story of the barracks, wondering if the windows of those rooms looked out above the massive stone walls. 'I prefer the dark. I spent a lot of time in solitary, Detective. You know what that's like, don't you?'

I stopped short.

'It's not polite to ignore me. You've sent perps to solitary, haven't you? How do you think you're gonna like the black hole?'

Rasheed was behind me now, holding the back of my neck as he prodded me along. At the last room in the long row, he let go of me and turned the knob. The door opened.

I stood on the threshold, letting my eyes adjust to the dark. Waves of nausea rolled in my stomach.

There were no windows in the room, no ventilation source that I could see. There was a pile of rope next to my feet, and I was sure that he would have something handy to gag me with, if he didn't use a piece of my own clothing.

'Take me somewhere else,' I said to Rasheed, trying to reposition myself, trying to turn around to face him. 'I'll do whatever you want. I promise. Whatever you want.'

We were inches apart now. He laughed at me. 'Oh, I do know that you will, girl. I know that you will.'

With the barrel of Mercer's gun, he pushed the frizzy hairs off my forehead.

'Just – just a different place than this,' I said. 'Upstairs, where there's more light.'

'No need to get all shaky on my account. You take off that jacket and I'll make you feel better, Alex. Alex, that's right?'

I had lectured to school groups scores of times. I had urged children – and women, too – not to get into cars with their abductors. The statistics were shocking. The likelihood of victims being found alive after they submitted to entering a vehicle was minuscule. The best time to fight was before being finally caged. If I was to escape from Troy Rasheed, gun or no gun, I would have to do it before he backed me into this room.

He put his free hand on the sleeve of my jacket and pulled on it.

'I'll take it off myself,' I said. That way, I could have better access to the knife.

'That's my girl. I'd like to put this gun down, but I can't do that until you're settled in, you hear?'

Now he was pulling at his lip again, kneading it between two fingers.

'I think I'm going to be sick,' I said, grabbing my stomach and bending forward as I dropped my jacket to the ground. I wasn't faking it. I was overcome by nausea.

'Not on my time, babe. You just breathe in some of this nice sea air and swallow hard.'

I leaned my head back and inhaled.

Rasheed make a sucking noise, then bowed forward, like he was reaching to kiss me.

'You're bleeding,' I said to him. 'Your lip is bleeding.'

He didn't take his eyes off me. He lifted his left hand and rubbed it across his mouth. 'Ain't nothing to be scared of, Detective. You might like the taste of blood.'

Troy Rasheed put his fingers up again, exposing the inside of his lower lip.

'That's my new one, sugar,' he said, showing me the tattoo, still so raw it was irritating the surface. 'I did that for my girlfriend last week. My old girlfriend.'

He laughed as he wiped his mouth again. I guess he had run out of room on his body to pay homage to each of his victims. Those were Amber Bristol's initials on his lip.

56

'Step inside, Alex,' Rasheed said.

I stood at the edge of the door, my back against the jamb. He pushed me and I swiveled halfway into the room.

He put the gun in his other hand, holding it to my stomach, and kneeled down to reach for the coiled rope.

I wasn't going to let myself be tied up. Not while I had an ounce of strength in me. With my left foot, I kicked at the pile of rope and heard it topple over, away from me.

'Damn it, bitch,' he said, grabbing at my leg to stop himself from falling with it.

I reached into my rear pocket with my right hand and withdrew the knife. I pressed the switch and the blade snapped open while Troy Rasheed tried to regain his balance and get to his feet.

'It's time we get down to business,' he said, lifting his head, his lips glistening with his own blood. 'C'mon, Alex. You be nice.'

He was on his knees, trying to stand, when his eyes met mine and he said my name again. I raised my arm over my head and plunged the knife as deep as I could into his chest. Blood spurted out through the hole in his shirt and Rasheed collapsed forward, driving the blade even deeper into his body.

57

Troy Rasheed was still screaming when I ran out through the gates of the fortress, crossed the drawbridge, and raced across the grassy lawn that sloped downhill. I didn't care whether he had laid traps that would ensnare or injure me. Anything would be better than the torturous death that he had planned.

I stayed on the cobblestone path, shouting Mike's name as loud as I could. The smooth, cold stones felt good beneath my feet, and the pebbles that peppered them barely slowed me down.

I veered to the right when I saw the roadway that led into Nolan Park, up to the Governor's House. In less than three minutes, I reached the porch of the old building. The door was wide open. I called for Mike and for Pam Lear, but the house was deadly still.

I stood on top of the steps, looking out on the quiet scene.

Then I remembered the old bell buoy, the one Mike and Mercer and I had passed on the first day. It was closer to the Governor's House than the Park Service office. I could be there in seconds, making more noise than this island had heard in centuries.

I flew down the steps and took off to the left, sticking to the cobblestone path.

The bright green and red bell buoy was more than twenty feet tall. The huge base on which it rested, once bobbing in the sea to warn passing ships, was waist high. I climbed onto it, resting the bloody knife on the ground, working my way inside the frame of the structure.

The brass bell resting in the metal grid was five times the size of my head. I grabbed it with both hands and stood back. With a deafening clang, the clapper struck against the side of the bell. It rocked from side to side, with a clamor that should have alerted anyone in the city that there was life on the little island.

Once it settled down, I released it a second time, then jumped down from the buoy and started on the roadway to check on Mercer and call for help.

I was running on pure adrenaline now. Halfway down the hill, I heard Mike calling my name.

'Coop,' he shouted. 'Where are you, Coop?'

He must have been standing in front of Leamer's office. The sound was coming from that direction.

'Stay where you are,' I yelled back. 'Don't move. I'm almost there.'

I didn't want Mike venturing out any farther into territory that might have been sabotaged by Troy Rasheed. I didn't want him to encounter that wounded animal, still armed with Mercer's gun.

I ran the rest of the distance as fast as I could. There was a black Bell helicopter dipping its nose toward the spot in the distance where Joe Galiano had let us off so many hours ago.

The instant I saw Mike Chapman jogging up to meet me, he

opened his arms and I fell into his embrace. It took him a few moments – and a reassurance from me – to realize the blood on my shirt was not mine.

58

'You look good there,' Mercer said to Mike.

Mike was sitting in Keith Scully's high-backed leather chair, smoking a Cohiba. 'You'd look good just about anywhere to-night, Mr. Wallace. If you're still seeing double, then you'd better keep your eye on me for a while. Blondie's a mess.'

It was late Tuesday evening and we were in the office of the police commissioner on the fourteenth floor of headquarters. Scully had left for another press conference with the mayor, this one announcing the capture of Troy Rasheed on Governors Island. The prisoner was still in surgery at Bellevue Hospital for the collapsed lung he'd suffered when I stabbed him. Pam Lear's parents had driven to the city from upstate New York to take her home.

I stood next to one of the large windows overlooking Lower

Manhattan and the East River. The city appeared to have resumed normalcy after the storm. Power had been restored, traffic was flowing with a regular rhythm, and the Staten Island Ferry was back in service. The water looked as smooth as silk.

Mercer had been treated for the injuries from Rasheed's detonation of the sting grenade. He and Russell Leamer had been knocked out, literally unconscious, when Rasheed opened the door of the office and threw in one of the small spheres, which exploded right next to them. Leamer remained in the hospital overnight for observation, with trauma to his visual cortex. Mercer's vision had cleared by late afternoon.

'Where did they find him?' I asked Mike, fixated on the placid scene outside.

I had been treated and released, too, like Mercer. I was only beginning to get details of the arrest.

'Right where you left him, kid. You not only need shooting lessons, but now we got to teach you some anatomy. Don't you know where a guy's heart is?'

Why did that question make me think of Luc?

'I wasn't aiming to kill him. I just wanted to get out alive.'

'You came pretty close to doing the job, Alex,' Mercer said. 'You clipped the left subclavian artery. Rasheed almost bled out on the spot.'

'And there I was, holding on to Pam,' Mike said, 'figuring he had gotten himself off the island or was holed up, not wanting to be found. She became hysterical when I tried to leave to see what was taking you so long.'

Mike wound up carrying her all the way to the small office. It must have been only minutes after Rasheed had forced me out. Once Mike had discovered Mercer and phoned for help, he started retracing his steps in a desperate effort to find me.

'You knew about Fort Jay?' I asked.

'I'd seen it years ago. I didn't know it had also been used as a military prison.'

'It was?'

'Yes. During the Civil War. But it was only for officers – Confederate officers. The magazine was directly behind the room Rasheed took you to. It's the building where all the ammunition was stored. That way, if the rebels stormed the island and tried to rescue their officers, the men would get blown up along with the entire fort. I'm just glad the sally gate was too rusty to close. We'd never have seen you again.'

I walked away from the window and sat across the desk from Mike. I shuddered at that thought. 'The what?'

'There's a huge iron gate inside the drawbridge.'

'Think of your knights in shining armor, Alex,' Mercer said. His head was resting on the leather back of his chair, a cold compress on his brow. 'Remember how they'd sally forth from their fortresses?'

'Fortunately, it hasn't been closed in years,' Mike said.

'And the dry moat?' I asked. 'For what?'

'Optical illusion, my dear lady. The bad guys storm the fort, infantry running up the hill, right at the counterscarp. They get to the crest and stop short – nobody needed to bother filling it with water, especially on an island that doesn't have any water source. The troops just keep coming, pushing one another off the grass into the moat, sitting ducks for the guys in the fort.'

I poured another glass of water from the pitcher on Scully's desk. I'd been parched all day. Nothing seemed to quench my thirst. 'When we will know about Kiernan Dylan?'

'Peterson will call when they're done with him,' Mike said. 'He's spilling his guts.'

Jimmy Dylan had phoned the homicide squad at six o'clock. His son wanted to cooperate once the news of Troy Rasheed's arrest flashed on the air. He had been staying in seclusion, even from his family, with a friend from high school, not far from the city.

'What's he got to say?' I asked.

'The kid was really sure his father killed Amber Bristol. That's what the cover-up was all about. That's why he panicked and left town.'

'But he cleaned out her apartment.'

Mike took his feet off Scully's desk and blew a smoke ring before he explained. 'Kiernan knew about his old man's dirty laundry. He'd met Amber at his father's bar, the Brazen Head. She started showing up at Ruffles after Jimmy Dylan broke it off. When Jimmy heard that, he told Kiernan to throw her out.'

'And Kiernan passed the job along to Troy Rasheed,' Mercer said.

'Troy, aka Wilson Rasheed. Kiernan asked a cop he was friendly with to do a name check. Came up no record, so no reason to poke around much more,' Mike said.

'When Kiernan told Rasheed to get rid of her – drive her home – he gave him the keys to his van. Next night, he says Rasheed told him Amber asked Rasheed to come back, that she was ready to pack up her things and go on home to Idaho,' Mercer went on.

'That's what we know so far. Kiernan gave him the keys the next night, too. Saturday night. Anything to get her out of town, out of his father's life.'

'And that's the night Rasheed abducted Elise Huff,' I said. 'You think Kiernan Dylan had anything to do with that?'

'So far, he's denying it. Wasn't even there when she showed up. But she walked into the hands of a killer,' Mike said. 'She was on her way to find Kiernan, and she came right up against Troy Rasheed. He'd had his first success the night before with Amber Bristol. He needed to feed his habit again.'

'And Connie Wade?' I asked.

'We'll have to see if Rasheed is talking when he comes out of surgery.'

'My money's with Nelly Kallin. Manipulation, not a blitz

attack,' Mercer said. 'He crossed paths with her somewhere the day she disappeared. Talked her into that white van. Offered her a ride back to school.'

Don't get into that car, I thought to myself. Don't ever get into that car.

'You think they have room service here at headquarters?' Mike said to Mercer. 'I'm famished.'

Mercer took the compress off, smiled, and reapplied it to his forehead. 'Unlikely, Mr. Chapman. Just fancier vending machines than the squad has.'

'I know, Coop's going to tell me she isn't hungry.'

'How would Troy Rasheed even know that dungeon was there? In Governor's House,' I said.

' 'Cause they used to give tours of the place when he was a kid. The men who lived there knew all that history. It wasn't a ghost island then,' Mike said.

There were footsteps coming through the outer office. Keith Scully and Guido Lentini were back from City Hall.

'You feeling a little better, Alexandra?' Scully said, resting a hand on Mercer's shoulder.

'Getting there.'

'Mercer?'

'One hundred percent.'

Mike got out of the commissioner's chair. 'Guido, don't you think a bit of medicinal Scotch is in order? I didn't want to open any of the cabinets here without a search warrant, but you could give me a hint.'

Scully was seated at his desk, ready to get back to work. 'Then get me a surgical update on Rasheed, will you, Guido?'

'You got orders for me, too?' Mike asked. He was much too wired to slow down.

'The mayor's going to push me too far,' Scully said. 'He wants me to let him know when Rasheed is ready to leave the hospital.'

'What's the problem with that?' Mike asked.

'He doesn't get the point. He wants to do a perp walk. Always looking for the photo op.'

I glanced at Mike and smiled. When he lost his temper and locked up Kiernan Dylan at Ruffles, over my objection, the amateur photograph had captured Troy Rasheed's image. That accidental perp walk undoubtedly saved some women's lives.

'Tell him to check with Coop before he does. You know how I hate to cross her.'

59

'Why aren't you answering your phone, Alex?' Joan Stafford asked. 'Why isn't your machine picking up messages?'

It was Friday afternoon and I was alone in my apartment. 'I'm being selective, for a change. I turned it off. That's why I'm calling to let you know that I'm okay.'

Joan had been checking on me every couple of hours after the news of our showdown with Troy Rasheed was made public.

'Just "okay"?'

'Better than that, Joannie. I promise you I'm better. I was a good soldier all week. Played by all the rules. I've been debriefed and re-debriefed. Every inch of me was examined by the doctors. My scratches and bruises were measured and photographed. I came home from the medical appointments the other night dressed in a hospital gown with Scully's trenchcoat covering me, so that my clothes could go to the lab and be cut up and analyzed for body fluids and trace evidence. The commissioner even insisted the department shrink try to have a go at me for a couple of hours.'

'Sounds like everyone except the forensic pathologists had a piece of you, and thankfully they weren't given the chance. So did you tell the shrink anything Nina or I don't know, darling?'

'I have no secrets from you, Joan.'

'Then come spend the weekend with Jim and me. We're driving out to the beach. You can rest there and I'll wait on you hand and foot.'

'I'm happiest in my own cocoon right now, about to get into a steaming hot bath, with scented bubbles up to my nose.'

'Alex, it's ninety-five degrees outside. Haven't you had enough heat?'

'I've got the air-conditioning going full blast, and I'm going to try to soak all the aches out of me.' I felt safe inside my home, after all the turmoil of recent days. I didn't want to leave for any reason.

'You'll starve to death if you're alone all weekend.'

'I think takeout was invented for me, Joan.'

She paused. 'You need this time by yourself, don't you?'

'I wasn't able to sleep for a couple of nights,' I said. 'Nightmares, flashbacks – I didn't even want to close my eyes. About four this morning, I gave in to it. I almost feel human again today. I didn't wake up until eleven. I still haven't gotten dressed. It feels wonderfully decadent.'

'Did you dream, Alex?'

With my left hand I unbuttoned the old shirt I was wearing. 'A very pleasant dream, actually, for the first time in several weeks.'

'In English or French?'

'Nothing that needed translation, Joan. A delightful foreign intrigue, but my lousy accent never got in the way of any action.'

'Then turn your phone back on. I've been running interference for you all day. You're driving your friends crazy with worry. And Luc can't get through. He called me to ask if you received the package he overnighted to you from his home.'

'I wasn't expecting any deliveries today. I asked Vinny not to call up.'

'Luc instructed the valet to leave it right in front of your door. Check while I'm on the line with you.'

I walked through the foyer and unlocked the dead bolt. I peeked out to make sure no one was in the hallway to see me, tousled and barely clothed, and swept up the newspapers and the light cardboard carton on top of them.

'Yes, Joan. There's something here.' I left the papers in the living room – there was no news I wanted to read about – and carried the box with me.

'Good. Take your bath. I'm so happy you're beginning to relax. Then open the gift later. And call Luc, will you?'

'I haven't forgotten all my manners, madame. I'll speak to you tonight, before I go to sleep.'

The bathtub was full. I closed the door and slipped out of my shirt.

'And Mike,' Joan said.

'What about him?'

'He's pretty anxious to talk to you, too. Like right now.'

'Somehow, being naked in a bubble bath doesn't seem like the most appropriate way for me to carry on an investigation, not even with my favorite detective. We had dinner last night with Mercer and Vickee,' I said. 'I'm entirely up to speed on everything I need to know.'

'Well, he sounds pretty desperate going through me just to get to you.'

I dipped my toe in the water but it was too hot to step in. 'Mike's riding high and deserves to be. He flipped Clarita Munoz yesterday. You know, the girl who was trying to get in to see me the day Kerry Hastings and I got rammed in the cab.'

'What did he do?' Joan asked.

'Mike helped with her interrogation. Got her to admit that it was her boyfriend – well, her ex-boyfriend now – Ernesto Abreu, who took the shots at me at Rodman's Neck a week ago. Part of Pablo Posano's posse.'

'But why did Abreu try it there?'

'Just what Mercer thought. The stuff of instant legends in the twisted world of the Latin Princes. What could be more macho than trying to take out the prosecutor Posano hates most at a police shooting range, with scores of cops around? Prove yourself to the man in the black hole. Maybe step up a rank in the organization.'

'Well, I think Mike's worried about you. About letting Rasheed get so close. About what almost happened to you. He was giving me that stuff about getting you right back in the saddle with another case so you don't get too frightened to try again.'

'I'll tell you something I didn't tell the shrink, Joannie. I couldn't even think of doing my work without the relationships I have that keep me grounded – Mike and Mercer, you and Nina, my friends in the office, and now Luc. I think of what Troy Rasheed did to the women whose paths he crossed and I know how blessed I am to be alive, to be unscathed.

'But now I need a few days alone, some time to see if I can ride the horse again without the help of anyone else. I need to test my own fortitude, my own resilience.'

Joan's tone changed. 'I understand, of course. I'm sure Mike will, too.'

'We've spent so much time together since these killings started that Mike's just having separation anxiety,' I said. 'He'll get over it.'

'Sure he will. And you know Jim and I are here for anything you need, Alex.'

'Some of my best thinking happens underwater, Joannie. I'll be fine. Speak to you later tonight.'

I put the portable phone on the sink, tested the temperature again, and lowered myself into the tub. I slid down, rested my neck against one end, and lifted my toes above the bubbles at the other. My thoughts drifted from the horrors of the last ten days to plans I had made for a September weekend on the Vineyard. I soaked for almost an hour, until my fears had lost their edge and the water had cooled enough to remind me to get out and dry off.

I draped a bath sheet around me and went into my bedroom. Luc's package was addressed with stickers that repeated the words *priority* and *urgent* on every side.

The tab stripped open easily and I removed a thin box, wrapped in white satin ribbon, from the carton.

I untied the bow and opened it. Inside was a short silk robe, the same aqua shade as the dress I had worn the last time Luc and I were together. It was trimmed with a delicate strip of ecru lace. As I picked it up, my towel slipped off onto the floor, and I wrapped the soft, sexy dressing gown around me, tying it with the aqua silk belt.

There was a card nestled in the tissue paper on the bottom of the box. I climbed onto my bed and lifted the flap.

Another key, this time a shiny new one, not a flea market antique like the first one he sent me. The end of it was tied by a ribbon to an airline ticket, one way, first class, to Paris.

'Dearest Alex. Come soon. Stay as long as you like. Meet you at the Plaza Athénée on *my* side of the ocean. Room 888 – the most beautiful view of the city and the Eiffel Tower. *Bonne nuit, ma princesse.* Luc.'

Those were the words he spoke when he kissed me good night for the first time, after Joan's wedding, at my Vineyard home. Every time I thought of him, called up his voice saying them to me, I smiled.

I was determined not to waste time worrying about the bad memories that were competing for space against so many strong, vibrant ones. I settled back against my pillow and dialed Luc's number.

ACKNOWLEDGMENTS

It seems that every day the city of New York reveals to those who love her some of the secrets that she has harbored for centuries. Whether it's her mean streets, ghost islands, or historic landmarks, I never tire of exploring her mysterious past.

I am grateful to the National Park Service and the Governors Island Preservation and Education Corporation for the introduction to their magnificent citadel, a hidden jewel for more than two centuries. As always, the *New York Times* archives have been an invaluable resource, as has Seitz and Miller's *The Other Islands of New York City*.

The New York City Police Foundation has done extraordinary work to make possible so many innovative programs for the NYPD. I thank them for the tour of Rodman's Neck and for instruction from the great men and women of the Firearms and

Tactics Section, especially Joseph Agosto and Elizabeth Mayer-Feinberg.

Abbie Shoobs of Tiffany and Company was gracious enough to tell me the history of the West Point rings and miniatures made by the great jeweler and of the West Point Ring Recovery Program, dedicated to returning these treasures to the families from which they've been separated.

This novel tells part of the story of a character called Kerry Hastings. I have taken the liberty of drawing some of her traits from the woman to whom this book is dedicated: Kathleen Ham. It is impossible to imagine the courage of Kathleen without letting her look you in the eye and describe in her own words what the personal toll of her battle has been. For thirty-two years her rapist was on the loose, and Kathleen lived in what she called her own private jail. The case went cold, but her courage never did. The man's conviction – and her willingness to go public about her ordeal – brought some measure of justice to Kathleen as well as inspiration to crime victims all over this country.

One of my proudest legacies at the office of the New York County District Attorney was the establishment of an offshoot of the Sex Crimes Prosecution Unit that I led for twenty-six years. The cold case unit is composed of two great prosecutors and friends – Martha Bashford and Melissa Mourges – who have mastered the art of solving violent crimes long after traditional investigative techniques have been unsuccessful. They and their devoted partners in the NYPD and the Office of the Chief Medical Examiner have used DNA to revolutionize the way rape cases can be prosecuted.

Thanks to Kerry O'Connell, another former colleague and friend, who tries a superb case and also introduced Coop to her Cohiba.

Every minute of working with Colin Harrison was an enormous joy for me. He is a master of his craft, generous of spirit, and wonderfully supportive. I shall always relish his check marks

– and the occasional double checks – with which he so kindly edited my manuscripts.

Phyllis Grann has long given me the gift of her friendship. I'm enormously proud and pleased to be in her professional hands now, too. I'm thrilled and honored to be welcomed so enthusiastically at Doubleday by Steve Rubin, for whom I have such great respect.

Esther Newberg gets all my gratitude for covering my back and easing my transition to a new home with her usual wisdom and humor. Thanks, too, to ICM's Kari Stuart and Chris Earle for their competence and good cheer.

Special appreciation to my mother, Alice, and all my family and friends, who understand my time spent at the keyboard talking with Coop, Mike, and Mercer.

And to Justin Feldman – my very own comeback kid – you're all heart.